Angel

He was her twisted guardian angel—someone she only ever saw and loved in the shadows. In the face of a deadly turf war, could she make him stay in the light...or will he disappear into the darkness forever?

Heart Chained

They have the perfect friendship—but their hearts refuse to let each other go. Will they be brave enough to admit the true ties that bound them...or will they forever be doomed to run in chains?

Shadow and Light

She was like the sun, on a day without clouds—he was only a shadow, steeped in a legacy of secrets. Can he tell her the truth about his heritage...or will he remain hidden in his blood-drenched past?

The Last Divide

Rivals, competitors, training partners—never friends. Brought together after 15 years by a passion that could put a raging storm to shame, will they finally reach out for a love long since hidden...or will the walls of the past keep them apart?

Our Love Replay

After years of loving each other from a distance, an acoustic songstress and a basketball superstar are reunited in the idyllic countryside. Burdened by secrets and the facade of fame, will they be brave enough to admit their true feelings, before the shot clock runs out?

Stories of Us

A ROMANCE NOVELLA COLLECTION

SHIRLEY SIATON

STORIES OF US
A Romance Novella Collection

Originally published as 'Angel' (August 2023), 'Heart Chained' (September 2023), 'Shadow and Light' (September 2023), 'The Last Divide' (November 2023) and 'Our Love Replay' (May 2024)

Copyright © 2025 Shirley Siaton Parabia

ALL RIGHTS RESERVED.
No part of this book may be reproduced or used in any manner without the prior written permission of the copyright owner, except for the use of brief quotations in a book review. To request permission, contact the publisher at books@inkysword.com.

This is a work of fiction. Names, characters, businesses, events and incidents are the products of the author's imagination. Any resemblance to actual persons, living or dead, or actual events is purely coincidental.

All brand and product names used in this book are trademarks, registered trademarks, or trade names of their respective owners. Inky Sword Book Publishing is not associated with any product or vendor in this book.

ISBN 978-621-8371-76-7 **(paperback)**

First Edition, January 2025

Published by Shirley S. Parabia
Cover by Artscandare Book Design
Interior formatting by Champagne Book Design

Inky Sword Book Publishing
Barangay Quezon, Arevalo, Iloilo City 5000
Republic of the Philippines
inkysword.com

Content Warnings

Warnings for explicit scenes, profanity, and mentions and occurrences of violence.

Recommended for mature readers 18 years old and above..

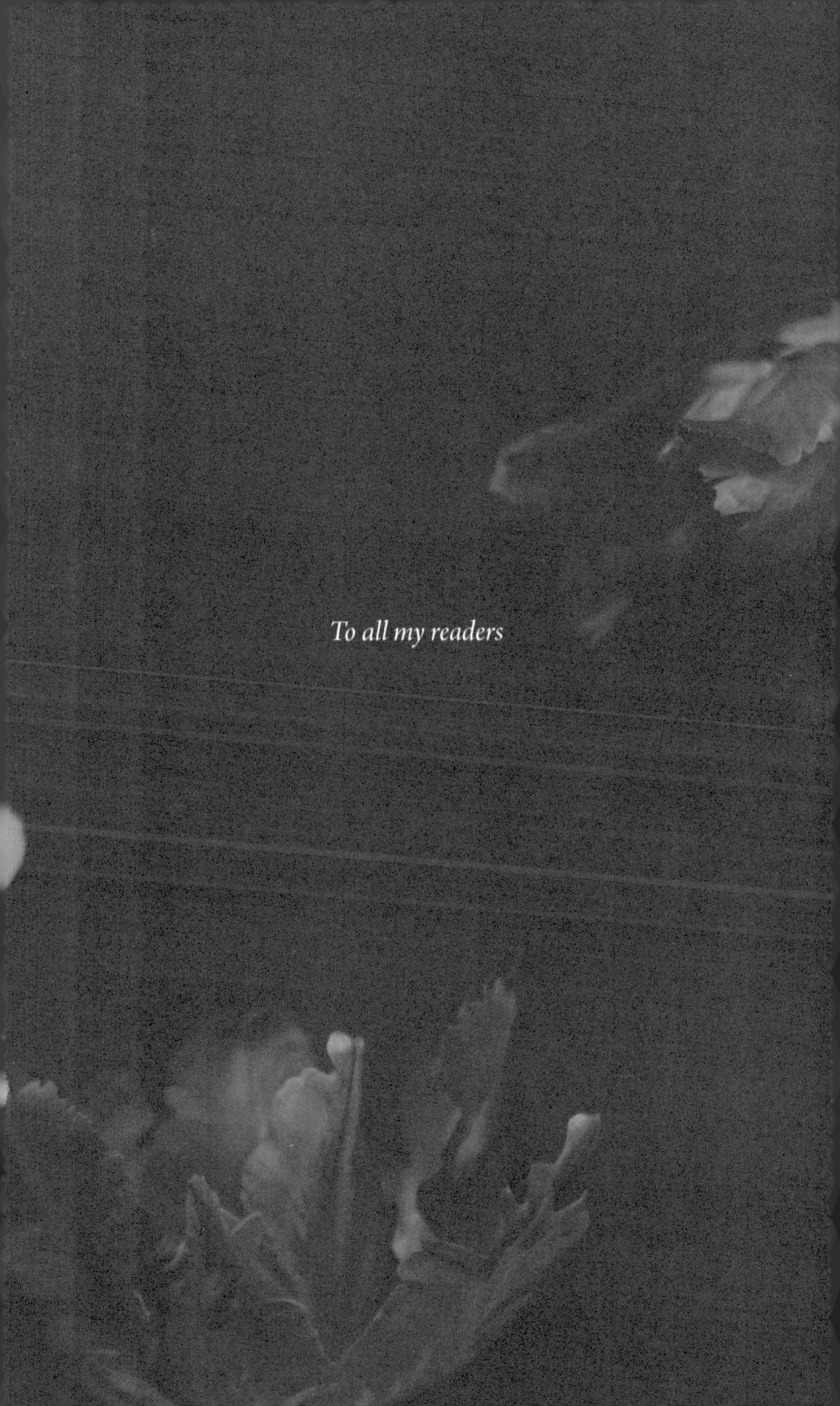

To all my readers

Contents

Content Warnings v

Book I: Angel xiii
Playlist xv
One: Stranger 1
Two: Criminal 9
Three: Farewell 23
Four: Reckoning 31
Five: Prison 39
Six: Storm 47

BOOK II: Heart Chained 53
Playlist 55
One: The Return 57
Two: The Secret 61
Three: The Rain 71
Four: The Race 75
Five: The Stranger 83
Six: The Turn 93
Seven: The Heart 101
Eight: The Chains 107
Nine: The Touch 111
Ten: The Light 117

BOOK III: Shadow and Light 123
Playlist 125
Prologue: The Prized Player 127
Act I: Falling 131

One: The Dark 133
Two: The Dusk 137
Three: The Distance 145
Four: The Divide 157
Five: The Dance 169
Act II: Fallen 187
Six: The Desire 189
Seven: The Dream 195
Eight: The Deception 199
Nine: The Deal 203
Ten: The Dawn 207
Epilogue: The Last Letter 211

Book IV: The Last Divide 213
Playlist 215
Prologue: Drawn 217
One: Reverie 225
Two: Return 233
Three: Rewind 241
Four: Resurface 253
Five: Restart 263
Six: Recall 273
Seven: Remnant 285
Eight: Revelation 299
Nine: Resonance 317
Ten: Restraint 329
Eleven: Recompense 339
Twelve: Remainder 347
Thirteen: Retrace 363
Fourteen: Restitution 375
Epilogue: Crossed 389

Book V: Our Love Replay	**399**
Playlist	401
Prologue: The Rain	403
Chapter 1: The Artist	419
Chapter 2: The Playlist	427
Chapter 3: The Sunset	441
Chapter 4: The Journey	449
Chapter 5: The Kiss	461
Chapter 6: The Garden	469
Chapter 7: The Memory	479
Chapter 8: The Game	485
Chapter 9: The Heart	493
Chapter 10: The Song	499
Chapter 11: The Secret	515
Chapter 12: The Dream	527
Chapter 13: The Confession	539
Chapter 14: The Promise	547
Chapter 15: The Eternity	559
Chapter 16: The Goodbye	567
Chapter 17: The Diamond	583
Chapter 18: The Gift	593
Chapter 19: The Victory	607
Chapter 20: The Beginning	615
Epilogue: The Story	625
About the Author	633
On the Web	635

A ROMANCE NOVELLA COLLECTION

BOOK I

Angel

Playlist

My Heart
Paramore

Secret Love Song
Little Mix & Jason Derulo

Dusk till Dawn
Zayn & Sia

Going Under
Evanescence

Hero
Enrique Iglesias

Put Your Arms Around Me
Texas

One

STRANGER

SHE GAZED AT THE SKY FOR PROBABLY THE umpteenth time in the past hour.

It was a starry night. The North Star and the many known constellations stood out clearly, brightly. The moon was bright and perfectly spherical. There was no chance of rain.

It was the kind of night for romance, at least for a teen-aged girl.

Stella Montero sat by herself at the street corner. The bench, with a newly dried coat of fresh paint, courtesy of a congressman, was right by the bus stop.

This was her favorite intersection, one she had grown up in. It was always brightly-lit by traffic lights and neon storefront signs. Green, red, orange, yellow and blue; it was its own kind of rainbow.

A gust of wind blew, stirring the street before her. Discarded newspapers and fliers flew by, tumbling on the stone pavement decorated by graffiti as colorful as the lights overhead.

Stella looked at the sky again. In mere seconds, it seemed to have grown murky and cloudy, as if someone had stolen the lights.

The stars were not the only ones that disappeared that night. Her hopes had gone, too.

Was it only this afternoon when Aaron called and asked if she wanted to go to the movies with him? Was it only a few hours ago when she, drifting on fluffy white clouds, had put on her best dress and favorite shoes and snuck into her mother's room to use her makeup and perfume?

She had already fallen from those clouds. More like stumbled, fell, and landed on the cold hard ground on her ass.

Six-thirty, the time she was supposed to meet Aaron Soler, had come and gone.

It was getting cold. She looked at her watch. It was already half past eight. She pulled her now-rumpled white cardigan more tightly around her body, shoving her hands into their shallow pockets. She would be an idiot if she allowed herself any more hope that he would show up at all. She had more self-respect than that.

"Stood you up, hasn't he?" The voice came out of nowhere, causing her to nearly jump out of her skin.

She sprang to her feet and backed a few feet away, hands clenching into fists as she turned to face the owner of the voice.

She had a box cutter in her bag, she thought, comforted. A girl who grew up in a city like hers knew how to protect herself.

He emerged from underneath the awning of an ice cream shop.

It was a boy. No, a man, tall and dangerous-looking as any predator of the shadows.

He had a thick mane of hair that fell past his shoulders. His skin was duskier than most, allowing him to blend easier into the night. Most of his face was still shrouded in the darkness; what she could see was about a third of his profile, sharp and harsh.

He was the most fearsome and compelling sight she had ever laid eyes on.

"Who are you?" It was almost a shriek, nothing like her own voice. "What do you want?"

He advanced into the light. His face looked even harder and older. There was a scar that ran the length of his right cheek, hidden in part by his long hair. He appeared to be in his early twenties, perhaps older.

"My name is Trey," he said, almost formally. "Hello, Stella."

She backed further away, hot and cold rushing through her veins at the same time.

"How did you know my name?" she demanded.

He gave a slight shrug, his shoulders rippling. "I asked."

She drew herself to her full height of five-foot-five, enough to intimidate most boys her age. It would probably have no effect on him, seeing that he was much bigger, but there was no harm in trying to appear braver than she actually was. "Asked who?"

"The people here. Everyone knows you."

"The people?" she echoed, stumped.

"You see them every day."

She stared, trying to understand what he meant.

Them? The people?

She blinked, slightly taken aback by the bright light coming out of the open doorway of the leather repair shop down the street. She shut her eyes for the briefest of moments. When she opened them, she saw the sweet old woman who ran the shop give her a smile and a friendly wave. Seconds later, someone else left the shop, the old man who did all the repairs by hand or using an ancient pedal machine.

She watched them lock up the shop and walk off.

She understood.

This was her intersection, her neighborhood, her city.

"Yes," she said, more to herself than to the stranger. "I see them every day."

"So you do."

She glared up at him, feeling infinitely more confident that she did minutes ago. "That doesn't explain why you're here, or what you want from me."

"With you? Nothing." Trey sat on the bench she had vacated, draping his arm over the back of the seat and extending his legs. With his dark shirt and jeans, he looked like a giant snake, coiled and poised to strike. "Why I'm here has everything to do with your friend, the pretty boy."

"Aaron?"

"We were tipped off by one of his sidekicks. They come here and pick up girls for their pot sessions. The last one didn't go so well. Joshua didn't want to be part of the repeat performance."

'Pretty boy' Aaron, who was supposed to be her date, was a senior and the most popular boy at their college. His father was the mayor of one of the smaller towns that bordered the city. Aaron always had a lot of boys in his entourage, mostly those from more affluent families; they moved around the school as if they owned it. Girls who got his attention instantly became the most popular ones at school. With her being only a freshman, his initial attentions had flattered Stella to no end.

"Joshua." She repeated the name, trying to jog her memory. "He's the one with the red car. He was supposed to pick me up tonight, with Aaron, and…" Her voice trailed off.

"Joshua Benitez won't be coming, either," he said. "As for Aaron Soler, let's just say his plans have changed."

Girls. Pot sessions. Repeat performance. His words kept echoing in her head as she stood stock-still on the sidewalk. This time, she shivered for real. The night breeze was nothing compared to the cold coming from within her

"Did you want to sit down?" Trey moved his arm out of the way and slid to one side of the bench.

Stella hurried over and plopped down next to him, before she collapsed from the sheer weight of information she was absorbing.

"How long has this…been going on?" So many questions popped into her head, but it was difficult to put them into words. This was the kind of urban cautionary tale picked up and sensationalized by late-night crime investigation shows. "How did you know about them? How the hell do I know you're even telling the truth?"

"I don't have to answer any of that, do I?" He leaned forward, placing his elbows on his thighs and clasping his massive hands between them. He turned his head and peered at her face. "Or would you really want me to?"

She found herself looking into his eyes. They were midnight-black, unblinking. Strangely, she felt no discomfort under his gaze; instead, she stared right back.

"I just wanted to go on a date with Aaron, you know," she said softly. "When he asked me out, I was on top of the world, everyone at school was looking at me. They all saw me. And Aaron…he actually knew who I was, he got my name right and everything."

"I'm sure he did." There was no sympathy or sarcasm in his voice. He sounded as if he didn't have to convince anyone of anything. "He knew Victoria, Yasmeen, Jennifer and Grace very well, too. Unlike you, they never stood a chance."

Stella didn't know the other three, but Jennifer Ang was a sophomore Aaron had dated the previous semester. She was a beauty queen, slated to compete in the national circuit of pageants that coming summer. Shortly after Jennifer and Aaron broke up, Jennifer's parents, who both worked abroad, had pulled her out of college in the middle of the year and brought her with them to Singapore. There had been rumors of a pregnancy, a party blunder that displeased her sponsors and ruined her image, an expulsion notice that was kept quiet…

"I knew Jennifer," she said. "She's a beauty queen who used to go to my college. She was his girlfriend for a while. She left town end of last semester."

"She got lucky. Grace was from about six weeks ago; she was studying Political Science in the university across town. She sat where you are sitting now. They saw her here before she got in the car with Benitez. She's in rehab now."

The strange reality of it all was overwhelming. In a matter of hours, she had been stood up in what was supposed to be the biggest date of life, her great crush had become a junkie who was bad news for girls, and a stranger from out of nowhere had appeared to be some twisted version of a guardian angel.

"Do you know where Aaron is?"

There was a crooked smile at the corner of Trey's mouth. "Do I really have to answer that question? The less you know, the better for you."

"I can't just sit here without knowing anything," she insisted. "If you want me to at least believe in what you're trying to tell me, then give me some answers."

"Soler won't be able to come here tonight. He and his friend are both at the docks. I brought them there earlier. We're trying to get them to sing. If they're lucky, they would get a little beaten down. If not…" He shrugged. "It's not like they even cared about what would happen to those girls."

"And you…you got them there?"

"It's my job. I work for the man who decided to put them there and, at the same time, get you out of something you wouldn't want."

She sat next to him, trying to keep her breathing even. She had somehow stumbled straight into the plot of a cheap action movie. At any other time, this would have felt contrived, even cheesy.

But she felt nothing like that.

This was a close call, not a joke. She could have ended up like any of those girls.

At that moment, Stella wanted nothing more than to see her mother. If anything happened to her, she could not even imagine her mother's reaction, the pain it would cause her. Even thinking about it made her feel *guilty*.

"I think I want to go home," she said.

The intersection was almost empty except for a few pedestrians and the familiar nighttime vendors who sold peanuts, duck eggs and green mangoes from their baskets. Most of the stores were already closed for the night. She had been there for almost three hours.

"I'll walk you there." He stood up the same time she did. Side by side, she barely made it to his shoulder. "Or wait until you get into a taxi."

"That won't be necessary," she said, flustered. "I live a few blocks away, near the commercial port."

"You can walk on your own if you want. I'll follow, anyway, and make sure you get there."

At any other time, she would have found those words creepy. She would have felt uncomfortable at the very least.

Tonight, however, was the kind of night that brought creepy to shame. If anything, she was past creepy.

With Trey, there was no feeling of discomfort, only a sense of awareness that he was more intimidating than everyone and everything else around her.

"Fine," she said, thinking she would rather have someone like him walking her home, rather than the less impressive assurance provided by her box cutter. "Let's go."

Two

CRIMINAL

She looked at the sky again, maybe for the seventh time in the past half hour.

It was still raining. It showed no signs of letting up.

Stella stood by the waiting shed next to the main gate of her college. She was still mercifully dry, if not for errant drops of rainwater, brought about by nasty gusts of wind, whipping against her skin and her white college uniform.

This wasn't rain, she thought. This was a full-blown storm, at least Signal Number Two.

Night had been upon them for hours, with clouds blotting out the sun since mid-afternoon. All the classes for the evening finished at seven-thirty. It was already past eight.

The campus would be locked up soon. She would have

to brave the storm on foot and wade her way through the flooded streets if she didn't want to get kicked out or get stuck. It was only a matter of time before the water levels got too high, if the rain didn't stop.

It was a simple, straightforward plan. Out the school and through the city's main street, where there was better drainage. She could use the buildings as shelter and sprint the last few hundred meters home past the plaza and the church. She would be soaked to the bone and maybe even get sick, but at least she wouldn't freeze to death outside her own school.

She turned to the other students huddled next to her, looking them over as she took off her shoes. There were three other girls and two boys, all looking as if they had the same predicament as she: brave the rain and flood, or wait it out. Her own choice already decided, she put her shoes in her bag and gave them a silent nod before walking out into the downpour.

It was easy enough to cross the road and make her way past the market. She was able to take shelter in the windows and awnings, up to and until she reached the main street.

By the time she made it to the intersection, the rain was so heavy she could barely see past a few steps in front of her. The shops had closed, with most of their lights and signs put out. What little light there was came from the streetlamps that still worked. She could feel water, cold and sticky, running in quick tiny currents under her feet. Blasted on all sides by strong winds, she could barely stay upright. It was like being in the middle of a sunken, vengeful city.

So much for her plan of using the buildings as shelter. She'd be lucky if she could make it past this junction. One wrong step could lead her into an open drainage hatch, if she didn't fall on her face, drown or get electrocuted first.

She stood in front of the sixty-year-old grocery store, squinting through the rain at a dim light coming from the window of a single shop across the street.

It was the old couple's leather repair shop. Were they still there? Could she possibly stay with them until this was over? Could she even cover that much ground without dying along the way?

Throwing caution literally to the winds, she drew her bag tighter against her body and sprinted full speed across the darkened road. Her bare feet burned from the roughness of the asphalt and the icy coldness of the flood.

"Hello? Can I please come in?" she called out, half-crashing, half-stumbling against the shop entrance. She pushed the wooden door open with all her strength and promptly ran into a wall.

She felt the wall give way a little, then something grabbed her upper arms, steadying her. It took her a second to figure out that she had run into someone, not something.

"Stella?"

It took a few more seconds for her eyes to adjust to the soft yellowish light inside the shop. Through a haze of stinging rainwater, she could make out a large black figure with equally dark hair and eyes. His face was the last thing that came into focus.

It was him.

"Trey?"

"What the hell are you doing here? Are you okay?"

She flinched at the harshness of his voice, or maybe at

the strength of the grip he had on her. She could barely move her upper body.

At least she could still move her head. She nodded. "I'm fine. Can you please let go of me?"

His hands loosened and fell away. She watched him take a step back, inwardly debating with herself whether or not this was all real.

"Did I hurt you?" Without taking his eyes off her, he picked up something from the front counter. It was an emergency lantern, the source of light she had seen through the window. The shadows in the room shifted as he brought the lantern overhead.

"No, it's okay," she replied, a little too aware of how closely they stood to each other. The repair shop had always been tiny, but now it felt considerably cramped and tight. "Where's Auntie Yolly and Uncle Frank?"

"They've gone home. Did you come here to see them? All the shops closed hours ago." There was a note of disbelief in his voice.

She shook her head. "I was going to take shelter here. It was the only place with the lights on. I thought I could get home on foot, but the streets are too badly flooded."

Exhaustion and cold started nipping at her joints. She leaned against the wooden counter and put her bag on top. Her uniform was drenched, the skirt stained by the flood waters.

It was only then that she noticed it.

The blood.

Next to the space where she had put her bag, she spied small streaks of dark red liquid. Her eyes followed the stains over the side, all the way down the floor, to the spot where Auntie Yolly would usually stand to serve customers. Concealed behind the wooden counter were two limp bodies leaning against each other, their faces split open like overripe watermelons.

She screamed.

She tried but never got the chance. He put his arm around her and brought her close to him, pressing her so tightly against his body that any sound she could make was muffled against his chest.

"Stella," he said, very calmly, almost soothingly. "Stella. Stella, look at me. Please don't scream. Just look at me."

She could feel her body shake violently at the gory sight she had just witnessed. She focused on his voice, the welcome heat of his body. She was fine. It was just blood. It wasn't her blood.

"Look at me, Stella," he repeated. "Don't scream. They're not dead. I won't hurt you."

Clutching at his shirt, she willed herself to open her eyes.

She could see, under the light of the lantern he held up, that he was looking at her, too, into her eyes. His own eyes smoldered like hot coals. She focused on them. He wouldn't hurt her.

"Good," he said. "Now breathe."

She breathed out, a long exhale that made her lightheaded. She held on to him, kept her eyes locked onto the somehow comforting familiarity of his face, as she tried to get her bearings.

"Please get me out of here," she heard herself say, trying very hard not to think of the bloody pulps next to her.

His face impassive, he let go of her and moved to the entrance to bolt it shut from the inside. When he was done, he gestured for her to go further inside the shop. "Let's go upstairs. If the water gets any higher, we'll be safer there."

Still feeling sick to her stomach, Stella carefully took her bag and did as instructed. Beyond the front of the shop, behind a thin plastic curtain, was the small workroom she was familiar with, lined wall to wall with tools and Uncle Frank's ancient pedal machine. To one side was a narrow flight of steps.

Guided by the light of the lantern, she was able to find her way to the mezzanine in record time. It was no larger than the downstairs area but had a higher ceiling. It appeared to be some kind of storage room for the shop's supplies. At one end of the room was a large glass window.

She put her bag on a shelf and made her way to the window. There was almost nothing to see, except the rain pelting against the glass and a very limited view of the flooded street outside. Most of the working streetlamps she saw earlier had gone out.

"You should sit down." Trey had put down the lamp on a tiny table and was bringing over a wooden stool for her. "You didn't have to see what you just saw. I guess you'd want an explanation?"

She settled on the stool, stretching out her legs and bare feet. She looked at him as he backed up and settled his large frame on the table next to the lamp. He looked bigger than she remembered; his hair was longer, too.

It didn't surprise her that he was talking so casually about the scene downstairs.

"Did you do that to them?" she asked, boldly.

"I did, just before you got here," he answered. "As I said,

they're not dead. They're just out. I remember doing the same thing to your old friends a while back."

She remembered that night vividly. After she'd reached home, she had looked over her shoulder to see Trey gone. She had tried not to think about what had happened and had not told anyone, not even her mother. In the Monday that followed, there had been a large ruckus at the college about the two boys and the rest of their circle getting arrested. None of their gang of nine ever made it back to campus. As far as she'd heard, the other boys had been caught in the act of using drugs and hurting girls from other schools. Stella had thought that maybe Joshua had sung a little too well, or maybe Trey and his boss had made him do so.

"What did they do this time? Drugs?" Stella tried not to think of all the blood splattered on the counter and the floor.

"They were going to burn this building down. They got into the shop by breaking the front lock. They probably wanted to make it look like an accident that started from here, with the amount of leather oil they were carrying. They could have easily taken out this entire block, too. These buildings may look like solid stone from the outside, but inside it's all old wood."

"Why would they want to do that?" She thought of all the people who had stores in the block. She had known most of them since she was little; if not by name, she recognized them by face.

"Territory. Those fuckers are not from here, they're not even from Visayas. They're the Zamora family from Manila. They want to control the Pier District, starting with the small businesses. With the livelihood of the people gone, it would be easier to buy them out."

Trey got off the table and walked the length of the room to look out the window himself. "They tried the same thing last month at the port, with the vendor stalls. We barely got there on time. Otherwise, they could have burned down nearly two hundred stalls and parts of the commercial port."

She lived there. Her house was a stone's throw away from those stalls. She used to eat there regularly. "The only thing I heard about the port was that there was a huge riot that broke out among drunks over videoke. It was all over the news last month. My mother warned me not to go there in the evenings once they start all the singing and drinking."

He looked over his shoulder at her. "It was a good story, wasn't it? The boys staged the riot so well and got all the attention. We were lucky at the time."

She hesitated before asking her next question. "What are you going to do about them?" She gestured vaguely downwards.

"We're tracking down their friends who could be in the other buildings. As soon as we could get through the flood, we're taking these sons of bitches to their quarters across town. It took us a while to find out where they're holed up. Turns out they live in the house of Greg Garces. He's got ties with the Filipino-American mafia. I wouldn't be surprised if he's the one funding this little takeover attempt."

Another cause, another enemy.

More blood.

Why Trey did what he was doing she had no idea. "What do they want from the Pier District? I've lived here all my life. Most of us in our neighborhood have. It's just boats and warehouses and shops, and tiny old houses like mine."

He turned to face her completely. "Whoever controls

the district controls the shipping routes and traffic. What goes in, what goes out, what everybody does in it. Most importantly, who gets to do business. All kinds of business."

"Somebody already does that, right?" She searched her memory for the name. It was a very old name, the elusive but notorious family that owned at least half of the district where she lived. "The Esguerras?"

"Raphael Esguerra. Ever since he took over a few years ago, other families and groups have been trying to take him down on all sides. A new leader usually takes a lot of heat. We've been putting out fires for a while now."

"You do dangerous things" she said. "You could get killed. Can't you just…quit?"

"And do what?"

"I don't know. Live and work somewhere else."

"Some of us can't just quit," he said with more emotion than she'd ever heard. "Some of us can't just give up the life we were born into. I grew up in the docks. I've lived here my whole life, too, just like you. I will do everything in my power to keep the Pier District from getting destroyed by outsiders, even if it means becoming a criminal to get rid of the people in my way."

His eyes left her then, as he focused his attention back to the window.

She stood up and picked her way over to the window, to see what he was looking at. It was still windy and raining heavily.

"I hope it stops raining soon. I want to go home. I've been at school since eight this morning."

"Aren't you cold? You look like you're going to be sick

soon." The concern on his face made her aware of their closeness.

All she had to do was reach out, to touch him, to make sure he was real.

Ever since that night at the intersection, she had thought about him constantly, wondering if he ever existed at all. She had wanted to ask others about him, but had decided not to. She knew if he'd been just a figment of her imagination she would be devastated.

She was soaked with rainwater and freezing all the way to her insides. She wasn't even aware she had wrapped her own arms around her body to keep herself warm.

"I'm fine. It was my fault. I forgot my umbrella at the library. By the time I came back to get it, I was too late."

"Here." Trey started unbuttoning his shirt. She stared, heat rushing to her face. She tried to move her legs, to step away from him, but she was frozen to the spot. His black shirt opened, showing a grey t-shirt underneath. He took off the polo and handed it to her. "Put this on."

She was blushing and she knew it. The grey shirt had a tighter fit on his body. His shoulders and chest were broad, contrasting with his flat stomach and narrow hips. His black polo ended up in her shaky hand.

"Thanks," she heard herself choke out.

"I'm sorry if there are any…stains on it. I don't have anything warmer."

His shirt was the warmest thing she had ever touched. It had a clean, fresh scent, something like pine, tinged with the sea. She slid her arms into the shirt, almost disappearing into its considerably larger size.

"It's fine. It's very warm. Thank you."

They both stood by the window in silence, staring out into the rain and the nearly invisible city street.

"How are you, Stella?" It had gotten so quiet, his voice almost startled her. "I didn't get to ask you earlier."

"Life goes on, I suppose," she said. "School has been busier since I was a freshman. Thankfully, no one tried anything since that night. I think everyone got a little bit scared with what happened to Aaron and Joshua."

"A little bit scared?"

"Scared shitless, then?"

"Better."

She smiled. "So, how are you?"

He held up his left hand to the light. His knuckles looked freshly skinned, with a little blood caked and dried on them. "Bloody after my little fun. I guess I'm fine."

She was tempted to reach out and touch his hand. She could only clench her own fingers into a tight fist.

"I don't think I ever got to say thank you," she said.

"For what?"

"For back then." She could feel herself blushing again. She really had to get herself under control. All this caused by someone she barely knew, someone who had the knack of appearing out of the darkness for her, whenever she needed it most. "And for now, I think."

He shook his head. "You're thanking me for showing you two half-dead bodies in a leather repair shop?"

"For being there, Trey. It means something to me, even if the thought had never crossed your mind. Don't be like that."

She was rewarded with the tiniest of smiles. "This is as much of a surprise to me as it is to you, Stella."

The moment was interrupted by his phone ringing. He

took it out of his pocket and answered. "Yes. I'm still here. Are you sure there's no one else out there?"

Trey looked out the window again. "Can you drop someone off first, then come back? Good."

"There's a car on the way," he said to her, replacing the phone in his pocket. "It can get through the flood. They'll take you home."

"That's great. Thanks." She looked around her, never at him. He would disappear again for goodness knew how long. She had to say it. "Will I see you again?"

He was already making his way back to retrieve the lamp from the table. He stopped mid-step and stared at her from over his shoulder. "What?"

"Will I ever get to see you again?" she repeated, as bravely as she could.

"Why would you want to see me? People don't usually like seeing me."

"I like seeing you," she retorted.

"Give me your phone." He walked back to her and held out his hand.

She reached into her bag, between rows of damp notebooks, and retrieved her phone. It was only slightly damp on the outside. The tiny device almost disappeared into his hand.

He looked at her phone's casing for a few seconds. It was made of shiny white silicone, decorated with a stylized drawing of a black archangel. He didn't comment. He turned it over to the screen side and started typing.

She heard his phone ringing again. "That's you calling. I'll save your number. Call me whenever you need, okay? I will answer."

She was tempted to say something in response when

he handed the phone back to her. Nothing came out of her mouth. Not even when she retrieved her bag and followed him down the stairs.

She stood as close as she possibly could to the entrance, the farthest from the two bodies behind the counter. Trey was talking on his phone again, to someone else, about meeting them in another district across town.

It barely took any time before the car reached the flooded main street. She saw its headlights approaching and turned to him.

Stella finally found her voice. "Thanks." She took off his shirt and handed it back.

He shook his head. "No, keep it."

"I don't think I can." *Even if she wanted to.* "My mother will ask a lot of questions. It's a very small house. And it's just the two of us."

"Don't worry. I understand." He took the shirt and put it back on just as she heard a muted honking from outside. He unlocked the shop's front door and held it open for her. "Take care of yourself."

"You, too." She walked past him and stepped back into the street. Once outside, she could see that the rain had calmed down. It was still pouring heavily, but she could barely feel the wind.

He followed her. "Tell Mario where you want to go. He'll drive you there."

A dark four-wheel drive had stopped outside the shop. It stood amidst the flood looking like a tank. A middle-aged man rolled down the window by the driver's side and was about to step out when Trey held up a hand and opened the backseat door himself.

"Good night, Stella." The rain dripped on his face and hair. He didn't even blink.

She finally reached out and got to touch his left hand, the one with the skinned knuckles. It felt warm, rough, strong. "Thanks again. Good night."

He nodded and shut the car door. He didn't move from the spot where he stood, not even when the giant car pulled out of the sidewalk and started making its way through the flood.

She never took her eyes off him. Not until the sight of him was swallowed by the darkness that stretched out behind her.

Three

FAREWELL

She looked up at the sky, then down at her watch. She sighed, trying to find a more comfortable position on the bench. Her legs and feet, clad in the black regulation stockings and low-heeled shoes of her school uniform, felt cramped. She felt warm in the white suit and regretted not changing into something cooler.

In the early evening, the intersection was the same as always, bright, messy and full of people rushing to catch a ride or selling food and trinkets. There was a thick, balmy breeze coming from the nearby waters of the docks, heavily tinged with salt. It was going to be a humid night.

Was it only a few years ago that she had sat on this same bench, shivering in a white cardigan, grappling with the dark realities of the world she was growing up in? It felt like a lifetime ago.

She wasn't surprised when someone suddenly took the spot next to her on the bench. She kind of expected it.

Stella had expected anything to happen since she got the text message from Trey last week. She had never called or messaged him in the past eighteen months since they last saw each other. She had not deleted his number, either.

It was the only message she had ever received from him.

Can we meet

Same place

Friday 6pm

She had called him back straightaway, just to make sure it wasn't someone else messing with her. He had answered after two rings, in that deep, raspy voice that sometimes followed her, especially when she walked alone in the city streets at night. Sometimes she dreamt of that voice, too.

For this Friday, she skipped her last class and told her friends she would meet them at the movies tomorrow evening. She had the foolproof reason of completing a report due that Monday.

"Hi, Stella." Trey, no longer a disembodied presence at the back of her head, looked surprisingly different. His long hair was tied back in a neat ponytail; he was dressed in a green polo shirt, blue jeans and brown shoes. He looked almost normal; his scarred face was as fierce-looking as ever, maybe even a little sharper with age.

Stella wondered how he thought she looked. She had definitely gotten taller since last time. Over the past few years, it was her height that brought her attention and sometimes opportunities neither she nor her mother had ever expected. A few months ago, she was approached by an events company to model for a local fashion show early next year.

"How are you, Trey?" she asked, politely. Light conversation had never been part of their interactions.

His Adam's apple was bobbing up and down. "I'm fine. Thanks for coming. I didn't think you would even answer my text. How have you been?"

She forced a smile, as strange as it felt to have normal small talk with him. "Good. Busy. Reports and exams take up most of my time. I'll be graduating this school year."

There was a rustle as he pulled out something from behind his back. She was certain he had gotten even bigger since last time; his shoulders looked wider in the more flattering cut and color of his shirt.

To her surprise, there was a small box of roses in his hands. There were three: one red, one pink and one white.

"I didn't know which color you liked, but I took a chance and picked roses," he said. "You always have on some kind of cologne that smells like roses."

"Yes, I like roses," she answered, taken aback. "Roses are nice."

If she had to list a hundred things this man was capable of doing, giving her roses would never even be a remote consideration, much less knowing how she actually smelled.

She reached out to take the box, trying to think of something else to say and failing miserably. She wasn't sure if she had intended to touch him, but her hands landed on top of his.

She looked up into his dark eyes and, sure enough, they were on her, too. She understood that look from a man, far better now than she did four years ago. No matter how mysterious he appeared to be, he was still a man, wasn't he?

"I wanted to see you," he finally said, breaking the silent, unmoving exchange between them. "I didn't want to leave town without telling you."

Her fingers closed around the box. It was made of white cardboard, plain yet sturdy, with a plastic display window to showcase the flowers inside. It was something she expected from someone like him: unadorned and straightforward.

"Where are you going?"

"Does it matter?"

"It does to me." She clutched the box closer to her, pressing it to the space between her chest and her stomach.

"I'm going to get a few things out of the way. North, mostly in Manila. We've lost a lot of good people to the Zamoras this past year. They haven't stopped trying to take over the Pier District."

His back heaved in what looked like a sigh. "It's only a matter of time before this escalates to an all-out war. But Iloilo is our home, we were born and raised here. We won't give it up, so we're bringing the war to them."

He was bringing the war to them, she thought.

Stella suddenly felt cold, empty, abandoned. The same way she had felt the first time she met him, on this very bench.

"You'll be back, right? You said before this is the life you were born into. You can't just leave, can you?"

There was that familiar tiny smile at the corner of his mouth. "It's not about leaving or staying. When I chose to do this, I knew I wouldn't be coming back. Sometimes, there are things we need to do that we can't just walk away from."

"I see," she said, evenly. "You'll be missing my graduation, then." It sounded stupid and pointless, but nothing ever made sense with him anyway. She could not even fathom how deep, dark and bloody the world he lived in was.

"I guess I will."

"I was a freshman when we first met, you know."

He nodded. "So, are you going to the senior prom with someone special?"

"Prom?" she echoed. "I haven't really thought about it. I don't have a special someone."

The idea had never really crossed her mind, not since what happened during freshman year. She had nothing against boys in general, but since then she had been averse to the young adult rituals of courting and dating.

Sure, there were a few boys who showed interest, some more than others. Darryl, whose family moved from another province at the start of their junior year, had been courting her shortly after he completed his first semester at the college. He was part of the student council and tutored younger students in Math subjects. Her mother liked him immensely. Stella didn't exactly dislike him; she just wasn't interested.

"It took me a while to trust boys again, after what happened. But I've learned a thing or two since then. I would stick an idiot in the throat with a box cutter before they could try anything funny." She had to smile through the heaviness in her muscles, a strange sensation considering how empty she felt inside.

They sat in silence for a while, before he stood up.

"I'm glad you're okay, Stella. At least I got one thing right in all of this."

Driven by a sudden sense of panic, she jumped to her own feet. "Are you going now?" she blurted out.

"I'm leaving tomorrow morning, so I'd better get ready." He was looking down at her with his mouth in a thin line. "I'm sorry if I bothered or upset you in any way. If there was someone I had to say goodbye to, it was you."

She felt something rise in her throat, bitter and painful and stinging hot.

Goodbye, she thought. It sounded so final and absolute.

Guardian angels were supposed to stay, weren't they? Wasn't he supposed to stay with her?

"I'm glad you told me," she said honestly. "It gave me a chance to see you. I thought I'd see you again sooner, after last time. But I'm glad you're here now."

"Me, too."

She swallowed hard, trying her best to stem the flood rising dangerously fast from within her. "It's early. I skipped my last class to meet you."

Before he could respond, she continued. "Let's eat something, okay? It will be my treat. I never had the chance to do anything for you."

Without giving him the opportunity to refuse, she grabbed him by the arm and pulled him through the throng of people milling the busy nighttime streets. She knew this place was part of him. This was home for Trey.

They had dinner of grilled fish and rice at a small,

open-air eatery on the docks. It was nice to see him doing something normal with her, for a change.

Or for the last time.

It was almost nine in the evening when the lights of the stores and restaurants started going out, signaling the end of the day. She thought back to the time she had sat at the intersection and looked at the dying stars as her own hopes died, too.

Trey was the only constant presence between then and now, between an innocent teenager's disappointment and her first real heartbreak.

Her twisted kind of guardian angel, who was leaving her life as soon as the day was over. She was determined not to lose any more time she had left with this beguiling man.

"You live near here, don't you?" She had her hand on his arm, a gesture she had dared to try earlier, as they walked on the open pier, the area where smaller passenger boats docked in the daytime. She had thought he would not want to be touched, but she was wrong. She was glad to be wrong.

"It's near the old Customs office," he said, a little too formally, nodding towards a cluster of warehouses a block away. "My boss bought a few buildings here to keep some of the cars and for us to stay in if we wanted. I didn't want to live out of town."

"Can I see your place?" Heat flooded her face at her own boldness.

He stopped in his tracks. "It's late. I should be walking you home.

"I don't want to go home. Not yet."

"What do you want, then, Stella?"

Before her mind realized what she was doing, her body and heart had already made the call.

Her school bag, with his gift of roses, slid off her shoulder as she let go of his arm to, finally, put her own arms around him. She could reach his shoulders, his neck; she had to stand on tiptoes and force his head down with all her might. And it worked.

She kissed him.

Four

RECKONING

She didn't think about it anymore. She just moved as she had always wanted to. She ran her hands over his back and his thick hair; she used her tongue to taste him, his lips, the inside of his mouth. The rest of her followed; her chest and her hips pressed against him, wanting more, maybe at least for him to touch her, too.

He understood.

She knew as much when he came to life, knowing exactly what she wanted, what she needed.

His lips moved against hers; his tongue was deliciously soft and snake-like as it twisted its way into the depths of her mouth. His hands were all over her. His fingers ran through her long hair, his palms burned a path through her skin as he wrapped his arms around her waist and started caressing her buttocks. It wasn't very long until she was pressed against him so tightly, she could feel him, hard and insistent, against her own softness. His fingertips glided inside her skirt as he lifted one of her legs to wrap around his hip.

She gasped when he touched that part of her, expertly reaching inside the modest underwear she wore with her school uniform. His fingers rubbed and stroked her as she moaned against his chest.

She denied herself the pleasure that was beginning to build and decided to come back up for air. She grabbed at his arms, still feeling him against her.

"Take me home, Trey," she whispered into the night. "Make me yours."

He was always more at ease in the shadows. She watched as he picked up her things with ruthless efficiency. This time, it was his turn to take her hand and lead the way.

He lived in a warehouse, one filled with auto parts. The lighting was sparse; except for a few fluorescent bulbs, it was the lights of the pier that danced with the shadows. He locked the door behind him and led her to a tiny corner where stood a small table, a portable chest of plastic drawers, a tiny refrigerator, and his bed, wooden, with a thin mattress on top.

He did not say anything; neither did she. He brought her to the bed and made her stand before him. He undressed her then, unbuttoning her blouse and skirt first and sliding them off of her. He fumbled a bit with her bra, but when he finally undid the clasp and took it off, she blushed deeply as he brought his lips to her nipples and suckled them hungrily. She would have fallen to the floor, easily, had it not been for his firm grip around her body.

When he was done, he lowered her stockings and panties

and, before she could protest, his lips, his tongue and his hands were on her, all over her. After a few moments, he lifted her to the bed, settling her gently on her back. His mouth came down between her legs again, as did his fingers, and she was at his mercy. She called his name, bucked her hips, spread herself further, dug her nails into his shoulders, until he brought her to the peak and she heard herself scream and moan in pleasure.

"You are so beautiful." She heard him speak huskily, from somewhere above her. It took a few seconds for her eyes to focus as she came down from what she knew was her first climax. She had read about it in romance novels, seen it in movies that made her blush, and even heard girls with boyfriends talk about it, but she had never expected it to feel like this.

She had never expected she would feel it with him.

In what little light there was, she could see him next to her on the bed, his dark eyes almost disappearing into the shadows. He was still fully clothed.

"Oh." Embarrassment sank in for the first time. Her hands came up, to cover her utter lack of modesty, but his fingertips were on her face before she could reach for something, like a blanket or pillow, to cover up with.

"You don't have to hide. Never from me." For the first time, she heard a tremble in his voice. She could barely see his face. His fingertips were gentle as he traced her cheeks; the skin on his hands was hard, rough and warm. She could smell herself in his touch.

She reached for him. Before she could wrap her arms around him again, he caught her wrists.

"I think it's time for you to go home." There it was again,

the shakiness in his voice. "I'll walk you there." He slowly let her go.

"No," she said, trying to lift her torso, to get a better look at him. "I want to stay with you."

He hesitated, then sat up, the cot creaking under his weight. "This is your...first time, isn't it?"

"Yes." Was there something she had done he didn't like? "What does that have to do with anything?"

"This is the biggest mistake you could ever make." His back was as stiff and unyielding as a mountain, his voice low and almost menacing.

"Mistake? Who made you responsible for my decisions?" Heat rushed to her cheeks and forehead. She grabbed at the thin striped blanket folded under the pillow she had been lying on and hastily wrapped it around her nakedness.

"Decision? You call this a decision? To sleep with me?"

"To be with you, Trey." She was close to tears. She slid off the bed and got to her feet. He still had his back turned to her. At least he couldn't see her so disheveled and hurt. "I want to be with you. It was my choice to make. Don't you dare tell me you didn't want it, too. I felt it. Don't you fucking dare deny it."

He put his hands on his thick legs and rose, almost painstakingly. "I'm not denying anything." He turned slowly, running his fingers through his hair, which had become half-unbound after their kisses. He kept his eyes hooded, gaze to the floor, or at least not on her.

"I've never wanted a woman as much as I want you. Look at you, Stella. How could I or any man say no to you?"

"Then don't."

"If only it were that simple. If only I were any other man."

"You will never be any other man," she said, almost impatiently. "Look at you, Trey. How could any man compare to you?"

"Any other man wouldn't leave you." It was almost a whisper.

That stopped her.

"Then come back." Her lips finally uttered the very thing her heart had known for a long time. "When all this is over, come back to me."

As soon as she finished saying the words, a lone tear slid down the corner of her left eye, landing and splashing on her naked shoulder. She was terrified he saw it.

That was the last shred of her dignity.

Somehow, that was also the last shred of his control.

As long as it took her to blink back more tears, he closed the distance between them. The way he grabbed hold of her around the waist was almost bone-breaking, crushing the breath out of her. His lips came down on hers like a clap of thunder, as powerful and overwhelming as he.

Her flimsy cover of a blanket fell to the floor, just as she gave him her complete surrender. This time, there was no waiting, no caressing, no gentleness, as she kissed him back like a woman starved.

Dimly, she felt her hands rip away at the last barriers between them, his clothing. It didn't take long for him to be just as naked as she. He looked beautifully inhuman in the dim light and shifting shadows; his skin was smooth where there were no scars, but he had dozens of them all over his body, mixed with what looked and felt like burn marks. His hair fell on her face like a velvet curtain, scented by the sea and his sweat.

They didn't even make it to the bed, or at least she did, halfway. He was inside her, a perfect fit, buried completely, as her legs went around his waist, his shadow looming over her. She felt him thrusting faster and harder by the second, heard him say her name again and again, and, finally, asked her to look at him.

Their eyes locked briefly, and she drowned at the ferocity and desire she saw in the way he looked at her, and his lips were on hers again. He thrust the hardest then, and he shouted as his body shook as if he had a hundred earthquakes inside him, from inside her.

He collapsed, draped across her, his hair and sweat and breath on her breasts. She could feel a slick wetness burning straight from him into her.

Her heart was pounding so loudly she could barely hear anything else. She put her arms around him and kissed the top of his head, feeling only tenderness as she watched him looking spent and vulnerable.

Is this how it was supposed to feel?

She never had any more time to think about it that night. She could only feel, only him. They made love again, and again, and once more. He was insatiable, as if he wanted every last part of her for himself, but, to her surprise, so was she.

By dawn, he had touched and kissed every inch of her, and she of him. She was straddling him, arms around his neck, his teeth and tongue on her nipples, when she saw the first strains of light filter in through the high windows of the warehouse. By the time she came in his embrace, moaning his name, morning was upon them.

He was on his back and she sprawled on top of him,

nuzzling his chest, when she realized it was the first time she was seeing him in the light of day.

"Come back to me, Trey," she blurted out, afraid he would somehow disappear. "No matter what happens, just come back to me."

He didn't respond, not for a long time. His arms went around her, so tightly, so protectively. She felt his lips on her temple, his heartbeat in her ear, his hands in her hair. She took these in, every touch, every scent, every sound, every feeling.

"I love you, Stella," he finally said.

Five

PRISON

I LOVE YOU.
   After he said the words, he slowly moved her to the bed and wrapped her in his blanket. She watched him dress in his usual dark clothing and take only a black backpack.

"It's yours now," he said, giving her the keys he had used the night before. "Do whatever you like."

Before she could protest, he brought his arms around her and kissed her deeply. With one last caress on her cheek and her hair, he was gone.

Trey.

She didn't even know his last name.

Stella got out of his bed, dressed and gathered her things. It was only when she finished locking up the warehouse that she felt the scalding pain in her throat, from last night, finally bubble to the surface, unleashing itself with her tears.

As she walked home, she didn't have the heart to check her phone, knowing that it was probably bursting with worried texts and missed calls from her mother. She would deal with it all later. All that mattered at the moment was she make it through the pain, see herself home alive.

She had no idea how hard she had been clutching his box of roses in her hands. She was just about to cross the intersection when it fell from her grasp. The box burst open, spilling the three roses onto the street, along with a small rectangle of paper.

She crouched down and slowly gathered the fallen items, fitting them into her school bag, feeling spent and raw as she did. The rectangle turned out to be a business card, with something written on the back of it by hand. The name was familiar.

RAPHAEL I. ESGUERRA, III
CHIEF EXECUTIVE OFFICER
ESGUERRA HOLDINGS

Trey's boss. There was a number printed underneath, which looked oddly familiar. It took her a few seconds to figure out that the mobile phone number was Trey's. She had looked at his number and only message from last week so many times.

Why was his phone number on his boss' card?

At the back of the paper, in bold, slashing handwriting, was a short message.

Call whenever you need.
There will be an ansfwer.
Trey

Unable to make sense of what she had just read, she fumbled with the rest of her things and slowly sat down at the bench by the intersection, taking deep breaths.

She slowly went back in memory, to what he had said in the time she was with him.

"Iloilo is our home, we were born and raised here. We won't give it up, so we're bringing the war to them."

"I work for the man who decided to put them there and, at the same time, get you out of something you wouldn't want."

"When I chose to do this, I knew I wouldn't be coming back."

"Some of us can't just quit. Some of us can't just give up the life we were born into."

Was Trey the boss he was referring to? Was he actually Raphael Esguerra?

Was he the Raphael Esguerra who protected her city?

Unable to stop herself, she took out her phone. The screen showed eighteen missed calls and almost double in unread messages. The battery was down to twelve percent. She scrolled through her contacts, found Trey's number, and called it. She felt an icy chill envelop her body, despite the warmth of the morning sun.

Her call was picked up after two rings.

"Hello, Miss Montero. Good morning." The voice was different, older, female. It sounded almost like her own mother's voice.

"Hello," Stella echoed. She suddenly felt disoriented. "Who's this? Is Trey there?"

"My name is Rhoda, Miss Montero. I work for Mister Esguerra. Is there something I can do for you?"

"Where's Trey? I want to talk to him. Please."

"I believe he has informed you he will be indisposed. He has given us instructions to be at your service, as and when you need."

Us? Her brain tried to cope with the words of the woman at the other end of the line. *At her service?*

Wherever Trey was, she had already gotten her answer.

"No, thanks," she heard herself say. "I just wanted to give him back the keys to his... house."

"Did you? I was under the impression he has given them to you, to access and use the warehouse as you please."

"No. Yes. I didn't understand what he was trying to tell me."

There was a pause from Rhoda. "Is there anything else you need, Miss Montero? I can send a car for you if you need to get somewhere, wherever you are in the city."

To her horror, Stella felt a few tears slowly escape her already stinging, sleepless eyes. "I don't need a car. I'll walk home."

"Very well, Miss Montero. Please call me if you need anything, anything at all."

"Goodbye, Rhoda." Stella disconnected the call. She mechanically picked up her bag and stood up. She could feel her legs extend unwillingly, still sore from her night with him. She was beyond tired.

Raphael Esguerra.

A powerful name, feared and respected in the world she lived in.

Trey.

The man who moved in and out of the shadows and into her life, into her darkest dreams and desires.

They were the same person. The only man she had given her heart and her body to.

She would have given anything to make him stay. She knew, however, that no one could tell someone like Raphael Esguerra what to do.

The very same person who told her he loved her.

She had never said she loved him, too, had she? Loved him the moment she first laid eyes on him all those years ago, stepping out of the darkness, under the bright neon lights of a street corner.

It was the only regret she had. It was a prison she willingly put her heart into.

She carried this regret in the days, weeks and months that followed, silently, guardedly.

When she reached home that Saturday morning, instead of greeting her with panic or anger, her mother told her that she received a visitor named Rhoda, the mother of one of Stella's classmates, earlier that morning. Rhoda had apologized for not calling to tell her that Stella was helping her daughter with an urgent term paper, help given at the last minute to a desperate classmate. After breakfast in a fast food restaurant with her daughter, Stella would be home.

She went to the movies that evening with her friends. On Monday, the student council started putting up posters for the senior prom, scheduled on Valentine's Day. She wasn't surprised to get asked by Darryl, whom she politely turned down. In the weeks that followed, she refused four more invitations.

It was almost Christmas when she first heard about it on the news.

It was hard to miss. A large explosion in Sampaloc, Manila had taken down almost four blocks of factories and warehouses. A hundred injured, twenty dead. Up to and until Christmas, there were interviews of a bereaved widow named Connie Zamora, clutching a brood of four children, mourning the death of her husband, business magnate Michael Zamora. Connie demanded justice for her family and the families of their employees.

The media and the police suspected terrorists trying to make a statement. Stella always looked at the sketches released to the public, but never found one she recognized.

Over the school break that December, just before New Year, she went back to the warehouse, on a quiet weekday evening.

It was the same way she had left it. She tidied up the bed, willing herself not to think of the person she had shared it with, and stripped the sheets for washing. She went through the plastic drawers and the refrigerator. The fridge had a few bottles of water and an unopened Snickers chocolate bar. The drawers contained an assortment of black and grey shirts, a few pairs of dark jeans, and shorts of different colors. All the clothes had been washed and neatly folded. In the bottom drawer was a plain ruled notebook and a few pencils. Nothing was written inside the notebook; there were only sketches that filled the pages, drawn in a neat, meticulous hand.

They were all sketches of her.

She spent the next hour crying on his bare mattress.

In January, she walked the runway for the first time, in a Dinagyang Festival fashion show. The designer was so impressed that she offered to design Stella's gown for the latter's senior prom, as part of her Valentine's Day portfolio.

February came with typhoons, one after the other. The rain on Valentine's Day reminded Stella of that night two years ago when the city was flooded.

The prom was at a seaside resort across town, in a covered pavilion with tall, thick glass windows that overlooked the beach. In spite of the weather, almost all her classmates and their dates had come.

Stella arrived with two other senior girls who didn't have escorts like her. All three of them lived in the same area and had opted to travel to and from the event together.

She made a stop at the bathroom before entering the venue. Pictures of the night were very important, according to the designer. They had contracted one of the prom photographers to take additional photos of her wearing the new dress.

The gown was made of deep red velvet, the color of blood. The neckline was cut low, off the shoulders, with small crisscrossing straps around her upper arms. The rest of the fabric was molded to her bodice and hips, then came apart by her left thigh in a slit, showing off her long legs, with the hemline almost brushing the floor.

The hairdresser had styled her hair half down, half up. It fell in waves all the way to the middle of her bare back. She had asked for three small roses to be put around the loose ponytail on top of her head. One red, one pink, one white.

'I love you, Stella.'

The words had echoed in her mind, heart and soul

countless times since she heard them, for the first, only and, possibly, last time.

Staring back at her in the mirror was the very image of a romantic heroine, draped in the colors of love.

But she wasn't that heroine.

She was Stella Montero, who didn't even have a date to the prom. She didn't have someone special. She already had something more than that.

She already had her prison.

Six

STORM

The prom was meant to last past midnight. The weather had other plans.

At nearly eleven that evening, Stella stood next to the glass door of the pavilion and looked up. She couldn't see any of the stars. The sky was almost completely covered in thick clouds. There was only the moon, cutting through the dark shroud with tiny yet sharp slivers of light.

The rain fell in a steady downpour, the winds picking up in speed with each hour that passed. A full-blown storm would be upon them soon.

She had spent the past few hours having her picture taken and getting congratulated by practically everyone present: her teachers, classmates and schoolmates, even visitors from other schools. She was, apparently, the frontrunner for Prom Queen.

She was not surprised when someone from the student council came over to escort her across the dance floor. It was the treasurer, a classmate of hers since freshman year named Vic. He guided her up the small stage and led her to a spot in a line where three other girls stood. Vic winked at her and mouthed, *"Congratulations. It's you."*

In one corner of the platform stood the male half of the prom court. Darryl already had the Prom King crown on his head. He was flanked by three other boys from her class who wore blue sashes as the first, second and third princes.

The emcee, a deejay from a popular local radio station, came forward dramatically, brandishing an important-looking cream-colored envelope. He took out a card of the same color and began to read out the names of the third and second princesses.

Stella felt the hug of the last girl standing next to her seconds after she heard her name being called as Prom Queen. The president of the student council came forward and put a pink and gold sash over her shoulder, followed by the college dean who pinned a bejeweled tiara to her hair. She was hugged and kissed by a few more people before Darryl stood in front of her bearing a bouquet of white, yellow and pink flowers, mostly roses. Photographers surged forward and snapped pictures at an alarming, blinding rate.

She could hear the strains of David Pomeranz's song, 'King and Queen of Hearts,' coming over the speakers. This was the traditional Prom King and Queen dance.

The crowd applauded. The catcalls, whistles and whoops were deafening.

The skies responded, splitting open with a resounding, bright burst of lightning. Thunder followed, echoing through the sudden darkness that blanketed the entire pavilion.

"The power just went out," she heard the deejay say loudly. "Everyone please stay calm."

Someone grabbed her hand, pulling her to the left side of the stage. She thought at first it was Darryl, but she was certain he was on the opposite side of the stage, where moments before he stood under the spotlight with an obnoxious-looking bouquet in his hand and a silly grin on his face.

Stella found her voice, her hand instinctively going up to prevent the tiara on her head from falling. She could use it as a weapon, too, just in case.

"What the hell do you think you're doing?" she demanded.

"Hi, Stella." The voice came from the deepest shadows of stage left, the only sound she could hear clearly even with the rising din of people talking in the darkness.

She knew that voice.

"Trey?" she heard herself respond, in what sounded like a desperate whisper. Maybe she had completely lost it now.

Cellphones and lighters began coming to life on the pavilion floor, allowing her to see more clearly.

A single streak of light moved across the spot where she heard his voice coming from, falling on his profile for the briefest moment.

That was all she needed to see.

She unceremoniously pulled the errant tiara off her head and tossed it aside, then jumped off the stage and into his arms.

She landed on his chest, her fingers clutching the fabric

of his shirt, her face burrowing into his neck, desperately taking in his familiar scent of pine and the sea.

Trey's hands were warm on her back. He was raining kisses on her hair and face. She knew the feeling of his lips on her skin.

"Let's get out of here," she heard him say.

Nothing in the world could stop her from going with him. She was not sure if he carried her, or she ran alongside him, but she found herself in a hut at the farthest end of the resort, cloaked by the night and the rain.

Before them, the surf crashed roughly against the shore. Their shelter of dried woven leaves made little consequence. They were both soaked to the skin.

It was only when he stood still before her, in the pale, thin light of the moon, was she finally convinced he was real. She reached out and touched his face, taking in all the planes and angles.

"I missed you so much," she said. "Whoever you are."

"It doesn't matter who I am. It never mattered to you."

He was right. It never did.

"What matters is that I love you." The words came out easily, as naturally as she breathed in the salty air and the heady scent of him. She touched the scar on his right cheek. She watched as he turned his head and started kissing her fingertips.

"You are so beautiful." His voice was equal parts passionate and tender, as was his gaze.

"So are you," she said, as she traced his lips and jawline.

"I came back to you," he said. "Do you know what that means?"

She put her arms around his torso, angling her ear so

she could hear his heartbeat. "That you really love me? That you missed me, too?"

"It means I am yours, Stella. I have been yours the moment I saw you sitting in that intersection. I couldn't stop thinking about you. I tried to draw you. I never thought I could even touch you. You're an angel on earth I would die to protect."

She could feel the tears welling up behind her eyes, from the flood of emotion that overcame her.

But she didn't have time for tears now.

She only had time for him, because she belonged to him, too.

She reached up and put her hands on his shoulders, the same way she had all those months ago. She didn't have to pull him down. He lifted her off her feet to kiss her.

"I am yours, too," she said against his lips. "*Raphael. Trey.*"

She let the names roll off her tongue. There was nothing strange about them. They were both him.

Stella kissed him, then, before she finally called him what she had really wanted to, all these years.

"*My angel.*"

BOOK II

Heart Chained

Playlist

Bring Me to Life
Evanescence

Everything
Alanis Morissette

One Last Breath
Creed

Into Your Arms
Witt Lowry & Ava Max

Here Without You
3 Doors Down

Gravity
Sara Bareilles

Stay
Cueshe

One

Trina

THE RETURN

He was predictable, and she liked it that way. With Vincent Tugade, she always knew where she stood, what to expect. Everything about him was practically routine.

That morning, she immediately knew, the moment she saw a small box of cookies on her desk, that he was back. He had spent most of the past two months working offsite in Pampanga, in rounds of audits to wrap up the tax year. Although he wasn't the only auditor who had traveled there, she knew he was the only one who would remember to get her a gift, usually a sampling of the local delicacies.

Katrina David smiled and, delightedly, made her way across the building floor, from Human Resources to the side of the external auditors, which everyone in their firm called Assassins' Block.

Vincent's office was at a far corner, smaller than most but with an expansive view of Pasay City. The walls were almost bare except for a few framed certificates and photographs. It was always scented with the strong black coffee he drank all the time.

He was seated behind his two computer screens when she walked in. He looked up when he saw her. He jumped to his feet and swooped down on her for a hug.

"Welcome back, VAT," she said, putting her arms around him.

Years ago, when he first joined the firm, she had found his initials to be a little too fitting for his profession. As a result, she began using it. Then it stuck.

His familiar warmth was always comforting, as was the cool, subtle scent of his cologne.

"You look so brown. Eaten one too many plates of *sisig*?"

He laughed as he kissed her on the check. "Jealous much? It's good to be back. How have you been, Trina?"

"It's been busy around here," she said, giving him a peck in return. "I had no one to complain to these past few months, though. You missed a lot."

Vincent Alcon Tugade was the poster boy for yuppie Manila. He had classic Filipino looks, from his brown skin to his proud face with the hard planes, broad nose and dark eyes. He always dressed simply and elegantly, in light shirts and dark slacks, with hair neatly combed back. He appeared trustworthy and competent, without being obnoxious about any of it.

"I'm sure I did," he said. "With you around, I'll catch up in no time."

She sat on one of the chairs in front of his desk, one leg folded under her, and leaned forward. "How are you? Did anything exciting happen in Pampanga?"

"If you call spending fourteen hours a day with ledgers exciting, by all means, it was very exciting. I had the time of my life."

"You're no fun, Vince."

"You're welcome to all the fun, Trina." His smile at her was nothing if not indulgent, like a patient adult to a restless child. "I'll stick to my balance sheets. I don't think I've got energy for much else."

She frowned at him, exasperated but unsurprised. If he wasn't Vincent, she would have felt patronized. They were about the same age, but she had long since accepted that he behaved like a much older man. Her own father, who was into Airsoft and war games tournaments, was more fun than him.

She pouted at him. "Well, you'd better have enough energy to dance at my wedding, at least."

His hand froze over the computer mouse, just as one of his eyebrows shot up into his hairline. It took a second before he said anything.

"Abella asked?"

"He's going to." Trina saw he was about to say something more, but she stopped him by interrupting. "Soon. Maybe this weekend. We're having dinner on Saturday night. He's pulling out all the stops, VAT. Five-star hotel, the works."

She watched him lean back in his chair.

Broad-shouldered, well spoken, neat, and fairly easy to fit in the bill of tall, dark and handsome, he would have been very cute, she thought objectively, had he not been so boring.

Mature, she corrected herself, loyally. *He's just mature.*

"Well, in exchange for the cookies, I'm claiming first dibs on the happy news."

Trina stood up and rolled her eyes. She would have liked to stay if not for their department's Monday morning meeting.

"I've got to go for our team meeting. I never knew those cookies had a price, though."

"Miss David, you have worked for this firm your entire professional life." He switched to what she called his Presentation Mode, which he usually assumed in meetings with clients. It was the most deathly serious and, somehow, also one of the most comical voices she'd ever heard. "You should know by now that everything has a price."

Maybe he wasn't so boring, after all.

Two

Vincent

THE SECRET

It was Saturday.

He picked up a dart from the coffee table in the middle of his apartment, aimed, and took the shot. The dart found its target, a small square of paper he had tacked to his reminders board.

Vincent walked up to the board and removed the dart. It had pierced right through the piece of desk calendar for that month, exactly where he had intended it to.

Today. *Saturday.*

He woke up that morning the same time he did every day, at five sharp. His apartment was close to Pasay City

Sports Complex, so on most days he would go for a run. Today was no different.

After his run, he returned to his place and cooked oatmeal and eggs for breakfast. If he was not working weekends or on travel somewhere, he preferred staying in. If he had the chance, he would go out on Friday and Saturday nights.

Tonight, he definitely was going out. He needed to get out.

He had received the announcement the night before, at eleven, by text message.

R1: 100% Stock Engine & Chassis

R2: Stock 4Stroke

R3: Stock 4Stroke Automatic

R4: Open to All Brands & Models

Track: Legal confirm 8PM Sat 22/4

Entry: TBC msg 9PM Sat 22/4

Vincent Tugade was a drag racer in the Manila underground circuit. His moniker, for many years now, was the King of Chains, from the insignia on the hood of his glistening black Dodge, paired with his signature leather clothing of the same color. His father had sketched this design for a race car back in the day; he had taken it upon himself to bring it to life.

He was into cars as far back as he could remember, spending long hours with his father at their garage during weekends, learning as much as he could about automobile design and engines.

Although his father had been a government tax official, his passion was customizing cars, which he had passed on to his son.

Vincent had been racing since he was eighteen, two years after his parents died from a freak traffic accident that involved a drunk driver ramming his pick-up truck into their own car. It was a bitter, ugly kind of irony.

He had uprooted himself and his little sister Veronica, ten years old at the time, from their province, and came to Metro Manila to live with one of their aunts, who taught at a Catholic private school. He had worked at the school as an errand boy at first, which led to the discovery of his near-prodigious understanding of numbers when he balanced the books of the school cafeteria and the uniform shop in less than a week.

Around the time, one of his jobs at his aunt's house was to look after her car, an ancient orange Toyota with manual transmission. He had been searching for a replacement for the stick shift at one of the shops in Makati when he overheard two men discussing an upcoming 'race.' That had piqued his curiosity in no time. Not long after, he had secretly souped up his aunt's ToyoPet and brought it for a run at an open race one night in late summer, just before he was due to start college.

By the time he graduated and got an Accountancy degree, he had garnered enough supporters and winnings to get his own car. An auditor's job allowed him more financial freedom to support his sister through university, buy a second car, and lease-to-own the condominium he now lived in.

Two years ago, his aunt had passed away quietly from a long-term illness. His little sister, after years of looking after their aunt, had decided to put her Nursing degree to good use and returned to their home province to take a high-profile clinical instructor job.

The glorious bachelor life allowed him to work as much as he liked with numbers during the day and race as much as he wanted at night. It was a simple delineation of the things he was good at.

He was on his second cup of coffee and was about to go downstairs to the parking basement to check his car for the night's race when his phone rang.

The name on the screen was the least expected of all. The presence of Katrina David was the only fluctuating value in the perfectly balanced books of his work and personal life.

He picked up the call.

"Hello, Trina." He tried to keep his voice as neutral as possible. "How are you?"

To his surprise, the response at the other end of the line was not the usual exuberant one he was familiar with. "Hi, Vince. I'm so sorry for bothering you. Did I call at a bad time?"

It was Trina, but she sounded so subdued it was like he was talking to an entirely different person.

"No, not at all. Everything okay?"

"You got a minute to talk? Please?"

No nicknames, no jokes, no comments on the absence of fun in his life. Maybe he had somehow wandered into a more depressing alternate reality after his early-morning run.

"Sure, of course. Anything for you." He took a seat on his couch. "What's up?"

"Nothing." There was a long, strained pause from her. "I mean, not nothing, but it's something I can't talk about with my parents or my friends."

"I'm all ears. What's this about?"

"James."

"Abella?"

The prick?

He wanted to tack on his opinion, but decided to keep his mouth shut.

The thought of James Abella, Trina's boyfriend, gave him the sudden urge to punch something. Vincent disliked him the same way he disliked racers who would rather spend money on a custom paint job than change their engine oil after a few races.

He had only met Abella three times at office functions over the past year or so but had long since formed the impression that the man was all flash, no substance. Perhaps a career in modeling did that to a person, but Vincent never generalized and only gave informed opinions. Since Trina was not a client, he kept whatever sentiments he had to himself.

"Has he done something? Are you okay?"

"Nothing like that. I'm fine."

He tried to be patient, thinking of the way he would usually talk to his little sister when she opened up about her relationships. "Okay, then, Trina. Just let me know if there's anything I can do."

Maybe, just maybe, run Abella over. She could pick which car I should use.

"Vince…what happens if I don't want to?"

"Don't want to what?"

"You know. The S-word."

He almost sputtered on his coffee. He slowly put his mug down on the table to avoid any further incident.

Damn. So much for your regular Saturday morning routine.

He held the phone away from his mouth as he took a deep breath before responding.

"I thought everything was done, dusted and double-ruled, all that. He was going to ask you to marry him, wasn't he?"

"He wants to take our relationship further, has wanted to for a while now. If he does ask me tonight to marry him and I say yes, he might want a..."

"Test drive?" He completed the statement and immediately regretted it.

"Yes." Deadpan and humorless, Trina had probably been replaced by an alien who happened to mimic her voice very well.

The silence on the line stretched for what seemed like hours.

There was only one response he could utter, the only one that mattered.

"What do you want to do?"

He heard a huge intake of breath, before she continued in a shaky voice. "I don't know. That's why I called you, to ask a man how he would feel if his fiancée refused to…you know."

This was dangerous ground. He would never speak for the prick.

"Has he asked you before?" He swallowed very hard before continuing. "Have you done it with him before?"

Fuck.

He could feel it. His face was going red. He was supposed to give advice on depreciation and inventory, not sex and relationships.

"No. Never. I tried, Vince. I can't…" Trina's voice trailed off.

He was tempted to ask why, but it wasn't the gentlemanly

thing to do. If there was one thing he knew about women, it was to give them space.

As Trina went on, she sounded more and more anxious with each word. "He hasn't asked me straight out. But what he does when we're alone, it's enough to tell me what he really wants. I know I'm supposed to like it. He's my boyfriend, after all. But I can't seem to get myself to give in."

He listened to her breathing for several long moments before he spoke, as gently and as patiently as he could. "Then don't give in, if you don't want to."

"Wouldn't that frustrate him, or make him angry? Turn him off?"

Vincent knew about frustration very well, but this was not about him. "If he really loves you and wants to marry you, he should damn well be willing to wait until you're ready."

"Would you wait, Vince?" Her voice was quiet. "If you were in his place?"

"You know me better than that. I would never even consider putting you in a predicament like this. That's not love, Trina. Not even close."

Damn it to hell.

This wasn't supposed to be about him. Not in the fucking least.

"I never thought of it that way," she said. "When James first became my boyfriend, I was so happy. Everyone kept telling me how lucky I was."

Not everyone, he wanted to correct her.

"He is so handsome and dreamy, you know? He is a famous model and all that. I thought I have to keep him happy, to keep him."

"Are you happy now?" That seemed to be the last word he could think of to describe her at the moment.

"To be honest, it's hard to be happy when your relationship is like a ticking time bomb. Lately, all I could think about is that it's only a matter of time before James asks. What if I can't give him what he wants? What if I make the wrong decision? What if he leaves me?"

It didn't sound like a healthy relationship. It sounded an awful lot like co-dependency.

"What if you think about what would make you happy, Trina?"

"Me? I don't know."

He couldn't blame her. Sometimes being in the safety of one's comfort zone mattered more than pursuing happiness. Sometimes the risk of getting out wasn't worth it, if it meant venturing into the unknown.

If it meant getting hurt.

"Once you figure it out, I get first dibs. I'll be here to listen. I might even splurge on some cookies. You know, those nasty sweet ones from Greenbelt you like so much."

He was rewarded by a small giggle. "Yeah, those."

"Think about what would make you happy, Trina, and make your decisions based on that. Not on what would make someone else happy, especially at your expense."

He hoped there was at least some clarity in her mind, or even a hint of a smile on her face.

"Thanks, VAT," she finally said. "You're the best, you know that?"

"Don't tell anyone, okay? My services are exclusive."

"To me?" He could hear the coyness, the humor, back

in her voice. It was the best he could ask for, under the circumstances.

"Always have been."

"See you Monday, Vince. I'm really sorry if I bothered you on your weekend."

"It's okay. You can bother me anytime."

Trina thanked him again and hung up.

He stood up, plugged the phone into its charger, and sat back down on the couch. He picked up his mug for a sip. The coffee was now cold and flat, almost bitter.

He felt just as cold and flat as he thought of Abella, with her.

Trina.

He first met her six years ago, when she did his pre-interview at the firm. She was the most breathtaking woman he had ever laid eyes on, an opinion the years had not changed. She had smooth caramel skin, an hourglass figure, and long wavy hair a deep shade of mahogany. Her face had a sincere warmth he could just stare at and drink in for hours.

His first impression was that she was the human equivalent of the Energizer bunny, someone who kept going and going and barely stopped talking while at it.

Instead of finding her lively manner annoying, he found himself warming up, to the point of allowing her to christen him with a new nickname. It was little wonder she was the one usually assigned to potential hires or new employees.

It was a wonder, however, how they became friends. The first thing he could think of was how she could so easily get him to open up, or at least talk. Other people at the firm, even his fellow auditors, gave him space to work and move around the office without much need for social interaction.

He had a reputation for no-frills efficiency, and he had to admit it commanded respect.

Trina did not give him the wide berth others did. She simply found her way into his life and settled in it, the same way she would barge into his office any time she wanted and sit in weird positions on the chairs facing his desk. Their friendship had lasted the better part of the past five years, to the point that his sister thought she was his girlfriend when Trina showed up at their aunt's funeral.

Now, he pondered the advice he had given her.

Think about what would make you happy.

Was he a hypocrite to give a confused woman this kind of advice, when he couldn't even apply it to his own life?

Then again, he wasn't the one in a relationship, not the one who faced the risk of a broken heart.

Or was he?

He knew from the moment Trina had started talking about things getting serious with Abella that his own heart was on the line. It was only a matter of time before it got ripped into shreds. He predicted it would either be at the sight of a ring on her finger or of the very woman herself in a wedding dress.

He was prepared for it, as long as she didn't know. He could face it, the same way he had faced life when it came to her.

Held back by chains of his own making.

Three

Trina.

THE RAIN

DONE, DUSTED AND DOUBLE RULED.
Vincent's words echoed in her mind as she lifted her chin and walked straight into the drizzling Manila night, ignoring the politely disguised yet obviously curious stares of the doorman and security guard stationed at the hotel's front entrance.

More like fully depreciated and written off.

She was a fool to think there would be at least some sort of compromise, that James would give her room to think about what she really wanted.

Instead, he had wined and dined her, then went in for the kill.

It shouldn't have surprised her.

The rain was the first one that month, adding insult to her already dreary state of affairs. The typhoon season was still months away, but, hell, anything goes.

Life seemed to be trying to throw as much crap as it could at her, all at the same time.

The hotel was located in the Bay Area, close to the metropolitan but posh and exclusive enough to merit its high profile and ludicrously expensive status.

There should be a few taxis around, in theory, but everyone drove their shiny, showy cars to and from this place, as far as she could see.

She was the only one walking.

She could wait inside for a taxi, but she had more pride than that. No way in hell was she staying.

Trina clutched her leather handbag tightly, debating whether or not to use it as some kind of umbrella, finally dismissing the idea as pointless.

Her little black dress and matching suede shoes had already gone to waste. She wished she had not splurged as much during her shopping trip that afternoon, in an effort to keep her mind off the conversation with Vincent and the inevitable with James.

The downpour had increased in intensity by the time she reached the main gates of the hotel. Half-blinded by rain water, she continued to plod onwards.

"I met someone else, Trina."

Those five words tolled at the back of her head like some kind of death knell.

James had gone on and on with his explanation. Perhaps he'd thought it would make her feel better, if there was a clear reason for their break-up.

"I thought you loved me, but I never felt it. She made me feel loved, in ways more than words could ever explain."

Feel it, my ass, she thought bitterly.

"I tried to make our relationship work but nothing ever seemed to get through to you. I hope you'll understand where I'm coming from. I've fallen in love with her."

The funny part was that she understood very clearly, maybe a little too well for her own good.

The moment her now-ex-boyfriend had finished his confession, she had stood up, with as much dignity as she could muster, and made the most regal exit she could from the restaurant.

She took pride in two things: First, she'd kept her head held high; second, she'd never cried.

She had no desire to cry. If anything, she could almost describe her feelings, after the initial hurtful blow of rejection to her ego, as a combination of relief and lightness, as if she'd just been unburdened of something ridiculously heavy.

"Think about what would make you happy, Trina."

She would give anything right now, if she could just talk to Vincent.

Anything to hear his voice, always a source of comfort and reason.

As soon as she got home, she'd try and give him a call…

A sudden, deafening screech cut through the fog of her thoughts.

She momentarily forgot her troubles as she, dazed and confused, faced the direction of the high-pitched sound.

A black car, with prism-like headlights, had stopped a few feet away from her. She stared as the car's wipers moved furiously, rhythmically, across the windshield.

She had not seen any cars coming her way. There was no one else outside, no one else on the road. Not in this weather.

She was meant to be on her own tonight, wasn't she? Chained to her own thoughts and, even more so, her regrets.

But it wasn't meant to be.

Four

Vincent

THE RACE

I*T WAS TIME.*
      Even after all these years, anticipation gripped him at the thought of a race.

The feeling was familiar: the slight acceleration of his heartbeat, the clammy sensation in his palms, the tightness in his stomach. Soon enough, nerves would give way to focus; and focus would eventually explode into all-consuming adrenaline once the flag came down.

In the dimly lit garage of his apartment building, the sleek form of his car, whom he'd named *Eskeleto*, stood before him, ready to carry him into yet another race.

He inspected every inch of the vehicle, ensuring its peak performance. He let his hands run over the smooth curves of the car, grounding himself in the present, as far as he possibly could from thoughts that threatened to invade his impeccably crafted sense of concentration.

Right now, he hated the accuracy and precision of his memory. Because of it, there were images of Trina floating at the fringes of his mind, clawing at the walls he had so carefully built to keep his emotions in check.

"Let's do this, old friend," he said to *Eskeleto*.

Just like the well-worn leather jacket he had on, the car's hood bore his insignia of a skull encircled by a chain and an antique pocket watch.

It was as fearsome a symbol as it was poetic; a juxtaposition of life, death, and the confines of mortality.

Time.

What he wouldn't give to have more time with Trina, before she went on with her life and rode off into the sunset with her male model.

He sighed.

He really was fucked.

He had no choice now but to deal with it head on, all cylinders firing.

He had to deal with the thought of losing Trina.

As the King of Chains of the Manila drag race circuit, he had one glaring solution to his current predicament: *Drive.*

Vincent slipped behind the wheel and switched the ignition, his hands settling comfortably on the steering wheel.

Next to *Eskeleto* stood his other car, the dark grey Toyota sedan he used to drive to work and other more everyday places. He'd named the car *T-Baby*.

Thinking about himself doing something so juvenile and lovesick was almost painful.

At least, *T-Baby* was there to stay.

As *Eskeleto* roared to life beneath him, he allowed the sound to drown out all else. With one last glance at his other car, as if bidding farewell to a part of him that still clung to the possibility of going in another direction, towards a different destination, he revved the engine and sped off into the night.

The city lights blurred together as he drove through the streets. He knew each race demanded every ounce of skill, focus and determination he could muster. He couldn't afford to give in to sentimentality or distractions.

He made it to the venue with time to spare. Situated next to Manila Bay, the track was abuzz with the frenetic energy of the underground scene, where the salty breeze coming in from the sea mingled with the scents of rubber and gasoline. The sounds of engines revving and people shouting greetings and good-natured taunts to each other were comforting to his ears, a welcome diversion from his inner turmoil.

He parked in his designated spot near the track, the area marked by a replica of his skull symbol using temporary neon paint. He took a deep breath and stepped out of the car to check in with the organizers of the evening's race.

"King of Chains!" a voice called out.

A group of younger racers, clustered along with their brightly colored sports cars, looked at him with awe and reverence.

"H-hey, boss," one of them stammered, extending a trembling hand. "Good luck tonight!"

"Thanks," Vincent replied, forcing a smile for their benefit. "Good luck to all of you. Let's have a good race tonight."

As he shook hands with well-wishers, he allowed himself to slip into his track persona: someone confident, untouchable, and utterly devoted to the thrill of the race.

"Vincent! Over here!" a chorus of female voices beckoned him from a nearby cluster of cars.

He turned to see a gaggle of beautiful women, some draped over sleek hoods and others leaning against gleaming fenders. A few cast sultry glances his way.

"Looking good tonight, Vincent," purred one woman whose perfectly made-up face he'd seen at almost every race for the past few years.

Her name was Alena; she drove a custom red Volvo that he was quite sure was also bulletproof.

"How about we celebrate your victory together later?" Her voice was heavily laced with suggestive promise.

"Sorry, beautiful, not tonight," he replied with a polite smile. "Got to travel for work tomorrow."

Though his reputation on the track often attracted such propositions, tonight his heart and mind were too preoccupied to entertain even the fleeting distractions of flirtation and casual sex.

"Always so focused," another woman teased, boldly stepping closer to ruffle his hair. It was Florence, an oil tycoon's daughter, who drove an import Lamborghini that probably cost more than a lifetime's worth of his salary. "That's what makes you the best."

"I'll make it up to you next time, ladies," he promised with a grin, though the words felt hollow to his ears.

As he turned away from the women and eventually found his way to the organizers, the clamor of the race track seemed to amplify within his head.

He *needed* tonight's race, more than he'd ever needed any other race before.

Trina.

The name echoed through this head, almost forming on his lips like a prayer for salvation.

His prayer was answered not too long after, when he found himself flanked by two other cars on each side at the starting line.

His opponents were mere shadows in his peripheral vision, their presence barely registering as his hands settled on the wheel with the familiarity of a swordsman with his trusty katana.

"Are you ready?" came a woman's voice through a megaphone. "It's time for the final race!"

That night's honorary marshal was a beauty queen from a neighboring country. She was unbelievably attractive in person, with a glistening black bob, legs that went on for days, and a tiny waist cinched in by the matching belt of her red dress.

She held up a racing flag in the air, her movement punctuated by excited cheers and roars of the crowd.

"GO!"

In an instant, the world around him melted away, fading into streaks of color as his car shot forward like a bullet from a gun. Adrenaline surged through his veins as he expertly navigated the twists and turns of the track.

As he raced towards the finish line, the cheers of the crowd reverberated in his ears, but none quite reached him.

He knew what was missing, but he also knew he had to keep himself in check long enough to finish what he'd started. The final stretch lay before him, a straight path to victory.

And, just like that, it was over.

Vincent and *Eskeleto* crossed the finish line, the other racers and their cars still dozens of meters behind.

The moment he stepped out of the car, he was surrounded by a boisterous crowd. He lost count of the handshakes, hugs, and kisses he was given, but he took it all in stride.

Somehow, tonight, he didn't feel the usual rush of victory. The end of the race, albeit one he'd won, felt like signing off the financial statements of a client at the end of a lengthy audit.

It was a job he did well, a job he'd completed meticulously and painstakingly. No more, no less.

"Nice win, King of Chains," one of his opponents called out, clapping him on the shoulder.

"Thanks, Phil," he replied, forcing a smile.

As the last remnants of the crowd dispersed into after-parties and the track finally fell silent, Vincent climbed back into his car.

Just as he started the drive back to his apartment, opting for a shortcut through the Bay Area, it began to rain.

The streets of late-night Manila stretched out before him like a labyrinth, but he realized there was no escaping the thoughts that haunted him, no matter where he went.

He could drive fast, drive away, or even drive endlessly. These were all tempting options, but he knew, in the end, escape was impossible.

Vincent knew he could never outrun his thoughts of her, tightly chained to his memories and his heart.

He didn't even get that far when he saw her in the middle

of the rain-slicked road. Shock mingling with disbelief, he dimly heard the tires screech as he hit the brakes.

Heart pounding, he stared at the drenched figure standing outside his car, illuminated by *Eskeleto*'s headlights.

It's not a mirage, he thought, his head spinning.

He would recognize the real Trina anywhere.

Was it a sign, or some kind of twisted joke?

There was only one way to find out.

He pushed the car door open and stepped out into the downpour.

Five

Trina

THE STRANGER

A MAN, DRESSED ALL IN THE SAME COLOR AS THE dark vehicle before her, stepped out of the car. His clothing was shiny, like leather. With his hair styled into spikes, he looked like a sleek nocturnal animal, or maybe the lead singer of a rock band.

"Trina? What the fuck are you doing here?"

The voice was very familiar, but the sight wasn't. The rain and the headlights danced around her like strobes in a disco, making her dizzy.

She had to make sense of this.

So she uttered his name, in both uncertainty and unabashed curiosity.

"Vincent?"

The man who sounded but barely looked like Vincent Tugade sloshed his way to her side, his eyes glittering even in the cover of night.

"Have you lost your mind, Trina? You shouldn't be out on the road like this."

"Vincent?" she repeated the name, not quite sure if she wanted to be right or wrong. "What are you doing here? Why do you look like that?"

"We have to get you off the streets." He held out a hand to her. "Come on."

She could only stare at him. The dinner, the near-accident, now this man. It was too much.

"Get in the car, Trina, please."

She backed away. She didn't have the energy to put up with more surprises tonight. "Just go, okay? Leave me alone."

"What are you doing?" He stepped closer and took hold of her arm. "I'm taking you home, okay? Please get in the car and we can talk about it."

He gave her that familiar indulgent smile, none too sincerely this time. She recognized him like this, vaguely.

"I don't think—"

Before she could continue, he had his hand on the small of her back and was guiding her to the car. Too weary to put up a fight, she allowed herself to be pushed, albeit gently, into the front seat.

He silently got into the driver's side. In the dim light, she could see his lips set in a firm line. He took off his jacket and gave it to her. He was dressed in a black sleeveless shirt underneath.

"Stay warm. I'll turn off the air conditioner."

"Thanks," she heard herself say.

"You're welcome."

He reached for the dashboard and started adjusting buttons and switches. His arms had well-defined muscles and an assortment of tattoos going all the way down to his forearms.

To stop herself from staring at him so rudely, Trina gave the jacket a shake and put it around her shoulders. She could feel her new dress soak water into the car seat. She buckled up when she saw him do the same. She clutched her bag and the seatbelt close to her as she looked out of the window at the rainy night.

The car hummed to life and started to cruise forward.

"Vince, I…" It took a while before she could work up the energy and courage to look at the almost-stranger next to her, much less talk to him.

"I'm sorry," she completed lamely, clenching her hands, feeling them shake with the residual cold.

He was quiet for several seconds. "For what?"

"For all the trouble. One thing after another went downhill. Before I knew it, I was out of there like my ass was on fire."

He shook his head, but kept his eyes trained on the road. "In a way, it's a good thing I was the one you ran into. The car's brakes hold up pretty well even when they're wet."

The thought of brakes was enough to make her feel even colder. Had it been another car, or another driver, she wasn't quite sure where she would be now.

In hindsight, she should have stayed inside the hotel and

waited for a taxi, or got James to drop her home, not wandered out into the rain like some tragic heroine in a cheap romance novel. The only real tragedy of the entire evening was the sorry shape of her pricey new dress and its matching shoes.

"Still, this entire drama is my fault," she admitted.

"Drama?"

"The walk-out, the emoting in the rain, the getting nearly ran over part. I guess I was too proud to put up with any more bullshit."

"I see." Vincent held on to the steering wheel with one hand, his other hand going up to rub out droplets of water stuck to his spiky hair. "I'm sure that wasn't how you had the night planned out, was it?"

"Well, no." She gave her eyes a little rub, still unable to reconcile the fact that this tattooed, leather-clad man was the Vincent she had known all these years. She didn't even know he had arms like that.

For the first time, she noted that this wasn't his Toyota sedan, but something else entirely.

The black car had metal panels on the sides, a convex roof and a windshield lined with what looked like steel reinforcements. The seats were wrapped in dark leather that matched his clothes. All over the interior, there were stickers and buttons with death motifs, such as skulls, chains and spikes. The buttons and gauges on the dashboard before her looked like the control panel of a mad scientist.

His voice was calm and measured as he spoke. "If I had known you were going to be at the hotel, I would have picked you up. You should have called me."

"I dragged you through the pathetic story of my

relationship this morning. I could never do that to you twice. Besides, I never thought you would be here, at this time. Like that." She gestured to all of him in general.

"Like what?" He glanced at her, tilting his head curiously.

"Like, different. Dangerous. You know, someone capable of running James over."

To her surprise, he smiled. "Whoever said I wasn't? All you have to do is ask."

She sighed. "That sounds very tempting right now."

His next words were so serious it was hard to discern whether or not he really meant them. "If you really want to do a number on Abella, we can turn back and get him. The track near the bay will be closed by now, but I'm sure I could get us in. I've raced there since they started building it, right after the mall opened."

Race.

VAT was a racer. Suddenly, the car, the clothes and the skulls all made sense.

"Thanks for the generous and potentially criminal offer, but I'll pass." She could feel the beginnings of a small smile on her lips.

They didn't talk for a while as he deftly wove the car through the Saturday night traffic of the city, taking shortcuts through tiny side streets. By the time they were out of the Bay Area, she felt calm enough to loosen her grip on her bag and the seatbelt and settle more comfortably in the front seat.

"You still live at the tower?"

"Yes. I'm surprised you remember."

He shrugged. "We should be there soon. I know a shortcut near the hospital. That should keep us away from most of the late night traffic."

"You're the best, VAT," she said, echoing her sentiments from earlier that day. "Thanks for putting up with my crap."

He didn't answer, but a little while later she felt his hand on her shoulder.

"It's not crap. I'm very sorry this happened." He gave a gentle squeeze before letting go. "You deserve to be happy."

She tugged at his jacket, pulling it more snugly around her. She never knew leather could feel so soft.

"At least James had the guts to call it off himself. I suppose he needed something I couldn't give. We both wanted different things. I stressed all about it for nothing."

Vincent shook his head. "Not nothing. I'm sure whatever you two had, it meant more to you than it did to him."

Trina looked out the window again. She could barely see a thing, except for torrents of water, thick mist, and flickering lights.

It was a fitting metaphor for what she had with James. What she thought she had with him. She never really saw what it was, just blurry lines and splashes of color. Everything she made out of it was her own interpretation, not the truth.

Her newly-ended relationship was a joke, if not a failure, from the very start. Marrying her was something James had never even remotely considered. She knew that now.

"James told me he met someone else while on a job in Bali months back. It doesn't take a genius to figure out he got what he wanted from her. Apparently they kept in touch after that."

The memory of her ex's confession was still fresh in her mind, spilling out easily. Trina couldn't even remember the other girl's name. "James said she was far less…I don't know, frigid than I am, I suppose. The exact words he used were 'cold' and 'walled off.'"

"Sounds like he thinks you're some kind of high security vault. One he doesn't have the access code to, the poor bastard."

"I never thought you'd ever feel sorry for him." She gave him a sidelong glance. "You hate his guts."

"Am I that obvious?"

"Kind of, especially as you offered to run him over if I wanted you to."

"That prick doesn't know what he's missing out on," he declared solemnly, in a tone that begged no argument.

Minutes later, they pulled up in front of a high-rise condominium complex. He parked in an open spot on the sidewalk, got out of the car, and opened the passenger door for her.

She shakily stepped out, her wet shoes digging into her skin as she walked carefully on the rain-drenched pavement. Her dress had dried partially, but it still clung to her body like a second skin. To her surprise, she felt self-conscious under the bright fluorescent lights of the building's main entrance as he followed her to the foyer.

"Thank you, Vince." She pulled his jacket off her shoulders and handed it back to him. "For everything."

"You're welcome." He reached out and took the jacket back. "Will you be okay? Can I get you anything, from the pharmacy or somewhere?"

"No, I'm fine. Thanks for the offer." No matter how he dressed, he was always reliable.

Tonight, he just appeared a little more exciting than usual.

It occurred to her how different it had felt to look at her ex-boyfriend's mestizo, camera-ready face, compared to the darker, harder countenance of the man before her.

With Vincent, she had always been at ease. She never had to second-guess herself or question her own actions and decisions.

His words in the car rattled around the back of her mind. *That prick doesn't know what he's missing out on.*

What if she asked herself that question?

What am I missing out on?

He was looking straight back at her. She had no idea what was in his head. She never really had. She'd always expected him, by default, to come through, listen, accept, and give—cookies, advice, time, his presence. He even came through for her at this time, without her asking, without him knowing, by sheer chance of fate.

Why did he?

Trina didn't know if she felt guilty, confused or overwhelmed. Perhaps all three. Seeing Vincent in a different light, in the rainy cold of reality, was unnerving.

She needed to put this entire weekend behind her, as soon as possible.

He stepped closer and wrapped one arm around her shoulders. He gave her a quick peck on the cheek; it felt familiar, yet, in her waterlogged state, she felt a little breathless at the contact. She could feel blood rushing to her head.

"Rest up, Trina," he said as he pulled away. "Call me tomorrow if you need anything, okay?"

She didn't let him pull away completely. Instead, she put her hands on his tattooed forearms. Still halfway in his embrace, she could see that his eyes were almost silver in color, not the greyish-brown she thought they were.

"Would you like to come up for some coffee?" Her own voice sounded higher-pitched, even shrill, to her own ears. She had no idea where it came from, but it was all her.

He hesitated. He was still predictable enough, but she had always liked that about him. She knew his answer before he said it, but she didn't quite anticipate the tension she felt emanating from his body.

"Sure."

Six

Vincent

THE TURN

WHAT THE FUCK ARE YOU DOING, TUGADE? Vincent mentally confronted himself as he followed her off the elevator. They had reached the seventh floor of her apartment building.

"My place is this way." Trina was a few steps ahead. He could see she was limping a little and dragging her feet. He thought of helping her, but the idea of touching her again didn't sound very smart at the moment.

He shouldn't have touched her like he had downstairs. They had always hugged and kissed each other chastely, but, tonight, it felt very different. For starters, she kept giving him wide-eyed looks, from all directions, as if she was seeing him for the first time.

Vince knew those kinds of looks. He had given her those before, many times over, when he was certain she couldn't see him. He had never stopped, not since he first saw her when she came out to the firm's lobby for his pre-interview.

He knew his feelings for her very well, had grappled with and successfully kept them buried under a platonic veneer. Trina, on the other, had no idea. If she did, she would probably be out of his life like her 'ass was on fire.'

It was a risk he could not take. He had too much to lose. Her friendship, her trust, and, above all, *her*.

Katrina David was someone he could never afford to lose.

With her freshly single from a break-up, this was the worst possible time to even consider that he had a chance. He would rather have himself run over on the track by the other racers.

Trina stopped at a unit numbered 704. "Home sweet home. Can you help me, Vince?"

He had to snap himself out of any delusional episode he had going. She was holding out her keys.

"The gold one, please."

He took the bunch rather abruptly from her grasp and moved closer to the door. As he bent over to unlock it, he felt Trina wrap her arms around his left arm as she leaned against him. Up close, he could see her wet dress hugging every curve of her body. Her cleavage was practically next to his face as she shifted her weight from foot to foot.

"I'm so tired, Vince," she said. "I think I spent next

month's salary shopping this afternoon for an outfit that I completely ruined."

Ruined? That was the last thing on his mind, looking at her in the little black dress.

He averted his eyes and thanked all existing higher powers when he heard the lock give way. He was too close for comfort. He would have that coffee and get himself the fuck home.

She did not let him go as they went in, clinging to his arm as she hobbled into the apartment and pointed out the light switches. He gave in to his earlier gentlemanly inclination and led her to the white couch in the middle of her living room. She heaved herself gratefully onto the seat and took off her shoes.

"Major ouch." She shook her head and made clucking sounds as she started flexing her toes and rotating her ankles.

He took the opportunity to step away from her. He could leave. She was fine. He had made sure of that.

"I think I'll call it a night," he said. "I'd better go."

True to form, Trina hopped back to her bare feet. "What are you talking about? Sit down. Let me get you that coffee. It's premium roasted Arabica. I'll even give you the rest of the beans, too."

He swallowed hard and seated himself hesitantly on the couch, next to the spot she had just vacated. He tossed his jacket to a nearby plastic chair. "I'm sorry about the wet clothes."

"I did the same thing to your car. Call it even between us."

He watched her disappear behind a curtained doorway. He looked around. The place was neat and orderly; the colors were a mishmash of white, brown, orange and yellow. Even on a rainy night, the place looked bright and alive.

Minutes later, he saw her head poke through the curtains. "Vince? Come join me in the kitchen. I put on some croissants, too."

"That would be great." He stood up and followed her into the next room. It was fairly compact, cozy, outfitted with sunny yellow tiles. Next to a small glass window overlooking the city, there was a wooden table with matching seats for three.

She gestured for him to sit on one of the chairs. She was quiet as she poured them both coffee. She placed a plate full of croissants between them and sat from across him.

"Thanks for looking out for me tonight. Goodness knows I have no business troubling you for anything. I honestly thought this morning was the end of it."

He took a sip of the coffee. It was strong and scalding hot. "Is that how you think of yourself, Trina? Trouble?"

He watched her take a sip of coffee, twitching a little uncomfortably in her damp dress as she thought about his question. He wondered if it would be appropriate if he suggested she change clothes, more for his state of mind than her own health and comfort.

"It seems I could never give anyone what they want from me," she declared thoughtfully. "I don't know if that's trouble or not."

"It's called making your choices, I believe. Definitely not trouble."

Trina shrugged. "Is it? James thinks I'm a cold bitch. My friends think I'm so flighty I couldn't even commit to their vacation plans. My own family thinks I'm all talk and no substance, that's why I haven't been promoted to HR Manager."

The rapid-fire honesty in her declaration was a heart-rending surprise. He was sorely tempted to close the distance between them and take her into his arms.

Instead, he took another sip of coffee. "Do you agree with any of them?"

She shook her head. "I love my job and I like people. I actually enjoy my work. If I were manager, I would have to spend the whole damn day writing reports, signing stupid forms, and talking to higher management. As for trips, I don't really want to go on a lot of them because traveling's so expensive and I want to pay off this unit as soon as possible."

Her down-to-earth practicality was something he admired immensely. "Can't argue with the numbers on that one."

"I know, right?" Her shoulders heaved in a sigh. "And James...well, tonight pretty much sums it all up. For the record, he broke it off, but I was the one who walked out first."

"There you go. You've made your choices. If people don't appreciate that, it's their problem, not yours."

She smiled at him for what seemed the first time that evening. "I think you're right."

"You should start thinking about what you want, rather than what other people want and expect from you. As I said, you deserve to be happy. Do what makes you happy."

If only he could do the same thing. If only he had the balls to follow his own advice.

Her smile brightened a little more. "This makes me happy. Having you here."

It felt as if she had stabbed him, front and center. To

disguise the tightness in his chest, he affected a grin and lifted his coffee mug in a toast. "To your happiness, Trina."

She leaned forward, wrapping her hands around her mug. Her eyes narrowed, focusing on him like laser beams, as if she was trying to read his thoughts.

"Why do you do this, Vince?"

"Do what?"

"This. You look after me. Without asking for anything in return."

He swallowed the bite of croissant in his mouth. "We're friends. That's what friends do."

"I don't really know anything about you, do I? I mean, you've never even told me you had a car like that, or you race…I don't even know if you have a girl waiting for you somewhere and, somehow, tonight her man's babysitting me instead. That kind of thing."

He had to smile at her words. She always gave him more credit than he deserved, especially with women. "You know there is no girl. There's no one. As for racing, it's something you don't exactly advertise when you work in a Big Four firm."

"Will you take me to a race next time?"

"I'll take you, just promise you won't tell anyone in the office. With that dress, you'll fit right in."

"This outfit has not been a total waste, then."

"No, not at all." After a quick glance at his watch, he got to his feet. All that talk about his personal life and the absence of romance from it was making him uncomfortable. She would prod and pry all the time, but when she suggested becoming part of it, even in a race, it made him feel exposed, vulnerable. "It's late, Trina. I'd better go."

She nodded and got up, too, following him back to her colorful living room. She handed over his jacket and a paper bag. "The coffee, as promised. If you do decide to bring it to work on Monday, save some for me."

"Not a chance," he said, grinning down at her.

Instead of responding by whacking him on the arm or giving one of her usual silly faces, Trina stared at him with wide, almost doe-like, eyes. She put her arms around his shoulders and invaded what little personal space there was left between them, never taking her gaze off him.

"Trina?" he asked, hesitantly, trapped but not exactly unwilling. "What are you doing?"

"What makes me happy."

With her fingers in his hair, she brought his head down for a kiss.

Seven

Trina

THE HEART

She heard his sharp intake of breath, felt a sudden tautness take over his body. Something fell to the floor, crunching under their feet. The world around them began to spin as she pushed her body against his.

This was something she had never wanted to do with James.

With Vincent, it was the exact opposite. The moment he gave her that big smile, there was nothing more she wanted in the world than to get all that leather off him and have him for herself.

She didn't want him to go.

The desire she felt was as clear as the sky on a bright, sunny day. There was neither confusion nor uncertainty. There was only the feeling she was exactly where she was meant to be, with the person she was meant to be with.

His arms, wonderfully warm through her damp clothes, went around her as he started to kiss her back, slowly at first, then with more urgency. He tasted of coffee and rain, of salt and a hint of sugar. She couldn't get enough of it.

In that moment, she realized what she had known, in the deepest and darkest corner of her heart, all along.

It has always been Vincent Tugade.

Kissing alone wouldn't satisfy her. She had never been more certain of something, ever. Her hands took a life of their own, moving beneath his shirt, until she could feel the hardness of his torso under her fingertips.

He didn't keep idle. He nipped at her earlobes and neck as he began to push the straps of the black dress off her shoulders, baring a wider path for his lips to trace.

She moaned when his mouth found its way to her collarbone. She dug her fingers into his back as he devoured the sensitive skin of her throat and chest.

She found her voice and, for what seemed like the very first time, the words to tell him what she truly wanted.

"Please don't go. Don't leave me tonight."

As if wrenched from a dream, he stopped, his hands still on her back, in her hair.

"Trina..." he breathed, his eyes clouding. "I'm sorry."

Her heart was still pounding so loudly in her ears, she

could barely hear him. She gripped his shoulders tightly as she fought to catch her breath.

"Sorry? Sorry for what?" She dared herself to look into his eyes.

His silvery gaze seared its way into her soul. She had to look away. She knew she would burn to a bittersweet death if she looked any longer.

"I can't do this, Trina." His voice was subdued, almost melancholic.

"Do what?" Her own response was just as muted.

"I care about you too much to do this now. You deserve so much better than this."

"Vince, please…" She didn't know what she was asking for.

She only knew, at that moment, that she didn't just want him.

She needed him.

He untangled his arms from around her body, but he stayed close enough to cup her face in his hands. "This isn't me rejecting you or us. It's about respecting your feelings and our friendship."

She leaned into his touch. He had to know. Just as she had to go through tonight to find out the truth for herself.

"There's something I need to tell you," she said determinedly, trying to ignore the shakiness and fear in her voice.

He reached for her hand and gave it a reassuring squeeze. "What is it?"

She took a deep breath. "It has always been you."

The words came out in a rush, so she chased after what little bravado she had left. "I never knew how to say it before, because you seemed so unreachable, so... grown-up and perfect."

Vincent didn't say anything, but he stared at her, unblinking, seemingly stunned by the weight of her words.

"Every time I was with someone else, I couldn't help but compare them to you," she continued. "That's why I could never truly be with anyone else—because they would always fall short of what I felt for you. They could never measure up to you, VAT. No one could."

When he finally moved, his reaction was the last thing she expected. He focused on helping her straighten her clothes, his fingers gentle as he smoothed out the creases from her dress like an attentive parent.

When he was done, he pulled her back into his arms for a gentle hug and pressed a soft kiss to her forehead. "Good night, Trina. I'll see you Monday."

Just as he took a step back, her anger flared.

"Good night? That's all you have to say?" She invaded his personal space once more, glaring at him, her raw vulnerability quickly replaced by indignation. "After all we've been through, that's all you've got to say? I don't think you've ever really cared for me, Tugade. All these years, and you never once showed me how much I meant to you!"

In sharp contrast to her biting tone, his response was soft. "That's not true, Trina."

"Isn't it? If you really cared, you would have been smart enough to figure out my feelings for you by now. You would have seen through all my smiles and my teasing, and you would have recognized that it was my love I was trying to hide from you."

"Trina, I..." The words seemed caught in his throat. His face was deathly pale.

He looked a bit like the skull on his jacket, she thought bitterly, stepping away from him and averting her eyes, unable to put up with all the uncertainty surrounding them like a poisonous fog.

"Trina," he began again, more slowly and quietly this time. "I don't just care for you. I love you."

His words landed like a physical blow.

Their meaning was so strong, she was almost thrown backwards onto the floor. Instead, she planted her feet firmly into her damp carpet, stubbornly staring at the wall before her.

Stubbornly refusing to accept what she had just heard.

Vincent didn't stop there. "Maybe that's why you couldn't see it. Caring is something clear, something easily understood. But love..." His voice trailed off, as if he was searching for the right words. "Love is so much more. It's complicated and messy and just plain fucked up. I could never figure out how to show you how I really felt. There's no formula on how to do it."

To her surprise, she felt tears well up in her eyes, taking down the last few pieces that remained of her battered pride. She prayed fervently he couldn't see them—or the pathetic look on her face.

There was a weighted pause before she heard him speak again. "Goodbye, Trina."

She heard a faint rustle as he picked up his jacket from the floor. After a few light footsteps and the creaking of her front door, he was gone.

When she finally had the strength to look, she saw that he'd left the bag of coffee beans behind.

It hurt to move from her spot in the middle of the living room. It was even more excruciating for her to walk to the door and lock it.

She did the only thing she could to ease the pain.

She sat on the couch and gave her tears permission to fall.

Eight

Vincent

THE CHAINS

H E FELT NUMB.
He was grateful he could still move after everything that happened in Trina's apartment. His entire body felt frozen and unwilling as he made his way back down the hall and took the elevator. He felt as if he'd run a marathon and then took a beating after.

Vincent climbed into his car and drove away from her building. Through the veil of the ongoing downpour, the streets were nearly empty in the late hour. The deafening roar of his thoughts seemed even more pronounced against the stillness of the world around him.

Why did he leave?

Trina had told him she didn't want him to go. He replayed her words in his mind over and over, each repetition making him question his decision more and more.

"It has always been you."

Wasn't he chained to her all these years? He had always felt that invisible bond connecting them, drawing him closer to her even when he tried to pull away.

"Fuck it all," he muttered under his breath, his hands shaking as he held the steering wheel as tightly as he could, fearing his self-control would slip away at any moment.

Why had he run away now, when she needed him most? Was it fear that held him back? Fear of admitting to himself and to her how much she really meant to him?

He breathed out slowly, trying to calm his racing heartbeat that mirrored the engine's purr.

"Trina," he whispered into the darkness, as if saying her name might bring him a measure of clarity. "I'm sorry, baby. I love you."

As soon as the words left his mouth, he realized that he was making a grave mistake. That the love he had kept bottled up for so long would remain unacknowledged if he didn't turn back.

He couldn't run away now.

He could never run away, in the first place, even if he tried.

Katrina David would always pull at his chains with a single glance, a soft smile, a teasing word; and he would be back right by her side, where he knew he'd always belonged.

Eskeleto's tires screeched on the pavement as he made an abrupt U-turn, his decision made. The streets whirred past him like a kaleidoscope, but all he could focus on was the burning resolve within him.

He accelerated, pushing his car to its limits, just as he would on the track.

But, this time, it was different.

It was a race he didn't want to win. It was a race he desperately wanted to finish.

It was a race he wanted to lose.

Vincent was done running.

I'm coming back for you, Trina.

In no time at all, he was parked outside her apartment building once more. He practically leaped from the car and sprinted to the entrance.

When he arrived at her door, he hesitated for only a second before knocking urgently, not bothering to check if there was a doorbell somewhere on the wall.

Trina opened the door almost immediately.

Her eyes were red and swollen from crying. Her face, which always had the most contagious of smiles, was drawn. She was still wearing her rain-soaked black dress, a little askew around her body after their kisses.

No matter how she looked, she would always be the most beautiful sight to his eyes.

He couldn't hold back any longer.

The words came out in a torrent of emotion. "I'm sorry for running away, Trina. Maybe I wasn't ready to find out how you really felt. It was something I wasn't prepared for... but it's also something I couldn't run away from. And that's why I'm here."

A sob escaped her throat as she flung herself into his arms, her tears warm as they soaked through his shirt. He held her tightly, feeling the weight of years of unspoken feelings finally pouring out between them.

His voice shook when he spoke, but he didn't care. He was done denying his own feelings, too.

"My heart has always belonged to you," he confessed. "In the racing world, they call me the King of Chains, but you have always been my Queen."

"Vincent," Trina whispered against his chest, "for someone so smart, you're an idiot."

He couldn't help but chuckle at her words, knowing the truth behind them. "I promise I won't run anymore, Trina. I'm here. I'll always be here."

"Good," she murmured, pulling back slightly to look into his eyes. "Don't you dare leave me again. And don't even think about leaving me tonight."

As their lips met in a passionate kiss, he knew he would never leave her side ever again.

Nine

Trina

THE TOUCH

After they kissed each other breathless on her threshold, Vincent spoke against her lips.

"No one is leaving tonight, Trina, as long as you tell me this is what you really want."

She nodded.

He smiled as he gently nudged her into the apartment, shutting the door behind them. Once he had closed them off from the rest of the world, he swept her off the floor and laid her down on the couch, covering her body with his.

Oh, god. She could tell what *he* wanted, felt it through those tight black pants that seemed molded to his long legs, as they resumed their heated kissing. Her own body responded as she shifted her hips closer, higher.

She put her hands on his cheeks and stared into his eyes, unable to stop herself from drowning in them. He was fascinating and so deliciously male. Why did she have to look at other men when she had him in front of her the whole time?

"This is what I've always wanted," she whispered. "I'm very sure."

His lips found hers again. His tongue delved into her mouth as his hands found their way through her clothing. He easily slid the dress off her, followed by her black lace bra and thong.

She had dressed for someone she had never desired, only to be undressed by the one man she had wanted—needed—all this time.

It was worth it, after all, she thought, as she felt him touch that intimate, soaking spot between her legs, felt his mouth close around each of her nipples in turn before making its way down to her heat. She squealed when she felt his tongue on her, her hips bucking wildly. She reached out for him, fumbling with his belt, only to growl and command him to take his clothes off, too.

When he stood bare before her, she marveled at the sheer sight of him. Without clothes, he was more muscle-bound than she'd ever imagined. His tattoos wound around his upper body like chains.

She held out her arms and he went into them. He was very gentle, his voice soft in her ear, promising he would never hurt her. His fingers coaxed her to open, drawing out her pleasure and her need. His lips were on her mouth, on her hair, on her neck, as she ground herself against him, knowing exactly what her body was reaching for.

His timing was exquisite. She felt herself stretch as he entered and sheathed himself inside her. She was the first to move, her hands going up into his hair, her arms locking around his upper back, her teeth grazing his shoulder.

He matched her movements as if they were in a perfectly choreographed dance, his hands on her hips and legs, guiding her body to meet and move against his. He was good, so good.

She felt it then, a warm, snaking sensation beginning to build inside her very core, wrapping itself around her, until she felt it explode between them and send shockwaves of pleasure throughout her body. She heard herself moan his name, followed by incoherent mewls and loud gasps.

"Trina, I love you," he whispered hoarsely, before she felt him tense up and move faster, harder, deeper into her. He made a throaty, guttural sound as his body convulsed on top of hers. She watched pleasure cross his features, savoring how tightly he held on to her, as if for dear life.

She put her arms around him as he slumped on top of her, burying his head between her breasts. She closed her eyes, basking in the bliss that still hummed throughout her body, and the familiar scent and warmth of the man she now had in her arms.

"Vince?" she said into his rumpled hair.

"Yeah?" His eyes were half-closed, his nose nuzzling one breast.

"I'm glad it's you. I've always wanted it to be you."

When she was rewarded by that grin again, and the

glitter of what she now recognized as desire in his eyes, she knew they were both in for a long, sleepless night.

In the hours that followed, they explored every corner of her apartment, their bodies coming together in passion and need as they made love over and over again.

From the couch, they rolled down to the living room floor, where he settled her on top of his jacket and put her legs on his shoulders, lifting her hips off the floor as he entered her more deeply than before. She, distantly, heard her loud moans, mixing with his own grunts and groans of pleasure.

With the city lights twinkling through the rain outside the windows, he pressed her against the wall and buried his face between her breasts, their bodies drenched with sweat as they moved and seized pleasure together.

In the kitchen, after they had both eaten more croissants, he devoured her then, using the magic of his tongue, lips and fingers to send her writhing in ecstasy on the tabletop. When he was done, she wrapped her legs around his waist as he took her once more, just as hungrily.

They moved to her bedroom then, where she insisted that she reciprocate what he had done for her in the kitchen. It was then she truly understood how much he really wanted her, and how good he tasted, as he came in her mouth, shouting her name.

In the darkest hours of dawn, their lovemaking became slower, more tender; their earlier desperation and urgency giving way to gentle exploration and intimate confessions.

As the first rays of the sun began to break over the city's skyline, they finally succumbed to exhaustion, collapsing into each other's arms.

As she watched him fall asleep in her embrace, she knew she would never run or hide from him again.

How could she, when her heart had always been his, bound to him with the invisible, unbreakable chains of a love that was there long before she knew it ever existed.

Ten

Vincent

THE LIGHT

T H E FIRST THING HE REALIZED, WHEN HE WOKE UP, was that he wasn't alone in bed.

Vincent found himself looking at long locks of mahogany hair spread out before him. They belonged to the woman sleeping next to him, spooned naked against his body. He still had one arm around her. Her bare buttocks were pressed against his leg.

He slowly reached over to push the hair away from her face. Trina looked beautifully content in sleep. In the morning light, he could see that her pink lips looked slightly swollen.

Morning light.

There was a small digital clock on the nightstand. It read 9:43.

He had overslept by almost five hours, in a bed that wasn't his.

This bed had sheets and pillowcases in white, orange and pink. A peach-colored teddy bear glared at him from its perch next to the digital clock.

So much for his routine.

But this was the kind of Saturday night and Sunday morning he could get used to.

They had made love all over her apartment, and moved to her bedroom afterwards. After savoring all of her, he decided she tasted like mocha, strong and addictive, with an undeniable hint of sweetness.

The last thing he could recall was Trina grinding on top of him, before he turned her over and took her from behind, tantalized by the perfect roundness of her butt the entire time. At some point, they fell asleep, the rain stopped, and the sun rose, in no particular order.

"Good morning." Her voice was sweet, shy, almost girlish. Her eyes were half-open, still a little clouded with sleep.

"Good morning, baby girl," he said, trying out the endearment for the first time in his life. It sounded right. It felt good to say it.

She turned to face him, her arms going around his neck with surprising familiarity. She kissed him square on the lips. "How'd you sleep?"

"Very good. I just woke up, too. I was watching you."

She blushed and buried her face in his neck. "Don't do that."

"Do what?"

"That thing with your eyes."

He had no idea what she was talking about. "Something wrong with my eyes?"

"No. Yes. Whenever you look at me like that, that's it. I'm gone." Understanding slowly dawned on him, as she began nibbling at his neck.

"Trina?" he prompted, tenderly, reaching for her chin.

"Yes?" She settled against the crook of his arm, as comfortably as she would sit in his office.

"What happens to us now?"

She looked at him with surprise in her eyes but said nothing.

He swallowed. He might as well get it over with, before nerves got the better of him.

"Would you like to be my girlfriend? I suppose, sooner rather than later, I would have to propose, too, seeing that we didn't use—"

She giggled, so merrily he forgot any apprehensions he had. She wriggled closer to him. "To all of the above, my answer is yes."

He kissed her soundly. "I love you."

"I love you, too, although I still can't believe I actually fell in love with someone who's secretly an idiot."

He had to laugh. It was refreshing to have his mental faculties taken down a couple of notches, especially when it came to matters of the heart.

She wasn't finished. "My only condition is that you've got to have the energy for this, Mr. Tugade. I don't want to have fun all by myself."

He raised himself up by the elbow and arranged his demeanor into what she called his Presentation Mode.

"Miss David, allow me to show you the real definition of energy. I hope you're ready for a demonstration."

With her laughter washing over him, he plunged into her waiting arms.

BOOK III

Shadow and Light

Playlist

The Unforgiven 2
Metallica

White Flag
Dido

Hold On
Limp Bizkit

Building a Mystery
Sarah McLachlan

Crash and Burn
Savage Garden

Sway
Bic Runga

You'll Be Safe Here
Rivermaya

Prologue

THE PRIZED PLAYER

MORNING CAME WITH A HOWLING WIND, THE KIND that carried dirt and muck that stuck on the skin and never washed out. It seemed to scream in pain. Arthur gritted his teeth. The storm, gone as quickly as it had come, was over, but everything in the campus was still drenched from the unforgiving intensity of the downpour.

It would be very cold on the field, not to mention muddy. The football pitch looked more like a swamp when he passed by it on his way to the college's main building.

Coach wanted them to start putting in more hours *now*, before first period, for the next intercollegiate football tournament game. Come rain or flood or any other calamity, they would defend their title all the way up to regionals, for the second year in a row.

He descended the steps to the main building's basement. It was a little past six in the morning. The prized player's first class started at eight and now he was most probably in his lair, practicing those deft knee tricks that brought tears to the eyes of the rival coaches.

As team captain, it was Arthur's job to secure the gear and inform the prized player about that morning's practice not getting cancelled in spite of the field's condition.

Not that he'd care either way, he thought bitterly

The prized player was a tireless machine, not a person. He'd show up, do the drills and rounds, and commit the plays to memory. Arthur often wondered what possessed him to turn down the position of captain, after bringing the team to two regional championships since he was a freshman.

Even as a senior, Arthur was only the distant second choice to lead the team this year. His numbers in goals and successful plays were pathetic compared to the prized player's, as was everyone else's. The man pretty much did not miss goals.

He typed in the door code and stepped inside the basement, which housed a collection of old school furniture and relatively new sports equipment. He knocked on the door of a smaller room inside, once a storage closet for cleaning equipment and a break room for campus cleaning staff, before the lay-offs.

This was now the prized player's residence on campus, because he didn't want to share his space with three other kids in the dormitory next door.

No answer. Arthur turned the knob, finding it unlocked, and pushed warily.

There was nothing in the prized player's room except a

sparse wooden cot, an equally drab three-legged table, and a portable clothes rack.

The team helped him load back the equipment only last night, he thought. *Knowing him, he wouldn't move out of this place. It's his lion's den, after all.*

Arthur knew that the prized player had some other stuff around, like dartboards, target posters, and sketches of exotic birds. They were all gone. Nothing was draped on the makeshift clothesline strung across the tiny room.

He stood there and assessed this new information for half a minute.

Arthur took a deep breath and closed the door. He retraced his steps in the basement, retrieving two footballs from the storage racks before he left.

He had better tell Coach that Aragon was gone.

ACT I
FALLING

One

THE DARK

It was dark.

In his world, somehow, it always seemed dark.

He gingerly lowered his body onto a lopsided stone bench overlooking the quad. His muscles ached and his sides burned from the run.

The campus was still cloaked in the night. He had been running for more than an hour, but the sky still resembled a blue-black canopy strewn with thick masses of clouds. Not a ray of sunlight breached his limited view of the horizon; it was still too early for that. The air was thick and heavy, and sullied by city dust.

Rain was coming.

He felt a detached, perverse satisfaction.

"Aragon?"

A female voice had said his family name. People knew him by that name.

Aragon.

A name full of history. His place of birth was far enough away, but he could still recollect the smells of gunpowder, the crisp click of a gun's hammer, the echo of death cries. They all came with his heritage.

His well-trained eyes made out her silhouette. The lighting in the campus was limited and the few functional lampposts badly needed their bulbs replaced.

"Jeri." Her name fell from his lips. After all this time, he was still surprised at the way he would say it. Softer, slower than his usual speech, and always with awe.

She was dressed in a white top and a denim skirt. The balmy breeze played with the strands of her long, wavy hair. She carried a black backpack, the size of which dwarfed her frame.

He wasn't surprised to feel his chest tighten, his heartbeat accelerate. "What are you doing here? How did you get in the campus?"

He watched her place the bag on the concrete pavement and take a seat beside him.

"I had to see you," she replied simply.

"How did you get in?" he pressed.

He lived on campus, in the main building's basement. He had first lodged in a boarding house, then moved to the dormitory after he'd secured a permanent spot in the college's varsity football team. He was not comfortable with the noise and activity in shared living spaces.

Coach had allowed him to hole up in the old janitors' break room, right next to the storage where the sports teams kept all their equipment. The old man could not refuse the simple request of the college's star athlete and pulled every string he could with Administration to make this strange request happen.

"Being in the Student Council has its benefits." There was a smile in her voice. "I couldn't sleep. I figured you would be here."

"I couldn't sleep, either."

Jeri slid onto the bench next to him. He opened his arms and she snuggled into them. She pressed her face to his chest, not minding his sweat-soaked shirt.

"I really missed you." Her voice was a melodious whisper in the stillness. "It's been so busy with your game and the debates…"

"I missed you, too. A lot."

The confession was a rare display of boldness in terms of expressing how he felt. This was a first for him, and he did it only for her.

"I wanted to call you earlier, but I knew you'd be sleeping," he went on as he touched her hair, wrapping the smooth strands around his rough palm. The contrast was undeniably appealing. "As always, the best option is to run. Wait it out until the sun finally decides to come up."

She giggled. "You're crazy, Aragon."

He had to smile at her declaration, knowing that the only witnesses were the darkness and her. "Maybe I am, because you're here with me and you're so fucking beautiful."

Her giggles dissolved into a breathless sigh as he leaned in for a kiss. Their lips met tentatively at first, before melding together with a passion that no amount of repetition or familiarity could dull.

As their kiss deepened, he found his hands on her body,

his fingers hungrily reaching for the softness and curves under her blouse.

She was in a similar state, her hands pulling at his hair as she pressed her body closer and tighter against his, practically melting into his heated skin.

"Crazy," she repeated, this time in a low growl.

"Come with me," he murmured against her lips. He stood up and took her bag, then held out a hand to her.

Wordlessly and without hesitation, she took it, her eyes wide and luminous in the semi-darkness.

He led her to his living quarters, their own little private sanctuary for more than a year now. When they were together, everything else held little consequence.

In those moments, she was the only one who mattered.

As soon as the locked door shut out the rest of the world, his lips found hers again, gently, but quickly growing more demanding and urgent.

He lost himself in the taste and feel of her, always reminding him of the tart sweetness of apples. It was something he could never get enough of.

For someone who had been taught his entire life not to get too attached to anyone or anything, he knew he had already lost this battle to her, long before he'd ever known what it was he felt for her.

The memory of the first time he saw her was striking in its simplicity and unforgettable in its intensity.

That day remained etched in his memory, the mark it made deeper than any of the arcane teachings that had been repeatedly drilled into him over the years.

From that day on, he knew, somehow, that he'd always belonged to the woman in his arms.

Two

THE DUSK

The Orientation Week of freshman year at the university dawned cloudy and rainy, perhaps an omen of things to come.

He was a stranger to most of the people around him, more so than usual, even in the boarding house where he stayed. He was surrounded by students from other provinces, but he still stood out like a sore thumb, with his accent and his reputation.

He'd been uprooted from the south, on a full football scholarship. The name Aragon had already made its way all over the country, a football player who had never experienced defeat on the field during his elementary and high school years. The universities had fought over him. He'd chosen this particular one because it was the farthest away.

He left his accommodation very early that day and spent the morning practicing on the field, alone, in the middle of the rain. He had a few hours before the start of orientation; he might as well do something useful. Any kind of training was beneficial.

The rain stopped and the sun broke through the clouds just in time for the freshman events to start. At the college auditorium, he joined the queue of new students quietly, hoping he wouldn't get noticed or singled out.

In sharp contrast to his desire to blend in, Jeri was one of the few brave souls who volunteered to be the freshman batch representative.

He watched her ascend the stage with grace and determination, her gaze sweeping over the crowd before settling on the microphone. Her smile was radiant and genuine. She had thick, dark brown hair that tumbled over her shoulders in waves, framing her round face like a halo.

"Hello, everyone," she began, her voice clear and melodic. "My name is Jerann Castelo, but you can call me Jeri. I'm here today because I believe in a better future for all of us, a future where every student has the opportunity to shine and achieve great things, no matter where each of us came from."

No matter where each of us came from.

He was struck and captivated by her words and the passion behind them.

The rest of her speech rang clearly, sincerely. "What is more important is where we are headed and what we can accomplish along the way. We can do this together if we help and support one another, starting today: right here, right now."

She possessed a magnetism that drew him in, the way her intelligent brown eyes seemed to pierce through his very core, seeing him for what he truly was. She had the gaze of a predator, but it was also warm and welcoming. It was a dangerous, intoxicating combination, one she was probably not even aware of.

It was no wonder she won with a decisive margin; she was a force of nature, a beacon of light.

He thought of her like the sun, a radiant star that burned brightly. It was a stark contrast to the shadows in which he had been trained to dwell, a nameless weapon cloaked in secrecy and anonymity.

Her presence wrapped around him like an embrace. It was a strange, but not unwelcome, sensation, one he got just by looking at a girl who stood and spoke on the podium.

He'd been taught to suppress emotions, to sever all ties to the world around him in order to survive.

Looking at Jeri Castelo challenged all of that.

He mustered the courage to speak with her, to his credit—or perhaps to his doom.

The auditorium was abuzz with excitement as the newly-elected freshman representative descended the stage after the announcements of the college dean.

"Congratulations, Jeri," he said, sidling up to her amid the throngs of students offering their well-wishes. His heart hammered in his chest, unaccustomed to such vulnerability with another person, but her smile eased the tension effortlessly.

"Thank you," she replied. "I appreciate it, uh..?"

"N—" He almost said his name in response, but before he could, a group of adoring girls and boys descended upon her, their voices clamoring for attention.

They'd apparently known her from her high school debate days, and their admiration was palpable in the air that crackled with energy and enthusiasm.

"Hey, Jeri! Remember us?" one of them called out. "We were in the Science High School across the road from you. We had an event on international trade policies."

And just like that, she was swept away by the tide of her admirers, leaving him standing alone in the crowded auditorium.

After that, he always watched her from afar, his gaze following her as she moved through the campus like a whirlwind. She gave him the regulation blue booklets for their quizzes twice during freshman year, whenever he forgot to buy them—the first time for a History exam, the second for an essay assignment in PE he had to write down fifteen minutes before the class started. He was particularly desperate on both occasions, and she graciously came to his rescue.

Her sunny presence was a constant in his life, shining on him brightly even as he retreated further into the shadows the more people paid attention to him and asked questions about his life before university.

He only ever stepped out of the shadows when it was time to play.

On the football field, he could be exactly as he was, without inhibitions or hesitation. While the ball was in play, he could assert his control, bend his body to his will, outsmart and outrun his opponents.

It was the only time he could let go.

He wished he could let go, too, when it came to what he felt for the girl whose presence he craved almost obsessively.

Sometimes, in the early evenings, he would see her seated alone under the fire tree in the campus quad, the bright blossoms a vibrant contrast to her pensive expression. There was a heaviness in her posture, a burden that seemed to weigh her down as she stared off into the distance, lost in thought.

It was in those moments, when the world around them turned momentarily insignificant, that he saw himself reflected in her eyes.

He wanted to reach out, to bridge the gap between them, but fear held him back—fear of rejection, of inadequacy, of the consequences that came with letting someone in, after so many years of being taught to do the exact opposite.

He did try, one time, at the start of their sophomore year, when she was running for a spot at the University Student Council.

It was dusk, but he knew she was not even halfway done with the day.

She was seated on a stone bench overlooking the quad, as usual, surrounded by a hefty stack of books and the large backpack she carried all over campus. It was a wonder how her petite frame managed to stay upright and even walk around.

It was now or never. He had to take the shot.

Before he could overthink the entire matter of approaching her, he found himself standing next to the bench.

"Hi, Jeri."

He was painfully aware that he cast a shadow over her. Swallowing hard, he stepped out of the way of what little light there was left before the sun completely set.

"Oh, hi." She looked up with a tentative, hesitant smile.

An involuntary shiver ran down his spine as their eyes met. An irrational thought struck him.

Does she know?

He didn't even know what to say. When he thought about it, the only thing he had in common with her was that they were both sophomores—and they had one class together that semester, Philosophy.

He said the only thing that came to mind as he took in the sheer amount of belongings around her. "May I sit with you?"

She made space for him by putting her books in her lap. "Sure. Can I help with you something? Is this about Math 100?"

He took a seat, careful to keep a respectful distance. "Math 100?"

She nodded. "I've been asked a lot lately about tutoring people in Calculus."

"No, not about Math 100, although I would appreciate the help if you've got the time."

Her smile was kind, but he couldn't help but notice the dark circles under her eyes, the drawn expression on her face despite the genuine light in her gaze.

"I'll have a look at my schedule at the Learning Center, but I'd be happy to slot you in if there are still free spots left."

"Thanks."

Silence fell over them, awkward and heavy.

He didn't know where he got the guts to speak first.

"I just wanted to ask if you're okay. I was passing by and, well, I noticed you've been looking a little…overwhelmed lately."

She studied him intently before saying anything in response. "Am I that transparent?" He wasn't sure if she laughed or sighed. "I guess I didn't realize anyone was paying attention."

"It's hard not to notice when someone's constantly on the move, always pushing themselves to do more."

She looked away, tightening her arms around her books.

He drew back, afraid he had offended her.

"Yeah, well, I've got a lot riding on this year," she finally said, looking back at him with a stiff grin. "I can't afford to slow down."

He doubted the sincerity of her words, but he knew he was in no position to question someone like Jeri Castelo. He chose not to say anything, shifting slightly in his seat to make a quick getaway before he inflicted any further damage. As he did, his shoulder brushed against hers. Her skin felt warm even through the worn material of his shirt

"I don't look okay, do I, Aragon?"

Her candid, murmured declaration was a surprise. He chose his next words carefully. "You don't have to carry the weight of the world on your shoulders, you know. There will always be someone who's willing to help. You've always helped everyone. It's your turn now."

She looked at him for a long stretch of time before speaking. "You make it sound so easy and straightforward. I guess that's what makes you such a great team player."

He was inexplicably flattered to know that she'd watched him play.

"Thanks."

"You're welcome. I guess I just need to find my balance, with everything that's been going on. It's too late to turn back once I'm committed to something."

"I know what you mean."

She glanced at her watch and sighed. "It's time for me to go. I've got Economics at six."

She made a move to stand up. Before he realized what he was doing, his hand was on her arm.

"Can I help you with those?" He gestured to the hulking backpack and pile of books between them.

Wide-eyed, she nodded. "Sure."

He needed no further prompting or instruction. He slung the bag over his shoulder and relieved her of the books.

"Are you sure it's fine with you? You're not off to practice or anywhere else, are you? I don't want to trouble you, honestly."

He shook his head and, for the first time in what seemed like the longest time, attempted a smile.

"It's okay. Happy to help."

He followed her across the quad and to the classroom.

"Thanks, Aragon," she said as soon as they reached the entrance.

"Anytime." It wasn't lost on him how the other students in the classroom stared.

"I owe you one. I'll let you know if I've still got that free Calculus slot, okay?"

She gave his forearm a squeeze before she turned and made her way into the room. Her touch felt like a white-hot brand on his skin.

"Sure," he replied to her retreating back. "See you around, Jeri."

The erratic pounding of his heart was strange to his ears. Even his breathing pattern had changed, just by being in close proximity to her.

If only you could show me what you really are, he said to her, silently, watching as she joined the others and once more changed into the vivacious girl everyone in the college was familiar with.

If only you could see me for what I really am, too.

If only we could let each other in.

Three

THE DISTANCE

His resolve held for a week, at best. After that, he knew he couldn't stay away from her.

Exactly seven days after they spoke on the quad, he found himself waiting outside Jeri's Economics classroom, carefully concealed beneath the shadows of a tree.

As soon as the final bell of the evening rang, she emerged from the classroom, as vibrant as ever, with an entourage of classmates from her political party. They were all laden down with campaign posters, her photograph beaming from all of them.

He wanted to approach her, to talk to her some more, but her companions commanded her full attention. He hesitated, uncomfortable with the idea of others observing their interaction. This was unknown territory to him; the presence of other people made him uneasy. He'd just as soon lose his nerve.

Instead, he opted to wait for her to finish, planning to offer to walk her home. Over the past year, he'd sometimes caught glimpses of her walking on the streets surrounding the university. She probably lived nearby.

He watched her and her team as they dispersed to cover different areas of the college. He chose to remain hidden, waiting for the perfect moment to step out of the shadows.

It was late in the evening when Jeri finally left the campus, laden down with her bag and books. With her head high and shoulders back as if she owned the world, her determined stride carried her towards the residential area. He tried to close the gap between them, hoping that she would see him and maybe even smile in recognition. Something held him back, an invisible barrier he couldn't bring himself to breach.

He knew what it was, at the back of his mind, although his pride would never allow him to speak of it.

Fear.

It was the same feeling he had a week ago, moments before he'd approached her on the quad.

Instead, he followed her from a safe distance, his eyes never leaving her as she approached the less crowded parts of the neighborhood. His thoughts raced, wondering how she would react if she knew he was trailing her like some sort of stalker. He'd been trained to recon and observe unnoticed, and now he used those skills only to see her safely home.

That was it, wasn't it?

To make sure she was safe.

As Jeri walked deeper into the dimly lit streets, his senses heightened. The sound of laughter reached his ears, quickly morphing into something far more sinister. The air grew thick with tension, and his pulse quickened in response.

"Hey there, cutie pie," a gruff voice called out, the words dripping with menace. Four men emerged from the shadows of an alley, surrounding her. "We just want your laptop and your phone, and you can be on your way."

She clutched her belongings to her chest. "Please," she begged, her voice breaking. "I need these for school. I'll give you my money, but please, let me keep my things."

The thugs laughed cruelly at her plight. "You're running for the Student Council, aren't you? You're very famous, even in these parts. You should be able to afford new ones."

His heart twisted; his breath hitched. It wasn't in preparation for the kill. It was something more raw and far less calculating.

It was an overwhelming sense of anger, heavily laced with concern. It drove him to admit that he could no longer remain a passive observer.

He couldn't stay in the shadows now.

She needed him.

It took him a single step to come out into the light, radiating from a nearby streetlamp. "Leave her alone."

The men turned their attention to him, their eyes sizing him up. Beneath their predatory sneers, he could sense their hesitation, an uncertainty in confronting a stranger who dared to stand up to them.

And he wasn't just any stranger.

"Who the fuck do you think you are, college boy?" one of the thugs growled.

"Someone who won't let you hurt her." His tone didn't waver as he felt Jeri's gaze upon him. He counted two knives, one retractable steel baton. The biggest of the men, in all likelihood their leader, didn't display any weapons. The leader probably carried a piece, too, but it didn't matter. They were nothing to him.

"Fine," snarled the biggest man, stepping closer to him with a menacing grin. "We'll just take care of you first."

As the leader lunged towards him, he reacted with barely a thought. His fighting style, as old as time, was subtle, fluid, like water flowing around an obstacle. There was no brute force in his movements, no unnecessary exertion of strength. It was as if he were simply stepping out of their way, guiding their own momentum against them.

"Fuck you!" the leader howled as he crumpled to the ground, clutching at an incapacitated arm. The others stared, momentarily stunned by the ease with which their companion had been defeated.

He didn't give any of them time to recover, or even express their regret at mugging Jeri or challenging him. It took him twelve moves to take the remaining three of them down. It would have taken nine had he wanted to go for the kill.

But she was there, watching him.

In mere moments, all four thugs lay sprawled on the pavement, with fractured bones and egos. They scrambled to their feet, their faces twisted with fear and pain, before fleeing into the shadows.

He stood silently, breathing his way back into a calmer state, before he spoke to her.

"Are you okay, Jeri?"

She nodded wordlessly, still clutching her books tightly to her body. Her eyes were wide, filled with residual fear mixed with gratitude and relief.

"Here. Let me take your things."

She offered no resistance when he moved to relieve her of her backpack and gently pulled the books out of her death grip.

"How...how did you get here?" Her voice was trembling, a far cry from her usual confident manner of speech. "It's so late."

"Football practice ran late. I was just on my way to grab some food when I saw you."

He was relieved when she didn't pry further.

"Thank you," she said quietly, barely above a whisper. "I...I don't know what could have happened if you weren't around. I could have l-lost everything. And I've worked so hard, too…"

Her voice trailed off, as if she'd seemingly stopped herself from saying too much.

"You're welcome." He thought it was the safest, most neutral response. "Do you live nearby? I've seen you walking this way a few times before."

"My grandparents live a couple of blocks away. Most of the time I walk to school." Her voice shook slightly. In the lamplight, he could see the hint of unshed tears in her eyes.

He could easily deal with four armed men, with his bare hands, but not with something like this. He didn't have the training to deal with an oncoming assault of emotions and tears.

He swallowed hard. "Can you walk? I'll take you home. Would that be okay?"

She nodded and, to his surprise, inched closer to him. He could feel her body heat, could see her flushed cheeks.

"Would you like to take my arm?" he offered, not sure why he did. It felt right to say it.

She accepted without hesitation. He didn't mind the weight of her things at all; he was very conscious of how close she was as they slowly made their way through the darkened streets, her hand resting lightly on his forearm. She smelled of something fruity and warm.

"This has never happened to me before," she said softly. "I know this neighborhood and most of the people around. I've lived here since I was seven."

"I'm very sorry this happened to you, Jeri."

"It's fine. It's a good thing you're here."

She stopped walking and let go of his arm when they reached a modest two-story house with yellow wood panels and a red galvanized-iron roof, nestled in a lane of similar-looking houses. "Well, this is me."

He took his phone out of his pocket and gave it to her. "Here. Please put your number in."

She took the phone wordlessly and typed in the digits as requested. As she did, she looked up midway through the task, twice, eyeing him curiously. As their eyes met, something stirred within him—an unfamiliar, yet somehow welcome, emotion.

She handed the phone back and he called her, waiting for her phone to ring. It played a beautifully melodious ballad, crooned by a woman with a haunting voice.

"That's a nice song."

"It's called 'Building a Mystery,' by Sarah McLachlan," she said, as she took her phone out of her pocket to cut the call. "It's been around for a while, but I really like it."

He glanced at the dimly-lit house before him and back

at her. "Promise me you'll call if you ever need anything. I'll be there."

"Really, I don't want to bother you. You've done more than enough and I—"

"Please, Jeri. Promise me." The imploring tone he heard in his voice was surprising even to his own ears.

"Okay. I promise."

A sense of relief coursed through him. He hoped she hadn't said it just to get rid of him.

"I guess I should be on my way."

Before he could react, she put her hand on his shoulder and tiptoed to kiss the lower part of his left cheek, her lips only able to reach as high as his jawline.

He felt like he'd caught fire, the contact leaving a searing heat as if she'd pressed a blowtorch right on the spot where her mouth was mere seconds ago.

"I guess." She took a step back and held out her hands. "Be careful, okay?"

He stared at her uncertainly for several long seconds.

Fuck.

Was he supposed to hug her now, or maybe kiss her back? Not that he didn't want to. He'd wanted to since he first saw her but...

"My things, please?"

Heat rushed up his neck and suffused his face, making him grateful for the cover of night. Heart pounding, he carefully handed over her backpack and books, hoping she wouldn't see that his hands were actually trembling.

"There you go. Good night, Jeri."

"Good night."

With a nod, he turned away from her and began to

retrace his steps to the campus. In truth, he still hadn't eaten anything since lunch, but now—

"Nick?"

Her voice carried quietly down the empty street.

Nick.

His first name was Nicholas, but none of his peers ever called him by it. Only the teachers who called the roll ever did.

He was Aragon to people in the university and this city.

She didn't even use his complete given name. Just Nick, as if she'd known him all her life.

He looked over his shoulder to see her still standing in front of the house, looking at him dead on.

"What is it?"

"Thank you. I'll never forget this."

He turned to face her, pushing his hands into his pockets to prevent them from doing something stupid—like close the distance between them again and take her in his arms.

He hesitated before launching into the question he'd really wanted to ask. "Can you do me a favor then?"

"Anything."

"Can we keep this between us? I don't want people to make a fuss."

"I understand. You can trust me."

He nodded. "Thanks, Jeri. I'll see you tomorrow."

"See you tomorrow, Nick."

His walk back to the campus was a blur, the idea of dinner losing its appeal the more he thought of what had just happened.

The fight, if one could even call it that.

The first time he'd shown an outsider even just a tiny glimpse of the true extent of his abilities.

The kiss.

The first time a girl had put her lips anywhere near him.

The promise.

The first time he had willingly offered his protection to someone without a price.

The name.

Nick. Spoken as if it were the most normal thing in the world for her to do.

He didn't realize he was already within the university's walls. He pulled out his phone, holding on to it tightly, as if it was tethered to the girl who was now hopefully safe and secure blocks away.

He took a deep breath and dialed her number. As he listened to the ringing sound, he felt tight knots form in his stomach, only to loosen when he finally heard her pick up at the other end.

"Hello, Nick?" she answered hesitantly.

"Hey, I'm sorry to bother you. I just wanted to check on you."

"Thank you," she breathed. "I'm…I'm fine. Just a little shaken, that's all. But I should be okay. I'm just getting ready for bed. What about you? Did you get any dinner?"

"Ah, it's fine," he replied, glancing at the deserted quad around him. "I'll be off to the gym soon."

"Really?" she sounded incredulous. "Do you ever sleep at all?"

He didn't answer, evading the question with a subtle deflection. "I'm just glad you're okay, Jeri."

"Well, I owe you one. I'll bring something nice for you to

eat tomorrow to make it up to you. I'm so sorry you missed dinner."

"Please, don't worry about it," he insisted, uncomfortable at the thought of someone going out of their way for him.

They spoke briefly about her campaign, and he couldn't help but admit that he would vote only for her, despite there being two available spots on the University Student Council.

"Your support means a lot." Her voice was now lighter, less tense. The more relaxed she sounded, the better he felt, too. "But I have to say, it's because of you that our university is back on the sporting map. It's like you've proven to the entire region that we're not just a bunch of nerds with our noses buried in books."

As their conversation continued, she asked about his well-being, if he needed anything or if there was any way she could help him, so far from home. The genuine concern in her voice moved him, and he understood why she was so beloved by everyone at school.

As they spoke, he walked to the bench on the quad where Jeri usually sat and assumed her place under the shelter of the tree. When they finally exchanged goodbyes and he waited for her to cut the call first, he realized it was barely an hour before midnight.

He stared down at his phone as if it could provide answers to the swirling questions in his mind.

What did he really feel for her?

Did she have any idea about it? What would she think of him if she knew?

What was he going to do about any of it, as someone living on borrowed time?

The stillness of the night wrapped around him heavily.

Most students would have been fast asleep by now, but sleep rarely came easy to him.

As he entered the dimly lit gym adjacent to the auditorium, he took a deep breath, inhaling the familiar scent of sweat and rusted steel that permeated the air. This was his sanctuary, a place where he could lose himself in his training and forget, if only for a little while, the real weight of his dual existence.

With each precise strike against the punching bag, each rep of the heavy barbells only he could lift, he tried to push all thought out of his mind, focusing only on the screaming of his muscles.

But thoughts of her persisted, even as he tried to punch and kick harder than usual, lift heavier than he normally would.

He paused in his training, pressing his face to the cold and grimy wall, trying to ignore the hunger that raged in his stomach.

"Damn it," he muttered under his breath, slamming his fist against the wall in frustration. The pain that lanced through his hand was a welcome distraction.

He needed not to think about time, about how he couldn't take it back no matter how strong he became, how hard he trained, or how much determination he possessed.

Time was his greatest enemy. He had already used up more than a year of it; he had less than three left.

Three years was nothing. It would all flash by in a heartbeat, and he would be dead again.

He was fighting a losing battle.

But he wasn't going down easily.

Four

THE DIVIDE

He found out they were both creatures of habit.

That small snippet of realization took down one more piece of the wall around him, as he unknowingly began to let her in.

The day after he'd walked her home for the first time, Jeri brought him a meticulously packed bundle of food: steamed rice, small cuts of grilled meat, and a piece of fruit. She turned up at the corner of the field right after the team's morning practice session. She repeated this the following day, this time with a small container of stir-fried noodles and vegetables clutched in her hands.

She became his tutor in Calculus, too, in twice-weekly sessions they spent in a corner desk just outside the library

Away from the confines of the Learning Center and the strict silence of the stacks, the spot always seemed reserved for her. Once he'd asked her if she'd signed him up officially as a tutee; she'd just shrugged and smiled.

He became, unofficially, her shadow. He walked her home almost every day, especially on those times when she stayed on campus until late in the evening. Even on days when football practice was supposed to drain him of energy, he found himself accompanying her on the darkened streets, seeing her safely to the yellow house with the red roof, which always seemed devoid of life.

As the days flew by, they became part of each other's daily routines.

Shortly before the University Student Council elections, he picked her up from her Economics class. They were once again subjected to curious stares, this time a little more openly. He wondered how she could live with such scrutiny every day.

"Hi." Jeri appeared at the doorway of the classroom, greeting him with a small smile.

"Ready for some Calculus?" He extended a hand, knowing she understood what he meant.

She turned over her backpack without question. "Always. Let's get you ready for a great score during the mid-terms. That way you won't have to stress so much on the finals."

They walked across the quad to their usual spot outside the library. As the night deepened, they delved into derivatives and integrals, her patience with him as saintly as her presence was soothing.

They were packing up their things when she hesitated before leaving the library building.

"I've been meaning to tell you," she said hesitantly, stopping on top of the steps that led to the quad outside. "I didn't want to talk about it before, but I thought you should know."

"What is it?"

Were people talking about him, to her? What did they know?

She averted her eyes from his before speaking, clutching her books to her chest and belly. This was her self-preservation reflex, using her books to protect her vital organs.

It was strangely endearing.

"Ever since we started spending time together, my campaign has picked up. People are taking notice, especially the sororities. I've gotten two invitations to pledge in the past week. They thought, well, that I'm your girlfriend." She swallowed hard and looked him in the eye. "I'm so sorry."

"Why?" He held on to her gaze as he relieved her of the books. She need not worry about anything hurting her, as long as he was around.

"Why what?"

"Why are you sorry, Jeri?"

She bit her lip and shook her head. "I don't know. For people misinterpreting our friendship, I guess. I just don't want you to think I'm using you or anything."

"Using me?"

"You're practically a celebrity in this school, Nick. Anyone close to you would have a higher clout than they'd ever have on their own. That includes me."

Had he been someone else, he would have laughed at the ridiculousness of the idea. But he could sense her anxiety, her fear of being misunderstood.

He didn't know the first thing about politics, but fear was something he understood intimately.

"How can you use me, when I'm doing all of this by choice?"

"Are you really?"

He nodded.

He wasn't even finished with his response before he found himself, laden down with her backpack and her books, in her arms.

She was hugging him. It was awkward and lopsided, but he didn't care.

"I don't care what people think," he said, uncertain on how to respond using his actions. He couldn't even move that much.

She gave him a squeeze before letting go. "Thanks. You're a really great guy, you know."

He felt a mixture of relief and loss once she broke contact. "Alright. Okay, let's get going."

The walk to her house was quiet and leisurely, with a few snippets of conversation in between; they talked about the start of the intercollegiate sports season, about the upcoming elections.

Life, for a while, was simple.

When they reached her house, Jeri hesitated at the gate as he handed over her things. She went on tiptoe as before. This time, he bent down so she could reach his cheek properly.

"That's better," she murmured against his skin before kissing him. "Thanks, Nick."

As soon as the books were in her grip, it was his turn to put his arms around her.

For the first time in his life, he hugged a girl.

He could feel the slight tremble in her body. She was wonderfully soft and warm to the touch.

"Good night, Jeri."

With her hands occupied, she leaned into him, her face nestling against the crook of his neck. "Good night. See you tomorrow."

As he walked away, the distance between them growing wider with each step, he felt the familiar buzz of his phone in his pocket.

Barely a moment had passed since their goodbye, and already she had sent him a message.

Thanks for your kindness

You're the best

He was about to text her back when the world around him shifted, a sudden chill creeping up his spine.

He was no longer alone.

Eight shadows materialized around him, some of their faces familiar. Half of them were part of the same group of men who had mugged Jeri weeks back.

This time, however, three of them brandished guns. The metal shone dully under the dim glow of the streetlights.

"Go back to whichever hell you came from, hero."

He recognized the leader, feeling a sudden pang of sympathy for him. If the would-be gangster thought he could save face, he was in for another disappointment.

An icy calm settled over him as he assessed the situation, his mind racing with possible strategies and outcomes like a high-speed game of chess.

He stared at the barrel of the gun closest to him. His voice was steady when he spoke. "Over my dead body."

The men laughed, their jeers echoing through the empty streets.

"If you think the tricks you used to impress your little girlfriend would work on us, you're fucking wrong, kid."

"Those tricks worked very well the first time. I can still remember how quickly you hit the ground."

"You're such a smartass, aren't you, college boy?"

"Just telling the truth." His jaw clenched as he inhaled deeply, drawing on his years of training to center himself before a fight.

He knew he shouldn't be doing this. He'd traveled so far to get away from it all, and yet here he was, letting himself get dragged right back into a world of violence. It was a vicious circle, one he couldn't seem to escape.

The fight broke out with a sudden ferocity, but he saw everything unfold in painfully slow motion. His fists connected with jaws and torsos, bones shattering under the force of his blows. He wove through the group of men, ducking beneath wild punches and countering with devastating precision. It was almost as if he had never left, the muscle memory of countless sparring sessions and battles awakening within him.

The fight raged on outside, but inside him settled a numbing realization. As he sidestepped and countered attacks around him, he accepted the inescapable truth: a normal life was never truly meant for him.

He was, after all, Cain.

Twin to death, forged in blood.

As he battled the men, dodged their knives and bullets with an almost insulting ease, he understood that as long as he lingered in the shadows, violence would continue to claw at him, always demanding to be acknowledged.

And so he lunged forward, disarming two of the men of their guns in one fluid, practiced motion. The cold weight of the weapons settled into his palms, feeling both alien and familiar all at once. They were imitation guns; cheap, soldered versions of the perfectly balanced Glocks he usually favored.

Fake gun or not, it would be so easy to pull the trigger, as natural to him as breathing. For a brief moment, he considered it.

Instead of aiming for the sweet spot between their eyes, as he had been trained to do, he shifted his aim, targeting the knees of the men before him. The gunshots rang out like muffled thunder, encrusted in rusty shells.

"Stay away from me and the girl." He stared down the last man standing, who still clutched his imitation gun with trembling hands.

"Or what?" the man challenged, a desperate defiance in his eyes.

Without hesitation, he fired again, the bullet tearing through the gunman's fingers, wrenching the weapon from his grip. Blood splattered on the grimy, trash-littered pavement as he turned away, as quickly as he had finished the fight.

He knew he had to move fast. Someone would have heard the shots, no matter how late in the night it was. Someone would investigate. It was only a matter of time.

With a heavy sigh, he bent down and collected the weapons of the fallen men, their moans and curses a grim soundtrack to his calculated actions. He found one of them wearing a fairly large jacket; he kicked the man over and ripped the jacket off him, using the fabric as a makeshift bundle for the guns and blades he'd gathered.

Moving with laser focus, he found an empty alley a few blocks away, just around the corner from the university. He entered the darkened area cautiously, ensuring he was alone before getting to work.

He didn't need light to guide his hands as he disassembled the fake guns and broke the blades off the knives' hilts. Using his powerful left leg, he kicked open a nearby manhole, the metallic clang setting his teeth on edge.

One by one, he dropped the pieces of his handiwork into the drainage, watching as they disappeared into the murky sewage below. The darkness swallowed the remnants of his violent encounter.

He was the only one who remained, aside from the eight men and their broken bodies. If they wanted a third round, he would gladly give it to them. This time, none of them would be walking away.

As he made his way back towards the university, the distant sound of police sirens pierced the night air.

His reaction to the sound was a first: his heart pounded in his chest, mingling with a rush of adrenaline and fear through his veins. In the past, he wouldn't have cared about the consequences—escaping and disappearing into the shadows would have been second nature to him.

But, now, things had changed.

Jeri.

With her long brown hair and equally dark eyes, with her smile and sweet little kisses. She'd hugged him earlier, hadn't she?

She'd brought him food every day, too, yet another burden for her to carry.

A random thought crossed his mind as he made his way through the darkened quad, his gaze brushing past the bench where she usually sat in the late afternoons.

More than half the books she always carried were not for her. They were for the people she tutored, including him.

The thought of being apart from her caused him physical pain, a gnawing sensation that ate its way from inside his chest.

He couldn't leave now.

He couldn't ever leave her.

Upon reaching his room, he sank onto the bed, his heart still racing. No amount of breathing techniques seemed to work in calming it down.

He knew there was only one way to deal with it.

He picked up his phone with trembling hands, skinned and bloodied from the fight, and dialed her number.

She picked up after four rings, her voice groggy when she answered. "Hello, Nick?"

"Hi, Jeri," he said softly. "I'm back on campus."

Something about his response must have sounded off to her. Her next words were more alert. "Are you okay? Have you eaten anything?"

The answer to both was a resounding no, but he didn't have to tell her. He hesitated for a moment, then forced a smile into his voice. "Yeah, I'm fine. I just wanted to say good night."

"Are you sure you're okay? Why don't you have some of those sandwiches I brought earlier? You haven't eaten them all yet, have you?"

The white plastic container with the green cover was on the tiny table next to him, already empty. Ever since she'd started bringing him food, he would wash those pieces of Tupperware religiously and returned them to her, squeaky clean and spotless, the following day.

"I have a few pieces left, thanks." He hoped the lightness he affected in his tone was enough not to make her any more concerned. "You're a lifesaver."

"I'll get some more food to you in the morning, okay? I'm so sorry our session ran late. Next time you don't have to worry about walking me home. Everyone at school will kill me if anything happens to you. Your coach will probably string me up on the flagpole."

"Nothing like that's going to happen," he assured her, cringing as the sterile fluorescent lights illuminated the torn, uneven skin on his knuckles. He'd have to make up some excuse about the punching bag ripping, then he'd have to rip the real thing convincingly. "I'm perfectly fine. I just wanted to say good night."

"Um…Nick?"

"Yeah?"

"Promise me you'll let me take care of you. You're so far from home and you're always doing something the rest of us can only dream about."

He didn't answer. He stared at the phone, as if she was speaking in a foreign language he didn't understand.

"Hello?"

"I'm here."

I'll always be here.

He desperately wanted to tell her how he really felt.

He was scared and lonely, hungry for her touch just as

much as his body craved sustenance. He was hurting inside and out, his limbs reeling from the exertions of his grueling training routine on and off the field, from the fight he could have easily ended with well-placed gunshots.

Most of all, he really wanted to be with her.

If only for a short while.

"You promise, right?"

"Right."

She paused. He thought perhaps she wasn't satisfied with his answer. She was, after all, a very intelligent person. It would only be a matter of time before she saw right through his lies.

He was relieved when she finally said something. "You sure you're okay?"

"Yeah. I'm fine, Jeri. Good night. I'll see you tomorrow."

"Good night, Nick. See you tomorrow."

She was gone, the line cutting to static, then to the cold dial tone of the mobile network.

He could only stare as the screen blacked out and locked, just like him.

His existence was blacked out and locked from the rest of the world

He lay on his tiny bed, clutching the phone to his chest, allowing an exhausted sleep to slowly claim him.

But it didn't take too long before he woke up, shaky and disoriented, because there really was no escape from the shadows, where he belonged.

Five

THE DANCE

It was a fateful Friday when everything changed. Anticipation hung heavy in the air as the balmy October day slowly gave way to a cool afternoon. He adjusted his red jersey one more time, unable to deny the real weight the Number 4 held for him.

Today was the day. Their first football game of the intercollegiate sports season and Jeri's fateful election for the University Student Council. He took a deep breath and glanced at the clock. It was time to meet his team for the pre-game prep and warm-up. They were last year's regional champions; the expectations this year were quite high.

As he left his room, a cacophony of voices and laughter filled his ears, but his eyes were drawn to one particular sight. There she was, waiting for him just outside the building.

"Hey, how are the elections going?" He closed the distance between them, still unable to understand how she could still think of him with everything else she was doing.

"I...I don't know yet," she stammered, clutching a Tupperware container tightly in her hands. "But I wanted to give you this. I'm sorry I didn't see you this morning. My party-mates and I had to be at the polls extra early to say hello and thank the voters." She hesitated before finally revealing the container's contents: spaghetti.

"Thank you." He took the Tupperware from her hands, noticing how they trembled. It just wasn't her hands. She was pale and her entire body was shaking.

Gently, he took her things and guided her to a nearby bench. "Sit down. You look like you need a minute."

As soon as they were seated, her eyes met his, and she began to cry. The sight of her tears tugged at something inside him, an ache that seemed to mirror her own pain. He wanted to reach out and comfort her, but the words caught in his throat, uncertain what to do with someone in tears. He could kill the cause of her pain, but that wouldn't really help in the long run.

"Do you...do you want to talk about it? Did someone hurt you, or say anything bad?"

Much to his relief, she shook her head. At least that was one less thing he had to worry about.

As her tears flowed, he hesitated for a moment before pulling her into an embrace. Without their usual barriers of bags and books, the sensation of holding her was new yet somewhat familiar; it was as if his arms were designed to cradle her smaller form. Despite her obvious distress, it felt good to hold her.

"Oh, god," she muttered. "You've got a game and here I am ruining you day."

"Don't worry," he said softly, trying to sound as reassuring as possible. "Just tell me what's wrong."

She sniffled, wiping away the tears that stained her cheeks. Her eyes darted around for a moment before they settled on his face.

"I'm scared, Nick. I'm scared shitless of losing, of failing, of being told I'm not good enough. I feel like I have no value if I don't do something meaningful with my life."

The raw honesty of her words cut through him, and he realized just how much pressure she had been under during this entire campaign. He thought back to all the times he had struggled with his own feelings of inadequacy, with the pressure that he had to be stronger, faster, better than everyone else.

"You mean a lot to so many people, Jeri. You don't have to prove your worth to anyone."

She shook her head, her eyes filling with fresh tears. "I feel like I only have value when people need something from me. That's why I tutor and help others. I want to show everyone that I'm not just...disposable."

Somehow, he felt offended on her behalf. "You're not disposable at all. How could you be, when you mean everything to me?"

Her eyes widened in surprise as his words sunk in, and for a moment, she seemed at a loss for a response. When she finally spoke, her voice trembled with uncertainty.

"Y-you mean you—"

"Yes," he interrupted, pulling her close again, this time without hesitation and awkwardness. "I mean it."

Her arms went around him as her tears soaked into the fabric of his jersey. "You're the only one who really understands, you know. It seems you always know why I need to do what I'm doing. You never question or doubt me. Lexie does, she thinks I'm trying too hard. She worries about me, but I think she's scared of how far and how hard I push myself sometimes. She thinks I might end up hurting myself"

"No," he said firmly. "While I'm here, I won't let that happen."

He knew her best friend tried to understand her, but even Lexie couldn't see past Jeri's relentless drive to succeed. He understood Jeri's need to prove herself, better than anyone else. He'd known it from the start, deep down, the first time he'd seen her speak at the podium during freshman orientation.

"I'll always try to help without asking for anything in return or judging you. Just tell me what to do. I'm yours to command."

Her eyes shimmered with unshed tears as she drew back to look at him. "Why are you so wonderful?"

"It's because of you, Jeri. I don't know what I'm doing half the time, but being with you just feels right. Everything falls into place, as if we're meant to be."

"Meant to be?" she echoed, her eyes searching his. "You mean...together?"

"I don't know," he admitted, shrugging slightly, "but it sure feels that way."

With that, she dove back into his arms. He held on to her quietly for several minutes, memorizing her breathing pattern, the heat of her body against his, and the warm, fruity scent of her skin and hair.

Leaning down, he dared to press a kiss to her forehead. "Let's have dinner together tonight. We can talk more then. I've got my stipend, so we can afford a full spread at one of the eateries across the road."

She giggled through the remainder of her tears, her hands warm as she squeezed his cheeks gratefully. "If I win, it will be my treat, but there's the annual mixer party tonight, remember? If you're coming, we'll see each other there. But make sure you eat first, okay?"

"Sounds perfect," he agreed, taking the container of spaghetti she had prepared for him. "Will you be at my game?"

"Front row," she promised, hugging him quickly before she jumped back to her feet. "Cheering the loudest for you."

He watched her walk away and gave her a wave before she disappeared around the corner of the main building. He crossed the quad and made his way to the classroom next to the field where his team had gathered to prepare for the big game.

The buzz of excitement and tension filled the room. His teammates immediately noticed the Tupperware Jeri had prepared for him, now a familiar sight; their teasing was good-natured and light-hearted.

"Hey Aragon, we're jealous," remarked a senior. "You've got a sweet girlfriend who's probably going to win the election, too. How does it feel to be The Man?"

A freshman chimed in, too, shyly, his eyes wide with admiration. "You've got everything, don't you, Aragon? We can only wish to have half of what you've got."

Before he could respond, their coach walked in, tablet in hand, and began outlining plays and strategies for the game against the maritime college down the road. They were rumored to have strong players this season, but some of those players carried an arrogance from being high school superstars.

After the meeting, they moved to the field to warm up with stretches and team drills. Before he put his phone away next to the makeshift bench at the end of the field, he gave Jeri a quick call to check if the results of the elections had been announced.

Her voice was still shaky from the earlier tension but much calmer. "No, not yet. One of my poll watchers told me I was leading the count about fifteen minutes ago. I'm sure the counting will be over by the time your game finishes."

"Can't wait." He could feel his chest expand, as if there was a balloon of emotion inside him. "Good luck."

"Thanks. Good luck to you, too." She hesitated, then added, "I'll be on the bleachers watching you play. I just wanted to say..." Her voice trailed off, and he heard her take a deep breath. "Never mind. I'll see you later."

"See you." He wanted to know what it was she was trying to say, but now wasn't the time. He put his phone away and joined his teammates on the field, his eyes scanning the bleachers for her face as the number of spectators grew.

The game started shortly, the roar of the crowd filling the campus as he took his position on the field.

He surveyed the opposing team. To their credit, it was a formidable, meticulously assembled line-up, far better than last year's. They had taller, bulkier players; it was an obvious attempt to stuff the roster with people who were physically strong and had a longer reach, similar to him.

As the first half of the game unfolded, he found himself relentlessly pursued by the opposing team's defenders. He could sense their frustration growing with every missed opportunity to stop him. They could fill their ranks however they chose, but they would always have to contend with his real training.

With a few minutes left in the first half, he saw his chance. The ball landed at his feet in a deftly executed pass from his team's vice-captain.

He wove through the opposition like a shadow slipping through cracks of light, the ball seemingly under his complete thrall. Time seemed to slow as he closed in on the goal, his focus narrowing until all he could see was the steel contraption and the grimy white net it held. He planted one foot, drew back the other, and unleashed a strike that sent the ball hurtling into the net.

Goal.

The crowd erupted into deafening cheers that shook the ground. As he jogged past the bleachers, his eyes locked onto Jeri's face amid the sea of spectators. In that moment, it was as if they were the only two people in the world. He waved to her and she waved back, her face splitting into a bright smile.

The second half of the game proved even more intense than the first. The opposing team held nothing back, their defenders swarming around him with more deliberate attempts to keep him away from the goal. They tried to injure him, several times, but he deftly evaded their attacks, as simple as countering deadlier assaults with firearms and blades.

He could feel Jeri's eyes on him, as sure as he could remember her asking if he thought they were meant to be together. As he took position for what could be the decisive goal, he thought of his real answer, and with a surge of determination, he launched the ball towards the right of the net, just a few inches out of the goalie's reach.

No one could stop him.

It was a goal.

The bleachers exploded in wild celebration. He was surrounded by his teammates, coaches, teachers, and classmates, all of them caught up in the euphoria of victory.

The roar in the field had barely subsided when another round of cheers broke out, this time originating from somewhere near the school auditorium.

"Castelo won!" someone shouted, their voice carrying above the din. "She got the most votes out of all the candidates!"

It seemed that today was a day of victories for both of them. Excusing himself from the merriment, he stepped away from the throng of people and retrieved his phone from the bench to call her. To his disappointment, she didn't pick up. Perhaps she was already caught up in her own celebrations.

In the aftermath of the game, the team gathered for an enthusiastic debrief, discussing their plans for winning the regionals once more and defending their title. After the meeting concluded, he retreated to his room, his phone still clutched tightly in his hand. He hesitated, wondering if he should call her again. He didn't want to impose on her well-deserved victory.

Before he could decide what to do next, his phone rang, displaying the name and number of the team's vice-captain, Arthur Posada.

"Hey, Posada."

"Hey, just calling to remind you to come to the college's mixer party tonight, Aragon. It's important we show our solidarity, and the administration will be there. You know how they like to see scholars putting in an appearance. Besides, they all want to see you."

He'd already decided to attend the party, but a reminder of his obligations to keep up appearances was the reality check he needed. He thanked the vice-captain and got ready for the night, dressing in his cleanest, newest blue polo shirt and jeans.

The college mixer was already in full swing at the auditorium by the time he arrived, feeling slightly out of place amid groups of chattering students and loud, thumping music. He wasn't one for social events and tried to avoid them as much as he could.

As he joined his teammates, he was met by an approving nod from his coach and the warm smile of the college dean.

"Congratulations, Aragon," the dean said, shaking his hand firmly. "You've earned that scholarship. Everyone here is proud of your achievements for the university."

"Thank you, sir. It's my honor."

"How is your family taking this? With you so far away but doing such great things for our school?" The look on the dean's face was equal parts sympathy and understanding.

"They are very proud, sir. My brothers can't wait to see me again so we can train together."

"That sounds like good fun," said the dean, clapping him on the back. "Enjoy tonight's party, Aragon. My old bones can only stay until ten, but you kids have fun the rest of the night. Make sure to keep it clean. We don't want the police digging around in the morning."

The dean excused himself and made his way to a group of teachers across the room.

He glanced over at his teammates, who were already enjoying food and soft drinks from the catering tables. He watched as a group of girls and other admirers descended upon them, asking the players to dance or engage in conversation.

Never comfortable with such attention, he quietly backed away from the crowd and, as always, inched into the shadows.

He surveyed the sea of people before him, as the flashing lights installed around the auditorium dipped and swung about in time with the music.

Where was she?

He was so caught up in his thoughts he never noticed the person who walked up to him and tapped his shoulder lightly. He turned around to see Jeri standing before him, her eyes bright, her cheeks flushed even in the dim light.

"Hey, Aragon," she said playfully, yet her voice wavered ever so slightly. "If you don't dance with me, I will kill you."

His breath caught in his throat at her words, surprised by the uncharacteristic boldness in them and the sudden rush of desire he felt towards her.

She had on a dress with green and white stripes that brought out the smoothness and pinkish tinge of her skin. With her hair arranged in loose waves around her face, she looked breathtakingly luminous, almost untouchable in her beauty.

"Alright, Castelo," he finally replied, trying to sound casual. "No need to threaten me with violence. I'll dance with you."

He hadn't really danced before, but he didn't care.

She didn't say anything when he took her hand. As they

moved onto the dance floor in the middle of the auditorium, a slow ballad began to play. He put his hands on her waist; in response, she rested her hands lightly on his shoulders.

"Congratulations," he said as they began swaying to the music. "Heard your victory was a landslide."

She smiled up at him, the pride in her eyes unmistakable. "Thanks. Couldn't have done it without you."

His arms tightened around her, drawing her closer. He wondered if she noticed.

"Congratulations, too," she continued. "You had such a great game. No one could stop you out there. It was amazing to watch. I'm sure you'll go all the way to the championships again."

"Thanks," he replied, pulling her even closer until she was almost completely pressed against him. He wondered if she could feel the raging reaction of his body from being so close to hers. "Is this okay?"

She let out a nervous laugh but bobbed her head gently. "Is it just me or do I feel like we've done this before?"

"Maybe in another life," he answered, his lips brushing her hair.

She sighed and closed the last few inches that separated them, her arms coiling around his neck, as high and as tightly as her height would allow.

"What about this life?" she muttered against his chest. The warmth of her breath through the thin fabric of his shirt felt undeniably intimate.

"You tell me, Jeri."

"I don't know. Her cheek settled comfortably on the spot where his heart was. "But I don't want this to end."

She had no idea how much he'd wanted to say the exact same thing to her.

I wish my time with you would never end.

But the song was over, leaving him breathless and unsure of what to do next.

She stepped back, avoiding eye contact. He averted his eyes, too. Acknowledging the intensity of the moment might make it too real—once he crossed that line, there would be no turning back.

"Nick, can we talk about what just happened?" Her hand found his in the darkness. Her touch was cold and slightly damp. He knew his reaction was almost the same.

"Of course." It was all he could say.

She led him to a secluded corner at the backstage area of the auditorium, past layers upon layers of dusty dark red stage curtains, their way illuminated by a few old lightbulbs. Away from the crowd, they found themselves alone in what looked like a broken-down dressing room. There were two chairs in front of the cracked mirror. As if in silent agreement, they both stayed on their feet. She still clung to his hand, a little too tightly.

"I feel like I've taken advantage of our friendship and your kindness," she began hesitantly. "You've always been so nice to me and I feel like I've insulted you. I'm really sorry. I think I got carried away. Today has been particularly overwhelming."

Her voice was barely audible over the distant hum of the ongoing party, but he could see the uncertainty and fear in her eyes in the semi-darkness.

What was she so afraid of?

He reached for her other hand, this time intertwining

his fingers with hers. He brought her hands up to his chin, as if keeping them next to his skin would warm her up.

"You don't have to apologize. We danced. That was all, wasn't it?"

She shook her head. "Was it only a dance to you? I don't even know how to act around you anymore. I don't know what I feel for you. I don't even know what we have between us. It fucks with my head so badly."

Before she could say anything more, he leaned in and captured her lips in a kiss.

It was his first kiss.

And he let go.

It was passionate and intense. Again and again, their lips met, each kiss increasing in urgency with which he craved her touch, her taste.

"Is this the real you?" she whispered when they finally pulled apart, her breath ragged and her eyes wide with wonder.

"Yes," he responded without hesitation. "It is, only with you."

He didn't say anything more as his hands moved to the straps of her dress, his fingertips brushing the softness of her skin as he slowly lowered the fabric to reveal more of her. He marveled at the curves and delicate lines of her body, everything that made her so perfect in his eyes.

"Nick, I..." she began to protest, stopping his hands in their path. "You know I'm not..." Her voice trailed off as she glanced down at herself.

"You're the most beautiful girl in the world to me, Jeri."

Tenderly, he explored her with his mouth. He started with her neck and chest, his tongue tracing circles around the taut nipples once her ample, perfectly round breasts found their way out of her bra. He settled her on the old dresser and kissed her lips before his fingers continued their journey downward.

"Trust me, you are perfect just as you are," he assured her, as he parted her legs, his hands tracing the curve of her hips before sliding her panties off.

He lifted the skirt of her dress and kissed his way from her knees upward, his tongue leaving a damp path along the way. His lips traced the curves of her inner thighs, inches away from the very heart of her that radiated white-hot heat. The scent of her engulfed him like an irresistibly intoxicating cloud; it was so uniquely her it was all he could do not to bury himself inside her.

He took a deep breath and pressed his lips to her core, his tongue joyously lapping up the taste of her as she moaned and writhed on the dresser, her partially exposed breasts bouncing, her legs parting wider to make way for more of the sensations he was giving her.

"Nick," she panted, her hips grinding against his mouth. Her hands dug into his shoulders and pulled at his hair in turn as her movements increased in urgency. Jeri losing control against a broken dressing room mirror was the most incredibly erotic sight he had ever laid eyes on.

It took one more suckle at her nub and one more deep stroke of his fingers before she let out a loud moan, finally getting to the peak he so desperately wanted her to reach.

Her body stiffened, then abruptly went limp in the aftermath of her climax. He caught her in his arms as she wavered from her seated position. He held her close, listening to her rapid heartbeat, their breaths mingling together as the lingering scent of her engulfed his senses.

He savored the sensation of her legs wrapped loosely around his hips, her arms draped over his shoulders, her damp hair plastered all over her face and his. This was the most intimate he had ever been with anyone.

He was the first to speak, his lips against her ear as he inhaled her now-familiar cologne, mingled with her sweat, from the throbbing pulse on her neck. "I've never been with someone before. I've never even kissed anyone. You're the first."

"Me, too," she breathed. "You're my first kiss…the first boy who's ever touched me. You're my first everything."

She pulled him close, kissing his cheek and burying her nose in his hair. It was a strange, yet deeply moving, gesture.

"I've never had a boyfriend before," she continued. "I've always been so focused on my studies, on helping others, on being a student leader. I never had time for…love. Definitely not this kind."

"Until now?" He felt something akin to hope stir in his chest.

"Until now," she confirmed, almost shyly.

Their lips met again, tenderly at first, then more urgently, hungrily. His hands found her exposed breasts once more, but before he could reach for the damp spot between her legs again, her hands slid into his shirt.

She hesitated briefly before going lower, her fingers finally daring to reach inside his jeans. "Is this okay?"

"Y-yes," he stuttered as his body coiled in anticipation.

She reached into his underwear and took him in her hand. He gasped and cursed under his breath, gritting his teeth.

Encouraged, she continued, rubbing and stroking him. He didn't know he could get any harder, but he did. He was almost at breaking point.

She slid off the dresser, straightening her clothes as she went, and pushed him against the wall. He was achingly aware she still wasn't wearing her panties; they were somewhere in a damp ball on one of the nearby chairs.

She went down on her knees and undid his zipper, pushing his underwear down just enough to free his rock-hard arousal. He groaned when she bent her head and took him into her mouth, her lips moving up and down his length in a maddening rhythm.

He felt an electric current shoot through him, and his entire body tensed as he climaxed right in her mouth. The waves of pleasure that coursed through his body were so strong they threatened to tear him apart. Her name escaped his lips in a raw, guttural moan, rumbling in his chest and through the dusty air of the backstage area.

She stood up and put her arms around his waist, as if to hold him upright.

"You're amazing," he whispered into her hair.

"So are you," she replied.

They kissed once more, tongues tangling, tasting each other with a newfound sense of closeness. He hardened again, almost immediately; this time, there was no hiding it from her.

"Jeri, what are we supposed to do now?"

"I don't know," she admitted, her fingers gripping his rumpled shirt tightly. "But I don't want us to end, whatever this is we've got."

I don't want us to end, he echoed inwardly.

They were an *'us'* now.

It was all he'd ever wanted.

Everything he'd ever needed, since the first time he saw her.

"Whatever you want to do, I'm here for you. I'll follow you anywhere."

"Would you?"

He nodded.

He felt, more than he saw, her smile.

He smiled back as his hand found hers in the shadows.

From then on, he never let go.

ACT II

FALLEN

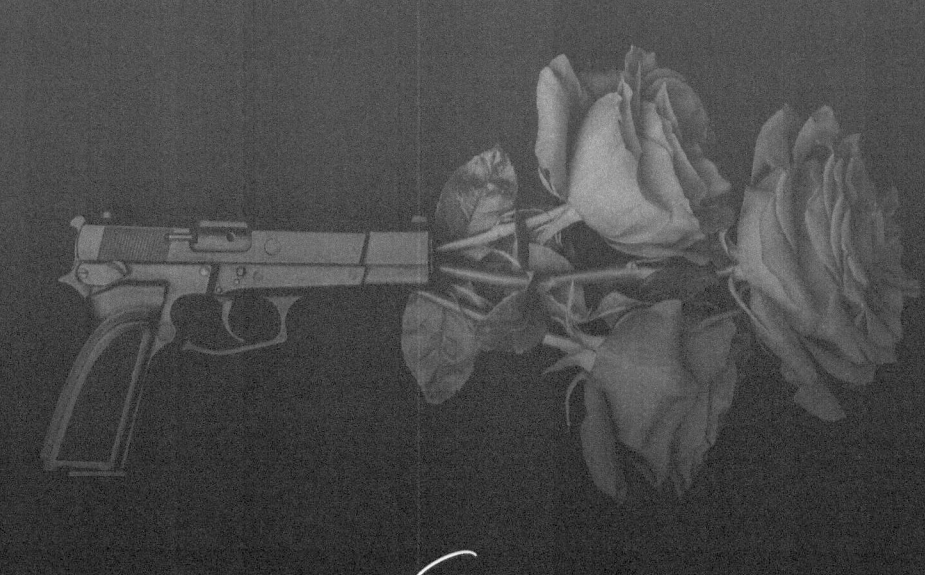

Six

THE DESIRE

H E HAD HER IN HIS ARMS, FOR NOW.

As he held her, he still marveled at how they both appeared to be so different from each other.

She was the epitome of intelligence and charisma. Everyone liked her—from the teachers, to the cafeteria staff, most if not all of the student body. She always had that ready smile and the time to listen to everyone's problems.

People believed that sleeping wasn't on her busy schedule, the same way she believed he didn't sleep at all.

Everyone knew that Jeri Castelo would rather stay up talking to someone in her trademark high-octane and witty manner, organizing events as a member of the University Student Council for the second year in a row, or tutoring other students in Calculus.

He was popular in another fashion: the star football player who never gave away much about himself.

The name Aragon struck fear in the football teams of colleges all over the region. Ever since his freshman year, he had brought the university an unprecedented steady stream of championships.

He was not, however, raised to become an athletic achiever. His training had aimed to accomplish more serious ends.

Deadly serious ends.

In his first year, their class had gone on a trip up the mountains as part of their Biology subject. While everyone had lugged bags of canned goods and other packaged foods, he had only brought clothes and minimal camping equipment.

Evening at their campsite, the teacher had asked, "Where's the dinner you're supposed to bring for yourself?"

"It's right behind you, sir." He had thrown his hunting knife, the blade whizzing a mere inch above his professor's head.

A wild chicken, an *ilahas*, had squawked and crashed to the ground in rapid succession.

He then had an entire roasted chicken for his dinner, served hot. No one shared his meal, or spoke to him for the rest of the trip. The teacher gave him a grade of 1.0.

After that, everyone dealt with him very cautiously. No one dared to test his temper, even though he had never once displayed it, on or off the field.

He'd liked things that way, or so he thought. The further he distanced himself, the better.

Only Jeri had dared break through the wall between him and the rest of the world.

Ever since that fateful night more than a year ago, he knew he had fallen in love with her, more and more deeply with each passing day.

She had not been of any help, either. She had wanted and loved him, too.

At the end of the evening they first danced and kissed, they had made love, nervously and tenderly, on his tiny bed in the main building's basement.

He had never imagined he would feel that way, when his body, lean and hardened by years of training, was intertwined with hers, soft and welcoming.

He remembered the first time he'd touched her hair, the first time he'd allowed himself to look into her eyes without any qualms, the first time he'd kissed her as much as he wanted to.

He remembered the first time she'd allowed him to take off her clothes and taste all of her.

It was only later, in the aftermath of their passionate encounter, did he figure out that she'd reminded him of apples.

Since then, he had been unable to distance himself or stop thinking about her, no matter how hard he'd tried to deny how he really felt.

Ever since their freshman year, the distance between him and the perfection that was Jeri Castelo had seemed impossible to bridge.

She shone as brightly and as purely as the sun, on a day without clouds.

He was only a shadow, a dreary mass of dark secrets.

But, for now, he felt whole, from her touch and her light.

Now was all he ever had with her, he thought, as his reverie of their time together melted away, bringing him back into the present, with her in his bed, wrapped in his arms.

Jeri peeled off his shirt, her fingers brushing over the eagle tattoo etched over his heart. He felt her hands run over his shoulders and his stomach. With a moan, she moved closer, climbing onto his lap and wrapping her legs around his waist as they continued to kiss each other.

He reached up and began to unbutton her blouse, slowly revealing her delicate skin. His eyes drank in the sight of her, his heart racing with the familiar combination of desire and fear, as if he was seeing her for the first time all over again. He unclasped her bra and gently traced his fingers along her curves before lowering his mouth to her nipples, licking and biting them softly, making her gasp.

He continued to explore her body, his fingers deftly unzipping her skirt and slipping it off along with her panties until she was completely naked before him. Her pinkish skin was flushed under the lights.

He focused on her inner thighs, coaxing her to open for him, his body humming with excitement as she gave in so willingly and sweetly to his unspoken request. As his mouth descended upon her, she cried his name out, her hands pulling at his hair.

"Please don't stop, Nick." Her voice was barely audible above the pounding of his own heart, as his arousal tried to fight its way out of the confines of his clothes.

But he was going to take his time. Patience was something he was very good at.

He began tentatively, by tasting her, his tongue tracing intricate patterns across her sensitive flesh. His fingers soon joined the fray as he brought her to the peak, a hoarse scream coming from her throat.

He held her close as she slowly came down from the heights of her pleasure. He kissed her hair and her cheeks as she trembled in his arms, panting as if she had run around the campus herself.

He didn't have to wait very long for her to catch her breath.

She reached for the waistband of his joggers, slowly lowering them to reveal his hardness.

His gaze never left hers as he gently positioned himself between her legs. He took a moment to make sure she was wet, using his length to tease her entrance. The sensation of her slick folds against him always drove him to the very edge, no matter how many times he had her.

"Fuck, you feel so good."

She cupped his cheeks and kissed him soundly on the lips. "So do you."

With those words, she put her arms around his shoulders and her legs around his hips.

He allowed himself to sink deep into her. He wrapped his arms around her tightly as he began to thrust into her, slowly, languidly.

They began to move together in a sensual rhythm. He could feel the tension building within him, the heat and pressure coiling tighter and tighter as he lost himself in her embrace.

"I can't hold back," he gasped out as he teetered on the brink.

"Let go," she urged him softly. "I'm here with you. I love you."

With the warmth and tenderness of her reassurance enveloping him, he lost control, surrendering to the tidal wave of pleasure that crashed over him.

"I love you, too," he heard himself say. "Now come for me."

As he thrust into her in the final throes of his own climax, he heard her cry out his name as she, too, gave her surrender.

For now, she was with him, as close as two people could possibly be.

For now, her light was his, too.

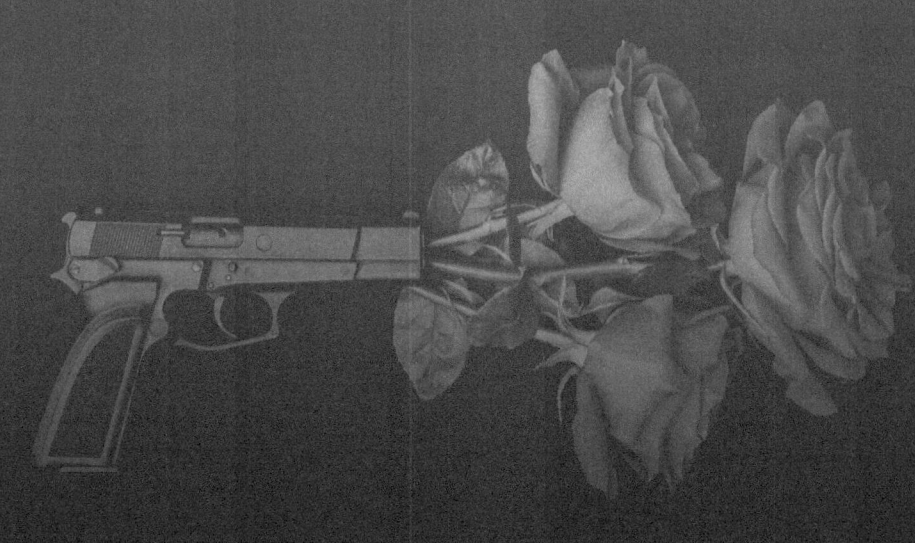

Seven

THE DREAM

WAS THIS A DREAM? His heart pounded as he gazed at the woman in his arms, their bodies tangled together on his narrow bed. His fingertips traced lazy patterns on her skin, marveling at the warmth of her that seemed to surround him completely.

When he finally found his voice, her name sounded like a desperate plea.

"Jeri."

She looked into his eyes, her own gaze reflecting his desire, before she cupped his cheek and leaned in to kiss him deeply. Their tongues danced together, exploring each other's mouths.

"Yes," she murmured between kisses. "Always yes."

With renewed vigor, he rolled them over, positioning himself above her once more. This time, she spread her legs wide, raising her hips to meet his mid-air. He slid his hands under her buttocks to lift her slightly, and then filled her in one quick surge.

He reveled in the sensation of her body fitting so perfectly against his, in the way she responded to his touch—and he to hers. He came with a thunderous roar, as she shook under him, her hair spreading all over his pillow as her breasts bounced enticingly with each of thrust.

It wasn't too long before he took her again, this time from behind, his hands gripping her hips tightly before moving to cup her breasts and caress her nipples.

After they recovered, he held her in his lap, their faces close as if sharing the same breath, as they exchanged tender kisses while they made love once more.

He didn't care if this was all only a dream.

It was a heady blend of tender emotion and fiery passion. He knew he would never tire of the feel of her body against his, the way her moans and sighs echoed in his ears, the softness of her arms around him.

He was completely and utterly lost in her.

Momentarily sated, they lay quietly in each other's arms.

"You should eat more," she declared out of the blue. "I need to bring you more food."

"Really?"

"Yes. I don't know where you get all that energy to move so fast, or kick that hard. Or to run so much every day." Her breath tickled the bare skin of his chest. "Or to do *this*."

"I don't know. Habit, maybe."

They both lapsed into silence.

She reached for his hands. He felt her delicate skin brush against his scarred and callused palms.

"It must be time for practice soon," she finally said.

He found his phone in the pocket of his discarded joggers. The display told him they still had a little more than an hour left before he had to go to the field.

He turned to look at her, naked in his bed, his blanket wrapped around her for modesty. "Would you like some breakfast?"

She nodded. "I'm starving."

He put his phone away and joined her, reaching for her underneath the blanket.

"Me, too."

As he took her back into his arms and kissed her again, he hoped he could stay in the dream long enough.

Eight

THE DECEPTION

THE SKY WAS STILL A DEEP, MURKY GREY WHEN THEY walked out of the main building. Morning, classes, and the rest of the world would be upon them soon.

She paused when they reached the middle of the quad, her eyes settling on the grassy field in front of them.

"The first time I saw you, you were practicing alone," she said softly. "It was the first day of freshman year. It was Orientation Week and I came in early. I wanted to introduce myself to people as they arrived. I saw you on the field when I walked up to this spot, right here."

He swallowed hard as he absorbed the weight of her words, the depth of the memory she now shared. All he could do was take her hand and listen.

"It was like watching something both magnificent and

deadly at the same time. It was raining, but you never even missed a shot. The way you moved, the way you stood there, on your own, defying the downpour...you didn't seem to care. You were just so focused and determined. But I never approached you because I thought...well, I thought you'd only be interested in tall, pretty girls, like the ones football players and jocks usually go for."

He felt a chuckle rumble through his chest.

Very few people had seen him smile. But she was the only one who heard him laugh.

She elbowed him in the ribs "What the hell's so funny?"

"You." He pulled her close as they looked at the field still blanketed by darkness. "Why do you always have to be so fucking *perfect*? You remember, know, and do almost everything."

Her breathing seemed to stop. It took moments before she could answer. "I was raised to be like that. No one could make up for my mistakes, if I was stupid enough to make them. When I moved in with my grandparents after my parents died, I learned this very quickly."

She paused, as if gathering momentum. "When I was little, my grandmother would slap my hands with a stick whenever I couldn't spell a word correctly. Or, sometimes, they wouldn't let me have dinner unless I could recite an entire speech without any mistakes. I got good at all of it. Then better. By the time I was eight, there was no more need for such discipline. I delivered everything they wanted."

"When I got older, my grandparents told me my mother failed them by eloping with my father. She had me when she was eighteen. And I...I couldn't fail my family."

The words had a pained, bitter edge. He could taste them

in his own heart. If there was someone who understood, only too well, how it was like to rise to the nearly impossible expectations and demands of their family, it was him.

"It gets exhausting. I'm doing a great job at it, though. There are so many people expecting so many things. I had to do all those things. I feel guilty when I couldn't. Sometimes it's like digging your own grave. But you need to do it anyway." Her voice sounded rough and strained. "Being perfect was the only way to survive, to keep having value."

The first few raindrops fell. He felt them on his arm. Then he realized they weren't from the sky. The droplets were her tears.

Something bubbled inside him. It wasn't rage, but a calmer desire to kill. It was part of him, his lifeblood.

Although he had vowed to himself never to take a human life again, he would break that for her, to spare her from any further pain.

But there was no one entirely responsible for the sort of torment she felt. Just like no one had to pay for his past and the choices he'd made, except perhaps he himself.

"I'm sorry..." His voice trailed off. He felt lame and helpless, as the familiar cold numbness ran the length of his spine. It was a feeling only pulling the trigger could relieve. "I shouldn't have said—"

"It's not your fault. Sometimes I just couldn't help but think about this, no matter how hard I try not to." She bravely swallowed back her sobs as he wiped her tears away. "I had it coming. I had it coming all these years. It was only a matter of time before I got burned out."

He waited for her to calm down. She could so easily collect herself, or at least appear to have done so. He was the only one who would always know and feel the trembling of her hands, the uneven beating of her pulse, even if she appeared perfectly composed.

She had looked like this during debates when she ran for the University Student Council a second time, when after she'd felt like ice to his touch. Everyone else had praised her composure and quick thinking, never considering the amount of control it took on her part.

With all the light she radiated, she still had the cold, dark parts, too.

Nine

THE DEAL

"I was raised to be the best, too," he admitted, slowly, cautiously. "I became the best."

Jeri's tearstained face had a look that showed the struggle to comprehend his words. She said nothing, but spoke volumes with wide eyes.

He knew at that point he had to explain, to make her understand.

There was no turning back now, not after everything they had shared.

"When I was in high school, I was known as Cain in the underground. My father chose that name for me. I was born with a twin brother, but my cord was around his neck when we were cut out…I choked him to death in our mother's womb."

"I didn't know..." She was grasping at words. "You never—"

He squeezed her hands in his, shaking his head slightly. It was his way of telling her it was okay. He would be okay, if he had her with him.

"I'm the youngest of five brothers, but I could outshoot all of them. I could take them all down hand to hand, too, by the time I was seven. I was faster and stronger. I was even better in most sports. A lot of schools offered everything from bribes to scholarship packages to my parents so I would go to their place, just so they could get all the football titles, even a National Games medal."

"My father told us that the mantle of the Eagle-Eye had to be passed down. He was almost sixty and it was about time for him to mentor the next one. All my uncles—everyone in my family—wanted me to take it. I was fourteen. The Eagle-Eye tattoo meant the world."

"That explains the eagle mark on your chest." Jeri placed her hand over his heart. "It's more than just a tattoo."

"Our family has been in the Philippines for more than three hundred years. You can say we wrote a lot of history in blood and no one ever knew. We are loyal to no one, except our own kin and land. That's how we had roots. The Eagle-Eye is the best of the present generation. He was entrusted to carry out the most dangerous missions."

He said everything without any pride. Then again, there was nothing to be proud of.

A series of frozen frames flashed in his memory. He drew in a sharp breath at how vividly he could remember the events of seven years past.

"My initiation rite was to kill a priest who had sexually

abused the son of one of our workers at the corn farm. The boy was eight, a *sacristan*. It was three-thirty in the morning…the priest was walking to Church to prepare for the *misa de gallo*. I got him with one shot, right between the eyes. It was Christmas—and my fifteenth birthday—when I became the ninth-generation Eagle-Eye. That's when I got the tattoo. Then my father said, 'You will be Cain now.'"

"There are twenty-nine others on my list; two of them were very young, maybe seven or eight years old. They were the children of a drug lord who thought he could smuggle *shabu* through one of the canning companies in our town. They saw me shoot their father. *Leave no witnesses.* That was in the rules."

"You killed people." Her voice was toneless. Not angry, afraid or accusing, just clear and audible.

"I left Surallah thinking I could somehow lose that part of me. I bargained for four years to finish college so there's time to think about it. No matter how hard you try, that side of you stays right where it is. If you try to get rid of it somehow, it will eat you up alive. You could shed your skin, but not your blood. You wouldn't have the strength to survive."

He realized she had not backed away, or showed any sign of fear or disgust.

Before he could say anything more, she looked straight into his eyes, unblinking. He could see the clarity in her gaze, behind the sheen of tears, in the soft light of the oncoming sunrise.

"I love you, Nick. Nothing's going to change that."

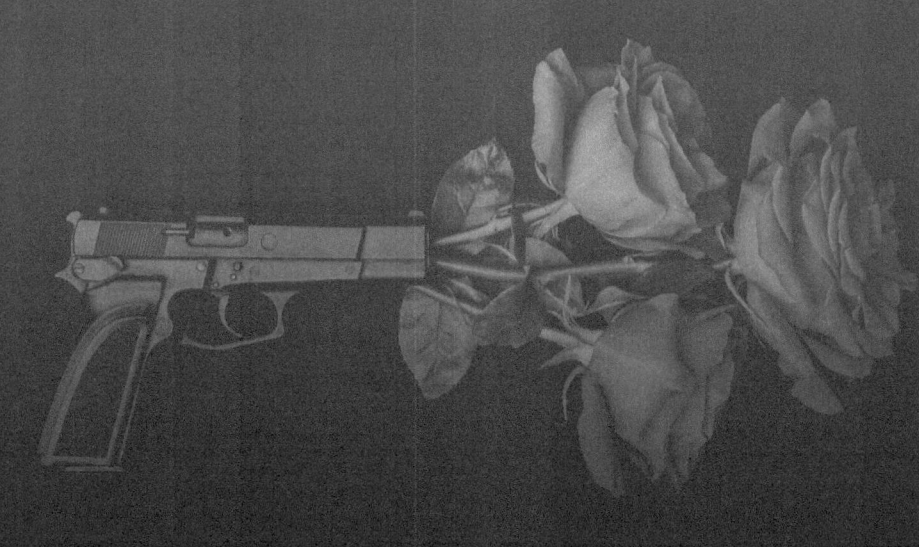

Ten

THE DAWN

N*ICK*.

He was only ever Aragon to everyone else. To Jeri, he'd always been her Nick.

The absence of revulsion from her took him aback. "I know I should have told you before. I couldn't, Jeri. I didn't want to lose you. I'm so sorry—"

"There's nothing to be sorry for." Her tone was firm, although she spoke in a voice so quiet it was almost carried away by the early morning breeze. "I loved you for what you are. I found in you a part of myself I thought I'd never find in anyone else."

He swallowed hard, ice and dread gripping his insides. "You're not angry, are you?"

She shook her head. "Why should I be? Because you told me the truth?"

"But I'm a...*killer*. You should be walking away right now."

Jeri did the exact opposite.

She put her arms around him. "I'm staying right here. I'm not going anywhere. Don't you know how good it feels to finally hear you talk about where you came from?"

"Jeri, I..." His voice trailed off. He had no words for her. He only had himself and everything else. He'd lay them all at her feet in a heartbeat.

She took his hand and placed it gently on her belly. "I love you for being the father of this child."

It took him a second to understand what she meant by both her actions and words. When he finally did, he felt all the air leave his lungs.

He could only stare at her as a sudden glow began to form in the pit of his stomach. It was the familiar warmth he had known only when he met her.

When he finally mustered some semblance of self-control, he said, "Are you...?"

He couldn't finish the question. The idea was too unreal, too beautiful, to speak of. Part of him feared it would disappear right before his eyes, along with her.

Instead, she smiled brightly. "Maybe six weeks now. A doctor who doesn't know my family confirmed it yesterday afternoon. That's why I had to see you. I could no longer keep this a secret." Her face, so breathtakingly beautiful to him, was a study in mixed emotions. "I had to tell you."

"I'm going to be a father," he said slowly, tasting the

word. He put his hands on her stomach, over her own. His own blood, now with hers.

Father, he repeated inwardly. A father.

She nodded.

This time, the first real drops of rain started to fall.

A droplet landed on his lips. He tasted sweetness and warmth. It bore none of the bitter taste and spilled blood of the past three hundred years.

A bolt of lightning streaked across the sky, followed by a loud rumble of thunder, just before the rain came down in earnest.

In silent agreement, neither of them suggested taking shelter in the nearby gazebos surrounding the campus quad.

Jeri stepped back and spread out her arms, giggling as she turned her face up to the downpour.

As he watched her spinning slowly under the rain, he realized that he was still half-stunned by her news.

She paused for a moment, her movements punctuated by a soft giggle. "Nick, I want to dance with you."

In that moment, his head cleared, as if someone had shone a light on the shadows of his burden. He took her hands in his and placed her palms over his heart, on the very same spot where his body bore the Eagle-Eye mark. "I love you."

She smiled and stood on tiptoe, pressing her lips to his. "For the first time in our lives, let's not be the best assassin or the perfect girl. Let's do the right thing and just be us."

He nodded. "Us," he repeated, trying the sound of the word rolling off his tongue.

He'd always liked the ring of it, remembering the first time she had used the word to describe what they had.

I don't want us to end.

The rain fell harder.

He basked in the sight of the woman who had looked him in the eye and never wavered, even after his confession and the deaths he had brought.

Instead, she embraced him and his blood.

She looked straight back at him, the same way she had the night of their first dance. The night she'd opened the door to his heart and, unwittingly, to his freedom from the shadows of the past.

Nicholas Aragon embraced her then.

Nothing more was said.

The rain crashed around them, drenching concrete, earth, steel, and their bodies.

When the sun finally rose, the thunderstorm came to an end. Only the wind was left howling, singing a dirge to the shadows as they became one with the light.

Epilogue

THE LAST LETTER

It was Lexie's habit, for the past two years now, to drop by the newspaper office every morning to check on messages and writing assignments.

When she arrived, on the dot, at half-past seven, the first thing she noticed was a folded note tacked to the corkboard. Her name was on it, in a familiar roundish script.

She took the paper off the board and unlocked the door.

The note felt slightly damp in her hands as she unfolded it. The paper seemed to have gotten wet in the heavy rain earlier that morning and was slowly drying out.

My dearest Lexie,

I've held on for years to what I thought I was.

I have become the perfect puppet to expectations that were never mine. It's time to cut the strings.

I gave them my entire life, until now. From today, it's my turn to live the rest of it on my own terms.

I will miss you.
Love always,
Jeri

She stared at the signature. Like her best friend's personality, it had an undeniable, inimitable flourish.

For a long time, Lexie stood in the middle of the empty office, her gaze seeing beyond the unlit space before her.

She went through the drafts left on the table for her to review, locked up, and headed to her first class of the day.

Along the way, she stopped by one of the trash cans on the quad and tore the letter to shreds. She watched the tiny white pieces fall from her hands like raindrops disappearing into the cold morning air.

"Be happy, Jeri," she whispered. "I'll miss you, too."

BOOK IV

The Last Divide

Playlist

Indestructible
Alisha's Attic

Konstantine
Something Corporate

What If
Kate Winslet

Someday
Nickelback

Moments Like This
Allison Krauss

Stay
Hurts

Baby Can I Hold You
Tracy Chapman

Prologue

Royce

DRAWN

WHY WAS HE NERVOUS?

School was over.

There were no more grades to reach and work hard for, no more competitive quiz bees, no more sports tournaments.

Royce Duran knew he should feel relieved.

Relief was the last word he'd use to describe what he felt at the moment. His pulse was racing; he was dizzy, and his throat felt closed and dry.

She was late.

In the late afternoon light, the football field before him

looked desolate and abandoned. The grass had grown a little too high and unruly; the ground was still muddy and partially upturned from the typhoon the week before.

He glanced at his watch, shifting slightly in his seat on the empty bleachers. She was usually punctual. Just as he began to feel agitated, he caught sight of her approaching figure.

Koreen Cisco was smaller than him by nearly a foot, barely reaching five feet tall. Her long, straight black hair swayed with each step. Even across the distance between them, her cat-like eyes bored into him like sniper rifles.

"Hey," she called out as she approached, her voice betraying a hint of the awkwardness that hung between them.

They were used to competing side by side and pushing each other to excel, but they rarely spoke privately or found themselves alone together.

"Hey, Koreen. Thanks for coming. Would you like to sit down?"

One of her dark brows shot into her hairline, an expression he associated with her uncertainty. She usually looked at him that way whenever he uttered an answer to a problem in Math class. Most, if not all, of the time, she would get the correct answer.

She settled on the same level of the bleachers, about two feet away from where he sat. She crossed her arms and regarded him with the same piercing, doubting look.

"This is weird, Duran. I thought you were screwing with me when you said you wanted to meet."

"Wouldn't dream of it," he replied with a smile, attempting to lighten the mood.

"Don't think I'm here to do you any favors. It's more

curiosity than anything else." She wrinkled her nose at him. "Be honest, then, what's this about? Something important?"

Her bluntness was one of the things he secretly appreciated about her.

"Not really," he replied with a shrug. "I just wanted to say goodbye."

"Goodbye? You're leaving?"

"Yep." He watched her reaction closely. "My family's leaving town."

"Why? Where are you going?" she muttered, her eyes downcast. "I thought you're staying in Iloilo. Get into law school and all that."

He nodded. "That was the plan. But things change. With the bank closing last year, it's been hard on my parents. My father found a new job in Manila. As for me, I was lucky enough my state university scholarship allowed me to pick any campus with an available spot."

"Wow," she replied. "Congratulations. Manila, huh?"

"Looks like it."

They were both silent for a while, watching the sun set over the muddy field.

She was the first to speak. "Well, I'm staying right here, getting my teaching degree."

"Being a teacher has always suited you," he said honestly, giving her a sidelong glance. "I've learned a lot from you, you know."

"Likewise," she replied, a small smile tugging at her lips.

"You know the best part about this? There'll be one less person around to annoy you."

She chuckled. "You're right. Things will be different without you."

"Yeah. Whichever way you look at it, we won't be around to annoy each other anymore."

They shared a light laugh, but, as the words left his lips, Royce felt a chill in the air that had nothing to do with the recent heavy rains. Their fierce competition over the years had created a strange yet undeniable bond. Separation was something new.

He took a deep breath and stood up with his hands in his pockets, feeling as though the fading light of day mirrored the closing chapter of his life in this city. He turned to look at the girl next to him, her glistening black hair catching the last rays of sunlight.

His greatest rival at school since first grade. His training partner in Karate since they were both six. They had shared valedictory honors in elementary and high school. They had both won regional kata championships in the past year.

She was practically part of him, wasn't she?

"Koreen," he began, hesitating for a moment before continuing. "I just wanted to say…I'm sorry for being such a pain in your ass since we were little."

"You're a good kind of pain, Duran—the kind that keeps me on my toes." She stood up and, to his surprise, moved closer to him. "Thanks for always pushing me a little bit more."

"You did the same for me," he admitted, acutely aware of the increasing tightness in his throat as he looked into her eyes.

Looking away, he unzipped his backpack and retrieved a small bundle wrapped in cloth. From the canvas bag, he pulled out his black belt in Karate, its fabric worn from years of use.

"I want you to have this," he said, holding it out to her. "With the way we've trained together over the years, our belts belong together, too."

She hesitated, her eyes flicking between the belt and his face. "This belt's yours. Why wouldn't you practice Karate anymore?"

"Maybe I will, but I'll have to start over at another club. If I do find a new one, I doubt it will be the same as the one we've got. I'd rather my belt stay with a champion, at my home dojo."

She looked at him closely for a while, her eyes thoughtful.

"Fine." Koreen relented after a moment, albeit reluctantly. "I'll hold on to it. For now. You can have it back anytime, okay?"

"Thanks." He nodded and put the belt back in its case before handing it to her. Their hands brushed against each other for a fleeting moment, sending a jolt of electricity up his arm. They both pulled away quickly, as if burned by the contact.

There had always been a barrier between them, something that the years and their fierce rivalry had put up between them. It was an invisible wall that stopped them from crossing into unknown territory, and now it seemed more impenetrable than ever.

"Is that all you wanted?" Koreen clutched the case of his belt tightly, her fingers tracing the embroidered letters of his name on the silken cloth.

Royce hesitated. "Yeah...actually, no." He reached into his bag once more and pulled out a black box containing a single white anemone, its petals lined with thin yellow, pink, and red stripes.

"This is for you." He held the box out with both hands.

Her eyes widened in surprise. "What's this?"

"It's an anemone," he replied, trying to sound casual despite the pounding of his heart.

"Aren't these supposed to be rare? And expensive, too…" Her voice trailed off as she looked at him and the box doubtfully.

He swallowed the lump in his throat, struggling to find the words to explain the significance of the anemone.

But the words never came, eclipsed by nerves and fear.

"Can you do me a favor and just take it?" he finally asked, his voice strained. "Don't you like it?"

"I like it very much." Her eyes never left the flower as she answered his question quietly and quickly. She reached out, her fingers brushing against the box before she took it from him. "Thanks."

"You're welcome."

Koreen held the box to her chest as if it were something fragile, not meeting his eyes as she spoke. "Does Kenneth know you're leaving?"

Her younger brother was one his closest friends, a basketball buddy since childhood. "He doesn't yet. I'll tell him and the others about the move during the game tonight. You're the first to know."

Her gaze moved to his face this time, making him feel very self-conscious. "I guess this is it."

He took a deep breath, feeling his head spin as he did. "Right. Just…take care of yourself, okay? And keep in touch. Let me know if you do decide to compete in the nationals."

She nodded. "Take care of yourself, Duran. Good luck with everything."

He dared to look into her eyes as he gave her an awkward gesture that seemed a cross between a wave and a salute. "Goodbye, Koreen."

Koreen seemed to want to say something more, but instead, she turned and walked away.

As he watched her retreating back, Royce desperately wanted to call out her name. He wasn't sure why, but he would have given anything to make her stop and at least look at him over her shoulder, for perhaps the final time.

Instead, he could only stare at the space she had gone into, long after she was out of sight.

One

Koreen

REVERIE

She stood in front of the classroom as she collected the last of the answer sheets, nodding appreciatively as her students stood in a quiet queue.

In life and in the classroom, Koreen Cisco prided herself on maintaining order and discipline. Today was no exception, as the weekly quiz in her Modern Algebra class wrapped up like clockwork.

"Thank you, everyone," she said as the final paper was handed to her. "I'll have these graded by Monday. Have a great weekend."

The final bell of the school week tolled. Murmuring

amongst themselves, her students filed out of the room, leaving her alone to gather her belongings and prepare for the next part of her day.

Her life was a whirlwind of activity. In addition to teaching, she also worked part-time as a Karate instructor at her old martial arts gym and as a trainer for a local BPO training center.

Growing up, Koreen had always been fiercely competitive and dedicated, excelling in both academics and sports. Her father, a math teacher himself, had passed away when she was in her first year of college, leaving her with the responsibility of helping her mother and younger brother. Through hard work and determination, she and her mother, who worked as an accountant for the city government, had managed to put her brother through medical school.

Even now, with her mother retired and Kenneth working as a doctor on a residency in another province, she continued to push herself in every aspect of her life. Her days were long and demanding, but she wouldn't have it any other way.

She knew no other way.

As she shouldered her bag and locked her classroom door, her phone rang. It was her brother calling.

"Hey, Ken. How's the residency going?"

"Busy, as always," he replied with a tired chuckle. "But it's good. I'm learning a lot, especially techniques on how to stay awake for seventy-two hours straight. How about you? How are things?"

"Same as always. Teaching, Karate, training…the usual."

"Always on the go, huh?"

She bristled slightly at his loaded comment, aware of the defensive edge in her own voice. "I enjoy it. Keeps me sharp."

"Yeah, but just make sure you're taking care of yourself too, okay?" His voice turned gentle, almost placating. She wondered if they taught this kind of thing at medical school: how to deal with stubborn patients—or older sisters. "Mama called me the other day and told me she's worried you don't seem to be slowing down at all."

"Slowing down?" she scoffed. "What for? Life doesn't stop just because we're tired."

"Well, she said you were working even when you were sick last time. You can't keep pushing yourself like that, Koreen. Your body might give up on you."

She rolled her eyes at his comment. "Ken, it was just a seasonal cold. Nothing to worry about."

"Still, you need to take better care of your health. Make sure you're eating well, getting enough sleep, and maybe consider taking a break every now and then. It wouldn't hurt."

"Alright, alright," she conceded, not wanting to prolong the conversation. "I'll try to take it easy. Thanks for looking out for me."

"Of course," he said, before pausing for a moment. "Oh, by the way, have you heard from Royce lately?"

"Royce who?" She waved goodbye to a small group of teachers exiting the faculty room. The day had ended for the people at school, but she was barely halfway done with hers.

"Royce Duran," Kenneth clarified.

The name stopped her train of thought.

Royce.

Memories of their fierce academic rivalry and intense kata training sessions came flooding back. He'd been part of her life for years, ever since they were four.

She still thought of him, after all these years, whenever

she demonstrated the Pinan sequences. No one could ever quite match his power in kata. She had the technique down pat, but sheer passion in every single move…Royce had that, and more.

"Uh, no," she managed to say, shaking off her reverie. "I haven't heard much from him since we graduated high school. Why?"

"He's visiting Iloilo for a business project or something. He reached out to me and told me he wanted to catch up while he's here. I'll see if I can get some of the old gang back together on a weekend to shoot some hoops."

Despite herself, her curiosity was piqued. "I've seen some of his posts online, but we haven't messaged each other or anything. He's still working in Saudi, isn't he?"

After finishing college in Manila, she knew that Royce had taken a job in Saudi Arabia. He had never come back to Iloilo City since he'd told her his family was moving.

"Yeah, he was still in Saudi when he messaged me, but he was getting ready to travel here. Maybe you'll run into him while he's in town."

"Maybe," she echoed uncertainly. After nearly fifteen years, seeing him again—in person—seemed a strange, distant possibility. He was only ever a face from her past, captured in old photographs.

"Anyway, I should get back to work," said Kenneth. "Take care of yourself, sis. And if you do see Royce, let me know how it goes."

"Sure thing. Take care, too."

As they said their goodbyes and hung up, Koreen couldn't help but feel a strange mix of emotions. She appreciated her brother's concern, but part of her bristled at the thought of someone telling her to slow down. She couldn't deny that she was overworked, but hadn't she been managing just fine all these years?

Her ultimate dream was to open her own BPO training center, a place where she could teach people the tools and tricks of the industry that had helped keep her family afloat since she was in college. She'd worked part-time as a call center agent and a medical transcriptionist while completing her Education degree.

Her dream business seemed more and more distant with each passing day, despite her tireless efforts. Raising funds was her greatest challenge; everything got more and more expensive as time went on, while her net income barely inched upward.

And then there was Royce—the boy who had once pushed her to her limits, both mentally and physically. What would it be like to see him again, after so many years?

He's a man now, she corrected herself. High school was a lifetime ago.

But his black belt was still with her, safely kept next to her Karate trophies in their place of honor, on a living room display shelf at her parent's home.

Lost in thought as she made her way to the parking area of the high school, Koreen barely noticed her phone vibrating in her hand again.

Glancing at the screen, she saw that it was from the gym. She swiped to pick up the call.

"Hey, Maggie."

"Hi, Koreen, I'm so sorry to bother you. I hope I'm not interrupting your class or anything." The receptionist's tone was both apologetic and urgent.

"No, it's fine. I'm done at school. I was just on my way to the training center. What's up?"

"Something important. We have a high-profile client who specifically requested a one-on-one session with you."

"Really?" Koreen was intrigued by the sudden request. She was no stranger to special sessions, but this came out of the blue. She usually saw these logged in her schedule at the gym weeks in advance. "I don't mind, but shouldn't I assess their skills first before accepting so I can prepare?"

"No need for that," Maggie replied, a little too cheerfully. "You know the client quite well, actually. It's Royce Duran. Leo told me you used to train with him."

Koreen's heart skipped a beat, and her grip tightened around the phone.

It had to be him, of course. After years of silence, it was typical of Royce Duran to simply reappear and weave his way back into her life, as if he'd never left.

She sighed, hoping Maggie wouldn't pick up her exasperation through the line. "When is it scheduled for?"

"Tomorrow, at four."

Saturday was her busiest in terms of teaching Karate. Starting at one in the afternoon, she had a kids' class, a thirty-minute kata technique session with some athletes competing at a local tournament, and an advanced class for brown belts and higher. Four o'clock was smack dab in between the last two, but she could manage it. She could do with the extra money.

"Fine. Book the session."

"Great," came the receptionist's enthusiastic response. "I'll see you tomorrow, Koreen."

"See you, Maggie. Thanks."

As she hung up and quickly made her way to her trusty red Corolla, her mind raced with thoughts about Royce, their history, and what his return meant for her and her hectic, carefully constructed world.

If it meant anything at all.

But there was no time to dwell on that now; Koreen had work to do. Her class with beginner transcriptionists was due to start in an hour.

She squared her shoulders, got into the car, and drove off, trying to ignore the pounding of her heart.

Two

Royce

RETURN

SUCCESS WAITED FOR NO ONE; NEITHER DID THE CITY before him.

Royce Duran stood by the window of his hotel suite overlooking the bustling streets of Iloilo. The cityscape stretched out before him, glistening in the late afternoon sun. It had rained on and off since he arrived three days ago, but, today, the clear skies were a welcome sight.

So much had changed in the past fifteen years in his hometown. Where before there were empty fields in the outskirts of the city, imposing buildings with modern architecture now stood in their place. These new buildings had become the hub for telecommunications companies, both local and international.

As CEO of Boundless Telecom, a Saudi Arabia-based business process outsourcing company, he was constantly on the move, planning the next big project for the company. This time, it was to establish a branch in the Philippines, in Iloilo City. This would be the third operations hub he would set up outside of KSA, in as many years.

It was a trip long overdue as well. Royce had not been in the Philippines for the better part of nine years.

Prince Khalid, his boss and the owner of Boundless, had urged him to take a break during his visit and charge his vacation expenses to the company. The prince's parting words, in a phone call before Royce flew out of Jeddah, still clung to the back of his mind.

You should think about getting married, too, my friend. Maybe now is the perfect time, after so many years of your hard work.

His phone rang, interrupting his thoughts. It was from his old Karate gym.

"Royce Duran."

"Good afternoon, Mr. Duran." The voice was warm. "This is Maggie. I'm calling to confirm that Miss Cisco has accepted your request for a one-on-one session tomorrow."

It was a shot in the dark, but her acceptance came as no surprise. Koreen Cisco was not the kind of woman who backed down from a challenge.

"Thank you. I'm sorry for such short notice. I'm glad she's accepted."

"You're welcome, sir. If you don't mind, please, Mr. Tuazon would like to speak with you."

Leo Tuazon, the son of the gym's owner and founder, had taken over since his parents retired.

"No problem, Maggie. Thanks again."

There was a brief rustle at the other end of the line, followed by a boisterous greeting.

"Royce, my man!"

"Hey, Leo. It's been a while."

"Yeah, it has. You know, we still have some of your old trophies displayed at the gym. My father never quite forgave you for leaving us to study in Manila. He lost a champion and a potential instructor."

Royce laughed. "He's still holding on to that grudge, isn't he?"

"Never got over it."

"How are your parents, though? Both good?"

Leo sighed. "Well, they're both doing okay. They prefer staying in the province these days. The city's gotten too crowded for them, I suppose. I do get them to go on Zoom when there's a promotion ceremony, just so they can see the kids."

"Ah, promotions. I remember those."

"I'm glad you're coming back tomorrow afternoon," said Leo enthusiastically. "And I'm even happier that you're reconnecting with Koreen. You two were the best we've ever had. No other club has ever had a year when they had two regional kata champions."

"Thanks for welcoming me back, Leo."

"Of course! And thank you for your generous

donation to the gym. The new training equipment will make a huge difference."

"Anything to give back. Always happy to help out."

They spoke about the gym and its former students and instructors for a few more minutes and exchanged goodbyes.

As he hung up the phone, Royce's thoughts drifted, inexorably, to Koreen.

What was her reaction to his request for a one-on-one? He wondered if she knew that he'd offered the gym double the charge of their usual sessions—and added a tip.

He'd seen her pictures on social media; she updated randomly and irregularly, mostly with pictures of inter-school math competitions, Karate tournaments, and the odd birthday greeting. She didn't seem to have much of a personal life.

Her brother, Kenneth, had been affectionately vocal on this.

"She's the same girl you knew, Royce. If anything, as a grown woman, she's more determined than ever."

He couldn't fault her for it.

If there was someone who understood ambition and drive very well, it was him.

His phone buzzed again, this time with a reminder for a conference call with the Boundless management team in Pune, India. It would be noontime there.

Performance data and notes on the Pune site had been linked to the reminder, too. With the amount of reports he could see, the meeting would take no less than two hours. His personal assistant, Yoshida, was nothing if not meticulous.

So much for reminiscing.

Royce's world moved too quickly sometimes. And he knew he'd built it in such a way that it didn't know how to wait, even for him.

His Saturdays were usually filled with informal meetings. Most of the time, he would have brunch with the prince or some of his contemporaries in Jeddah. These luxurious meals weren't technically downtime; casual conversations inevitably swirled towards business.

Sometimes, Royce would be travelling for a site visit, a conference, or a meeting out of town, to strike yet another deal. It was strange to wake up and not be concerned about getting ready to get to work, for a change.

He wasn't really certain if it was a welcome one.

That Saturday, he rose with a tight sensation in the pit of his stomach, far more pronounced than any tension he'd feel before potentially striking a deal worth millions of dollars.

The only meeting in his schedule that day meant far more than any contract won for Boundless.

The thought of seeing Koreen again was somewhat unnerving.

Did she still have his black belt?

They hadn't kept in touch much since their last meeting at the football field all those years ago, only occasionally seeing each other's updates online. Other than her liking a few of his posts, mostly pictures of work functions and events, their interactions had been very limited.

He'd lost count of how many times he had wanted to reach out to her before, even with just a message or a phone call, but something had always held him back. It was the unseen yet undeniably powerful wall that had always stood between them, time and distance be damned.

Their school and training days were long behind them, but their belts, together in her keeping, still symbolized some kind of connection.

Or did they?

Perhaps this kind of sentimentality came with age, or the fact that he was back in a place he still considered his childhood home.

Instead of dwelling any further on his wandering thoughts, he glanced at his phone. Even though it was the weekend, there was always something at Boundless that needed his attention. Work didn't disappoint. He needed to answer a few emails.

Afterwards, he had breakfast at the hotel's poolside restaurant and visited the construction site of Boundless Tower, which wasn't far from where he was staying.

Once he got back to the hotel, he began to get ready for his training session with Koreen that afternoon.

It felt strange that, for the first time in his life, he didn't have the proper attire for Karate anymore. He'd long since outgrown his gi, kept with his old belongings at his parents' house in Manila.

Ordinary exercise gear would have to do. He was grateful he always brought gym attire whilst on travel. Squeezing in an hour or two for a workout was always a welcome respite from his hectic schedule.

He was zipping up his bag when his phone buzzed

with a message. He glanced at the screen to find a text message from Kenneth Cisco.

> "Hey man! How's Iloilo so far?"

He typed out a reply, trying to keep his tone neutral.

> "Good. Saw the site for the Tower. Glad it hasn't rained since yesterday."

> "Great! Koreen knows you're back, by the way."

Kenneth's words jumped out the screen.

The mention of her name in the message brought about an unexpected rush of nerves. Booking a training session with a phone call was one thing; being referred to by her own brother was something else entirely.

> "Can't wait to catch up with you. Let me know about that basketball game. I'm meeting Wesley tomorrow for drinks."

It was the best response he could muster, without sounding too evasive.

As he waited for the car that would take him to his old Karate gym, he looked at his reflection in the closet's full-length mirror. He'd chosen to wear a simple black shirt and sweatpants.

Even in nondescript sportswear, he still looked formidable enough. He had grown to his full height of six feet by the time he turned twenty-one. Over the years, he'd put on at least sixty pounds of muscle on what used to be his lanky teenaged frame.

He still looked like someone worthy of Koreen Cisco's attention.

Mercifully, the phone rang.

"Your car is ready, Mr. Duran," the polite voice on the other end informed him.

"Thank you. I'm on my way down."

With a final glance at his reflection in the mirror, he took a deep breath, steadying himself for the encounter that awaited him.

It was time to step back onto the mat.

Three

Koreen

REWIND

Her Saturdays were usually fueled by coffee and determination.

Today was no different, except there was a significant amount of anxiety thrown into the mix. She'd barely slept the night before.

At sunrise, Koreen gave up and got out of bed. She headed for the living room, to the shelf where her mother kept their awards and certificates along with a massive collection of framed photographs.

For the past fifteen years, she'd kept Royce's belt on the shelf next to her trophies and their picture together, taken moments after they had both been awarded their kata championships. She had never imagined the day would come that the belt would actually be returned to its owner.

She took out the canvas bag embroidered with his name, untouched after so many years. The black belt had been neatly folded inside, but there was something else she'd kept along with it.

In the thin light of dawn trickling through the windows, her fingers reached into the bag and settled on a piece of cardboard folded in half. She slid it out carefully and placed the canvas bag back onto the shelf.

It would be the first time in years she'd mustered enough courage to look at *it* again.

She could still remember the white anemone with its beautiful, colorful stripes. It had dried to a clump of thin, light brown petals that looked more like leaves, a piece of its original cardboard box the only thing holding it together.

The summer Royce had left for Manila, she had held on to his parting gift with the utmost care, guardedly and devotedly, until the flower had drooped over her hands. She'd then kept it and a piece of the box with his belt ever since.

They were all meant to be memories: the anemone, the belt, and Royce Duran. Nothing more.

She put the cardboard piece inside the frame with their photo, locked away in a time long past.

Koreen took the canvas bag and closed the shelf's glass door, determined to go on with the day as if it were any other.

Morning came and went too soon. After downing two cups of coffee and finishing a piece of toast her mother had practically force-fed her before leaving the house, she found herself outside Nelly's tailoring shop on the city's old Main Street.

She had asked the seamstress, who made the school's uniforms for decades now, to alter an extra karategi they had sewn for the Tuazon school. The outfit was originally meant for a Criminology major who was a kumite athlete, but he'd pulled out of a competition weeks ago due to an injury from his intensive police training.

Late yesterday afternoon, Koreen had decided to pay for the uniform in full, hoping it would be ready within the tight overnight window she'd given.

This karategi was for Royce.

She had looked up his photos on social media to get an idea of how much he had grown since high school, using her vast experience to gauge his uniform size. It felt strange, almost invasive, to see him living a glamorous, high-flying life in those photos.

A life so different from her own.

Koreen sighed inwardly. She felt old and, somehow, left behind.

She pushed her thoughts aside and entered the shop. "Good morning, Nelly."

The seamstress, sharp-eyed and ageless with neatly-coiffed gray hair, was already hard at work behind her sewing machine.

"Ah, Koreen!" The older woman flashed her a big smile as she got to her feet. "Good news, dear. The girls and I managed to finish everything last night, including your rush order."

She let out a sigh of relief. "Thank you so much. You're

a lifesaver. I'm so sorry again for troubling you about that additional uniform at the last minute."

Nelly waved her apology aside. "You never ask for favors, so I was pretty sure this is very important to you."

Koreen could only nod, trying to ignore the flush rising up her neck.

Two of Nelly's assistants walked into the room, wheeling a large rack full of neatly-pressed children's karategi in various sizes. Moving with practiced ease, they took the uniforms off their hangers and folded them into big white boxes.

The seamstress reached for a much larger karategi hanging at the far end of the rack. Standing next to it, Koreen was practically swallowed by the sheer amount of fabric.

"This one is quite big," Nelly said appraisingly. "I was surprised when you said you wanted to buy out De Silva's competition gi and size it up even more. Who is this for, anyway?"

"It's for a former student of the gym. I'll be teaching him later today."

"Really?" Nelly raised an eyebrow, clearly intrigued. "Tell me more about this mystery man."

Koreen hesitated slightly before answering, hoping Nelly couldn't see the heat that had somehow found its way into her cheeks. "His name's Royce Duran. We were in the same class back in high school, and, well, we've trained together since we were kids. I'm pretty sure his old uniform's from here, too. He's worked in Saudi Arabia for years, but he's back in town for business of some kind."

Nelly's gaze was unwaveringly, unabashedly curious. "Interesting. Is he single?"

She shrugged, trying to hide her discomfort at the direction the conversation was taking. "I'm not sure, but that's really none of my business. I just need to make sure this karategi fits him. He was a kata champion once. We won our titles at the same tournament, the same year."

"Wow, very impressive. So nice of you to get this organized for him."

Nice wasn't exactly how she'd treated Royce Duran in the past, but Nelly didn't have to know that—or anything about their history, for that matter.

"Anyway, I should get going soon," Koreen said, changing the subject. "My class starts at one. Thank you again for your help, Nelly."

"Of course, anytime. Let's get all these boxes ready to go."

They watched the assistants finish their task of packing up the uniforms. Before they could close the last box with Royce's new karategi inside it, Koreen stepped forward, her stomach churning at the task she was about to do.

"Just a second, please." Before she lost her nerve, she retrieved the canvas case with his black belt from her handbag.

She carefully placed the embroidered fabric on top of the gleaming white uniform. "This belt belonged to him when we trained together. It's time to give it back to its owner."

Nelly smiled as she closed the box and gestured for her assistants to seal it. "Maybe that's not the only thing that belongs to him."

Koreen blushed but didn't respond, opting to act as if she didn't hear what the seamstress said. Instead, she bid Nelly goodbye and helped the assistants load the boxes into her car.

The drive to the gym was a blur, the gravity of that afternoon's session hanging above her head like a specter that refused to leave her alone.

She could still recall his parting words vividly.

"With the way we've trained together over the years, our belts belong together, too."

Before she realized it, she was in the parking area outside the building. Leo and Maggie were already there, waiting for her and the uniforms to arrive. Their excitement was palpable as they chatted about Royce's upcoming visit.

"Royce made some generous donations for equipment, Koreen. We can finally buy a couple of those inflatable dummies the little kids could practice on." The hero-worship was evident in Leo's voice. "He even paid more than twice the usual rate for a one-on-one session with you. We really needed that money."

"I know, Leo," she replied gently, as she retrieved her bags from the passenger seat. The act of giving back to the gym was not entirely unexpected, but the fact that Royce had paid extra for a session with her seemed a little too much. "It's good news for the gym."

She couldn't fault Leo for agreeing to the session. The gym was struggling financially, largely because he had tried not to increase fees for their students, leaving barely enough money to keep the facility afloat.

"His company must be doing so well," chimed in Maggie, as she reached for some of the boxes in the backseat. "One of my cousins has already put in her job application online with Boundless. They seem to be hiring for a lot of positions."

"Can you imagine," Leo went on, his eyes sparkling, "both you and Royce performing a kata sequence together? I'd give an arm and a leg to see that!"

Koreen shook her head at his enthusiasm. "Let's not get ahead of ourselves."

Maggie raised an eyebrow as piles of boxes teetered

precariously in her arms. "It's not every day we get two champions in the gym. You're both legends. This is the kind of thing that goes viral on the Internet."

"I'm too old for those, Maggie," she replied dismissively, trying to keep the conversation grounded.

But both Maggie and Leo pressed on, insisting that having her and Royce together, after all these years, under their gym's roof at the same time was truly a big deal.

"Fine, whatever you say," Koreen finally conceded, embarrassed at their excitement and keen not to be late for her first class. "Now, please help me unload these uniforms. I still need to change."

As she walked into the gym and got ready for her classes, the weight of seeing Royce again grew heavier in her mind with each passing second.

She steeled herself against the onslaught of uncertainty. She had her responsibilities to focus on. She was determined to face them all—and the man from her past, too—head-on, just as she always had.

Koreen's muscles ached as she walked around the mat of the gym's main training area. Sweat beaded her brow as the thick, humid air wafted in through the open windows. The few wall and ceiling fans installed around the facility offered very little relief against the sticky mid-afternoon heat.

Her class for primary-grade children was arguably the busiest and the most exhausting on the Tuazon school timetable, but she wouldn't have it any other way.

Ever since her arrival at the gym that day, she'd focused

her thoughts and energy on her students, closely assessing their progress to distract herself from what awaited her later. Her heart swelled with pride when one of her shyest pupils, a nine-year-old girl, executed a flawless, perfectly targeted roundhouse kick.

At half past three, she thanked the athletes who came to her kata technique session and wished them good luck in their upcoming competition. As soon as they had all dispersed to go home or change in the locker rooms, she made her way to the gym's tiny staff room.

She couldn't deny she wasn't tired, but adrenaline coursed through her veins, making her feel almost giddy. It didn't help that she hadn't really eaten much today, except for that piece of toast this morning.

She sat down on a plastic stool and took a minute to force down a banana and a small bottle of water. Her stomach rumbled in protest. She had no time or desire to eat anything more substantial.

Peeling off her damp karategi, Koreen took a deep breath for the first time in hours. She slipped into a fresh uniform, pulling the fabric taut across her shoulders. As she arranged her hair into a neat bun, she caught a glimpse of herself in the mirror. The reflection staring back at her still held traces of the champion she once was—someone fierce, powerful, and unstoppable.

She emerged from the staff room at ten minutes to four. Another class was in full swing, led by Ace, a fellow instructor who worked at a nearby merchant marine school. She paused for a minute to watch the mid-level teenaged students as they attacked and defended in turn through their shadow-sparring exercises.

Other than the people in the class, the gym was empty. Older students usually didn't have parents or guardians hovering nearby. Maggie's desk at reception was deserted, and Leo had disappeared as well.

"God, I've missed doing this."

At the sound, her heart leaped into her throat. The words were spoken softly, meant only for her ears. Before she even laid eyes on him, she knew who the owner of the voice was.

Royce Duran's presence was undeniably imposing, as always. This time, she had to look way up to see his face.

He had always been athletic and strong, but now he stood before her as a man fully grown, the difference between their sizes and stature more significant and pronounced than ever. It was clear that he had continued to train and develop his body through the years.

His hair was shorter than before, now looking much like a crew cut. He had a very thin, perfectly-trimmed beard and mustache that gave him an exotic, intimidating air.

But it was his eyes that, as always, commanded her attention.

Even after fifteen years, she was familiar with his eyes, as if she'd last looked into them yesterday. Royce Duran's eyes had the deadly, unyielding focus of a seasoned predator.

Those same eyes were now smiling down at her.

"It's nice to see you, Koreen." His voice was deeper than she remembered.

She was at a loss for words. Her hands clenched into fists as she attempted to regain her composure.

"It's good you're on time, Duran." Her response came out colder than she'd intended it to sound.

It was as if she had some kind of standoffish reflex when

it came to talking to him. She could still remember herself telling him on their high school's football field that agreeing to meet him was weird. She'd never realized, until it was too late, that he'd only wanted to say a proper goodbye.

"Wouldn't miss this for the world." His response was warm, almost friendly. "How have you been?"

"I'm fine," she replied, a little too quickly for her own comfort. "Busy as always, but fine. And you?"

His gaze never left her face as he answered. "It's good to be back in Iloilo. It's even better to be back in the gym after such a long time. I didn't realize how much I missed being here."

She was the first to break eye contact, averting her attention to the sparring teenagers in Ace's class. "Welcome back."

"Thank you. I'm glad you agreed to this session at such short notice. Starting Monday, I have meetings lined up, so this weekend is really the only one I've got free before all the craziness starts."

"Craziness?"

"Ah, yes." He chuckled softly. The sound sent shivers down her spine. "I'm back in town for business. I'm setting up a new operations center for my company, Boundless Telecom. We're planning to house an army of agents at a dedicated facility, providing translation and transcription services to clients in Europe and the Americas."

She nodded. "Sounds like a big venture. I could recommend a few of my trainees based in the city if you're looking for people to hire. They're hardworking, disciplined, and quick learners."

"Always teaching, aren't you?" There was an unmistakable smile in his voice.

"It just sort of fell into place. When my father died shortly after I started college, I found work in some BPO places to help my mother out."

"I'm very sorry about your father," he said, his tone now serious and sincere to her ears. "He'd always been kind to me. I'd never forget how well he could make a kite out of newspapers and barbecue sticks."

"Thanks."

Side by side, in strangely companionable silence, they watched the students in the class wrap up their sparring exercises.

Koreen glanced up at the clock. "It's time for us to train. Are you ready?"

"Always."

The way he said that one word seemed to hold a deeper meaning than merely being prepared for their session.

It didn't matter what he meant. She squared her shoulders and inclined her head towards the other side of the gym, a smaller enclosed training space that Leo had booked for their session.

As she looked up into his eyes, she could feel her heart hammering against her ribcage with equal parts anticipation and trepidation.

There it was, back from the dead: the familiar competitive fire within her began to burn—bright and undeniable.

"Alright, we'll see what you've got. Let's get started."

Four

Royce

RESURFACE

He looked around the gym where he'd spent countless hours training as a child and as a teenaged boy.

Royce had come in for his session early, unnoticed by all with the exception of Leo Tuazon, who had fawned over him a little too much. It had been a surreal experience, to see his martial arts school almost the same as it was before.

Seeing Koreen, however, was the most unsettling experience of all.

She had always been petite, but now she barely made it to his shoulder. She still kept her black hair long, piled high on top of her head. He'd always had the opinion that all she needed was a crown to complete the appearance of a warrior queen. Her brown eyes, cat-like and unapologetically intelligent, looked as determined as ever.

The fifteen years that stretched out between them seemed to have wavered; the gap it had created strangely closing, as if no time had passed.

"Lead the way," he replied, lowering his head slightly in a gesture of respect.

Koreen nodded, seemingly satisfied with his response. She brushed past him and made her way to a smaller, partially enclosed training area, the same place where they had both practiced their kata all those years ago.

He could see his younger self, standing beside her, their eyes locked in the mirror. There had always been an unspoken challenge between them as to who could deliver the sequences more flawlessly, more precisely.

Out of earshot of the ongoing class across the floor, she paused by the threshold. He'd expected her to bow before entering, as was custom. Instead, she crossed her arms over her chest and gave him a once-over.

"Before we get started, I want to know what kind of martial arts training you've been doing."

Somehow, her question made him feel vulnerable, almost inferior.

"I've barely done any Karate training since I went abroad. I did dabble in Taekwondo in college, but even then, I've always been drawn to Karate more. Maybe because I've studied it since I was four."

"I can understand why," she replied, nodding. "I tried training in Sanda, too, in another gym, after high school. I came back to Karate eventually. It felt like…home to me, I suppose."

He was surprised at how agreeable he and Koreen seemed at the moment. He didn't want to push his luck, but perhaps they had both matured over the years.

"Which brings us both back here, now." He gave her a small smile.

Instead of smiling back, she raised an eyebrow and looked him up and down again, shaking her head disapprovingly. "Is that what you're planning to wear for our session?"

"Uh, yeah," he replied, glancing down at his sports attire, slightly taken aback by her question. "I don't have a karategi anymore. I outgrew my old one a long time ago."

Koreen's lips formed a thin line as she shook her head. "That's unacceptable. Follow me."

Before he could respond, she led him to a locker near the changing rooms. She opened the tiny steel door and gestured to a karategi hanging inside. It was a pristine white, adorned with the logos and colors of the Tuazon school.

"This is for you, Duran," she said, gesturing to the uniform. Her chin was lifted, but her gaze seemed focused on something above his shoulder. "Take it."

Too surprised to say anything, he reached inside the locker as instructed and pulled the karategi out. It became clear that the uniform was tailored perfectly to his size.

"Koreen, how did you…?" His voice trailed off as his mind raced to find the right words to show his appreciation. Their history together made it difficult for him to express his gratitude—or any other emotion.

But she wasn't finished. From the same locker, she

produced a small canvas bag. He could see his name embroidered on the worn fabric.

It was his black belt.

"Here. It's time you have it back."

Time seemed to stand still as his mind flashed back to their awkward farewell at the football field fifteen years ago. He had so much left unsaid back then. Even until now…he still didn't have the words.

He reached out to take the belt from her, and when their hands touched, he didn't pull away this time. Instead, he squeezed her hands gently.

Koreen's hands seemed smaller and more delicate, but no less powerful.

"Thank you." It was all he could say.

"It's the least I could do, to honor a former champion of the school." The expression on her face was unreadable.

He let her hands go but found himself unable to look away from her eyes.

She was the one who took the step back.

All of the sudden, he felt it.

It was the same thing that had always stopped him from reaching out to her on social media—the very thing that had prevented him from calling out her name across the field.

"It will only take a minute for me to change," he said instead.

"Good."

Without another word, she turned and walked away.

The invisible barrier between them had asserted itself, once more.

THE LAST DIVIDE

He wasn't certain if the mirror was lying or not, but Royce liked what he saw.

He had no idea how Koreen had managed to estimate his size with such precision. The new karategi fitted him perfectly, the fabric falling against the lines of his body as if it knew exactly what kind of movements to expect from his limbs.

With the black belt tied just above his hip line, he looked as if he'd always belonged in the uniform.

As if he had never left.

He took a deep breath and exited the men's locker room, quickly making his way back to the enclosed training area.

She was waiting for him, standing in the middle of the room with her hands clasped behind her back.

"Wow." He took in the familiar sight of the mirrored walls and the dark blue rubber mats on the floor. "This place hasn't changed much."

"Leo replaced the mats a few years ago, but that's about it," Koreen said in a quiet voice. "The business barely makes any money, but he's trying not to increase the fees for the students."

He'd thought as much, the moment he'd seen the weather-worn sign outside and the slightly dilapidated state of the office furniture in the gym's reception area.

"Stubborn just like his parents, huh?"

She smiled; it was a tentative upward curving of her lips, but it was enough for him.

"Yeah. I suppose Ace, Jonah, and I are just as stubborn. We refuse to leave him."

Leo had pointed Ace out earlier on the floor. Royce didn't know him, but he knew Jonah. She was a few years older than he and Koreen, and a kumite champion back in the day.

He chuckled. "To keep a place like this running, he needs people like you. He's very lucky you're all with him."

She didn't respond, but her eyes searched the room before finally settling on him.

"So, what's your goal for this session, Duran?"

He hesitated for a moment before answering honestly. "My goal was to see you."

Her eyebrows shot up, and various expressions flickered across her face in quick succession: surprise, confusion, curiosity. "What do you mean?"

"Exactly that," he replied with a shrug. "To see you. To train with you, like before."

She regarded him silently for a moment before she spoke. "Alright, then. You need to warm up first. We'll start with some kata sequences once you're ready."

He stood before her and bowed, indicating he was at her bidding. As she rattled off a series of exercises for him to do, he watched her face closely.

Just like before, he couldn't tell what she was thinking. Was she pleased by his admission, or did it make her uncomfortable?

As he began his warm-up, she watched him wordlessly, her eyes tracking his every movement. The rest of her looked as elegant and stoic as a marble statue.

The gym echoed with the sound of other students practicing their own techniques, but he didn't really pay much attention to anything else. As he moved under the watchful eye, her opinion of him was the only thing that mattered.

His muscles ached as he finished the warm-up, sweat trickling down his face and back. He looked over at her, trying to gauge her reaction.

"You're in pretty good shape for a man your age," she told him bluntly.

"Thanks," he replied, wiping sweat from his brow, unwilling to admit he was one burpee away from collapsing. "But you look to be in way better shape than me. I guess a good kata sequence would prove my point."

If he knew her well enough from their shared childhood and youth, he might still be able to push a few of her buttons.

She didn't disappoint.

Koreen hesitated for a moment, this time her eyes flashing and narrowing in turn. She looked slightly uncomfortable, as if he'd crossed an invisible line.

"I'm better now," she bit out. "Better than I used to be."

Her reaction—and her words—gave him immense satisfaction.

"Only one way to find out, isn't there?"

This time, she took the bait, almost hungrily. "Why don't you do the entire sequence with me, then, Duran? I assume you still remember Pinan One to Eight?"

"I'll try," he responded with downcast eyes. "I'm sure I'll remember if you're by my side."

She turned to face the wall-length mirror and gestured for him to take his position to her left.

As they stood side by side, Royce marveled at how little had changed between them. Time had not faded the way they both held themselves, the intensity that radiated from each of them.

"Get ready." Her words cut through the still, tense air between them like a knife.

His eyes met hers in the mirror. "Before we begin, if I do the entire sequence perfectly, I owe you dinner for being such a fantastic sensei."

She seemed taken aback by his comment, but before she could respond, Maggie walked into the room, carrying a towel and a bottle of water.

"Are you going to do the kata?" Maggie asked, her mouth dropping open in surprise. "Together?"

Koreen shot her a pointed look, but confirmed with a terse, wordless nod.

Excited, Maggie called out for Leo, announcing that they had to take a video of this.

"Our two champions, guys!" Her voice rang throughout the gym.

Maggie's enthusiasm was highly contagious; soon, Ace and his class of teenagers had gathered around the enclosed area, eager to witness the showdown.

Royce's heart hammered in his chest as he glanced around the room, taking in the sea of faces before him. He could count at least forty people; more than half of them already had mobile phones in their hands, cameras trained towards him and Koreen.

He swallowed hard, feeling a tight knot of anxiety forming in his stomach. Speaking before the Board of Directors of Boundless was nothing compared to this.

This was not what he had expected when he'd challenged

Koreen to perform the kata sequence with him. But now, he knew there was no turning back.

With a deep breath, he met Koreen's gaze in the mirror, finding quiet challenge and a resigned determination in her eyes. She leaned closer, her voice barely audible above the excited murmurs of their audience. "Don't you dare let me and this school down."

She moved to resume her preparatory stance, but paused midway and tilted her head to the side. "Besides, you're a champion, aren't you, Duran?"

If he knew how to push her buttons, she knew how to push his, too. It was an exchange as old as time.

"Wouldn't dream of disappointing you," he whispered back.

"We'll find out soon enough," she said simply, straightening. "Let's begin."

As they bowed and started the kata sequence at her command, he pushed all thought aside, focusing instead on Koreen's graceful form beside him.

They still moved in sync, their bodies mirroring each other's strikes, blocks and kicks. Over the years, he'd done this sequence countless times on his own, just to make sure he never forgot. It connected him to this place, to his childhood, and, most importantly, to her.

This time, it felt very different with a live audience, in his old martial arts school no less.

It felt very different with Koreen by his side.

As they progressed through the steps, Royce felt the strain in his muscles, his body slick with sweat from the exertion. He knew he couldn't falter; the stakes had never been higher. He wasn't just performing for an audience, or even a score.

He was performing for himself—and for her.

By the time they reached the end of the sequence, his knees trembled and his breath came in ragged gasps. But he stood tall, refusing to show any sign of weakness, after they took the final bow to mark the end of Pinan Eight.

Before she could react, he stepped forward, filling the space before her.

He bowed deeply, making sure he never lost eye contact even as he made the ultimate gesture of respect, humility, and gratitude.

"Sensei," he said, the single word carrying the weight of everything left unsaid between them.

The gym erupted into cheers and applause, the sound deafening in its intensity.

He didn't move until she bowed back.

Only then did he straighten and turn to face the rest of the room, smiling and bowing to an audience he didn't quite see.

All he could see before him were the years falling away.

The raw, undeniable bond between him and the woman who had always been his equal—and, oftentimes, superior—in so many ways.

The fierce battle for supremacy that had always seemed to divide their world into two.

For now, he was certain, whatever it was that connected and separated them in equal measure, had never truly faded.

Five

Koreen

RESTART

"Excuse me, Miss Cisco?"

Koreen looked up from the stack of quiz papers she was grading. It was late afternoon. All the other teachers had left for the day. She was savoring a rare moment of solitude in the faculty room before going to the gym later for her grueling Thursday night kumite class.

One of her senior students in Modern Algebra had poked his head through the half-open doorway. He was wearing a school jersey, probably still at practice in the courts near her office. "Yes, Paul? How can I help you?"

"There's someone asking for you. He said he was a classmate of yours."

"He's here?" The words escaped her mouth before she could stop herself. She had forgotten about Royce's dinner offer.

That wasn't entirely correct. She had tried very hard not to think about him or their on-the-spot kata demonstration at the gym that past weekend.

If not for Leo, Ace, and the students present, she would have walked out right then and there. Royce had expertly goaded her into accepting a challenge she had no business considering from the very start.

She was an instructor, fourth dan black. She should not have allowed herself to fall for his bait of doing the kata with him, especially to a live audience, most of them with camera phones in hand. She was supposed to have more dignity and restraint than that. Kata was meant to be sacred, not the object of a random challenge or something to post on the Internet.

"Hey, Paul. Is your Ma'am Cisco in there?" She heard a deeper, older male voice coming from the corridor.

Paul's head disappeared from sight. "Yup. She's right in there, Mister Duran."

A few more words were exchanged, before she heard a set of receding footsteps.

"Good afternoon, ma'am." It was Royce's turn to poke his head through the doorway. "Although you look more like a student, I'm getting a very strange sense of *déjà vu* right now."

She glared at him. "Did you come all the way here just to throw jabs at my age?"

"Not really, considering I'm two months older," he

answered, deadpan, walking into the room. "I tried calling and sending you messages. I thought I might have gotten your number wrong, but Kenneth told me it was correct."

There was nothing wrong with the number he'd been calling or texting. She had deliberately avoided his calls and not opened any of the messages he'd sent. She had known it was him trying to reach her since Monday; she'd gotten his number from Maggie's records.

His session had been completed. He was supposed to be busy now, wasn't he? He should just carry on with his business in town and leave her alone.

She shrugged. "I must have been busy at the time. Would you like to have a seat?"

She gestured to the chair in front of her desk. Regardless of what she felt at seeing him again and her reaction to last Saturday's events, she didn't want to appear rude.

"Thanks." He strode into the room, his presence dwarfing everything else in sight.

It was a presence that was impossible to ignore.

Today, he wasn't in sports attire. Instead, he had on a perfectly cut aqua-colored polo shirt and dark blue slacks. His feet were encased in what looked like black leather boots, shiny and expensive-looking. He looked sleek, but understated enough not to be ostentatious.

Royce had always held himself with quiet dignity, which made him appear more mature than most of their peers. As a man, he moved with more confidence. He looked like someone with the world at his command.

Maybe it was.

He settled gracefully in the chair in front of her desk, tilting his head to look at the papers she was marking. "Algebra?"

She nodded. "Modern Algebra. I also teach Trigonometry and Calculus."

"Always teaching."

"Yeah."

She finished grading the quiz paper, and looked up. Her breath hitched the moment they locked gazes. It was as if he'd never taken his eyes off her the moment he walked into the room.

"What brings you here? I think I'm the only teacher left around for the day, except maybe Coach Porras."

"I saw him when I came in. He's the one who asked Paul to take me here."

"I can schedule a visit for you, if you like."

He shook his head. "That's not why I'm here. I came to see you, to make good on my dinner invitation."

His words at the gym echoed in the back of her head.

"My goal was to see you."

She didn't know what to make of it. Competing against the younger Royce Duran was easy. Dealing with the gentleman who had taken his place was something else—something very unnerving.

"I thought you were joking." Koreen sighed and shook her head. "I honestly believed you didn't mean any of it."

"I meant what I said. I'm sorry if you thought I was trying to pull some kind of stunt on you. At our age, we should have already outgrown whatever bad blood we had between us by now."

She put down her pen and pushed the papers on her desk to one side. This was not the kind of conversation she wanted to have, much less in the faculty room of all places.

"It's not bad blood. It's not even about whatever's between us."

"Then what's this about?"

"You. Your intentions." She got to her feet as soon as she uttered the words. Sitting behind the desk felt suffocating all of a sudden. She had to put some distance between them; at least she should be relieved that she still had enough energy to move.

It was strange to see him looking up at her. "My intentions?"

"Why are you doing this?"

"As I said, I wanted to see you."

"Why?"

"We haven't seen each other in fifteen years. Besides, it's not every day someone goes out of their way to get a karategi done for me, much less a perfect one. I have not even thanked you properly for that—or for keeping my belt all these years. I'm just trying to be friendly."

They had been rivals, competitors, training partners. Never friends.

There had always been a line between them—an invisible divide that bisected the world.

That is, until he said goodbye fifteen years ago.

Until the anemone he'd given her—the first flower she'd ever received from a boy—wilted and fell apart in her fingers.

Her pride would never, ever allow her to admit that she'd cried that night. In the morning, she'd cut a piece of the black cardboard box and stashed the petals inside it, to be kept along with his belt in the years to come.

"You don't have to thank me," she replied, stepping away

from her own desk. She tried to avoid looking into his eyes, but couldn't help it. "You don't owe me anything."

He regarded her with an unreadable expression on his face, his dark eyes unblinking. "On the contrary."

"What makes you say that?"

"Last Saturday, when I first saw you, you gave me the best business epiphany I've ever had in years. Without knowing it, you managed to solve a very big problem of mine, in the space of a single conversation."

Koreen shook her head. All those years working so hard abroad had probably unhinged him. "What the hell are you talking about?"

"Boundless Tower is our biggest operations site to date, and we need the best person to run it. I believe you would be that person."

This was the last thing she had ever expected him to say.

"I want to offer you the position of Country Manager," Royce continued, a little more animatedly. "To oversee the place as it is built and supervise the operations once everything is up and running."

A job, she thought dazedly, finally managing to piece together the meaning of his words. *A very big, important job.*

Managing Boundless Tower in her own hometown would be a far cry from having her own tiny BPO training center. At this stage in her life, she could barely afford a single whiteboard with her savings, much less the computers, peripherals, and software required. She didn't even want to think about how much it would cost to rent a decent facility.

It was the biggest possible shock he could have sprung on her. So much so, that all she could do was stare at him, dumbstruck.

THE LAST DIVIDE

"What made you think that?" she finally asked, cautiously, aware that her voice was shaking.

He shrugged. "The Tower in Iloilo will be one of Southeast Asia's biggest and most advanced outsourcing facilities. If I had to trust my dreams and lifeblood with someone, it would be the smartest, hardest working person I know. You."

She shook her head. "You're crazy."

"There's no one like you, Koreen. Let me make that very clear. I knew a little bit about your background in the industry, but when I found out you were training people as well, it just clicked." Royce stood up slowly, his gaze never leaving her face. "I was going to make you the offer over dinner, under circumstances much better than this."

For the longest time, and she could never really fathom how long, they both stood in the middle of the faculty room, wordlessly sizing each other up.

"I need some time to think about it," she heard herself say, after what seemed like the longest pause. "If that's what you're really asking."

"Yes, it is. Take all the time you need. I'll be around for at least a few months if you want to clarify anything. You have my number, don't you?"

She flushed as she nodded, the meaning behind his seemingly casual question clear. He knew she had been avoiding his calls and messages. Time and distance seemed not to have diminished Royce Duran's ability to get into her head and under her skin.

"I'll have my assistant message you the link to a private folder with the job description and offer. There will be some forms for you to complete, too, once you decide to accept the offer."

"Great." The single word escaped her awkwardly. Somehow, she felt cornered and embarrassed, like a child caught in a blatant lie by a grown-up. He still had the talent for effortlessly one-upping her, even as an adult. "Looking forward to it."

"Thank you."

"You're welcome."

He gave her a smile. "So, what about dinner? Does tomorrow sound good?"

For a moment, she considered refusing his invitation, but she couldn't think of a good enough excuse, considering he had just offered her a job that most people could only dream of. The sooner she had dinner with him, the sooner she could go on with her simple, straightforward, hectic life.

"I have a class at the training center until seven-thirty."

"I'll pick you up after, if you don't mind sending me the location."

"I'll do that."

Before she knew what he was doing, before she could step away, Royce had closed the distance between them. "I promise, no business talk. I'm glad I got that over with today."

He was so close she could have sworn she could hear his heart beating loudly, or maybe it was her own. She wasn't quite sure which, but, at that moment, she was more concerned with catching her own breath.

This was no longer the same Royce Duran from fifteen years ago. This older, stronger, bigger version was decidedly harder to deal with.

But she was still Koreen Cisco, wasn't she? She could always handle him.

She stood straight, lifting her chin until they were eye to eye. "I'll see you tomorrow, then."

His grin caught her off-guard as he echoed her earlier response. "Looking forward to it."

Six

Royce

RECALL

The night was humid, the air thick with a heaviness that settled on his skin as he stood outside the training center. The wind whipped around him, carrying with it the sharp scent of impending rain. It was almost eight in the evening. Across the road, the car from the hotel and its driver idled patiently.

Royce watched as the trainees trickled out after their classes, laughing and talking, discussing weekend plans and job applications. He smiled inwardly when he heard one of them mention that he and a few friends were applying for jobs at the new Boundless Tower.

As the number of students exiting the building began to dwindle, he approached a group of girls.

"Excuse me, ladies, do any of you happen to know Miss Cisco?"

The trio looked him over, eyes wide with curiosity. They nudged each other, giggling, as if to determine which of them had to respond to his question.

Finally, one girl managed to shush the other two, long enough for her to answer. "Yes, she's our trainer. We just finished our class."

"Why are you asking?" another girl chimed in, before she was elbowed.

"I'm waiting for Miss Cisco," he replied smoothly, with what he hoped was a reassuring smile. "I thought perhaps she had forgotten about me."

"She actually dismissed our session five minutes early," said the first girl. "But she asked us to stay behind."

"Wait, are you her boyfriend?" The third girl's eyes were alight with what looked like mischief as she exchanged knowing glances with the others. "We helped her get ready…for your date."

"See?" The second girl looked as if she had just hit the jackpot, her grin almost reaching her ears. "I told you she's got a hot date. Good thing we convinced her to let us do her makeup!"

"Wow," murmured the third girl, eyeing him up and down.

"She should be out soon," said the first girl, her eyes shooting daggers at her companions. Without another word, she grabbed her friends' hands and pulled them away.

A chorus of excited chatter followed the girls as they walked off into the night, disappearing into the shadows as the lights of the building began to go out one by one.

Royce resumed his wait, amused and bemused at his encounter with Koreen's students.

Offering her the job as manager of the Philippine operations of Boundless was a bold move, but she was perfect for it—someone he could trust completely. Her passionate, persistent, determined nature had been a constant ever since they were children. She was the kind of person who put her heart and soul into everything she did.

There was no denying how much he admired her for it. Or admired *her*.

Regardless of what he felt, he hoped she would accept the job. The idea of having her in his life again was a welcome one.

In an almost dreamlike haze, he saw her emerge from the building. Carrying a simple black bag, she was dressed in a shimmery black dress and strappy heels. The dress hugged her body, while her long hair cascaded around her shoulders in soft curls. Her cat-like eyes were even more striking with the makeup she wore; her full lips were painted an enticing, deep shade of red.

His breath caught in his throat; his heart pounded so hard he felt as if he'd been punched, thrown, and kicked all at once.

Fuck.

Desire coursed through him, undeniable and strong in its sudden intensity, leaving him momentarily disoriented.

He could only think of two words.

So beautiful.

She had always been a strikingly attractive girl, but the Koreen who now stood before him, with a somewhat concerned expression on her face, was on another level entirely.

"Duran?" Her voice carried a hint of uncertainty. He probably looked like a big, bumbling idiot. Hell, maybe he was even drooling.

He was grateful there wasn't that much light left for her to see him clearly. He was surprised, to put it mildly, and highly aroused. All he wanted to do was take her in his arms and maybe to his hotel room. In reality, if he tried, she'd probably put him in the hospital with a few well-placed strikes.

Forcing himself to focus, he stepped forward with a smile. "Koreen, you look stunning tonight."

"Thank you." Even the sparse light could not disguise the blush tainting her cheeks.

"Here, let me take your bag." He offered his hand, and she hesitated for just a moment before surrendering it.

Unable to resist, he bent down to kiss her cheek, inhaling the fruity scent of her perfume. He braced himself for a punch or a sharp retort, but it didn't come. Instead, she placed her hand on his shoulder, returning his kiss, her lips warm against his skin.

"Are you ready to go?" It took all of his self-control to keep his voice steady.

She nodded, her thumb grazing his cheek. He realized she was wiping away a trace of her lipstick. "Yes, I am."

He took her hand and, together, they crossed the road to the waiting car.

THE LAST DIVIDE

The car pulled up to the grand entrance of Royce's hotel, its opulent architecture even more dazzling under the warm lights of the building façade.

"This place is incredible," Koreen murmured, her eyes wide as she took in the sights before her. "I could never afford something like this on a teacher's salary."

"Consider it my treat." He smiled at her, feeling a sense of pride in being able to share this luxury.

As they stepped out of the car and made their way to the grand lobby, he noticed the appreciative glances she drew from other guests and staff alike. A feeling akin to pride swelled within him.

She was a rare gem. Strong, smart, and beautiful. No wonder he had found his way back to her, after all these years.

The hotel manager greeted them warmly as they approached the bank of elevators.

"Your table at the poolside restaurant is ready, Mr. Duran," he said, shaking Royce's hand. "We have also prepared a backup option indoors should the weather take a turn for the worse. There are reports of heavy rains and potentially a storm coming later tonight or early morning."

"Thank you," Royce responded. "I just hope the weather wouldn't affect the progress of the Tower's construction too much."

The manager nodded. "Let's hope so, sir. For what it's worth, I'm glad you chose this area to build your project on. We have the least flooding in the city proper. That's why our owners chose to have the hotel here as well. It's one of the safest places to be."

The manager led them out to the poolside restaurant, where the staff whisked them off to a prime table situated close to the water. The subtle glow of the pool lights reflected off Koreen's glimmering dress, giving her an ethereal appearance that made his heart race. He wanted nothing more than to touch her, to make sure she was really there with him.

To make sure that she was the same girl he'd known since they were both four years old.

"Please, have a seat." He pulled out her chair, ignoring the two waiters hovering nearby. He was going to stay as close as he possibly could to her, everyone else be damned. She sat down gracefully, her eyes never leaving his as he took his own seat across from her.

"Would you like something to drink?" he offered, gesturing for their waiter.

She looked at the drinks menu on the table before her, shaking her head a little bit. "I'm not much of a drinker. I don't even go out very often. Too busy."

Her sheepish admittance made him laugh. "Don't worry, I'm much worse. I don't even have time to go out. I only drink socially, outside of Saudi. Sharia Law prohibits alcohol."

They settled on mocktails, a decision that seemed to make her relax visibly.

"I've noticed from your social media that you travel a lot," she said, her cheeks flushing as she realized how that might sound. "I mean, for work, obviously."

He reached across the table to pat her hand reassuringly. "Yes, I do travel quite a bit," he admitted, surprised when she didn't pull away from his touch. "It's part of the job, but it also gives me the chance to experience different cultures and meet new people. And eat a lot of food."

She smiled. "I can see that. If you didn't quit martial arts, you could easily get a job in the WWE."

He grinned right back. "Never too late to consider a career change as a pro wrestler, then?"

She regarded him seriously. "You might last a few good years, give or take, if you get back into training. But that's only my opinion, in case you get bored of the high-flying CEO life."

"Tell me about your work, Koreen," he encouraged, leaning back in his chair and sipping his mocktail. "Kenneth mentioned you're always on the go."

"He did, huh?"

"The kid's quite proud of you. He could only hope to have half of your determination. Hospital residencies are not for the faint of heart."

"He's learning," Koreen relented grudgingly. "But he's still got a long way to go."

"But you've gone all the way and back, haven't you?"

"You mean aside from teaching at the high school, gym, and training center?"

He nodded.

"That's just the bare minimum. I tutor kids in Math on Sundays, and I do one-on-one sessions in Karate whenever I could. Sometimes, I get invitations to teach BPO courses remotely, too."

"It sounds like you genuinely enjoy teaching, don't you?"

She nodded enthusiastically. "I do. It's the idea of helping someone learn something new and amazing that keeps me going. Once they have the knowledge, it can't be taken away."

He watched her entire face glow as she spoke about

teaching. He had never seen someone so passionate and breathtaking, all at the same time.

"My dream is to have my own BPO training center someday," Koreen continued, a touch of wistfulness in her voice. "Maybe one that's subsidized, so kids with less money can afford it and still find work in the industry."

"At Boundless, as its country manager, you would have so much more," Royce said, allowing business to creep into their conversation, unable to help but put his best offer forward. "You could give more people opportunities like that. This is the very reason why we chose Iloilo instead of any other city for our third international operations center. The potential of the local talent is incredibly high and, of course, this place will always be my hometown."

He quickly caught himself and added, raising his hands in mock surrender, "I promise not to mention anything business-related anymore tonight."

"It's okay." She smiled, seemingly relieved. "So, have you visited your old house or seen any of your old friends while you've been here?"

"Actually, my old house has been demolished along with a few others to make way for apartments. But yes, I've managed to catch up with Wesley and Owen over the past week. I'm looking forward to seeing Kenneth and some of the old basketball gang maybe next weekend. He told me he'd asked for a few days off."

Just as they were settling into a comfortable rhythm in their conversation, the waiter arrived to take their order.

Koreen hesitated and glanced at him, clearly uncomfortable with the expensive menu. "Go ahead, pick for me, please."

Royce took over smoothly, ordering starters and mains while telling the waiter they would consider dessert later. As they were left alone again, he felt the time was right to address the earlier moment of honesty between them.

"I meant what I said yesterday," he said quietly, leaning a little closer to see the reaction on her face. "I was telling you the truth."

"What truth?" she replied cautiously, her eyes searching his face.

"That the reason I'm here is to see you." He held on to her gaze as he spoke, to make sure she wouldn't see him falter. "I couldn't come back to Iloilo and not see you. It's been such a long time…and this dinner is long overdue."

Her surprise was unmistakable; she drew back into her chair slightly as she visibly paled at his declaration. He didn't want to make her uncomfortable, but he would rather be honest to someone like Koreen Cisco. She deserved no less.

"The last time we saw each other, we were kids," came her measured response. "We didn't know anything back then."

"Maybe a thing or two," he responded with a smile. "We should give ourselves more credit. Once upon a time, we were unstoppable."

She returned his smile hesitantly. "What do you want, then, Duran? Can I even give it?"

He welcomed such bluntness. It made her special. "Can we start over as adults, become friends? We have too much history to ignore, don't we? We practically grew up together."

"Friends," she echoed, her fingers playing with the edge of the tablecloth, eyes fluttering open and shut as if her thoughts were on rapid fire. "I'd like that. We're too old to try and keep one-upping each other all the time."

"I can't entirely promise the not one-upping each other part," he replied, relieved. "It's become too much of a habit."

A light, almost carefree laugh escaped her lips. He found himself mesmerized by the sound. He reached out across the table and, this time, took her hand in his with a gentle squeeze.

"You should smile and laugh more, Sensei. It makes you even more beautiful."

She blushed and dismissed the compliment with a wave of her free hand. "Come on, Duran. You don't need to flatter me. You know it wouldn't work."

"Trust me, I'm not flattering you. I'm surprised there's no one around to beat the shit out of me when I asked you to join me for dinner."

Her cheeks turned a deeper shade of pink as she shook her head. "I've been single for a long time. I'm too busy. There's no time for a relationship."

"I see." Royce felt an even deeper sense of relief at her words, understanding only too well the challenge of balancing one's professional and personal lives. "I can relate. I suppose we have chosen our paths, haven't we?"

The meaning between them was not lost, as they stared at each other across the table, the already humid air thickening with tension. Before either could say anything more, their exchange was interrupted by the arrival of their food. The waiter set plates filled with colorful dishes in front of them, the mouthwatering scents wafting through the sharp evening air.

"Thank you," he said to the waiter, who nodded and

retreated discreetly. Turning back to Koreen, he gestured to the feast before them. "Please go ahead and begin, Sensei."

She nodded and smiled in return, letting his hand go to pick up her fork, but not without giving it a squeeze first, making his breath catch again.

Even as they began to eat, he couldn't deny the almost palpable electric current running between them, a spark re-ignited from a childhood rivalry forged years ago, now transformed into something else entirely.

Seven

Koreen

REMNANT

She sipped the last few drops of her coffee, taking in the sight of him.

All evening long, Royce had been relaxed and attentive, and so effortlessly funny. She had never really seen him that way before. Then again, she had never really spent any time with him before, not like tonight.

He was only supposed to be someone from her past; a boy who'd been a constant presence in a childhood long gone, now a man of power and wealth meant to be a distant, glittering presence on her social media feed. He wasn't supposed to be seated from across her, much less touching her hand as if they had been friends for years.

The way he looked at her, however, was a different matter.

Under his gaze, Koreen felt both self-conscious and wanted, vulnerable and powerful.

"Are you ready to head home?" He put down his own cup on the table and gestured for the waiter to take the bill folder.

Around them, the restaurant was already empty, with the staff beginning to set up the tables for breakfast the following day. She was glad it hadn't rained that evening, despite the pronounced humidity in the air and occasional streaks of lightning on the evening sky.

She watched as Royce took his infinite black credit card and replaced it in his wallet. She'd seen how much their bill was minutes ago; it had been eye-wateringly exorbitant. The tip Royce had added on was almost as much as their bill, but she knew better than to comment.

Instead, she focused on the warmth of the rich black coffee settling in her stomach; on the smile of the handsome, expensively dressed man with her. She could allow herself to pretend for a few more minutes, couldn't she? Pretend that she belonged in his world.

Before she could answer his question, the restaurant staff began to gather around their table, approaching Royce with smiles and murmured words of gratitude, most of them speaking on behalf of loved ones who had gotten jobs at Boundless Tower. The restaurant manager came over, too, and profusely apologized for the interruption, but Royce waved it off.

"It's okay, Joey. I'm happy to hear so many people have found jobs with Boundless. That's exactly the reason why we decided to set up our operations here."

She watched the exchange, both impressed and touched by the genuine respect and admiration the staff held for Royce. As the employees dispersed, leaving them alone once more, she finally found her voice.

"No," she said, surprising even herself. "I don't want to go home yet. I want to go dancing in the club."

I don't want this night with you to end, she wanted to add. *Not yet.*

Royce raised an eyebrow, clearly surprised at her declaration. "Dancing, huh? We've never done any dancing in the past, have we?"

She shook her head. "You're not too old to try and find out who's better on the dance floor, are you, Mr. Duran?"

The challenge in her words was unmistakable. Oh, she still knew how to bait him.

His eyes widened in surprise, but he quickly recovered, a playful smirk tugging at the corner of his lips as he shook his head.

"I knew you're not the kind of man to back down," she teased.

"Very well, Miss Cisco." Royce stood up, offering her his arm. "Then what are we waiting for?"

The hotel club was a different world compared to the serene poolside restaurant. It pulsed with vibrant lights and thumping beats, the sheer energy of the place a welcome rush to Koreen's senses.

Royce guided her through the crowd of dancing bodies with a confident hand on her back, his body brushing against hers as they walked towards the bar. His warmth and the protective—almost possessive—way he moved made her giddy.

"Two glasses of red wine, please," he told the bartender, turning to her with a grin. "We'll need some liquid courage before hitting the dance floor. Or would you prefer something stronger?"

She shook her head and accepted the glass he handed her. "I didn't take you for the shy type, Duran."

"Trust me, I'm not," he replied, raising his glass in a toast. "To us."

She didn't question his meaning; instead, she settled onto the stool next to him, allowing her body to relax against the wooden countertop as she savored his warmth next to her.

As they sipped their wine, they reminisced about their shared childhood, laughing over stories of their intense rivalry at school, and how they had always tried to outdo the other in science fairs and quiz bees.

She was only too aware that, as the conversation went on, he began to touch her more casually, his hand brushing her arm or resting on the small of her back as he leaned in to speak. Each contact sent a thrill through her, making her heart race faster than she'd like to admit.

She began to relax into his touch and his presence, almost leaning against him by the time they finished their drinks. He welcomed it, seemingly, sliding his arm around her waist to hold her up and keep her close at the same time.

"You've been talking a big game all night, Mr. CEO," she said against his shoulder, feeling the world around her sway slightly. "Time to put your money where your mouth is. Let's dance."

"Challenge accepted, Sensei." The smile on his face was almost a sneer as he took her hand and led her onto the dance floor.

The music was fast, but he held her close, his hands firm on her waist. They swayed together, their bodies pressed tightly against one another as they tried to keep up with the beat.

"Sorry," Royce murmured in her ear. "I'm not much of a dancer. This is one thing I'm going to concede with no regrets."

Koreen laughed. "I can't dance to save my life, either. Give me all the hardest forms sequence of any martial art, any day."

"Nobody can beat you at any kata," he agreed with a grin, his arms around her tightening. "Not even me."

As the music pulsed around them, people swaying and twisting to the beat, he pulled her even closer, pressing their bodies together she could almost feel his body heat seeping into her, weaving its way through the barrier of their clothing. His cool, citrusy cologne, mixed with the light musky scent of his sweat, was intoxicating to her already overwhelmed senses.

She couldn't bring herself to deny that there was an electrifying connection between them, a magnetic pull she couldn't quite resist.

So she gave in, her hands settling on his chest, fingers digging into the fabric of his shirt, as she leaned against him and welcomed the thrum of his heartbeat against her ear. She sighed as she swayed against him, aware but not caring that their movements were out of sync with the rapid tempo of the music.

"Hey, are you okay?" He drew back and lifted her chin with a gentle hand. He looked sheepish and slightly uncertain, as if he didn't know what to say or do next. The change from his usual confident demeanor was surprisingly endearing.

"Must be the wine," she replied lightly, trying to deflect her attraction onto something external. "So much for liquid courage."

They shared a moment of laughter, the tension between them disappearing for a few seconds. But the moment of levity was gone as quickly as it had come, replaced by a surge of desire that ignited every fiber of her body.

"Maybe we didn't need it," Royce said softly, his thumb tracing her lower lip, before his arms reached around her to pull her back in. "Maybe we had it in us all along."

Before she knew it, their lips met in a tentative, exploratory kiss. Koreen found herself surrendering to the passion that had been simmering beneath the surface all evening. The kiss deepened, growing more urgent and intense as she allowed herself to get lost in his arms.

She registered the fact that he'd lifted her off the floor, so smoothly and effortlessly. She marveled at his strength, even as her body instinctively responded to his touch.

"Can we go?" she gasped when they finally broke apart, her breath coming in short, uneven pants.

"Of course." His voice was strained and tight as he set her down gently, his hands lingering on her waist and venturing downward to trace the curve of her hips, as if he couldn't let her go completely.

Their eyes met, locking wordlessly. Her hand slipped into his, so naturally it felt like he'd always been meant to hold it. He brought her fingers to his lips and pressed a brief kiss to her knuckles.

With a nod from her, they turned to leave the dance floor, pausing only to grab her bag from the bar. Royce's grip was warm and firm was they walked out of the club.

Her steps were slightly unsteady from the mix of alcohol and raw emotion coursing through her. She clung to him as he guided her to the elevators.

It was only when they were inside that she noticed that they were going up, not down towards the lobby.

He was taking her to his room.

Her heart pounded as they stepped out of the elevator and into the dimly lit hallway. She hesitated, swallowing hard as she let his hand go. "I know where we're going."

He paused mid-step and turned to face her, his eyes searching his face. "Hey, if you don't want this, it's okay. I'll take you home right now. I thought…well, I thought you wanted this as much as I do."

She stared in shock at his confession, her pulse quickening even more. "Is that why you asked me out? Because you wanted me?"

"Yes," he admitted without hesitation. "You're the reason I came back to town, the reason I wanted to build Boundless Tower here in Iloilo."

"What are you talking about, Duran?" The words escaped her even as her mind tried to process his previous answer.

"I've always admired your brilliance, Koreen." His voice was soft, tinged with what sounded like sadness and self-doubt. "I wanted to be someone worthy of you, when the time came that I could finally be with you."

"Be with…me?" The idea sent her reeling; it was a surprise that she was still on her feet, steady enough to remain standing.

He nodded. "I was hoping you'll give me a chance, but I'll understand if you don't want to. I'm sorry if I crossed any lines."

"You want to be with me? Is that what you're saying?"

His broad shoulders heaved in a sigh. "I'm surprised you haven't realized this."

She stood there, rooted to the spot, her world shifting beneath her feet. The intensity of his gaze made her feel exposed.

"I never knew." Her voice trembled as her mind struggled to up. "Why didn't you tell me before?"

He looked away for a moment, as if gathering his thoughts, before meeting her gaze once more. "I did, with that flower I gave you years ago. I needed you to understand that I've always wanted to be with you, no matter what you felt for me."

The memory of that single anemone surfaced in her mind; the petals wilting until she couldn't hold on to them any longer. As the flower fell apart, so did she. She could still remember the sleepless nights she'd cried over Royce Duran, cried over losing her chance at telling him how much he really meant to her.

Fifteen years later, the same person stood before her and, yet, she could only see her own uncertainties.

He spoke softly, his face unreadable in the sparse light of the corridor. "It took me weeks to find that single anemone, but I never gave up because I wanted you to have something special. If you'd asked me to stay back then, I probably would have found a way. You meant that much to me."

Tears began to fill her eyes, blurring her vision as she struggled to comprehend the enormity of what he was saying.

Royce wasn't finished, his voice becoming more unsteady as he went on. "When I left my belt with you all those years ago…it meant I left part of myself with you, too. I'd never be whole again until I was back with you. I wanted to tell you before I left, Koreen. Believe me, I did my best."

A strangled sob escaped her throat. "You're crazy! You're fucking crazy, and this doesn't make any sense."

His face contorted with exasperation, his hands balling into fists at his sides. "What the hell do you want me to say? How the fuck can I make you understand?"

"I don't know!" she cried, wiping angrily at her eyes. "I just—I have to go. I'll get a taxi."

She turned on her heel and sprinted down the hallway. She could feel his eyes on her as she fled to the elevators.

"Koreen, wait!" Royce called out, but she refused to look back.

As the elevator doors closed behind her, she leaned against the cold steel wall, her legs trembling beneath her as sobs racked her body.

But she refused to fall.

She stumbled into the hotel lobby, her heart sinking as she

spied the heavy rain pouring outside, clearly visible through the windows and the glass doors of the main entrance.

Koreen blinked away tears and readjusted her bag on her shoulder, trying to regain her composure while approaching the front desk. A young woman with wire-rimmed glasses was manning reception at the late hour, tapping away at her computer.

"Excuse me, miss," she said in the clearest, strongest voice she could muster. "Could you please call me a taxi? I need to go home."

The receptionist looked up at her and glanced out the floor-to-ceiling windows of the lobby, concern furrowing her brow. "I'm afraid it might be difficult to find a taxi at this hour with the weather being so bad, ma'am. If you're willing to wait, I'll do my best."

Koreen nodded, then ventured further, remembering the sleek vehicle that had picked her up from the training center earlier. "What about the hire cars?"

She could only imagine how much they would cost, but, in her desperation, money was the least of her worries.

"They're based offsite, but I can try and get one for you in the morning as soon as their office opens."

A quick glance at the digital clock on the wall indicated it was almost midnight. Koreen sighed resignedly, forcing herself to bear up. "That's fine. I'll take whatever's available first."

"You came in with Mr. Duran, didn't you? Would you like for me to call his room, let him know you're down here?" The receptionist's gaze was mostly sympathetic, but there was a touch of curiosity in them as she mentioned Royce's name.

Koreen shook her head. "It's fine. I don't want to bother him. I'd be happy to wait right here."

"Of course, ma'am. Please let me know if you need anything. I'll try and make some calls for your taxi."

"Thank you." She turned away from the front desk and looked around the warm lobby, trying to figure out the best place to settle in for the night. With the way the rain pelted against the glass and the wind howled outside the thick walls of the hotel, the storm had made landfall in the time frame predicted.

She pulled out her phone from her bag, wincing when she saw there was no signal from her mobile network. The strong winds had probably knocked out the nearby tower.

She spotted a small balcony overlooking the city, sheltered from the rain by a tile roof, and decided to try and get a signal from a better vantage point.

She stepped outside, feeling stray droplets of rain land on her arms and feet, soaking through her dress and shoes. No luck. The service bars on the screen remained hidden.

Koreen was about to return to the dry, welcoming lobby when Royce appeared beside her on the balcony.

The concern she saw in his eyes sent a sharp, stabbing sensation right through her chest. The last time she felt something close to it was at the football field all those years ago, when he'd asked her to let him know about her decision to compete in the nationals.

With Royce's departure from Iloilo, followed a few months later by her father's death, she'd withdrawn from the nationals and quit Karate. She'd then joined another club and tried to learn Sanda, another martial art. If not for Shihan Tuazon and his wife, who had visited her at home to offer her a part-time teaching job, she would never have returned to Karate.

"Please don't send me away, Koreen."

She could hear the defeat in his voice, as present-day Royce took a few tentative steps closer.

"I won't," she replied, her voice coming out hoarsely, from the cold and the stinging remnants of her tears. "I just want to leave. I'm tired."

"Fine, you can go whenever you want. I won't hold you back." He stepped directly into her line of sight, oblivious to the rain falling on his clothes and hair. "If you could just be honest with me about one thing, I'll leave you alone. I won't bother you again."

Curiosity mingled with her exhaustion as she looked up into his unyielding eyes, inwardly telling herself that she could survive this moment, survive this night. "What is it?"

"Can you remember what you did with that flower I gave you? Did you throw it away? Please tell me."

Memories of the delicate anemone and the hidden emotions it represented flooded her mind. She opened her mouth to answer, but no words came out.

Royce sighed, his shoulders slumping as he accepted her silence as an answer.

"Of course you threw it away," he said quietly. "What else would you do, right?"

She looked away, unable to look at the pain clearly etched on his face. She felt the same pain inside, multiplied by a hundred. She was familiar with it; she felt it every single time she looked at their photo on the shelf.

"Look," he continued, taking a step back and glancing towards the interior of the hotel, "if you want to stay here tonight, I'll pay for a room for you. In the morning, I'll arrange for a car to take you home. It's the least I can do after all the trouble."

He paused, as if waiting for her reaction. After a few seconds without a response from her, he went on, in a much softer voice, "Goodbye, Koreen. I'm glad I got to see you again."

With that, he turned away from her and began to make his way back into the lobby.

"Royce."

His name escaped her lips, the sound almost foreign to her ears. She'd never called him by his first name before.

Only now. Because now was all she had.

"Wait," she called out, her voice cracking with emotion in that single word.

He heard her. She could see the tension in his back as he stopped just outside the balcony door.

Tears filled her eyes as the past bubbled and burst its way to the surface of her heart. "I never threw the flower away. I held it every night until it fell apart, and I kept the petals… with your belt. They were my memories of you. The only ones I could hold."

Her words hung heavy in the air between them. Time seemed to slow, too, as the years and the rain-drenched world faded away and she could see only him, right there in front of her.

Slowly, he turned to face her once more.

"Say my name again. Please."

She knew, then, that everything had changed.

"Royce," she repeated.

Without another thought, she rushed towards him,

her heels echoing loudly against the rain-slicked tiles of the balcony.

She threw herself into his embrace, seeking solace in the strength she'd always admired. He caught her effortlessly.

"Royce," she said once more, before her lips crashed against his, with a desperate passion that put the raging storm to shame.

Eight

Royce

REVELATION

THE FORCE OF HER CONFESSION HIT HIM LIKE A tidal wave.

She'd kept it.

All these years, she'd kept it with her.

Disbelief washed over him as his world tilted on its axis, leaving him breathless.

"Koreen."

Her name was swallowed by the rain, the howling wind.

It didn't matter.

Instead, he asked her to repeat his.

So she did.

The sound fell on his ears like a gentle caress. He had never been 'Royce' to her. He'd only ever been 'Duran.'

Before he could even comprehend what was happening, she sprinted across the balcony, her hair whipping wildly. She hurled herself into his arms, and suddenly, everything felt right.

Royce could scarcely feel his own muscles as they instinctively moved to catch her. She fit into his arms perfectly, as though he was always meant to hold her, protect her, *love* her.

She said his name again, both a plea and a command, and he obliged. Their lips met and they were kissing hungrily, years of pent-up emotion crammed into a single act.

Her body trembled against his as she clung to him tightly. She pulled back to speak, her breath warm against his cheek, in a broken whisper. "I never knew. I never understood…I thought I'd never see you or touch you again."

Her sobs tore at his heart, and for the first time, he saw her vulnerability beneath the fierce exterior. A wisp of a woman, heartbreakingly beautiful, smart, and strong, held together by the sheer force of her own will.

He could feel the urgency in her grasp, the longing in her voice. This was the first time he had seen her lose control. He pulled her closer; she could fall apart and he would be with her every step of the way.

"I'm here, Koreen," he murmured into her hair. "I'll never leave you again."

"This is real, isn't it?" she sobbed against his shoulder, her tears soaking through the material of his shirt.

"More real than anything I've ever known," he replied, his lips brushing against her forehead tenderly.

"This isn't even possible…" she breathed.

He could feel her trembling in his embrace, so he lifted her off the ground, unwilling to let her slip away from him again. "Do you want me to kiss you again, like in the club? Just to make sure this is all real?"

She nodded slowly, her eyes never leaving his face. "Yes."

His heart skipped a beat at her agreement. He'd fantasized about this moment for years. And now, here she was, their lips just inches apart. He leaned in, their mouths meeting in a fiery kiss that stole the air from his lungs.

He felt her arms wrap tightly around his neck, her legs encircling his hips, closing the space between them. Through her tears and their veil of raindrops, she kissed him back with reckless abandon.

He slid his tongue into her mouth, tasting her sweetness—a flavor he had never imagined possible. As their tongues danced together, he tightened his hold on her, his hands tangling in her hair.

She welcomed his touch, her hands fisting in his shirt. The kiss was raw and powerful, untamed and unrestrained.

As they parted, breathless and panting, he realized this was what he had been missing; the taste of her on his tongue, the feel of her softness against his hardness.

"Do you still want me?" Her question was tentative, her voice quivering with the cold and something else, something undeniable that bound them to each other.

"More than anything." His answer, in contrast, left no room for doubt or argument. "I've always wanted you. Ever since we were children, ever since I understood what a boy could feel for a girl."

Her eyes widened. "But I thought you never saw me as a girl, only as someone who just one-upped you at every turn."

He laughed, planting tender kisses along her jawline. "You're the most beautiful woman in the world to me, Koreen. I've seen so many people, but none of them could ever compare to you. Nobody could ever outshine you."

As they kissed again, Royce felt her body rubbing against him passionately. He was already painfully aroused, and he couldn't keep his distance any longer. His body burned for hers. "Would it be okay if you stayed with me, Koreen? Just… be with me."

She nodded eagerly, her eyes glistening as she reached up to touch his cheek. "I want to be with you, too. More than anything."

He smiled at the way she echoed his earlier admission and carefully set her back down on the rain-soaked balcony, straightening their disheveled clothes before placing a protective arm around her.

He led her across the lobby and to the front desk. The receptionist looked up as they approached, an apologetic smile on her face.

"I'm really sorry, ma'am," she said to Koreen. "I tried calling a taxi for you, but none of them could get through the city. It's starting to flood outside."

"Miss Cisco won't be needing the taxi after all, Stephanie," Royce said. "She'll be staying the night as my guest."

The receptionist nodded. "Very well, Mr. Duran. I'll make a note on your booking."

"Could you please call Mrs. Cisco and let her know that her daughter will be spending the night at the hotel? It's best for her safety. I'll ensure everything is taken care of."

"Of course, sir. Can I have Mrs. Cisco's number?"

Koreen hesitated only briefly before providing her mother's

number. As they left the reception area, they found themselves hidden from sight, waiting for the elevator. The momentary privacy provided them with an opportunity to resume their passionate kissing.

His hands cupped her face as he whispered between kisses, "Do you want this, Koreen? I could always book a separate room for you if you'd rather."

Shaking her head, she touched his face again, her fingers tracing the contours of his lips.

"No," she said, almost shyly, a pink flush staining her cheeks. "I want to be with you. And...I've always wanted this."

A warm smile spread across his face as they stepped into the elevator. He kept her close to him and pressed soft kisses to her hair, never letting her go as they ascended to the penthouse.

Once they were in the hallway, he swept her off her feet and into his arms as they made their way to his suite. Fumbling slightly with the key card, he was rewarded by the sound of her giggles and the sensation of her lips brushing against his jaw and neck.

"I really like you with a beard," she murmured, her breath warm against his skin. "You look like a very rich sheikh or something."

He chuckled at her comment, finally managing to unlock the door and step inside. He immediately switched on the 'Do Not Disturb' sign before carrying her to the bedroom and gently laying her down on the bed.

"I'm done controlling myself around you, Koreen."

He didn't know if it was meant to be a precaution or a promise, but it was the truth. She needed to hear it.

"I don't want to hold back anymore either," she replied

softly, her fingers playing with the hem of his shirt. "We've already wasted so much time."

He reached out to caress her face. "I agree. Let's not waste any more."

He lowered his lips to hers, initiating a tender kiss that quickly grew more passionate. His hands moved down her body, deftly unzipping her dress and sliding it off her shoulders and arms. The shimmering fabric pooled around her waist, revealing a black strapless bra.

"You're so beautiful, Sensei," he whispered against her skin as he trailed kisses down her neck, nibbling at the soft flesh.

The scent of her perfume and the sweet taste of her skin reminded him of strawberries. He could feel her pulse quickening beneath his lips.

He reached behind her and unclasped her bra, pulling it away to reveal full, round breasts. He stared at them in wonder, unable to believe that someone so petite could have such perfect proportions. His fingers traced the curve of her breasts before his mouth followed suit, licking and sucking at her nipples until they were pebble-hard.

As he continued to worship her breasts with his mouth, his hand snaked its way down her body and between her legs. To his delight, she was wet and ready through her panties. Using the pad of his thumb, he began to rub her in slow circles, matching the rhythm of his mouth on her nipples. Her moans grew louder, her fingers digging into his back as she writhed beneath him.

"Tell me," he whispered, drawing back for a moment. "Have you always been mine?"

"I've always wanted to be yours," she replied, her eyes

dark pools of desire in the dim light of the room. "But there were…others."

"Others?" he echoed, reaching around the cover of her damp underwear and sliding a finger into her slit, eliciting a squeal.

"Other men," she gasped out. "Two…a long time ago."

"Tell me about them," he urged gently, inserting another finger into her and increasing the tempo of his ministrations on her nipples.

Panting, she ground against his hand as she spoke, her breasts bouncing on his face. "One was a PE teacher I met at a tournament. We broke up after six months…and he left town. The other was a Korean Taekwondo instructor…he was a fling during a martial arts conference in Manila. This was…oh…years ago."

White-hot jealousy coursed through him at the idea of those unknown men seeing her naked, touching her, *having her*. A low, almost angry growl escaped his throat as he increased the pace of his fingers inside her. "Did either of them ever make you feel like this?"

"No, never like this," she managed, her body tensing. Her hips lifted off the bed, as if reaching for something more.

"Are you sure?" he asked softly, sliding up to give her a feather-light kiss on the lips. He slid his other arm under her and raised her torso off the pillows. "What about this?"

Without warning, he slid his tongue into her mouth, just as he redoubled his efforts between her legs.

The feeling of her draped over his arm was almost too much. Her long hair, soft and damp, tickled his skin. Her bare breasts were crushed against his chest. Her mouth was hot, her core even hotter. There was nothing more he wanted to do than tear off her dress and take her.

But he'd waited fifteen years; he could wait fifteen seconds more.

Koreen was moaning incoherently against him, into his mouth, clutching his arms for dear life.

He knew she was almost there, at the very edge. He slowed the pace of his fingers, causing her to groan in protest. He slanted his lips against hers before he spoke again. "And what about this, Koreen?"

He'd had his fair share of women, but he'd never felt the need for affirmation as he did with her now. He should have been her first, he thought with a twinge of regret and self-loathing. They should have been each other's first—and last.

She was panting, both in urgency and frustration, but he knew her pride would keep her talking.

"Only you, Royce," she whispered into his neck. "Only you."

Satisfaction coursed through him at her admission. "Good. Now let's begin."

He pulled the last of Koreen's dress away and slowly rolled her panties down her legs, kissing the path of the silken fabric as it brushed against her skin. She squirmed as he did; he wasn't sure if she was ticklish or highly aroused. He would like it very much if she were both.

With Koreen now completely naked before him, he wrapped his arms around her and kissed her soundly.

"My queen," he said against her lips. "You're mine now. You'll only ever be mine."

"Always yours, Royce," she whispered, her breath sweet and warm on his cheek.

He kissed her deeply once more before settling her back down on the pillows.

"Now, open wide for me," he commanded, his voice hoarse with need.

With her eyes never leaving his, she obediently spread her legs, revealing the glistening curls at the apex of her thighs.

"Wider," he said, and she complied, baring herself completely to him.

The sight of her like this—open, waiting, wanting—was almost too much for him. He wanted to do nothing else but devour her, every sweet inch of her, but he knew he needed to take his time.

He lowered himself between her legs, bringing his hungry mouth to her sensitive flesh. He began slowly, teasing her with his lips and tongue, making her buck beneath him.

"Royce," she whimpered, her hands gripping the sheets.

"Tell me what you want, Koreen," he murmured, his mouth an inch away from her wet, heated core. The sound of his name on her lips made his pants feel tighter. He was now very, very hard.

"Your mouth, your tongue…all of it," she panted, grinding against his mouth as if there was no tomorrow.

"Can you take it?"

"I…"

Before she could answer, he began to increase his pace. He explored every inch of her, using his hands, lips, and tongue. Her moans grew louder as he brought her closer and closer to release.

"I can't… I'm going to…" she gasped, her legs trembling on his shoulders as her hips ground against his mouth. With her head lolling back and her hair spread on his pillow, her lips parted and her face tight as she sought her own pleasure, he'd never seen anything more beautifully erotic.

"Let go, Koreen," he urged, his fingers digging into her thighs as he lapped at her like a starving man. "Give yourself to me."

With a strangled cry, she shattered in his arms, her body shaking with the force of her climax. He drank her in greedily, savoring every last drop.

As he waited for her to come down from the high of her orgasm, he slid up next to her and cradled her in arms, pressing gentle kisses to her hair and cheeks. He could still taste her on his lips, making it difficult for him to think about anything else other than how much he wanted to be inside her.

He didn't have to wait very long.

As soon as she got her bearings and breath back, Koreen grabbed him by the collar, pressing her naked body against his own fully clothed one.

"Kiss me," she demanded, her eyes gleaming in the dim lamplight.

He obliged, his lips capturing hers in a searing kiss. As they broke apart, she shifted her position in a perfectly executed mount, straddling him and grinding her heat against his rock-hard arousal.

"My turn." Her voice was soft, but her fingers were steady and urgent as she began to unbutton his shirt. Once his chest was exposed, she dove in, licking and nibbling at his pecs and nipples.

"Fuck, Koreen…" His fingers tangled in her hair as a groan escaped his throat. The sensation of her warm mouth and teeth on his flesh was maddening.

"Be a good boy, Duran," she murmured against his chest. "You need to warm up properly."

He wasn't warm; he was on fire. He gritted his teeth as her hands wandered south, from his chest to his stomach.

She unbuckled his belt slowly and slithered her way down until she was between his legs. "Have you ever imagined me doing this to you?"

"Fuck, yeah," he bit out, his body tensing in anticipation.

She slid his slacks and underwear just low enough to free his arousal from its confines. She raised an eyebrow at the sight of him. "And what about this?"

The way she'd asked the same question as he had earlier only served to make him even harder. She took his cock in her hands and brought it to her lips, her tongue swirling at the tip as she cupped his balls and squeezed delicately.

"God, yes," he gasped, unable to contain himself as his hips bucked in response. "All the time."

"Really?"

Before he could utter a coherent answer, she took him into her mouth, sliding the whole of him in and out between her lips.

"Fuck, Koreen…" He had no words except for these two, as pleasure built rapidly from within him.

She knew exactly what she was doing, and she was doing it so damn well. He held on to her hair as her mouth increased its pace; silken locks fell around her face and brushed against his skin, compounding the assault on his senses.

Before Royce knew it, he was tipping over the edge, his body wracked with an intense climax. With a muffled moan, she swallowed every last drop from him, her eyes meeting his with challenge and satisfaction. He watched hazily as she got up and pulled off his pants and socks.

"My queen," he called out, his voice hoarse in the aftermath of his explosive orgasm.

She smiled, her tongue flicking out to lick her bottom lip as she went on her hands and knees. This was the first time he fully understood what the phrase 'the cat that swallowed the canary' meant. "Yes?"

"Come here," he rasped, holding out his arms.

She crawled to him until she was splayed over his much larger frame like a blanket, the weight of her settling across him deliciously. The sight of her full breasts in front of his face was enough to make him go hard again.

"I like this. You're like a very hot beanbag, literally and figuratively. With a beard." She giggled, her tongue flicking out to trace the facial hair on his jawline.

"I like this, too."

She nuzzled his neck. "Can I ask you something?"

"Anything," he replied, his hands exploring her back, lowering to cup her toned backside.

"Are you...really single? Do you have a girlfriend? A fiancée? A wife waiting for you back in Saudi?"

He laughed. "No, I don't have any of those. I had a girlfriend in college, but it barely lasted a year. My only serious relationship was about seven years ago; she was a Serbian air hostess. We started out great, but she wanted a rich man to fund her lifestyle...and I've only ever wanted one person all along. Apparently, she's now the second wife of some Bahraini financier." He shook his head slightly at the memory of Yulia, glamorous and demanding, who could never seem to quash the memory of the woman now in his arms. "Since then, I haven't had any relationships. My schedule barely gives me any free time."

"And this one person you wanted all along…?"

"She's with me now. Right here."

He heard her take a deep breath against his shoulder. He tightened his arms around her in response.

"No one could really quite live up to you, even when you're so far away." Her voice was almost swallowed by the muffled sound of rain. "I always end up comparing every guy with you…and no one even comes close."

The honesty he had always admired now tugged at his heartstrings, refusing to let go. "I guess that settles it, then."

"Settles what?"

"That you've always been mine, Koreen."

She brushed her lips against his in a feather-light kiss. "I guess there's only one thing left to do, then."

"What's that?"

"Isn't it obvious?" Her voice lowered to a sultry whisper. "You should take what's always been yours."

He immediately understood what she wanted, what she needed. He kissed her back before flipping her over, pinning her beneath him.

He'd never been this aroused in his life, never felt such a primal, insatiable need for another person before. It was all-consuming, and he knew he would never be sated.

"I should, shouldn't I?"

She nodded, her eyes never leaving his.

He pinned her arms above her head, lacing their fingers together as he slid his length along her slick folds. Their eyes locked, and he could see his raw hunger mirrored in her eyes as he began to push inside her. She gasped, her teeth sinking into his shoulder, her grip on his hands tightening until he thought his bones might break.

"Mine," he said into her hair, filling her completely in one thrust. Her mouth met his passionately, tongues tangling, as he started to move inside her, his hips snapping against hers with a force that made the bed creak beneath them.

She met each of his thrusts with equal fervor. The sounds of their moans and heavy breathing filled the room, punctuated by the distant rumble of thunder outside.

"Royce," she gasped, her back arching. "Don't stop… please, don't ever fucking stop."

He couldn't have stopped even if he'd wanted to, not with his name on her lips like that. The world seemed to narrow down to just the two of them, their bodies locked together in a dance of desire.

"Koreen," he groaned, feeling his own climax building like a storm within him. He could no longer hold back, and with one final thrust, he came with a shuddering cry, collapsing on top of her.

For several moments, they lay there, panting, his heart pounding loudly against hers. Their lips met, and he kissed her feverishly.

"Again," he murmured, feeling the fire within him reignite with alarming speed.

"Yes."

That was the only thing he needed to hear. He lifted her legs, folding her knees to her chest as he slid into her again, the new angle eliciting a whimper of delight and surprise. They moved together in perfect harmony, until they were both trembling from an earth-shattering release once more.

He took her from behind next, as he stood by the edge

of the bed, his thrusts going deeply into her as she went up on her hands and knees, her backside his for the taking. The sight of himself driving into her butt almost made him pass out from the pleasure that followed.

But they weren't done—not even close.

She pushed him back onto the bed and straddled him with a wicked grin. She moved with the confidence of a goddess, her hips undulating and bouncing in perfectly timed movements that drove him to the brink of insanity. He fondled her breasts and tweaked her clit, coaxing wave after wave of pleasure from her body, and she finally gave in, taking him to the peak with her.

With a cry that seemingly echoed throughout the hotel, she finally collapsed on top of him, whimpering and shaking.

"Always mine," he said as he pulled her close, not even sure if she heard him.

"Yours, Royce," she answered shakily, her eyes fluttering shut as she curled into his body as if she had always belonged there.

Entwined in each other's arms, they both drifted off to sleep.

Habit made him open his eyes even before first light. His body had learned to adjust to his routine, and he demanded nothing less from it.

The lights flickering outside the bedroom window showed it was still dark. The heavy rain displayed no signs of abating; the sound now an almost soothing staccato he was getting accustomed to.

The dim orange lamplight cast a gentle glow on Koreen's face as she slept in his arms. The sheer sight took Royce aback. He watched her with wonder, unable to shake off the feeling that this was all just a dream and any moment he would wake up alone. But as her chest rose and fell with each breath, he knew that this was real—she was right there, and she was his.

As if sensing his gaze, she stirred, her eyes slowly drifting open. She looked up at him with a sleepy smile.

"Hi." He smiled back and kissed her on the forehead, inhaling her light strawberry-like scent, now mingled with their night of passion.

"Hi." Her voice was husky as she reached up to trace her fingertips along his jawline.

His body responded to her touch, desire already stirring within him.

"Shower?" he suggested.

"Yes, please."

With a grin, he scooped her up into his arms and carried her to the bathroom. As water cascaded over their bodies, they couldn't keep their hands off each other, fingers exploring every inch of bare skin they could touch.

She pressed herself against him, her breasts rubbing against his chest as she reached up to pull him into a kiss. Their mouths moved together hungrily as the water streamed down around them.

Unable to wait a second more, he picked her up, her legs wrapping around his waist as he pushed himself inside her, their lovemaking taking on a new urgency beneath the spray of the shower.

Later, still damp and flushed, they tumbled onto the

plush carpet of the living area, the full-length windows offering a view of the dark, stormy skyline of the city.

He laid down on the floor and pulled her to him, whispering a request in her ear that made her laugh and blush. She relented without hesitation and, before long, she was on top of him, her wondrous mouth moving up and down his length, as he licked, sucked and fingered her from a new, tantalizing vantage point.

She wanted something, too, but it was more of a demand. She pushed him down onto the plush beige couch and guided his length inside her once more. It was a different angle; her breasts pushed against his face, her clit rubbing against his pelvis.

In a pleasure-induced high, he watched her ride him with wild abandon, his hands reaching up to cup her breasts and thumb her nipples. The sensations were overwhelming, pleasure building within him like a tidal wave.

"Move with me, Royce," she panted. "I can't get enough of you."

"Neither can I," he admitted, his hands gripping her hips as he thrust up into her, their bodies meeting and, finally, coming together.

Once he got feeling back in his legs, he carried her to the bed and slid in next to her, pulling the thick comforter over their exhausted bodies.

But Koreen Cisco always knew how to one-up everything. As they lay there, spooned together, she shifted, grinding her backside against him. He heard a groan of desire escape his lips in response to her invitation.

He reached around to finger her soaked core once more. Once she was ready, he entered her from behind, lifting her leg to allow himself deeper access, and began to caress her clit as they moved together.

The pleasure they reached left them both breathless and, for the time being, spent. As she succumbed to sleep, her soft snores filling the room, Royce held her tightly, his fingers combing through her hair, his lips raining kisses on her skin, even as he felt sleep claim him, too.

His last thought was that, yes, she'd always belonged with him.

Nine

Koreen

RESONANCE

She stirred from her slumber, heavy warmth enveloping her like a blanket. As the haze of sleep lifted, she realized it was Royce's arms around her, his snores somehow a rhythmic, comforting sound to her ears.

In the thin morning light that seeped through the slightly open electronic blinds, Koreen took in the sight of the man who held her so tenderly—his short dark hair, chiseled jawline covered with a hint of beard, and his muscular frame that was equally intimidating and reassuring.

The rain and wind still raged outside, but nothing could

dampen the heat that fluttered in her chest as memories of the previous night surfaced. It had been incredible, so much better than anything she'd ever dared imagine; his body entwined with hers, his desire for and power over her overwhelming. She felt a blush creep up her cheeks as arousal stirred within her at the thought of all the delicious things they did to each other.

As she traced her fingers lightly over the contours of his face, now sharpened and hardened by time, she realized this was her first time waking up in a man's arms.

In Royce Duran's arms, of all people.

His eyes fluttered open, and he looked at her with a drowsy frown. "Don't wake me up, Koreen. I don't want you to go."

"Who said I'm going anywhere?" she replied softly, wrapping her arms around his neck and snuggling closer.

He pulled her tighter against his chest, the beat of his heart a steady rhythm in her ear. No sooner had she settled comfortably did she realize he was asleep again.

He'd always been steady and strong, ever since they were children. Tears prickled unbidden at the corners of her eyes as she thought of how many times she'd wanted to have him with her, only to realize that he was gone from her life.

For a moment, she gave in to the indulgence of ignoring the storm-drenched city outside their own little world, focusing only on the feeling of his skin against hers, the scent of him mixed with soap and their passion.

Later can wait, she decided, her fingers dancing lightly over the curve of his shoulder and down his arm.

The world can wait.

For now, she had Royce, and that was enough.

As she lay in the protective cocoon of his embrace, afloat between sleep and waking, memories of their shared past began to surface.

There was a time when they were both eleven years old, when her unnamed feelings for him had first taken root.

She had been training tirelessly for an upcoming regional junior kata competition; she'd worked hard for two years just to qualify and make it through the city-wide and provincial rounds. Her life at that time was filled with challenges—her brother Kenneth was in the hospital, very sick from dengue fever, while her mother stayed by his side and her father scrambled to gather enough money for his medication. Koreen was left to navigate the world alone, commuting to and from the gym each day.

One evening, after an especially grueling training session, Royce had found her huddled in a corner of the gym as they waited for a special technique class with their school's Shihan, Mr. Tuazon. He'd pulled out a sandwich and a packet of juice from his bag, offering both to her without hesitation.

Hunger had made her swallow her pride back then; she'd taken the food with a soft word of thanks and immediately started eating, to appease the angry monster gnawing at her insides.

"How are you getting home tonight?" He'd sat beside

her, mimicking her huddled position a little awkwardly. His limbs had started growing and filling out; he looked less like a boy and more like a young man.

"I'm going to commute," she'd replied between bites of ham sandwich, trying to sound nonchalant, as if she was completely fine being on her own.

After training, Royce had insisted on making sure she got home safely. That night, he walked her to the jeepney stop, a different one from his own. Along the way, they came across a fishball vendor. Royce had ended up buying out the entire cart, as they both devoured the street food, with all its different sauces, until they were bursting.

She'd wanted to ask him how he knew about her struggles, but something had stopped her—her willingness not to admit that she was exhausted from running around on her own, perhaps, or that his help was more than appreciated.

His help was needed, and she'd never even asked.

Just before they parted ways, he'd pressed a twenty-peso bill into her hand without a word. By the time she realized he'd given her money, the jeepney she was on had already driven off, leaving him standing on the pavement.

It was in that moment, watching him from a distance as the night swallowed his lanky frame, Koreen realized how special Royce truly was.

The nightly walks to the jeepney stop became their silent, unofficial ritual for two weeks, until the kata competition came and went. As she stood beside him to have their picture taken, silver medals hanging proudly from around their necks, Koreen had wanted to say thank you, but the words never came.

They never did, not in the way she wanted to say them.

Back in the present, nestled in his arms, she felt warmth spread through her chest as the memory played out in her mind. How strangely and deeply their lives had intertwined back then—and how intense their connection had become now.

She allowed her eyes to open and settle on his sleeping form next to her. Still overwhelmed by the depth of emotion welling up inside her, she leaned in and pressed her lips to his, wanting to convey what she still couldn't find the courage to say.

Thank you for everything.

You have no idea how much I missed you.

A sole tear rolled down her cheek, as she thought of the most important thing she wanted him to tell him, but never could.

I've loved you for the longest time.

Koreen didn't realize she had fallen asleep watching him. As she once more stirred to wakefulness, she felt his gaze on her.

She found herself looking into his dark eyes, their depths still hazy with sleep. A smile tugged at the corner of his lips, and she couldn't resist leaning in to capture it with a lingering kiss.

Royce gave an appreciative moan. "This is the best way to wake up."

Kissing him with increased fervor, she felt her body respond to his touch as if it were the most natural thing in the world. Unable to help herself, she straddled him and she took his length into her body, the sensation of being filled by him exhilarating.

She rode him hard then, his hands gripping her hips tightly, guiding her movements as she brought him to the brink.

When she could no longer hold back, she surrendered herself to the waves of pleasure that crashed over them and promptly collapsed onto his chest.

"Good morning, my queen," he greeted her softly, brushing a strand of damp hair away from her face.

"Good morning," she replied, still breathless from their passionate encounter.

They lay in silence for several long moments, listening to the sound of the rain outside and their own breaths.

She was the first to speak. "Royce?"

His hands were idly twirling locks of her hair. "Yeah?"

"You told me you didn't have time for a relationship," she ventured. "But you're here with me…and you seem to have time. You asked for me at the gym, saw me at school, took me to dinner…" Her voice trailed off; she didn't want to appear assuming, or give herself any hope.

"This is my last shot with you, Koreen," he answered without hesitation. "I couldn't let you slip away from me without trying to be with you. As you said, we've already wasted so much time."

Her eyes stung as his words sunk in. "Why did you wait so long?"

His hands found her waist and, before she knew it, she was back in his arms, the warm comforter thrown over both their naked bodies.

Royce didn't speak at first, but continued his caresses, his fingers feather-light as they stroked her hair and skin.

"I wanted to make sure I could give you everything you've ever wanted," he finally said. "You're the only person who's ever made me feel like this…the only one I'd do anything and everything for. I never felt that with anyone else, only with you."

She closed her eyes, letting his words wash over her.

"Koreen…" His fingers were on her chin. "Please look at me."

She did, afraid of what she knew she would see. Afraid that, if she looked, she would be forever lost.

"Before I left, my boss, the owner of Boundless, told me something I've never even considered before. After I saw you, I realized he was right, all along."

"Right about what?" Confusion joined the myriad emotions already churning within her.

"Maybe you should consider getting married to me. I can't imagine being with anyone else. Being married to you would be heaven. Don't you think it would be heaven if we were married?"

She froze, her body rigid with shock. *Get married?* The thought had never crossed her mind before, but now it hung heavy in the air between them.

Swallowing hard, she grabbed a pillow and hugged it to her body, as if to shield herself from the immensity of what he was offering and the decision that lay before her.

Royce didn't miss a beat; as they lay side by side, he spoke passionately about how perfect they were for each other, how they complemented and fired each other up, and how together they were invincible. As he talked, his voice both soothing and persuasive, she found herself torn between wanting to give in to the idea and resisting the urge to succumb to something unknown, something beyond her control.

When he finished speaking, Royce reached out and caressed her cheek. She found herself weakening at the adoration in his eyes. "Look at you. My perfect warrior queen."

She reached up and caught his hand, feeling the warmth of his skin and the steady pulse beneath. With a smile, she pressed her lips to his fingertips.

Still aching with longing for him, she slipped out of bed and wrapped herself in a robe she'd found in the closet last night but never got to use. She didn't need it then. She had the comfort of Royce's embrace.

She approached the glass windows of the bedroom and used the control to open the electronic blinds, revealing the gray, flooded cityscape below.

Numbly, she stared out at the dark, brooding sky. For the first time since she'd stepped into his suite, she felt cold, even underneath the thick, fluffy white robe.

Marriage.

Royce's wife.

Spending every night in his arms, building a life together. As beautiful and tantalizing as it sounded, she couldn't shake the feeling that it was all part of his plans, not hers.

Everything had been his plan.

As if sensing her unease, she heard Royce get out of bed.

"Hey." She felt the warmth of his voice in her ear, the heat of his naked body against hers. He wrapped his arms around her from behind, resting his chin on her shoulder. "Are you hungry?"

"Yes, I'm starving." She met his eyes in the glass, forcing a smile.

The sincere smile she got in response lit up his face. "Me, too. Let's get some breakfast. Or lunch. I'm not even sure what time it is."

As he spoke, she could feel his arousal pressing against her. His hand gradually found its way under the robe, slowly reaching for her breasts and heat as he used his other arm to pin her against his body. Each touch ignited a fire within her, making her wet, her nipples hardening under his touch.

"Royce…" she breathed, torn between the desire coursing through her and the weight of her own uncertainties.

"Be my wife, Koreen," he whispered against her neck, undoing her robe and letting it fall to the floor. He turned her around and effortlessly lifted her into his arms.

"Marry me." He entered her slowly, guiding her to sink into him. "Together we can do anything. You know that."

Koreen had no answer. Instead, she wrapped her arms around his neck, her legs encircling his hips. Their bodies entwined perfectly, echoes of the previous night on the balcony when they had first kissed. She lost herself in the heat of the moment, moving along with him fervently, desperately. Their lips met again and again, tongues tangling and breaths mingling.

He pushed her against the cold glass, the contrast between the chill and his warmth more pronounced as he drove into her with an intensity that left her gasping for air. She matched him stroke for stroke, climbing higher, needing to have all of him, before she had to let go.

"Koreen," he groaned, his grip tightening on her waist.

She knew he was close; so she kissed him, hard, feeling tears rise to her eyes as she ground herself harder against him.

She knew it, then, as she gave her body to him, so willingly, holding nothing back.

She had always been his.

She reached the peak with a shudder that weakened her limbs, just as she felt him tense up within her, thrusting almost feverishly as he came. She held on tightly, her lips tasting the salt of his sweat as she buried her face into his neck, nibbling at his skin.

As their breathing slowly returned to normal, she disentangled herself from his embrace and pushed him to the floor.

On her hands and knees, she focused on the storm still raging outside the window.

"Again," she whispered, knowing he would rise to the challenge.

Never one to back down, Royce sank to his knees behind her. She moaned when she felt his lips and tongue lap at her dripping core before entering her from behind. His body covered hers, one hand grabbing her hair while the other firmly squeezed and pinched her breasts. He nipped and kissed the back of her neck and shoulder as he took her again, fiercely, mercilessly. She felt herself teetering on the edge, ready to shatter into a million pieces.

He went faster and harder, his hand moving to rub roughly against her clit. His voice was a growl in her ear as he said once more, "Marry me, Koreen."

She didn't respond; instead, she allowed herself and her heart to break.

He followed her, his breath hitching, his body convulsing above her with the force of his own release.

Together, they collapsed on the floor, Koreen face down and Royce sprawled atop her, still partially within her. She bore his weight without complaint, reveling in the feeling of him hot and pulsating inside her.

"You're mine, aren't you?" His voice was raw, almost vulnerable.

"Always."

Royce slowly brought himself up to a seated position. He pulled her up with him, his hands firm on her hips.

She climbed onto his lap, and their eyes met. So many questions and no sure answers.

If this were a Mathematics test, it would be a dismal failure, she thought darkly.

She embraced him, her lips finding his. She willed him not to say anything and ruin the moment.

But he did.

"Will you marry me, Koreen?"

The words were hopelessly fragile, ready to shatter under the weight of her answer.

Despite all her self-control, a lone tear slid down her cheek, cutting a path through the sheen of their mingled sweat on her skin.

It was a question that resonated with all the dreams she'd locked away in her heart for so long. But something held her back, something decidedly stronger.

Her answer was tremulous, broken, but ready.

"No."

Ten

Royce

RESTRAINT

It wasn't a sensation of tripping or falling—or even crashing.

It was *nothing*; the absence of everything. A blank numbness that closed in from around him. There was no more tension or emotion.

There was only emptiness, as the life he'd imagined for so long was seemingly ravaged and washed away by the storm outside.

But he still held on to her; his body was still fighting, unable to let go. "Why? Why won't you marry me?"

At least she still looked at him straight in the eye, her

own gaze filled with something akin to sorrow. "I'm sorry. I can't keep up. This is all too much, too fast."

His arms tightened around her.

Please, don't, he wanted to say it so desperately, repeatedly, until she succumbed.

A lifetime of competition, of striving to be better than one another, had led them here. He had dedicated years to proving himself worthy of her, to becoming the man who could stand beside her as an equal. And now she was slipping through his fingers like sand.

"Koreen, aren't we meant to be equals?" he said instead. "To complete each other?"

She shook her head, her hair falling across her face. "You've always been the better half. You've always been the one looking out for me, giving all of yourself. I…I have nothing to give."

Their lips met in a desperate, searing kiss, and for a moment, time stood still. But then, with a quiet sob, she began to untangle herself from his embrace.

"That's not true," he insisted, grasping for any lifeline that might bring her back to him. "I don't want anything from you. Just you. You're all I've ever wanted."

She didn't respond, and as she stepped out of his arms, Royce felt the chasm between them widen, the wall between them rise and reinforce itself a hundredfold.

He could only stare as she moved around the room, the stillness between them heavy and oppressive. She avoided his gaze as she began to gather her scattered clothes. With each piece she collected, his own heart twisted more and more painfully in his chest.

To distract himself, he awkwardly stood up from the

floor and picked out fresh clothes from the closet. The sound of her sipping water filled the room as he dressed quickly, feeling the weight of their unspoken words suffocating him. She was seated on the bed, rummaging through her bag.

He watched as she pulled out a comb and ran it through her hair. The simple act seemed to hold so much more meaning now. He felt a sudden urge to reach out to her, to close the distance that had formed between them.

"Do you want to eat something?" His voice broke the silence. It was the voice of a stranger.

"Yes." Her eyes met his for the first time since she'd stepped away from him. "If you could arrange for a car to take me home after, that would be great."

For a fleeting second, he entertained the thought of ordering in, of keeping her in the room with him, making love to her again and again. But instead, he nodded and reached for the phone.

"Good afternoon."

"Good afternoon, Mr. Duran." It was a different receptionist from last night.

"I'd like to book a table at the restaurant for lunch, please, and request a car to pick up Miss Cisco at three this afternoon."

"I'm really sorry, sir." The voice at the other end was deeply apologetic. "The storm is still at Signal Number Three. The streets are flooded, and no cars could get through the roads."

He glanced out the window, watching the rain and wind still whipping through the city mercilessly. Everything in his sight seemed doused with a bleak gray color.

"It's okay. We'll have lunch, anyway. Please let me know if any transport will be available."

"I will, Mr. Duran. Thank you for your understanding."

He hung up the phone, resisting the urge to bring his fist down on it. Why was everything fucked up, all of a sudden?

"Can't get home, can I?" She took a few hesitant steps in his direction.

"No. Better to call your mother and tell her what's going on."

She nodded and pulled out her phone from her bag. "At least there's service now."

To give her privacy, he retreated to the living area and sank onto the plush armchair. He could hear her soft voice as she spoke on the phone.

The sound both comforted and tormented him as he thought about their lovemaking, his proposal, and her rejection.

Too fast? They'd both waited a decade and a half.

He waited for Koreen to finish her call. As soon as she was done, she walked into the living area, clutching her bag and hobbling a little on her heels. "Sorry to have kept you waiting. Mama is on her own, so…"

"It's fine. Is she okay, though? Does she need anything?"

"Our area rarely ever floods, thank goodness. She's alright, just worried about me. She wanted to talk to you and say thanks, but I told her you're in a separate room." She flushed a little as she spoke, her eyes meeting his for a moment before darting away.

In a different world, they would damn well be engaged by now.

"You can tell her whatever you like, Koreen. I don't really mind."

"Um, listen…I can find a cheaper room or something, so I won't be a bother." She looked uneasy as she spoke, fidgeting a little with her bag.

"No." His response was immediate and just as forceful, surprising even himself. "You can stay here. Use the bedroom. I'll sleep on the couch."

It was the least he could do since she couldn't get home because of the storm. He'd give her the greatest comforts he could offer. He wanted to keep her close, too, selfishly, even if it was just for a little while longer.

"You don't have to do that. Besides, it was my decision to stay last night…" Her voice trailed off, her cheeks reddening a little more.

He didn't answer. Instead, he watched as she looked down at herself, her rumpled black dress from the previous night clinging to her body.

"Do I look okay? This is a bit much for lunch, isn't it?"

He took in her appearance, strong and beautiful, pained to see her so unsure of herself. "No, it's fine. You look perfect." He hesitated before adding, "The world should be yours, Koreen."

She shook her head, dismissing the compliment. But he could tell it had affected her, the color on her face still evident. "Are you ready to go eat?"

She nodded, and he offered her his arm. The elevator ride was silent and charged, like a bomb waiting to rip their world apart.

When they reached the lobby, the hotel manager greeted them with apologies for the storm. Royce waved off his concerns, insisting that the storm was beyond anyone's control.

The manager nodded, turning his attention to Koreen. "We are very sorry Miss Cisco can't get a car, but we will provide everything she needs during her stay."

"Thank you." Koreen smiled and thanked him, her manners impeccable. Royce felt oddly proud to see her so composed.

As they walked and took their seat at the restaurant, he watched her and the other guests 'stormed in' right along with them. In sharp contrast to the silence between him and Koreen, everyone else in the dining room was talking animatedly.

They both ate without speaking; the clink of silverware on plates their only exchange. She seemed to enjoy the meal, eating heartily despite the heavy atmosphere. He was pleasantly surprised to see her appetite match his.

They matched each other in so many ways, both pronounced and intimate.

"Are you okay?" he asked gently, breaking the silence once he had signed the bill.

She nodded. "Thank you for the meal."

"You're welcome. Do you need anything else? What would you like to do? There's a gym and an indoor pool. There are books in the gift shop, too."

"I'd like to make time to read again soon," she said, a little wistfully.

"Reading is one area I can't keep up with you in."

She gave him a small smile. "I used to read mostly shorter romance books and you had a thing for thrillers, so there's really no comparison, is there? I remember you liked John Grisham a lot. You wanted to be that lawyer in *A Time to Kill*."

The fact that she could recall his favorite book growing up was more than enough to break his heart. "I got a signed copy from the author. One of my friends in Saudi got me one for my thirtieth birthday."

"That's so cool. I'd like to see it someday."

At the back of his mind, he knew that someday might never come.

Another awkward silence settled between them. The other guests in the dining room slowly trickled out, sharing their concerns about the storm and showing each other photos on their phones.

"We can have a look at the books in the shop," he offered.

She shook her head. "It's okay. I should go back to the room and get some sleep. I should call my brother and some of my friends to check on them."

As they made their way towards the elevators, her phone rang. She glanced at the screen before answering.

"Hey, Leo."

In the relative silence of the elevator, Royce could hear Leo Tuazon's voice on the other end.

"Hey, Koreen. Just wanted to check if you're okay. Are you at home?"

"No...I'm stuck somewhere else. With a friend. How about you?"

"I'm at home. It's not so bad here in Molo, but I'm closing the gym for at least a few days. The whole area is flooded, and I'm pretty sure the ceiling would have leaked by now if it hasn't already caved in."

"I'm so sorry, Leo."

"It's okay. You know how it is."

"Have you heard from the others?"

"Jonah went to Maggie's last night before it got too bad in Tagbac. Ace and his family are okay."

She sighed in relief. "We're all safe. That's what matters, right?"

"Yeah. We'll just have to deal with whatever comes our way next."

"Stay safe. Let me know if you need any help."

"You, too. I'll be in touch once the storm clears. Take care."

Koreen exchanged goodbyes with Leo before she hung up. She replaced the phone in her bag and was quiet the rest of the way.

Once they reached the penthouse, she immediately noticed a basket of fresh clothes provided by the hotel. "Oh, wow. I really didn't expect this."

"Please, make yourself comfortable." He tried to keep his voice steady despite the pang of longing that almost caused him physical pain. If it were up to him, she wouldn't need any clothes.

Now they behaved as if they were strangers stuck in a room together. He watched her carry the basket into the bedroom, shutting the door behind her. Minutes later, he could hear the muffled sound of the shower. He wanted nothing more than to join her.

But he'd fucked it all up, hadn't he?

Royce settled behind the desk set up in the living area and opened his laptop. Work was always a reliable means of escape. He sent emails to his assistant and managers, the clack of the keyboard momentarily drowning out his thoughts of the woman only one wall apart but seemingly worlds away

THE LAST DIVIDE

from him. As the afternoon went on, he could hear the faint murmur of the television from the bedroom.

As the gray day gave way to a pitch-black night, Royce finally closed his laptop, having exhausted himself with work. He stood up, stretching his limbs before checking on Koreen.

She had fallen asleep on the bed while watching Netflix. An episode of *Cobra Kai* was still playing at low volume.

He slowly approached the bed and pulled the blankets around her sleeping form. He switched off the TV and closed the blinds, plunging the room into darkness.

"Goodnight, Koreen," he said.

He tried to stop himself then, but even his pride could not hold him back from saying the words he'd wanted to confess for so long.

He might never have the chance to tell her again.

"I love you. I always have, and I always will."

Eleven

Koreen

RECOMPENSE

WHERE WAS SHE?

It took Koreen a few seconds to get her bearings as she stirred awake, still wrestling with the leaden weight of her dreams. Her face felt cold with moisture; as she reached up to touch the skin, she realized they were teardrops.

She willed her eyes to focus as she fumbled under the pillows for her phone. Her hands closed around the ice-cold device quickly, only to find out it had gone dead while she slept.

With a sigh, she reached over to her side and managed

to switch the lamp on. A quick glance at the hotel phone revealed it was almost one in the morning.

Even with the protection of the comforter, she shivered. The temperature had dropped significantly since she'd gone to bed, and she was clad only in the plain white underwear provided by the hotel. Her eyes scanned the room, landing on two light dresses that hung on the closet door, which she'd unearthed from the complimentary basket earlier. They looked like something one might wear to the beach, not in a freezing suite in the middle of a typhoon.

She went into the bathroom and tried to put on the robe but found it still damp from her earlier shower. Frustration gnawed at her as she fumbled through the closet, fingers finally brushing against a soft cotton t-shirt. Realizing it belonged to Royce, she hesitated for a moment before pulling it over her head, desperate for warmth.

Memories from the previous night flooded her mind; their bodies entwined, having each other until dawn. The scent of him still lingered on her, from the bed they had previously shared.

He was outside, wasn't he? He'd said earlier that he'd sleep on the couch.

She needed to see him, even if it was just for a moment.

Her steps silent on the plush carpet, she padded across the suite to the living area. She paused in the doorway, her breath catching at the sight before her.

In the dim lamplight, she could see Royce asleep on the couch, clad only in shorts, oblivious to the chill around them. He looked a little awkward crammed onto the cushions, his long legs and large frame a little too big even for the oversized couch.

The blinds of the floor-to-ceiling windows had been left open, revealing the shadows and lights of the darkened, water-logged city around them. Guilt and regret descended on her as she watched his chest rise and fall with each slow breath. Her fingers itched to touch and trace his muscles.

Royce stirred, as if knowing he was being watched, one hand reaching into the semi-darkness for something—or someone. All she had to do was step closer and she would be in his arms again.

The arms of the vulnerable-looking, half-naked man before her, who had bared his heart to her and offered everything he had, everything he was.

They had always competed against each other and trained together, ever since they were children, but he'd never been cruel to her or treated her badly. He'd always treated her like a gentleman. She was the one who had kept pushing him away, afraid of losing herself to her own feelings.

Fuck it all.

Her hands clenched into fists, wanting to hit something so badly in frustration as she recalled the way he'd looked at her on the football field, trying to tell her something she hadn't been ready to hear. But now...it was too late, even if she listened.

He had already reached a point in their lives where she'd never be his equal. He had the world now, while all she had were memories and the burgeoning realization of her love for him.

A love she would cut clean, too. She had already decided she wouldn't accept the job at Boundless. She had her life, and he had his.

She knelt beside his sleeping form on the couch. Up

close, she could see that his beard had grown uneven. She found comfort in its imperfection. It made him seem more human, less untouchable.

"Hey," she whispered, reaching out to touch his cheek. "I'm sorry, I fell asleep."

"Uh," Royce mumbled, shaking off sleep. His eyes widened slightly in surprise, perhaps at her unexpected tenderness. "It's okay."

"Did you have dinner?"

"No, but I'm fine." He rubbed his eyes as he slowly pulled himself up to a seated position.

"Would you like me to call downstairs for some food?" she offered hesitantly.

"It's okay; I'd rather sleep." The smile on his face looked forced. "Work knocked me out."

Koreen nodded, pained at the awkwardness between them. It was as if they were strangers, tiptoeing around each other's feelings. "Maybe you should move to the bed. It's more comfortable. I can sleep here. You could fit two of me on this thing."

Royce shook his head. Her heart ached at the distance that stretched between them, even if they were shoulder-to-shoulder. She wondered if he could see it in her gaze.

To distract herself, she reached for a bottle of water on the coffee table and opened it before gently slipping it into his hand.

"Have some water."

"Thanks."

As he drank, she embraced his arm, urging him to move to the bed. He hesitated, then declined once more.

It was a stubbornness she knew and understood all too well. Neither of them were willing to concede their independence.

But then they both gave way, just a little.

"Stay here with me," he said, putting the empty bottle down on the side table and holding out his arm to her.

It was a beautiful surprise, like a parting gift. She knew this might very well be their last night together.

"Okay." She scooted over and curled up next to him, welcoming the warmth of his body against hers. She listened to the rhythm of his heartbeat, its steadiness grounding her to this fleeting moment.

One last night with him. A memory I could lock away in my heart.

As if sensing her thoughts, he pulled her closer.

"Koreen, I...." His voice was hesitant, but his gaze never left hers. "I've dreamt of this moment—seeing you come to me, wearing my shirt. I bet every man has this kind of fantasy."

He could not have hit her any harder.

The tears she'd been holding back for hours finally welled up in her eyes, spilling down her cheeks. He reached out, wiping them away with his thumb.

"It's okay," he murmured as he pulled her back into his arms.

Finally, Koreen cried.

She cried for the kind boy who had bought her all the fishball she wanted to eat and given her a twenty-peso bill; the young man who had stolen her heart and bound her to him with a black belt and a white anemone.

She cried for the man he had become.

The man who now held her so tenderly; a man who conquered her heart, body and soul in one fell swoop.

She didn't know how long she cried; the shadows danced before her eyes as his whispers and caresses became tender music to her senses, a tune she would never forget.

When she was finally spent, she allowed herself to melt into him, committing to memory the feel of his body pressed against hers.

"I promise, I'm not going to ask you to marry me again." Royce's voice sounded as if she were underwater. "Let's just be here together until our time is up. No strings attached."

"I'd like that." She reached up, this time trying to memorize the angles of his face with her touch.

"Can I tell you what's going to happen when the storm's over?"

She nodded.

"When it's over, you're going to go home. And I'm sure you're going to tell me you're not accepting the job at Boundless."

She didn't have the energy for denial. "How did you know?"

He smiled sadly, brushing a strand of hair from her face. "I know you better than anyone, Koreen. You're a queen—you go all or nothing. You run the world as you'd have it, not the way I'd want it to be."

Her heart swelled with love and admiration for this man who understood her so completely. Wordlessly, she nodded.

"I have to be honest, too. I wanted this so much. I'm sorry if I came on too strong. That was never my intention. I only wanted to show you what I could give."

"Please don't apologize," she said, her words muffled against his shoulder.

"Okay." With that, he pulled her up to his lap, burying his face in her hair.

Nothing more was said.

THE LAST DIVIDE

As morning drew closer, she felt their breathing syncing with each other's as they slowly drifted towards sleep.

Koreen stirred first, tugging at his hand as her feet found the carpet. "Come to bed. You should rest."

"Alright." There was a hint of weariness in his voice but he followed as she led him to the bed, guided by the soft glow of the bathroom light she'd left on earlier.

They stretched out next to each other, eyes locking, before she inched closer to him, seeking his warmth once more.

He pulled the covers over them and hesitated for a moment before asking, "Can I hold you? Like last night?"

She could feel a bittersweet smile form on her lips as she nodded her assent. There was no place else she would rather be. As his warmth seeped into her own skin, she turned her face towards him, her eyes meeting his. "I'm sorry, Royce. I'm really sorry."

He shushed her with a kiss on her nose. "You said no more apologizing, right?"

"Right."

"Then don't be sorry, Koreen." He reached for her hair, combing his fingers through the strands with an almost reverent air. "Just let me love you, like last night, too."

"Please," she whispered.

He kissed her deeply, his tongue dancing with hers as he cradled her face between his hands. She put her arms around his neck, as if clinging to a beautiful dream.

This was the dream that made her cry.

Everything else around them faded away, leaving only

their passion, tempered by longing and hurt and the inevitability of time. It was a slow exploration, a rediscovery of one another.

She felt his hands trace her body, his touch gentle yet unyielding, his desire evident in the way he held her as he took her over and over again.

Her own fingers roamed across his skin, reacquainting herself with his sheer power, his steady strength. She held on to him as tightly as she could, giving in to the need and pleasure that he coaxed from her body, allowing herself to drown in his kisses and his touch.

In those moments, she allowed herself to believe that, after a lifetime of competition and then separation, they were meant to be together.

But the dream had to end.

The first light of dawn began to filter through the curtains, signaling the end of the storm. As they lay entwined, spent in their desperation, time seemed to slow, too, as if reluctant to break them apart.

She knew the world outside would, soon enough, rear its cruel head. She knew she would be made to believe, yet again, that nothing lasts forever.

Not nothing.

Koreen Cisco knew how to one-up fate, too.

My love would last forever.

For the final time, she took Royce in her arms, whispering his name, etching every sensation and emotion deep into her heart, where her memories would remain long after the sun had risen.

Long after they had said goodbye.

Twelve

Royce

REMAINDER

His world moved at a relentless pace, and time was a ruthless taskmaster.

For Royce, the days and nights ebbed and flowed into one another. He used to be fueled by dogged determination and unabashed ambition; now, he moved out of habit.

He knew if he stopped, it would be the end of him. So he didn't.

He took in the progress that had been made since the typhoon finally left Iloilo City. The construction site of Boundless Tower stretched out before him, the chaos of cranes and trucks filling the air with a cacophony of mechanical noise. A gust of wind carried the scent of upturned earth, damp gravel, and freshly cut steel.

He hadn't allowed himself much time for reflection these past few weeks, as he had been working nonstop—changing schedules, making arrangements, and ensuring that everything would be back on track as soon as possible.

In the wake of the storm, he'd made the best decision he could.

As soon as air travel was possible again, he'd called in two of his best: Jesse Lozada, who managed Boundless Jeddah, and Kotaro Yoshida, his personal assistant.

He'd appointed Lozada, a fellow Filipino from the neighboring region of Cebu, as the manager of Boundless Philippines. Yoshida followed shortly, meant to stay in Iloilo for a few weeks to provide support.

"Royce-san." Yoshida appeared next to him, clad in safety gear. The young Japanese man lowered his head respectfully. "Do you really wish to leave the Philippines so soon?"

He was speaking Nihongo, a subtle sign that the conversation would veer towards more personal territory.

Royce inclined his head and gave a small smile. "Your concern is appreciated, Yoshida, but this is for the best. We have more business to bring in and more operations centers to build."

"Ah, but Prince Khalid made it very clear he wishes for you to stay longer," said Yoshida delicately. "He has given orders for you to take a vacation at the company's expense. Rushing back to work will displease him."

"I'm not rushing back. I will be staying with my parents

for a few days in Manila. I need to return to Saudi to appoint Lozada's successor. You know this."

"Nine years away is a very long time," Yoshida went on, his eyes lowered in deference. "I have served you for six years, and I have never seen you take a break."

"Thank you for your honesty, Kotaro-san, but my decision is final. I'm sure you and Lozada will keep things running smoothly here."

Yoshida nodded and didn't press the matter any further. "Of course, sir. I have also confirmed with your lawyer that the investment offer is in place. As soon as the other party signs the contract, the funds will be wired. In fact, the funds are ready now."

"Good. Please have Attorney Panes contact them after I have left the country."

"Of course, sir." Yoshida reverted smoothly to English, bowing again. "I wish you safe travels. If there are any changes to your schedule, I will ring you immediately."

"Thank you, Yoshida. I'll see you back in Saudi."

After his assistant had said goodbye and disappeared back into the construction site, Royce slowly made his way out, surveying the damage that the place had sustained from the storm. The ground was still muddy and uneven, but overall, the situation seemed manageable.

Lozada was waiting for him by the hire car, standing with an air of confidence and a big smile that immediately put Royce at ease. A BPO veteran who had supervised some of the earliest call centers and transcription facilities in the Middle East, he'd been all too happy to finally work in his home country.

"Leaving us so soon, sir?"

"I've done what I needed to do in Iloilo, Jesse. It's your turn now."

Lozada didn't mince words. "Well, I'm happy to report that it's not as bad as it looks. If there are no more big storms like the one we had weeks back, we could call in more trucks of sand and gravel to patch up the damage and carry on with the construction. I've been talking to the engineers and they told me the ground is quite stable. I've also scheduled another team to have a look after the weekend; one of them worked on our Pune site, too."

"Very good. And the recruits?"

"Already taken care of," Lozada assured him. "We've finalized our schedule at the Convention Center to begin orientations for the new staff. Hands-on training will take place at a computer college in the city during nighttime after classes. They have equipment our recruits could train on in the meantime."

"Keep me posted daily, Jesse," Royce said, clapping him on the shoulder. "I made the right decision bringing you home."

"Thank you, sir." Lozada's face broke into a wide grin. "I'm just glad to be back in the Philippines. My wife and children are excited to come to Iloilo."

"I'm happy for you and your family." Royce held out his hand; the other man took it and shook firmly. "Thank you again for everything."

"You're welcome, boss." Lozada stepped aside as the driver opened the car door for Royce.

"Take care of Boundless here for me, Jesse," Royce said through the window, giving the other man a nod in farewell.

"I will. I won't let you down." Lozada gave a jaunty wave. "Safe travels!"

As the car pulled away from the busy construction site, Royce watched the sunset illuminate the unfinished skeleton of Boundless Tower. In his mind's eye, he could already see the strong yet elegant and graceful lines of the completed skyscraper. It had been designed to mimic the appearance of a queen, proud and regal.

Koreen would have been perfect here.

He had imagined her managing this facility, with her impeccable background in the industry, her incomparable work ethic, and, most of all, her fierce dedication to excellence.

In another life, she would have been his wife, his queen. But she had always followed her own path, and he couldn't help but respect her for that.

The sky was already a deep, velvety blue when Royce arrived at the hotel. He knew work was still ongoing at the Tower, with its construction in multiple shifts. He would have wanted to stay longer, but he took comfort in the presence of Lozada and Yoshida there. They were men he could trust with the project.

It was time for him to leave; the rest of the world awaited him. He would be alone, once again, but then that was the world he'd built, wasn't it? It kept moving, waiting for no one.

As he made his way across the lobby, his gaze fell upon a familiar face seated on one of the plush beige sofas near reception.

Kenneth Cisco stood up with a broad smile and made his way over. The years had not dulled his quickness. Before Royce could adequately react, the other man had pulled him in for a tight bear hug.

"Duran! So good to see you, man!"

Royce recovered by giving him a thump on the back. "Good to see you, too, Doc."

They had been friends and basketball buddies since elementary school. Kenneth was two years younger but a great player, a wily point guard who'd commanded Royce's respect.

Kenneth stepped back and regarded him curiously. "You look like one of those rich princes from Dubai. Which car do you drive again?"

"A *Mercedes S*," he answered automatically. It took him a second to realize that the younger man was joking. "Fuck, you were kidding, weren't you?"

Kenneth chuckled. "You are serious. Damn. I was pretty sure you had one of those. I wasn't wrong, was I?"

"You hit it right on the head," Royce conceded. "What brings you here, Doc? I'm glad I got to see you before I leave tomorrow. My flight's at eight in the morning."

"Tomorrow? Already? We didn't even get the chance to have that game with the gang. Damn typhoon had me stuck in San Jose. Couldn't travel with all the flooding and landslides on the road."

"There's already someone running the Philippine operations of our company, so it's time for me to go." It wasn't completely true, but it would have to do. "No rest for the wicked and all that."

"Yeah, sounds about right." Kenneth smiled, glancing at his watch. "I have to pick up my girlfriend at eight. Do you think you can spare an old friend an hour for a drink? I promise not to drink you under the table like I did last time when we won that summer league championship. The fun of underage drinking."

"One drink," Royce relented with a laugh. "I barely drink these days."

"One drink, then," Kenneth agreed.

They went to the hotel bar, settling into chairs by the window overlooking the city. Royce made Kenneth pick the drink. They ordered Black Label whiskey.

"I'm glad I made it on time before you left," Kenneth said as soon as their glasses had arrived. "I'm only in town for the weekend to see my girlfriend and family, so I thought I'd drop by to say hello. I have to be back at the hospital early Monday morning."

"Let's drink to the time we have now, then." Royce raised his glass.

"Cheers." Kenneth lifted his own glass and met his with a resounding clink.

They sipped their whiskey in companionable silence for a few minutes, watching bolts of lightning skitter across the early evening sky.

"I believe thanks are in order, too," said Kenneth casually. "I have to thank you for looking after my sister during the storm."

Royce swallowed his sip of whiskey; a little too hard it scalded its way into his throat. He hoped Kenneth hadn't noticed his wince of pain.

"Don't mention it," he replied in what he hoped was a dismissive tone. "We had dinner to catch up. Before anyone knew it, no one could get a car in or out of the hotel."

"Still." Kenneth tipped his glass in his direction. "Our mother was worried sick, but she was very reassured that Koreen was stuck here with you."

Royce shrugged, forcing a smile. He wasn't quite sure

how Kenneth—or his mother—would react if he knew the truth. "I'm glad I could help."

"By the way, Royce, how did you survive two nights with Koreen?"

The question was meant to tease, but memories of those nights—his body entwined with Koreen's, his lips on hers, his hands on her skin, himself inside her—threatened Royce's composure. "Koreen was fine, no trouble at all. She spent most of her time eating and watching *Cobra Kai*."

"I'm surprised you got her to slow down," said Kenneth, chuckling lightly. "She's always on the move—teaching here, working there. Did she try to use your computer to run an online class or something?"

Royce shook his head. "Never once mentioned it."

"Wow." Kenneth shook his head incredulously. "Perhaps the storm happened for a reason, just to hold her down for a while."

"How is she now? Still keeping busy, I bet." The question had to be asked, or Kenneth might start wondering what had really happened during those stormed-in nights.

Kenneth sighed. "Yeah, she jumped right back onto the swing of things once she could drive around town again. She was actually the one who dropped me off here."

"I see. She's got one of those transcription classes, then?" He was quite sure Koreen had not mentioned to her own brother—or anyone else—about the job offer at Boundless and her subsequent refusal to accept it.

"She was going to the gym. I think she's training some kids for a tournament. They're all working late these days, to make up for when the gym was closed for a week."

"Yeah. I heard her talking to Leo about the gym taking damage during the storm."

As they went back to sipping their drinks, Royce's thoughts went back to the morning the storm ended.

He had held Koreen in his arms as they watched the sun rise over the flooded city. They had breakfast at the restaurant, subdued and peppered only with small talk. An imposing four-wheel drive with an equally no-nonsense driver had then appeared on the driveway, sent by the owner of the hotel for Royce to use as he pleased.

Their separation had been simple and bittersweet. The last thing he could recall doing was kissing her on the forehead before helping her into the massive black vehicle. She had touched his cheek lightly before she'd pressed her lips against his skin. The last thing he remembered seeing was her in a pink sundress, a scarf awkwardly draped around her shoulders, waving goodbye to him with a tiny smile on her lips.

"You were always good for Koreen, Royce," Kenneth said earnestly, interrupting his thoughts. "I mean, I couldn't say anything all those years ago; I was a kid, but now…"

"What do you mean, Doc?"

Kenneth shrugged. "You've always kind of looked after her when we were growing up. You're pretty much the big brother we both needed, really. "

Royce shifted in his seat, feeling the weight of the words. "What makes you say that? Koreen and I have been competing all our lives."

"Competing?" Kenneth scoffed, shaking his head. "Man, you were looking out for her. You were always in the same space where she was, just to make sure she wasn't alone. That's a real man."

Kenneth's voice was tinged with nostalgia and admiration as he spoke, never taking his eyes off Royce. "Our father, God rest his soul, always praised you for being there for Koreen. Remember that time I got dengue and was hospitalized for more than a month? Fuck, I almost died back then."

Unable to speak past the tightness in his throat, Royce nodded.

"Koreen told us you were there for her, especially when she competed in the junior kata championships for the first time. You're the reason she made it through. You were looking after her the whole time. That's something."

Royce stared into his glass, the amber liquid swirling and dancing in the dim light of the bar. For a few moments, he lost himself in the memory of being eleven years old: walking Koreen to the jeepney stop after practice, asking his mother to make an extra sandwich for her, giving her as much of his meager allowance as he could.

It was love—that very act of caring for her, protecting her, and making sure she was safe. At eleven years old, he knew he loved that fiery girl who had always challenged him. And he…he'd just always wanted to be with her.

"That's a long time ago," Royce said, setting his glass down on the table. The sound seemed to echo through the hushed conversations around them. "We were kids."

Kenneth nodded. "Yeah, we were kids. But sometimes I'd like to think that some things never change. Makes us who we are, right?"

As they sipped their drinks and night descended over the city, they let memories wash over them: their old group, the friends they'd made, and all the tournaments they'd played. Life was much simpler back then, when all they had to worry about were grades, girls, and basketball games.

Kenneth checked his watch and sighed as he set down his empty glass on the table. "I have to get going. I'm picking up my girlfriend from the hospital. She's got a residency here in Iloilo, lucky for her."

"Of course." Royce gestured to a nearby waiter for their bill. "This one's on me."

"Alright, man, but next time I'm taking you to the coast for some good old beer and videoke." Kenneth leaned back in his chair and gave him a mischievous look. "Since you're treating, I'm going to tell you a secret about Koreen."

"A secret? I'm not sure I'm the right person to share these things with." Royce tapped his credit card on the machine offered by the waiter.

Kenneth laughed. "Oh, but you're the perfect person."

As soon as the waiter was out of earshot, Kenneth carried on gleefully. "Don't worry, it's nothing incriminating. Just a little insight into how she thinks."

Curiosity got the better of him. "What's the secret?"

"Did you know that Koreen deliberately failed her Calculus final in your last year of high school? She didn't flunk, of course—her grades were too high for that—but she brought down her grade low enough so you could catch up. You both ended up having the same average, both becoming valedictorians."

Stupefied at the revelation, Royce could only stare. "When—and how—did you find out?"

Kenneth grinned. "Just before they announced the honor roll for your graduation. I overheard her talking to her best friend Dara in her room. The principal had talked to her about it or something, maybe asked her what happened. Koreen was crying, but she kept telling Dara it was worth it. 'He' was worth it." He used his hands to form quotation marks, emphasizing the pronoun.

Shock descended on Royce. "Why would she do that?"

"I told you, you're good for her. She slows down, brings herself back down to earth. She doesn't want to be alone at the top, man. It's lonely up there."

"But...this doesn't even make any sense. She would never fail a Math test."

"You know how Koreen is. She can do whatever she sets her mind to. On top of that, she only does what she wants. Who knows what goes on in that big brain of hers." Kenneth shrugged, rubbing the back of his neck. "But for you, she did a total one-eighty without even thinking. She made you valedictorian, too, I think, so she wouldn't be alone. I don't think she'd do it for anyone else."

The weight of Kenneth's words settled heavily on Royce's shoulders, and for a moment, he was speechless.

How had he never realized just how deeply their bond ran?

Finally, he found his voice. "I think I should say goodbye to her before I leave. Sounds like the right thing to do, doesn't it?"

"Definitely." Kenneth stood up and held out his hand. "She should be at the gym until eight or something, if I heard her correctly."

He stood up, too, and shook Kenneth's hand. "Thanks, man."

"Keep in touch, okay? And don't stay away too long."

Royce nodded. "I'll do my best. If you or your family need anything, I'm just a message away."

With a strong slap on his back and an energetic goodbye, Kenneth was gone, disappearing into the Friday night crowd of the hotel bar.

Alone to confront his thoughts in the wake of his discovery, he decided there was no more time for him and Koreen to keep on pretending, hiding, or denying.

She had to know how he really felt. He owed it to her, to himself, and their shared history. He was going to break down every single wall between them, until there was nothing left but the truth.

Because he knew, at the very heart of it all, there was love.

It was a love everyone saw except for them. A love that had bloomed in childhood and grown alongside them; a rivalry that wasn't truly a rivalry at all. It was two people constantly seeking each other, bound by an invisible thread that stretched across the walls and distances that kept them physically apart. Where one was, the other had to be, too.

Koreen had already given in to its power many years ago—and he never knew until tonight.

With hurried strides, he made his way to reception and asked for his car. As he waited, rain began to fall, soft droplets that left a damp chill in the air.

When his car arrived, Royce slid into the backseat and gave the driver directions to the gym. As they drove off into the night, the drizzle intensified.

At the back of his mind, he registered the potential impact of the inclement weather on Boundless Tower's construction, but this fleeting thought was quickly swallowed by the urgency of seeing her again.

Koreen.

The rain was already falling in torrents, punctuated by cracks of lightning and loud thunderclaps, by the time they reached the gym's street. As the Tuazon school came into view, Royce spotted a lone red Corolla parked in front. He remembered her car from his session at the gym weeks ago; he'd seen her get into it with about half a dozen duffel bags and drive off.

Relieved and overwhelmed, he dismissed the driver for the night once his feet hit the pavement. His pulse quickened as he, oblivious that he was drenched head to toe, ran up the steps. He had no idea there were so many.

He tried to catch his breath as he stepped onto the worn blue carpet of the reception area. There were barely any lights on. He couldn't see or hear anyone in the facility.

The place was empty, except for Koreen.

Illuminated by the white fluorescent bulbs, she stood alone in the enclosed training area where they had done the kata together weeks ago. Her back was turned to the entryway as she erased notes from the whiteboard. She was still clad in her karategi.

"Hey, Asha, forgot something?" she called out, vigorously rubbing out lines written in black marker. "You left your Squishmallow. I kept Shantira with me. I know how much you love her."

She turned, eraser still in hand, smiling and pointing to a fluffy blue toy draped over her bag on the floor. "She's right there—"

Her voice caught when she saw him, shock and confusion flickering across her face.

"Hi, Koreen."

"Royce? What the hell are you doing here?" Her cheeks flushed a deep shade of pink, her eyes wide with surprise.

"I…I just want to ask you something."

He saw her take in his drenched appearance; he was still half-breathless from his mad dash through the rain and up the steps. He probably looked like a crazed stalker. If she beat him up right then and there, he couldn't blame her.

"What is it?" Her voice was shaking.

Was she afraid?

He braced himself for the worst—her fists, the eraser, even the whiteboard—but he kept on speaking.

"Does she know how much I love her?"

Thirteen

Koreen

RETRACE

THIS WAS THE DREAM THAT MADE HER CRY.

She remembered it now.

She'd first dreamed it at the hotel, in the big bed that had witnessed their seemingly insatiable passion.

She'd dreamt it again in the weeks that followed. After ten or more restless nights in a row, she'd taken the black cardboard cut-out and the dried anemone out of the picture frame and kept them in her bag, with every intention of throwing both away when she had the chance.

It was a dream of holding Royce Duran in her arms—until he vanished into thin air. In that dream, he was never really there to begin with. She'd imagined it all: his voice, his cool citrus scent, his touch, their lovemaking.

Even in her waking hours, the dream followed her incessantly.

Tonight, he stood before her, chest heaving, raindrops glistening on his skin and hair like tiny diamonds. Of course this was yet another version of that dream.

The real Royce would never be here, at this time, looking like that.

"Koreen." He spoke again, almost pleadingly, his eyes wild as they seemed to devour the sight of her. "Do you know how much I love you?"

She took a step back, the eraser falling from her grasp as her hands and knees began to shake uncontrollably. "I don't know."

"Do you want to know?"

She held up her hands. If only he'd have mercy and stay away. "Let's not do this."

"Not do this? My flight's tomorrow. I can't leave Iloilo again without telling you the truth. Do you want us to do this in another fifteen years?"

She shook her head, pain shooting through her as if he'd just struck her in the solar plexus. "Please, Royce, I don't have the strength to do this all over again."

"Then let me give you mine," he insisted, taking a step towards her. "Why won't you let me in? Why can't we be together?"

"You know why. You're on top of the world now, but I can't go that high. I would lose myself."

"Never." The word was uttered with such raw determination, making her flinch. "You'll be with me."

"I've been the only person I could count on for the past fifteen years. If I lose that person...what would happen to me?"

He advanced further, reaching out to her with both hands. "Nothing. That's not going to happen. But why can't you be with me? You belong in my world. We belong with each other."

"Your world is perfect," she countered, tears prickling at the corners of her eyes. "It's a glittering dream of wealth and power...but mine is full of struggle and uncertainty. All my dreams keep slipping away. You were the first to slip away—and I couldn't stop you. Since we were kids, I tried to keep you with me, wherever I was. You made me feel whole, as if you're the best parts of myself. When I was with you, I was always better, happier, stronger. When I lost you, I didn't know what to do."

She felt a tear escape, tracing a hot path down her cheek before she could stop it. She put her arms around her body, fearing she'd fall apart into pieces too small to put back together.

"You know what happens when you take out someone's heart, right? They stop breathing. That's what happened when you left. With Papa gone, too, I quit Karate...I only came back because they gave me a job. In college, I never even made it to the dean's list. It didn't matter that much, because you weren't around. I just ended up working, day after day... until I couldn't stop."

"Koreen...why the fuck didn't you tell me? You should have just called and told me to come back to you."

She shook her head. "A little too late for that, isn't it?

Look at what you've achieved. Everything you are now…I don't have a place in a world like yours."

His eyes flashed angrily, his jaw clenching so hard his face looked distorted. "But you do. All of this won't mean anything if you're not with me. I pushed myself to be the man you deserved to have."

"Why would you do that?"

His impatience mounted; she drew back as she saw fury ignite in his eyes. Without warning, Royce stalked towards her, grabbing her arms firmly before she could react. Tears streamed down her face, but he was relentless.

"Because I love you. I loved you before I even understood what it meant. I loved you since we were children, since Shihan Tuazon paired us up and told me you were the best in kata, and I could only hope to be half as good as you."

Royce's grip softened as he continued, his voice so quiet it was barely a rumble in her ear. "He made us training partners because he knew you would challenge me, that you'd make me better. And he was right—you did. All those years, we made each other better. Now, give me a reason why we shouldn't be with each other for the rest of our lives."

Through her tears, she looked into his blazing eyes and shrank back from the intensity she saw, only to be held in place by his unyielding arms.

This was the person she had loved her entire life.

She took in his scent, the mingling of his sweat and the pouring rain around them, and listened to the racing of his heart. She knew in that moment that the heart in that powerful body of his had always been hers.

That heart didn't know the meaning of giving up.

"I…I don't want to lose you again," she whispered,

leaning into his embrace, allowing herself to collapse against his chest.

It was everything she had ever wanted. To be loved by the only person she had ever wanted to love her.

"You won't." His answer was immediate, firm, giving no quarter for doubt. "You never fucking will."

"I should have told you that I loved you, all those years ago," she said, a little wistfully. "I didn't know how to. I was too afraid...I didn't want to be weak. I didn't want you to laugh at me."

He cradled her face in his hands, his thumbs brushing away the tear tracks on her cheeks. To her surprise, there were drops of moisture trickling down his face, too. Sweat, tears, or rain—she wasn't sure, but she didn't really care.

"Do you still love me, Koreen?"

She smiled, unable to help herself. "Yes. I love you more now."

"Damn it to hell, woman." He uttered a few more curse words as he sank to his knees before her, wrapping his arms around her waist, burying his face in her stomach. "Was that so fucking hard to say?"

She giggled, euphoria coursing through her as she embraced him right back, her nose burrowing into his short-cropped hair. It tickled, causing another stream of teary giggles.

"No. I know exactly what I want from you, too."

His eyes widened as he lifted his head and looked into her eyes. "And what's that?"

She looked down at him; this strong, intelligent man who never gave up on her; the boy who had looked after her when she was alone; the boy who had been too afraid to say his feelings, too. And now, the man he had become—brave enough to tell her the truth.

"All I've ever wanted was you, Royce." The echo of his words from the hotel proposal resonated within her, reminding her of how desperately they had both longed for each other. Their bodies had been more straightforward, knowing exactly what the other wanted. "I don't need anything else. You've always been enough for me, from the beginning. More than enough."

"You got me. I've been yours since we were six years old, you know."

She took his face in her hands, her fingers tracing the shape of his beard. "Maybe all we ever needed was each other, from the very start."

"You're right," he said softly. "That's all we've ever needed."

"Can I…can I have you, then? Just you?" It was the simplest of questions, causing the most complex mix of emotions inside her: joy, longing, regret, fear. She realized she was trembling, but she knew he was there to hold her up.

He reached up, caressing her cheek tenderly. "You can, Koreen. You never had to ask."

She bent down to kiss him, their lips meeting passionately. The kiss quickly grew heated, their hands hungrily reaching for each other, desperate and feverish after their recent painful separation.

As they kissed, his hands deftly opened her kimono, revealing her camisole and sports bra underneath. He wasted no time in sliding his fingers beneath the layers of fabric, releasing her breasts to the cool night air.

"I miss you," he murmured against her lips, his breath hot and heavy.

"I miss you too," she groaned, feeling heat pool in the pit of her stomach as she pressed her body tighter against his, her nails digging into his back.

His mouth left hers, trailing a path of hot, open-mouthed kisses down her neck and across her collarbone, finally reaching her breasts. His tongue flicked over her nipples, teasing them as he alternated between licking and sucking.

His hands moved lower, expertly undoing the ties of her pants, allowing them to pool at her feet. He lifted her out of them, leaving her clad only in her underwear and half-open kimono. His eyes roamed over her body as he lowered her damp panties, leaving her completely exposed before him.

He leaned in towards her folds, his breath teasing her sensitive skin. With one hand supporting her waist, he raised her leg slightly, granting his mouth better access. He buried his face between her thighs, his tongue eagerly seeking out her wetness.

The sensation of his lips on her was electrifying; the pleasure he was giving her mounting quickly as she ground against him. She could dimly feel her exposed breasts bouncing as she moved wantonly, but, at the moment, the world was theirs—and theirs alone.

"Please, Royce," she gasped, as she felt the first waves of her climax drawing closer.

Her plea made him redouble his efforts to push her over the edge. His mouth worked in sync with her increasingly desperate movements, bringing her higher and higher, until she couldn't hold back any longer.

"Come for me, my queen," he whispered against her, his tongue flicking over her nub.

That was all she needed. With a final cry of his name, she climaxed, her body trembling with the force of her release.

She collapsed in his arms, momentarily breathless and weak-kneed. He held her easily, his hands rubbing her back, his lips whispering soothing words into her hair.

But that was only the beginning.

As she slowly came to her senses, she felt his hands gently pulling off the rest of her clothes until she stood naked before him. At the corner of her eye, she could see her bare body, proud and glistening, reflected in the mirrors.

She watched as he stood up and swiftly removed his pants, freeing his erection from the confines of his clothing. The sight of him, strong and virile, made her heart race.

"Come here," he commanded as he lowered himself onto the floor once more, opening his legs for her.

She straddled him, feeling the blazing heat of his rock-hard length pressing against her entrance. She put her arms around his neck, using his strength for support as she slowly lowered herself onto him, gasping at the feeling of completeness as he filled her.

She looked into his eyes and saw only burning need. This man...he would have all of her and more.

"Royce, I..." she began, but he silenced her with a kiss.

"Ride me," he urged, his hands gripping her hips as she began to move.

She moaned as she felt him thrust deeper into her, their bodies finding an instinctive rhythm together. This was their own sequence of passion—perfect and powerful.

He licked, caressed, and bit at her breasts as she rose and fell against him, their skin rubbing together deliciously.

"I love you," he breathed between fervent kisses to her neck and chest, his fingers digging into her hips as he drove himself deeper inside her. Her body tightened around him, the intensity of their connection leaving her teetering on the edge of ecstasy.

"I love you, too," she gasped, her orgasm washing over her like a tidal wave. Her head rolled back as the sensations sent her reeling, losing what little control she had left.

Moments later, he followed her over the edge, his body tensing as he poured himself into her, grunting her name into her breasts.

She clung to him as he crashed to the mats, their bodies still entwined. She listened to his heart pounding against her ear, his breath coming in gasps.

"There goes your fifth dan, Sensei," he chuckled breathlessly. "So much for having two champions together, huh?"

"Oh, shut up, you." She gave his shoulder a playful shove, but he caught her hand instead and kissed her palm.

"I love you, Koreen."

"I know." She lowered her head and pressed her lips to his, tasting herself on his mouth.

"You do, don't you?" The desire she could see in his eyes was unmistakable. They weren't done yet; this reunion was too intense, too long-awaited to be satisfied so easily.

He helped her roll off him and pulled her to her feet, a sly grin on his face. "Ready for another round?"

She nodded, not knowing what he had in mind but more than willing to oblige.

Without another word, he swept her into his arms and

brought her towards the mirrors that lined one wall of the training area. As soon as he set her down, she ripped off his shirt and jumped onto him, arms around his neck, legs around his hips.

He laughed as he caught her by the waist and peeled her off him. "Later for that, love. I've always wanted to do this."

He set her down so she faced the mirror, and stepped around to stand behind her. She could already feel his hardness against her leg.

"Royce…"

"Hands on the mirror." He gave her a gentle push towards her own reflection, her breasts pressing up against the glass. "Higher."

As she followed his instructions, he drew closer, his chest pressing against her back. His hands roamed down to her heat once more, teasing and coaxing. Her body responded in kind, making him whisper his appreciation against the back of her neck.

His hands found her breasts, his thumbs flicking over the nipples. Her hips bucked, her backside seeking his hardness. She knew now what they were up to.

He entered her from behind, surging into her in one sure, firm stroke. She cried out against the mirror, her body adjusting to his size, the angle new and the mounting pleasure earth-shattering.

He thrust into her and she met him, again and again, their reflections seemingly dancing in the fogged glass as the lights flickered and wavered overhead. The sound of their moans and skin slapping against each other filled the gym, drowned out by rainfall.

"Eyes up, Koreen," he murmured, his voice rough with exertion. "Stay with me. Be with me."

The rest of the world fell away as they locked gazes in the mirror. He didn't miss a beat; he kept up his pace, owning and mastering their rhythm and her. She followed his lead, finally surrendering herself to him.

"Yes, my queen, that's it." His hand slid up front, rubbing her core in firm circles, the pressure of his touch and the friction of his strokes sending her hurtling towards the inevitable.

"Royce…oh god!" She reached the peak in a hoarse scream, her body trembling against the glass.

With a final groan and his deepest thrust, he joined her, his own release exploding within her as he buried his face in her neck, his breath ragged against her skin.

And, outside, the rain grew into a storm.

Fourteen

Royce

RESTITUTION

HE WAS HERS NOW.

He felt himself shatter as he thrust deeply into her body. Dimly, he heard his own voice, groaning her name, as his hips gyrated against her backside, unable to let the waves of pleasure subside just yet.

They collapsed together on the floor, their bodies slick with sweat, his arms still around her. She turned to face him, her hands running through his hair, her lips raining kisses on his burning cheeks.

"I love you, Royce," she breathed into his shoulder, still clinging to him like a lifeline.

Their lips met once more, tender and adoring, yet still filled with an insatiable hunger for one another.

"I've always loved you, Koreen," he answered, kissing his way down, from her lips to her jawline, from her chin to her collarbone. He'd missed her sweet strawberry scent so badly.

As reality settled over them, she disentangled her limbs from his and, shyly, gathered her discarded uniform and underwear from the floor. Her cheeks flushed a rosy pink, she giggled as she darted naked towards the locker room, leaving him to pull up his pants and attempt to reassemble his torn shirt.

He gathered her black bag and the blue stuffed toy off the mats and made his way to the main hall of the gym, waiting for her to finish.

A few minutes later, she exited the staff room, dressed in a t-shirt and jeans, her long hair tied back. Illuminated by flickering bulbs and flashes of lightning, she was breathtaking, even more than the night he'd first brought her to the hotel for dinner. He took her into his arms and kissed her.

This time, there was no hesitation on her part as she responded in kind, meeting his lips with her own, just as enthusiastically.

"I've got her," he said, holding up the stuffed animal that had sparked their entire encounter. It was only then that he came to notice it wasn't only a toy; it also had the straps of a backpack.

"Shantira." She smiled affectionately. "She belongs to one of my kata juniors. Asha considers her a lucky charm."

"Asha is right about that. Does she know where I can

get my own Shantira—or perhaps a hundred of her, to be sure?"

"I'll ask," she replied with a light laugh, taking the backpack-slash-toy and draping one of its straps over her shoulder. "But, tonight, she's coming with me. With the way the rain's going, I won't be surprised if this part of town floods again soon."

He nodded. "Where do you want to go? Home?"

She looked up into his eyes, reaching over to stroke her thumb over his lips. "I don't really know. I just want to be with you. I…I missed you."

"I missed you, too." He pulled her close. His heart clenched at the thought of him being away from her again, but he didn't want to think about it now. "I'm leaving at eight tomorrow…Tell me what you want to do until then."

She took his hand as she looked at the stormy world through the gym's windows, the rain drumming a relentless rhythm on the roof above them.

"We need to go. If it starts to flood, my car won't be able to get out of this part of the city." She hesitated for a moment. "Maybe I can drive you to the hotel? We can stay there safely from the storm, like before. I don't think I'll be able to get home at this rate."

He felt a smile tug at his lips, at the poignant memories of the precious, fleeting time they had spent together in his room. "Let's do that."

Hand in hand, they descended the steps. Still familiar with the workings of the facility, he pulled down the steel doors over the entryway and waited for her to lock up.

"I hope another storm won't destroy this place." Koreen's voice was tinged with wistful affection as she replaced the keys in her bag and ran her hands over the metal door. "It means so much to so many people."

Royce surveyed the foundations of the building. The ceilings and walls might eventually give in, but the structure itself was inherently tough and stable, made of thick steel and pure gravel from an older time. "Sometimes you have to take damage to see how strong you really are."

With their fingers entwined, they braved the storm together, walking towards her car. The downpour had become much heavier since his arrival at the gym.

She drove through the rain-slicked streets with a determined cast to her face. The windshield wipers fought a losing battle against the pouring rain, but, in the end, they made it through.

Upon arriving at the hotel, they silently agreed to head straight to his room. The moment the door clicked shut behind them, he pulled her into his arms once more.

"Koreen," he whispered. "I have always loved you."

She didn't answer, but her arms went around his stomach as she pressed her face to his chest. He hoped she could hear that his heart knew and spoke only her name.

They stood together in their momentary shelter from the storm, until he gently broke the silence.

"Let's do this properly, my queen. I want to do this right."

He picked up the phone and ordered a big dinner for the both of them. As they waited, they settled in front of the glass windows, watching the cityscape being battered by rain and wind.

The food and drinks arrived, and they ate in comfortable silence, occasionally sharing a smile or a touch.

The unspoken truth of his impending departure hung heavily between them. Somehow, acknowledging it would make it all too real—so neither of them did.

Once they finished eating, Koreen took her phone out and called her mother. He discreetly got out of her way, tidying their plates back onto the trays and placing them outside the main door to be picked up.

When he was done, Royce found her by the wall, plugging in the charger for her phone.

"Is your mother okay?"

She nodded. "Kenneth and Debbie are with her. It's a good thing they decided to bring some dinner home to her."

He took a seat on the couch and opened his arms for her. She joined him and, together, they returned to watching the storm, holding on to each other.

After a while, he spoke, unable to contain his curiosity any longer. "Koreen…is it true that you deliberately flunked our last Calculus exam in high school?"

She froze, but she didn't say anything, just turned her face away from his slightly.

"I always did wonder, you know. Your grades were definitely higher than mine during senior year. Something must have happened that made us get the same average in the end. Is it true?"

In the soft light of the living area, he could see a tinge of red on her cheeks. She remained stubbornly silent.

He tried again, sensing the truth behind her evasion. "Did you make yourself fail, so I could catch up?"

"How did you find out?" she demanded, giving him a

wary look as she drew back. "Dara was the only one who knew, and she's in the US now."

He reached up and tweaked her nose. "Does it matter?"

She hesitated, pushing his hand away irritably. She crossed her arms over her chest, not meeting his eyes. "Oh, for fuck's sake. Yes, I did."

He tried to pull her back towards him, causing her to retreat to the other end of the couch. Undeterred, he scooted over and promptly covered her with his body. She tried to push him off, but he used his weight to keep her pinned down.

"Was it worth it?" he murmured, his mouth a few inches away from hers.

"It was," she replied, still avoiding his gaze.

"Koreen."

"What?"

"Love you."

"God, stop it already. You were worth it, okay? I couldn't bear it if you weren't with me. I switched half the integers and misplaced a lot of decimal points. That damn test still haunts me until now. But then, I think of you… and it's okay."

It was his turn to freeze. Kenneth's revelation had surprised him, but the raw, almost angry, honesty in Koreen's admission hit differently.

The depth of her feelings, captured in that simple confession, humbled him.

"Did you know that Dr. Briones actually talked to me about it? I told her I was exhausted and got confused with some of the questions. I don't think she believed me at all, but no one could do anything."

A failure. A white lie. A strike against her own brilliant intellect and reputation.

All for him.

She made another attempt to push him off. He was well aware that she was perfectly capable of breaking his neck or gouging his eyes out from her position, but she didn't. She probably really did love him.

"Royce, I can't breathe. You weigh a ton."

Still dumbstruck, he lifted his body off hers. She slid out from under him and crossed the room to an armchair, where her black bag sat with Shantira. He watched her pull out a small object and walk back to him.

Instead of sitting down, she stood before him, holding out her hand. In her palm was a battered piece of dark-colored cardboard. "Here."

He finally found his voice, amidst all the shock. "What is it?"

"It's the flower you gave me all those years ago." She unfolded it to reveal a clump of shriveled petals. "Your anemone. You gave it to me in this cardboard box."

"Koreen, I..." The words disappeared in his throat, swallowed by emotions too many to name.

"I used to keep it with your belt," she explained, almost dreamily, as if lost in memory. "Then I kept it with our picture. When I got home from the hotel last time, I took it out."

Her fingers smoothed the dried anemone tenderly. "I've been carrying it with me for weeks. I thought about throwing it away when the time felt right, but that moment never came. I just couldn't let it go. But now I could."

He reached out to touch the fragile petals. So many years, so much time, kept in a single memento.

"Why?" he choked out.

"Because I have you now."

He took the cardboard and the old flower nestled within it from her hand, setting the past aside, carefully, on the coffee table. When he pulled her into his arms, she didn't resist.

"We have each other now," he corrected gently.

She nodded as she nestled against him, all her earlier irritation gone. "I've only ever wanted you, Royce. Not what you have, not what you can give—just you."

He leaned down and captured her lips in a kiss. It started slow and gentle, their mouths barely touching. But the intensity grew quickly, like a wildfire.

They undressed one another, carefully peeling off layer after layer until they were bare in each other's hands. He scooped her up into his arms and carried her to the bed.

She made him lie down next to her, and lost no time by placing tender kisses on his chest before descending further down his body. She knelt between his legs, her fingers lightly stroking him before she slid his length between her lips.

The sensation of her mouth engulfing him sent shockwaves through his entire body. He fought to keep his eyes open, needing to see her as she brought him closer and closer to the edge. The warmth of her breath, the wetness of her tongue, and the rhythmic suction drove him to the brink—and beyond.

"Koreen," he gasped, gripping the heavy wooden

headboard so hard he, dimly, heard it crack. He heard nothing more as the intensity of his climax overtook him.

As the last shudders of his orgasm ebbed away, he reached for her, worshipping her skin with caresses and kisses until she was soaking wet and ready.

"We have all night, my queen," he said, burying his face between her breasts. "Let's make the most of it."

She ran her hands down his back as she pushed her hips and chest upward, all his for the taking. "I want that, too."

And so they began, their bodies moving together, exploring every inch of heated skin. Over and over again, they lost themselves in each other.

They made love on the bed, the soft sheets tangling around them as they writhed in rhythm with the rain. They made love on the floor, the plush carpet cushioning their movements as they explored new positions and angles. They made love against the glass windows, the cool surface contrasting with their burning passion, and on the desk, her body draped over the wood as his tongue teased her before he took her again, sinking deeply into her core.

He lost count how many times he had her—it could be ten, or twenty. After a quick shower where he ate her out against the tiles, under a stream of warm water, he carried her back to the bed.

He wasn't sure who dozed off first, but they were awakened by a persistent ringing sound. He thought at first it was his alarm, set for four in the morning.

"Your phone," Koreen muttered as she stirred in his arms, still clinging to him, one leg draped over his hips.

He fumbled sleepily with one hand, reluctant to let her

go with the other, before finally locating his mobile on the bedside table.

The name on the display wrenched all the sleep out of him. Royce sat up, bringing Koreen along. She groaned in protest but adjusted her position, still half-asleep.

The clock read a few minutes past three in the morning. He swiped to take the call. "Yoshida."

"I am very sorry to bother you, Mr. Duran." His assistant's voice sounded wide awake.

"It's alright, Yoshida. Everything okay?"

"I have just been informed by the airline that your flight to Manila has been cancelled because of the storm. I tried to find you another, but all flights in and out have been grounded until further notice."

A sense of relief washed over him, followed by a looming uncertainty in what could come next—the state of Boundless Tower, his decisions in running the company all over the world, his love for and future with the woman in his arms.

"It can't be helped. In the morning, please tell Jesse not to push any work on the Tower until the flood has subsided." Both Yoshida and Lozada were staying in another hotel, closer to the building site.

"Yes, sir. As for your flight, shall I book you on the next available one out of Iloilo?"

He took a deep breath, taking a few seconds to look at Koreen next to him. Her cat-like eyes were now wide open, watching him closely with a mix of hope and trepidation.

"Sir?" Yoshida's voice broke through his trance.

"I'll let you know what's going to happen next,

Kotaro-san," Royce replied in Nihongo. "I may need to take that vacation, after all."

"Of course, sir."

"Stay safe. Thank you."

Yoshida murmured a welcome before hanging up.

"What happened?" Koreen asked after he'd put the phone away.

He took her chin into his hand. "My flight's been canceled because of the storm. I'm not going anywhere today. I don't think I'm going anywhere for a few days, at least."

A smile broke across her face, more radiant than any sunrise. "I don't think I'm going anywhere for a few days, either."

He chuckled, nuzzling her neck, kissing his way down to her breasts. "Sounds about right."

"We've been so stupid, you know," she said softly, even as her body eagerly responded to his touch.

Curious, he looked up at her. "What makes you say that?"

"From the beginning, everything was telling us we were meant to be together—getting paired up in Karate, how we both did so well in school, our failed relationships, these storms."

He listened closely, allowing her words to wash over him. By the time she mentioned the weather, he was grinning, his lips seeking her nipples. "No complaints from me."

"I'm serious, Royce. How many storms have to happen before we realize that?"

"I'm serious, too. I was the one who wanted to get married, remember?"

She huffed in frustration. "That's not even what I meant, but you're right. Why do you always have to one-up me in everything?"

"Because I love you. Because that's what we're meant to do to each other." As soon as he was done speaking, he dove right back into her, kissing and licking her nipples until they were rock-hard.

"Royce Duran—"

He didn't let her finish. His hand had sneaked its way into her folds, causing her to squeal in surprise.

"Stay with me, my queen," he said, moving his fingers in and out of her, using his palm to tease her nub. "Stay with me until this storm is over."

Nothing more was said as he moved between her legs, teasing her entrance with his arousal before he entered her. He brought her legs high and wide, driving into her wetness until their moans filled the room.

Sated, they lay back on the pillows, still breathless from their release.

Even in their blissful post-coital state, Koreen Cisco asserted her supremacy. Even in love, she knew how to one-up him, too.

"I don't want to stay until this storm is over," she said, her voice muffled by his skin as she pressed against his chest. "I want to stay until the next, and the one after it. I go all or nothing, remember?"

He nodded, wrapping his arms around her. "I like the sound of that."

"What about this?" With one quick movement, she was on top of him. "Do you like the sound of this, too?"

She reached for his hardness and sank onto it, glorious

and sure in her movements as she rode him, grinding and bouncing, to a tidal wave of ecstasy.

And, yes, he did like the sounds they both made.

As they finally lay next to each other, drifting off to sleep, legs entwined, he reached out to touch her. As he ran his fingers through her hair and down her cheek, she reached out, too, her hand landing on the spot where his heart was, ever only beating for her.

"I love you, Koreen," he told her.

Her eyes drifted open, a smile forming on her lips as she replied, "I love you, too." Moments later, she was fast asleep, her hand still firmly in place.

It was then that he realized that the gap between them had never truly been a wall.

It was a bridge, one they had been too afraid to cross. All they really needed to do was reach out to each other.

With their fear gone, replaced by love, they had finally found their way, closing the last divide between their hearts.

Epilogue

Koreen

CROSSED

It was the end of another week—and she looked forward to the next.

Koreen watched her students gather their laptops and tablets, smiling as she listened to their enthusiastic chatter about job interviews and weekend plans with friends, acknowledging and responding as they bid her goodbye.

Once everyone had left, she took a moment to draw a deep breath and look around the classroom, making sure everything was ready for tomorrow's longer, more intensive weekend sessions. She was making her way out when she was met at the threshold by a trio of girls from her old BPO training center. They had followed her when she'd opened her own facility months ago.

"Miss Koreen!" Althea exclaimed, bouncing on her toes with excitement. "You have a visitor waiting in your office!"

"Really? This late?" It was closing time; her session had been the last one for the day.

"Trust us, you'll want to see him." Jane giggled, nudging her friend knowingly.

"Alright, alright." Koreen shook her head in amusement. It was probably the security guard who went around the building before his night shift, selling something his wife had made, usually rice cakes, to the tenants.

She began to walk towards the door, but before she could leave the room, the girls descended on her like a pack of eager stylists. They straightened her clothes, spritzed her lightly with cologne, and applied powder and lip gloss.

"Good?" Someone took out her hair from its ponytail, fluffing up the locks to fall over her shoulders.

The other two girls standing in front of Koreen nodded seriously, like a panel of judges.

"With the amount of time we were given, we did excellent," May, the group's *de facto* leader, said approvingly.

"Okay, that's enough," Koreen laughed, gently pushing them away. "Thank you, girls. You should be going home now. Don't forget, we have skills assessments on Monday. Good night."

After waving goodbye to the girls from the small hallway as they exited the center, Koreen headed to her office.

Her office.

The thought always made her feel a swell of pride at

what she had accomplished. What once had been a dream was now a reality; her small business was thriving. Located in a cozy office building adjacent to the almost completed Boundless Tower, it may have been tiny—with only three classrooms, a reception area, a staff room, and her office—but it was successful. Most importantly, it was hers.

Named Unison, her facility operated on a unique business model. Their training programs were bespoke to the needs of partner corporations. Her students, trained on specific required skill sets, with a syllabus approved and subsidized by each hiring company, were funneled into Boundless and other call and transcription centers. Most of the time, they would quickly be placed in supervisory positions. In her new space, she was able to cultivate a new generation of leaders.

As she reached for the doorknob, she smiled at the modest nameplate before her.

KOREEN T. CISCO
Owner/Manager
UNISON TRAINING & PLACEMENT

"Good eve—" The words caught in her throat as soon as she laid eyes on her 'visitor.'

Seated on one of the small chairs facing her desk, idly perusing brochures, was Royce.

He looked up when she entered, a mischievous glint in his eyes.

"Hey there," he said casually, as if it were perfectly normal for him to be sitting in her office halfway across the world from where he was supposed to be. "I really like what you've done with the place."

"What are you doing here?" Heat suffused her cheeks and stomach at the sight of him only a few feet away.

"I'm here to see my girlfriend," he replied with a smirk, clearly enjoying her surprise. "Besides, a partner can check on his business anytime, right?"

"Yeah, you can," she grudgingly admitted. He did own half the business as the one who had provided the capital and corporate contacts. "But why didn't you tell me you were coming home?"

"Where's the fun in that?" He grinned, standing up and closing the distance between them.

Koreen couldn't help herself; she practically leaped into his arms the moment he was within reach. Their lips met in a passionate, explosive kiss—from months upon months of pent-up longing and desire. All propriety vanished as Royce reached over to lock the office door, his fingers deftly sliding the bolt.

As they continued to devour each other, he cleared her desk with a single, powerful sweep of his arm and lifted her onto it with a growl. They fumbled with buttons and zippers, pushing enough of their clothes aside to allow their bodies to join together.

"God, I've missed you so much," he groaned into her ear as he drove into her with a force enough to break the table she was on. She welcomed every thrust and lick and kiss, meeting each with equal fervor.

"I've missed you too," she panted. "I love you so much."

With one last suckle on a partially exposed breast, he

turned her over. Bending her body over the desk, he lifted her skirt and pushed her legs apart.

"I missed this," he murmured as he reached from behind to tease her opening with his fingers. "I dreamt of doing this to you every single fucking night."

She gasped when he entered her, the sensation of being stretched and filled making her heady.

"Then what are you waiting for?" she breathed, feeling his hands tighten on her hips.

He didn't answer, but instead began to move inside her.

It was heavenly; she could barely hold on to the edge of the table as he pushed her to the brink and, with a final shout of her name, followed closely behind.

He collapsed on top of her. She could feel him shaking from his climax, feel his warm release dripping down her leg.

"I love you," he said, nuzzling her hair and the back of her neck. "I'm so glad to be home."

As the last echoes of their passion faded, he helped her up and they quickly dressed in silence. Decent once more, he pulled her into his arms for a chaste kiss on the forehead. "Ready to head out?"

Koreen nodded. Together, they locked up the training center and made their way to the outdoor car park. As they stepped into the cool night air, she glanced at the glittering Boundless Tower in the distance. It had become her habit over the past few months; the sight of the magnificent building made her feel closer to him.

Royce noticed her gaze and put his arm around her shoulders, pausing to look at the Tower himself.

"She's ours now," he declared.

"Ours?"

"Boundless Tower," he clarified without hesitation. "Or what used to be."

"What do you mean, used to be?" She looked at him and the building, and back again.

Even with the limited lighting in the car park, she could see the grin on his face. "I bought out Boundless Tower from Prince Khalid, Koreen. I asked him if he was willing to sell it and he agreed, on the condition that I make him a foreign partner in the business."

She stared at him, slowly processing his words. She reached for his hand and gripped it tightly.

"I quit my job in Saudi," Royce said, his smile widening. "I'm not the CEO of Boundless Telecommunications anymore. That's why I'm back…I came home."

"Really?" Her heart thundered in her ears at the realization that he was staying—with her, for good.

He nodded. "I wanted to come home to you…so here I am. Surprise."

With a cry, she launched herself into his arms, sending her bags crashing to the pavement. Their lips met again and again, as she laughed and cried in his embrace.

"I'm going to rename the business, too, and the Tower, of course," Royce said, setting her down gently back on her feet and wiping her tears away with his thumb.

"Rename it? To what?"

"Crown. Fit for a queen."

Koreen felt a blush rise to her cheeks. "I like it. No, I love it."

The happiness on his face was unmistakable as he

spoke. "I knew you would. You gave me the idea when I first invested in your training facility. I thought it was brilliant; to have a business of your own, no matter how small. I took a page out of your book, Koreen—I didn't want to be an employee forever, either. I wanted my own place to belong to."

She hugged him tightly around the torso. "You belong with me."

"Exactly." His arms went around her shoulders as he pressed kisses to her hair. "So, where to next?"

"Wherever you want to go, as long as we're together."

He smiled slyly. "Good, because I'm staying at my old room. I thought you'd want to go there for dinner."

She laughed, but the meaning behind his words made her shiver in anticipation. Yes, she would have dinner, and then she would have him.

"I miss that room," she admitted.

He kissed her nose lightly before he let go to pick up her scattered belongings. Hand in hand, they walked to her car.

Upon arriving at the hotel, she was surprised to see him practically leap out of the passenger seat, offering his hand with an infectious grin. She took it, giggling at his enthusiasm.

"Royce, slow down, we haven't even eaten yet," she teased, though she found herself matching his pace, moving through the familiar halls a little breathlessly.

"I have something better planned. Something very special."

He hoisted her into his arms as soon as they exited the

elevator at the penthouse level. He didn't let her go until they were inside the suite.

Hands on her waist, he steered her in the direction of the bedroom. Her breath caught as she spotted a single white anemone, partially wrapped in black paper and tied with colorful ribbons, sitting in the middle of the giant bed.

She turned to him, unable to read the expression on his face. She'd given him the dried petals all those months ago…Her vision wavered and blurred and, suddenly, she was sixteen years old again.

She was on a storm-ravaged football field, unable to say anything—not even goodbye—to the boy who owned her heart.

"Koreen?"

Royce's voice broke through to her in the present, sixteen years on. She turned to the sound and there he was, tall and strong, sure and steady, next to her.

"Can you please get that for me?" He inclined his head towards the lone flower, a small smile on his lips.

Without a word, she stepped forward and carefully picked up the anemone. As she did so, something cold and hard slid into her palm.

Startled, she opened her hand to reveal a gleaming platinum-white ring. It was adorned with a square-cut black jewel.

"It's a diamond." His voice was hoarse and shaky.

When she turned to look at him again, he was on bended knee, his head lowered.

"Royce…" She reached out with her free hand, running her fingers through his hair, smoothing the beard she had grown to love so much on him.

He put his hand over hers, his gaze slowly moving up to her face. "I couldn't find a cardboard box this time around. But I thought…maybe this would be a suitable replacement."

Tears pricked at the corners of her eyes as the full weight of his gesture hit her.

This time, I will listen.

I will let him know how I feel, too.

This time, she wasn't afraid anymore.

She crossed the last few inches that separated them, never taking her eyes off him as he slid the ring onto her finger.

"It is," she said. "Yes, it is."

BOOK V

Our Love Replay

Playlist

Everywhere
Michelle Branch

I'm With You
Avril Lavigne

Far Away
Nickelback

Private Emotion
Ricky Martin & Meja

No Promises
Shayne Ward

Walk Away
Solid HarmoniE

214
Rivermaya

Prologue

THE RAIN

Tara

In an odd dance of black and grey swirls, thick clouds gathered overhead, promising a downpour that would soon drench the pathways of the university.

Sighing, Tara Galvez tore her gaze away from the sky and turned her attention to the retreating back of her best friend. She raised a hand in farewell just before the other girl disappeared around a corner, in a quick getaway before the heavy rains hit.

Jasmine's parting words lingered at the back of her mind, both a comfort and a challenge. *"You really should share those poems with other people, just like your grandmother says. They're too beautiful to stay hidden in that tiny notebook of yours."*

Alone now, she felt the familiar wall of shyness close around her. She hugged her canvas bag closer to her body, feeling the first whispers of wind nudge her along, urging her toward the library before it closed for the day.

Moments later, with the reserved History book snugly under her arm, Tara headed towards the closest campus gate, hoping the traffic wouldn't be as bad as Jasmine had feared. As she made her way down the library steps, she nearly collided with a lanky boy in a red varsity jacket. He was an upperclassman, all limbs and hasty apologies as he darted past, his backpack swinging haphazardly from one shoulder. She blinked in surprise, watching as he disappeared towards the grounds in the opposite direction. It was then that she noticed a large rectangular notebook lying on the concrete.

"Excuse me! You dropped something!" she called out, but he was already too far away to hear her.

Sighing, she bent down to retrieve the fallen item. As soon as she touched the dark blue linen cover and thick spiral-bound cream paper inside, she realized it was a sketchbook. Curiously, she flipped through the pages, each one filled with pencil strokes so vivid they seemed to pulse with life. Flowers rendered with delicate lines bloomed around majestic mountains; bodies of water rippled and rows of coconut trees swayed across pages; and faces captured in silent conversation stared back at her.

Debating whether or not to follow the young man, she glanced towards the direction he'd disappeared, then up at the sky. Dark clouds loomed closer, reminding her of her own need to get home. The best thing to do would be to get to the jeepney stop immediately. She could hand over the sketchbook to the college office in the morning. Not that it was something expensive or anything...

Or was it?

Before she could think twice about it, Tara found herself scurrying in the same direction as the upperclassman, the sketchbook clutched tightly to her chest. The distant echo of bouncing basketballs drew her onward, until she caught sight of the open-air court at the end of the grassy field.

Of course. With his varsity jacket, he could very well be part of the team. She'd heard about the city-wide intercollegiate basketball tournament opening game next week. Everyone in her class had seemed very excited about this, talking about another championship.

The sidelines were packed with people, many of whom were girls, all eagerly watching the team practice despite the imminent rain. She squeezed through the throng, murmuring apologies right and left. As soon as she had a clear view of the concrete court, she spotted the sketchbook's owner almost immediately. He was clad in jersey number one, tearing down the court in a blurry zigzag while dribbling a basketball with his left hand.

Tara looked around her tentatively before turning to address an older girl standing next to her. "Excuse me, do you know who the boy wearing number one is?"

The girl responded with an openly curious stare. "Why do you ask?"

She swallowed, feeling her cheeks grow warm under scrutiny. "Um, I need to return something that belongs to him."

"Seriously? You don't know who he is?" The girl shook her head disbelievingly. "That's Lucas Delgado. He's a junior and the star player of our varsity team. He pretty much single-handedly made us win the city-wide tournament for the past two years. Everyone here wants him, and everyone else out there, too. He's that hot."

Both girls watched as Lucas moved across the court, skillfully evading his teammates and effortlessly sinking a three-pointer. Tara felt an unexpected flutter in her chest as she took in his lean build and the way his wavy black hair stuck to his forehead from sweat. It was easy to see why he was so popular.

"Call out to him," the girl urged. "If you got something for Lucas, he won't mind. He's nice, too, you know. We have a few classes together."

Tara felt heat rushing up her neck at the mere thought of talking to jersey number one. "Uh, no, it's okay. I think I'll just wait until the end of practice."

"Suit yourself." The older girl shrugged and turned back to watching the players, eagerly chatting with other people around them about the team kicking the butt of the maritime academy down the road from their college.

Tara retreated to the shelter of a nearby acacia tree, careful to keep Lucas in her line of vision. As the minutes passed, her mind wandered to the beautiful sketches she had glimpsed, wondering how someone so talented on the basketball court could also have such a gift for art. It seemed almost unfair, and, yes, undeniably intriguing.

Just then, Lucas made an impressive layup shot that sent the crowd into a frenzy of cheers and applause. She couldn't help but join in, her heart racing as she watched him turn away from the ring and look in her direction, a smile on his face. The fleeting contact made her realize he had deep-set, distinctly piercing dark eyes; he also had a dimple in his right cheek. But, as quickly as Lucas had glanced her way, he ran off again, this time to guard his opponent at the other end of the court.

The first droplets of rain splattered against the ground, darkening the earth and turning the sky an ominous shade of gray. The drizzle quickly escalated into a full-scale downpour, sending spectators running for shelter.

To her surprise, her feet remained rooted to her spot, her eyes never leaving Lucas as the practice game continued without missing a beat. Lightning streaked across the sky, followed by a loud thunderclap.

"Practice is over!" the coach finally yelled. "Everyone, head inside!"

Determined not to lose sight of jersey number one, Tara fixed her eyes on his tall form as he gathered his belongings and jogged off the court with his teammates towards the main college building. She couldn't let this opportunity pass her by; she had to return his sketchbook.

"Lucas!" she called out, but her voice was drowned out by the rain and the rumble of thunder overhead. Resolved, she followed him, her sandals squelching as she made her way gingerly around puddles.

As she stepped around a tree, its branches and leaves swaying in the wind, Tara's foot slipped on the muddy path. She cried out in surprise as she toppled onto her backside, her things falling from her grasp. Strangely, the sketchbook remained glued to her grip, as if unwilling to be let go.

"Are you okay?" Lucas Delgado stood over her, rain dripping from his hair and basketball jersey. He had her canvas bag and borrowed History book clutched in his hands.

She blinked up at him, taking in the look of concern written across his face. It took a few seconds for embarrassment to sink in, a few more for shock to follow.

"Y-yes, I'm fine," she stammered, her throat tightening as she attempted to push herself upright. Pain shot up through her left ankle, causing her legs to wobble beneath her.

"Here, let me help you." He extended his hand, and she gratefully took it. As she rose, he noticed his sketchbook in her other hand, his eyes widening in recognition. "Is that my mine?"

"Sorry," she mumbled, her face burning despite the coldness of the falling rain. "I saw you drop it earlier, and I wanted to return it to you."

"Don't be," he replied, shaking his head. "Thank you. And I think these are yours." He handed over her bag and library book with a small smile.

Then, without warning, he scooped her up into his arms, eliciting a surprised gasp. Ignoring her, he went on conversationally, as if he did this with people on a regular basis. "You shouldn't be walking on this slippery path. There's an open classroom nearby where we can wait the rain out."

Lucas carefully made his way out of the field and onto the wet pavement, his hold on her as steady as his heartbeat beneath her ear. As the rain continued to pour around them in a thick veil of water and wind, it felt like they were the only two people in the world.

"Hang on, okay?" He was looking down at her with a gentle smile. It felt strange to hear him say it, considering he was the one doing the heavy lifting. "We're almost there."

She nodded, ducking her head behind her bag so he wouldn't see how flustered she really was. It took a few more long, rain-drenched moments before he stopped in front of a partially open doorway that led to an old classroom next to the cafeteria.

"I have Biology class here," she said lamely, acutely aware of the heat and closeness of his body.

"Good enough, then." He used his shoulder to push the

door open, stepping inside the dimly-lit room. He made his way straight to the teacher's table up front and carefully lowered her onto the wooden surface.

"Are you okay?" he repeated, this time examining her more closely, his dark eyes searching hers.

"Y-yes," she managed to say through her dry throat, struggling to retain a semblance of composure. "Thank you."

"You're welcome." He made his way back towards the entrance and attempted to switch on the lights. He cursed softly when nothing happened.

"I think the power's gone out," she offered.

"Yeah. Good thing I'm with you and not my teammates."

The comment made her blush, but she chose not to clarify what he meant by it. Instead, she tried a safer topic. "My best friend's gone home. I hope she doesn't get stuck in traffic. She lives in Jaro, so it's a two-ride commute."

"I live in Jaro, too. How cool is that? I'm trying not to think about how long it will take me to get home." He grinned sheepishly and pulled up a chair by her feet, sitting down and placing his backpack next to her on the table. "What's your name?"

She decided she liked having him close, even though all she ever did was redden and stutter at his proximity. He had a solid, reassuring presence. She got the same feeling looking at his drawings earlier. No wonder she'd followed him to the court. "Tara Galvez."

"Nice to meet you, Tara. I'm Lucas Delgado." He offered a friendly grin that melted away most of her nerves. "You were at the court earlier, weren't you? I saw you by the acacia."

"Um, yes. I picked this up at the library after you dropped it. You were in a hurry so I don't think you heard me calling out." She handed his sketchbook over, careful not to let her hand touch his. "I followed you to return it."

"Thank you. That's very kind of you." His eyes and face lit up as he flipped through the pages. "This is my favorite one. It has drawings of my father's childhood village in Antique province. I try to add more every time I visit, which is not very often these days."

Moved by the wistful tone in his voice, she imagined him roaming through the rural landscapes, capturing the beauty of life in pencil and pastel. She could see it now… Lucas seated on top of a grassy hill, sketching intently with a furrowed brow; herself next to him, writing poetry in her own notebook as a gentle breeze ruffled her hair.

"Let me take a look at your foot," Lucas said suddenly, jolting her back to reality. He put the sketchbook in his bag, the look of concern back on his face. "May I? It's the left one, isn't it?"

Blushing even more furiously, she nodded her assent, her eyes carefully trained at a spot on the wall above his head as she shook her wet sandal off.

With sure hands, he lifted her compromised foot and examined the ankle with gentle presses and light twists. "It doesn't seem too bad. Good news is that it's not even sprained. You should be fine after resting it for a bit. I'll stay with you."

"Thanks." She tried to quell her embarrassment at the easy familiarity and openness he treated her with. She could hardly believe that this kind, attentive young man was the same star athlete who took over the basketball court and captured the attention of so many girls.

"Are you a freshman? I don't think I've seen you around

before today." He gave her ankle a reassuring pat before moving backward to a more respectful distance. The girl on the court earlier was right; he really was nice.

"Yeah, I just started this semester." She tried to muster a smile, hoping it made her look less awkward than how she really felt.

"Welcome to the college, then," he replied warmly, his eyes crinkling at the corners as he smiled in return. "I hope you're enjoying it so far."

"Thank you. I am." *Especially now*, she wanted to add, but couldn't find the guts to say so, not in a million years.

"Great! You should come see our games. Next week we'll be mopping the floor with those maritime snobs next door. Just because we're part of a state university doesn't mean we're all scrawny nerds, right?"

She nodded vigorously, unable to look away from the animated expression on his face. "I heard the girls talking about it earlier. No, we're definitely not all scrawny nerds, that's for sure."

Lucas leaned back in his chair, seemingly satisfied at her response. This time, his gaze zeroed in on her curiously. "So, Tara, tell me about yourself. What do you like to do in your free time?"

She hesitated before giving him a truthful answer, hoping she didn't sound like a 'scrawny nerd.' "I, um, I like to write poetry and sing."

"Really? That's awesome. You must be really talented. Are you joining the theatre group, then?"

"No," she mumbled. "I can't do all that dancing I've seen them do. Besides, these are just hobbies, nothing more."

He shook his head. "Still, I'd love to hear you sing someday, maybe even read some of your poems."

Before she could respond, he noticed her shivering from the cold air seeping through the windows. "Hey, you're getting soaked. Here, take my jacket."

"You don't have—" she protested weakly, but was interrupted when he took the garment off and draped it over her shoulders. The warmth from his body radiated from the shiny fabric, instantly enveloping her.

"You know, your hair's really beautiful," he murmured, adjusting the jacket by gently flipping her hair over it. "Like you."

Her breath caught in her throat, her heart pounding so hard she thought it might burst from her chest. She didn't know how to react to his compliment, so she simply stared at him, admiring the dimple on his cheek as he looked at her with a soft, almost dreamy, smile.

"Better?" His eyes lingered on her face for a moment longer before turning to the drenched campus outside. "You should be warmer now."

"Thanks," she muttered, her cheeks burning with a mix of embarrassment and gratitude.

They sat in companionable silence for a little while longer, watching as the rain began to subside. When the downpour eventually turned into a light drizzle and the fluorescent lights overhead flickered back on, Lucas stood up and stretched his long limbs.

"Looks like the worst is over." He turned back to look at her as he slung his backpack over his shoulders. "We should get going. Get a move on before it pours like hell again. You're okay getting home, aren't you?"

Disappointment, unbidden and unstoppable, crept into her, causing tightness in her throat. "Yeah. I live in Molo, so it's just one ride from the highway."

"I'll walk you to your stop, then." He held out a hand, the gesture so casual it was hard to believe they didn't know each other two hours ago.

Trying her best to ignore the storm of unfamiliar sensations within her, she took it, feeling the strength in his grip as he helped her to her feet. She slid on her damp sandals, grateful for the absence of pain from her ankle, as she watched him shake off rain water from her bag and the History book.

"Thanks." She held out her hands for her belongings, but he shook his head.

"I got it," he said, in a tone that begged no argument. "You're okay to walk? Do you think you can use my jacket as your umbrella? It will keep you dry for the most part."

With her things safely in his hands, he led the way out of the classroom. The college lay quiet and serene in the aftermath of the downpour. They walked along the rain-slicked, glistening path illuminated by the yellow-orange glow of campus lamps, their footfalls echoing against the empty buildings.

They crossed the highway carefully to Tara's jeepney stop, Lucas moving to either side of her against the oncoming traffic. Once they reached the waiting shed, half of its cement seats dampened by rain, he gestured for her to sit on a relatively dry corner. "Here's hoping you can get a ride soon."

She shivered slightly, feeling the cool air on her damp skin. She reached to remove his jacket from her shoulders, with every intention of returning it.

"Keep it," he insisted, shaking his head. "I'll feel better knowing it got you home safe and warm."

"Thanks," she murmured, sliding her arms into the garment's expansive sleeves. It was several sizes too big for her, but the heft of the extra fabric felt almost like an embrace.

Silence descended on them as he sat down next to her. She gazed out into the drizzling night, watching droplets of rain reflect the lights of the highway and the vehicles passing by, listening to the hum of engines and the patter of water on concrete.

She glanced at Lucas and, strangely, his eyes met hers squarely. He gave her an effortlessly reassuring smile; his gaze seemed to hold a thousand secrets, alluring and mysterious. An unfamiliar warmth spread through her chest and down to her stomach, an involuntary response of her body that both terrified and thrilled her.

Finally, a Molo jeepney appeared and he stood up to flag it down, the vehicle stopping before them with a screech of its brakes. He handed over her things, his fingers brushing against hers for a fleeting moment.

She found herself wishing she could hold on a little longer to his touch, maybe even stay in the cover of the rain; hidden by water, wind and shadows, suspended in time.

"Good night, Tara," he said softly. "I'm sure I'll see you around. Thanks again for giving my sketchbook back."

"Bye, Lucas." With one last look into his eyes, she climbed aboard the jeepney, settling onto the only vacant seat at the edge.

As the vehicle pulled away, she watched him wave, remnants of his smile still on his face, his tall figure growing smaller as the distance between them increased.

She didn't look away until he was out of sight. She leaned back against the seat, feeling the steady thrum of the engine beneath her as the rain-soaked city rolled by outside.

She clutched her bag and History book tightly to her chest, both still bearing traces of the warmth of his hands. She closed her eyes, as if to calm the whirlwind of emotion and confusion within her, all caused by their chance encounter.

Although she couldn't see anything, her heart seemed to know something for certain—whatever it is she had just shared with Lucas Delgado, this was only the beginning.

*It was three A.M.
I began to cry
Remembering what I left unsaid*

*Remembering how I last saw
You as you walked away
It was three P.M.*

~ Excerpt from 'Time's Three'
Lyrics and music by Tara Galvez
I Remember You, Esta Melodia Records

Chapter 1

THE ARTIST

Tara

A GENTLE BREEZE RUSTLED THROUGH THE TREES, carrying with it the sweet scent of fresh blooms. Tara walked along the winding path of Galvez Farms, savoring the feeling of her hair dancing around her face as she hummed softly to herself.

As she passed a cluster of coconut trees sheltering a patch of earth she'd chosen as her personal garden, her fingers instinctively traced the delicate petals of the gold and white flowers she had planted weeks back. The vibrant colors seemed to sing to her, bringing a sense of peace and inspiration. This was her sanctuary, the place where she had hoped to find her music…and, perhaps, herself.

She paused in her walk and leaned against a tree, the strains of a new melody on her lips. She let her eyes flutter close, as she thought of the chords she needed to write down the minute she got back to the villa. Just then, her phone buzzed in her pocket, momentarily breaking her creative trance.

Tara pulled out her phone to see Jasmine's name flashing on the screen. She could feel a smile tugging at her lips, a momentary reprieve from the pressures of composing the next big Spotify hit. "Hey, gorgeous."

"Hello, yourself. How's Asia's Acoustic Angel doing so far away from the studio? Spread your wings yet—or did being too far away from city life clip them?" The voice of Jasmine Samontes carried through the line as if she were right there on the farm path, eagle-eyed and equally sharp-tongued.

"If I do decide never to leave the farm, it's all your fault. You won't believe it, Jas. I've just finished another song for the album. It's all coming together so beautifully here."

"Really? That's amazing!" If there was one constant thing about her manager, it was the ability of knowing exactly what Tara needed, even before she realized the same herself. "I told you this would be the perfect place to find your inspiration. Where it all began and all that…and how's everything else going, girl?"

"You should see the flowers I've planted, Jas. They're absolutely stunning."

"Ah, I can only imagine," Jasmine sighed wistfully. "I miss those days when I still had time to visit the farm. Send me pictures, though. And when you're ready to rejoin the old ball-and-chain, please come back with some of your magic *biko*, will you?"

She laughed at the request; her grandmother's secret recipe of the traditional sticky rice cake was legendary—and Tara knew how to make it perfectly. "Of course. Least I could do after you put everything on the line for me."

"This is about you, Tara." The response was uttered gently, but there was steel behind it. "It's about making sure that magic in you gets the chance to shine. Not all of us have something as special. I'm just glad I was able to convince the studio you needed this time off. Besides, there won't be a 'line' without your music. So, yeah."

She swallowed at the sincerity and determination in Jasmine's voice, feeling guilt churning in the pit of her stomach. "Thanks, Jas. I needed this." *More than you'll ever know.*

"Honestly, you don't have to thank me. I'm just doing my job."

"Still, it's the best idea we've had in all these years. I thought without my grandparents this place would feel different. It does feel different…but it's like they're still with me, somehow, telling me to let the world hear my voice."

"Trust me, I can feel it," Jasmine replied enthusiastically. "Just remember, don't rush the process. I know that's just not gonna cut it for you. The songs will come when they're ready, and when they do, they'll be all the more beautiful for it."

Tara could feel hot tears trying to fight their way out from behind her eyelids. Yes, she needed the time, but the real reason wasn't as simple as her best friend thought it was.

It was a reason that had haunted her since her second album, *I Remember You*, reached platinum a few years ago. It was a reason that had haunted her since the studio began planning an international concert tour to celebrate her tenth year as a recording artist, to coincide with the global release of her much-anticipated third album.

"I hope you're right," she said, praying Jasmine couldn't hear the tremble in her voice. "I hope I don't let you down. And everyone else, for that matter."

"You won't, songbird," came Jasmine's firm response. "Now, just focus on making some more of your beautiful music. I can't wait to hear it all."

"As you say, boss. By the way, how's everyone? Your parents? Jared?"

"Mama and Papa are keeping busy as usual. You know how they are, academia is life. And Jared's out of the picture. Life's too interesting for me to be tied down to a nerdy sound engineer who plays *Fortnite* in his spare time." Jasmine's tone was dismissive and no-nonsense.

"You okay?"

"Why wouldn't I be? I'm having fun right now keeping the media at bay. They pretty much think you're off on a much-needed vacation before your big tenth anniversary celebration, preferably somewhere exotic. Beaches, white sand, margaritas, all that. They don't know you're working on your biggest album yet. And they definitely don't know you're in Antique."

Tara giggled. "Let's keep it that way for the rest of the year."

"I'll do my best, songbird, and then some. Listen, enjoy your time there. When you're ready to return to us, we'll be waiting."

The words landed with the finality of a staunch businesswoman who knew the rhythms of the music industry as well as her own heartbeat. Tara could only wish she had her best friend's command of the world around them, as well as Jasmine's unshakeable belief in her and her talent.

After they exchanged goodbyes, she slid her phone back into her pocket and resumed her walk towards the farm's main villa, her eyes lingering on the white walls perched like a pearl amidst the emerald sea of coconut leaves.

The sun was already high in the sky, lavishing warmth on her skin as she, as always, made her way alone. Soon, as was now her routine, she would sit down on the dining table for lunch, a solitary meal in the company of her thoughts and memories.

Her thirties had arrived quietly, more poignant than she would ever dare to admit. Her fourth decade in the world was heralded by the loss of both her paternal grandparents. Even with an impressive lineup of hit songs and countless sold-out appearances, within her grew a sense of isolation and uncertainty. Not even Jasmine's constant encouraging presence and the adoration of her fans could alleviate the heaviness in her heart.

In an attempt to distract herself, Tara pulled out her phone and checked her meticulously curated social media accounts, tagged in numerous discussions with varying speculations on her current whereabouts. Her last public appearance had been in the New Year's Eve countdown show of a popular TV network. Some claimed she had eloped with an unidentified non-showbiz boyfriend, while others insisted she was ensconced in some far-off resort, most likely overseas, penning songs inspired by the sea.

If only it were that simple and straightforward. With a sigh, she replaced the phone in her pocket, a sad smile forming on her face even as her eyes took in the almost dream-like coordinated swaying of fronds in the breeze.

Creating music about love was a far cry from the romantic life people believed she lived. In truth, her career had always been a demanding companion, leaving little room for anything else. Her only true confidantes had been her guitar and her worn leather-bound notebook. Even Jasmine and her parents—her lifelines to reality—remained shielded from the depths of her innermost fears.

As she stepped through the wooden sliding doors that led to the villa's spacious living room, her gaze fell on a framed cut-out from her college paper's literary section, proudly displayed in its place of honor on her grandparents' wall. The cut-out, flanked by childhood pictures of Tara and her brothers, featured her first published poem, 'The Voyage,' accompanied by a delicate drawing of a boat sketched by none other than Lucas Delgado.

Lucas.

The kind, talented boy who saw something special in her poetry. He'd drawn every single illustration for the paper to match her poems for two years before he left school and started his glittering basketball career. Her grandmother had all those other poems with Lucas' illustrations compiled in an album, tucked away on the shelves of the villa's library.

Tara recalled the shy, quiet girl she used to be, hiding behind her guitar and notebook, pouring her heart out into her music and poetry. And there was Lucas, who had carried her to safety and warmth that fateful rainy evening her freshman year. She had wanted to talk to him again after that night, but never had the chance.

Her fingers traced the lines of the drawing, each stroke

evoking admiration for the boy whose smile remained a sweet but heartrending memory, always filling her with longing for what could have been.

If only.

If only things had been different. If only she had said something to him after that night.

"I hope you've found happiness," she murmured to the framed poem, aware of how ridiculous she'd look and sound to anyone else watching.

Tara's thoughts turned inevitably to Lucas Delgado of the present, now a household name in Philippine basketball. The staff of Galvez Farms and their families—hell, the entire village and town itself—rooted for Lucas and his team. Whenever his team had a game, everyone asked to go home early to watch it.

She had followed his career closely since he'd graduated, cheering him on from afar. Outside of the hardcourt, he was the star endorser of the liquor brand that owned his current basketball team; he also represented a casual clothing line and an international cologne brand. She had seen his pictures at those glamorous galas and parties, beautiful actresses and models draped over his arm, and had wondered how he was doing in his personal life. She knew he was successful—a franchise player, touted to lead his team for a third Philippine Cup championship in the coming months—but what about his heart?

Was he the same gentle soul she met back then, who didn't hesitate to help a girl he didn't even know? Did he have someone who saw him not only as a sports superstar but a gifted artist, whose illustrations told stories a million times better than words ever could?

A tear slid down her cheek as she brought her fingers to her lips and pressed a kiss to Lucas' signature. Her heart swelled with a mix of admiration and pride for this man she now barely knew, but whose presence always lingered in the delicate, most guarded depths of her memory.

"Good luck, Lucas," she whispered. "I wish you all the best. Always."

She forced herself to turn away, telling herself this would be the last time she'd cry over someone who had most likely forgotten about her a long time ago.

But she knew her heart, as always, refused to listen.

Chapter 2

THE PLAYLIST

Lucas

THIS WAS THE KIND OF PLACE ONE CAME HOME TO. Lucas Delgado could not blame his parents one bit for their choice of retirement home, as far as it was from the town proper. As he drove the rented SUV towards the sprawling bungalow he'd only seen in pictures before, he could feel a sense of relief, a lightness he couldn't last recall ever experiencing in the big cities.

"Hey man, you made it there yet?" The voice of Derek Torreblanca, his closest friend and teammate for six years now, rang through the car speakers as they conversed over the phone.

"Yeah, almost at the new house," Lucas replied, his eyes

taking in the groves of coconuts that lined the wide dirt path. "It feels good to be here. This is the first time I'm visiting this side of town and, man, it's even more gorgeous than my father's home village."

"I can almost smell the coconuts from here," said Derek with a hearty chuckle. "Enjoy your time off, brother. You deserve it. Your parents okay?"

"They're great. Retirement suits them very well and they've settled nicely in the village. How's Bali treating you and the fam?"

"Ah, it's paradise," Derek sighed contentedly. "You should see the kids splashing around in the pool, laughing and having a blast. It's moments like these that make everything worthwhile, you know?"

A flicker of envy stirred in Lucas's chest at the thought of Derek's family life, but he quickly stifled it. Instead, he focused on the lighthearted banter that came so naturally between them. "Yeah, well, maybe one day I'll find my own paradise."

"Who knows, maybe this visit will lead you to the woman of your dreams, Delgado. I haven't lost all hope for you, you know. Not yet, anyway."

"We'll see about that, Torreblanca, although you're beginning to sound like my parents. It's mildly disturbing."

"Hah! With good reason."

Lucas would have rolled his eyes had he not been driving on his own. "Seriously, though, I've been meaning to ask. Do you think we're ready for a three-peat?"

"With you in top form? With Cordova at the helm? And with me keeping those overgrown Fil-Am kids off your back?"

The confidence in Derek's voice was overwhelmingly

high. Lucas felt his hands tighten on the wheel at the thought of the upcoming Philippine Cup Conference—and their team's defense of the title for the second year in a row.

"I'll say we've got a very good chance," continued his friend. "So don't overthink it. We just need to stay focused and give it our all out there, just like before. What else can we do?"

Lucas took a deep breath, hoping he'd eventually have the same confidence at the end of his vacation. "I guess you're right."

"At my age, of course I'm right. But for now, you enjoy your time off, okay? Take care of yourself and give my regards to your parents."

"Thanks, man. You too. Say hi to Janice and hug the kids for me, will you?"

"Of course. Talk to you soon."

The call ended, leaving Lucas alone with his thoughts as he parked in front of the bungalow. Slowly, he stepped out of the car and unloaded his duffel bag from the back seat, careful not to shock his right knee at the change in position after many hours of driving.

He took a deep breath, welcoming the clean taste of the country air into his lungs. The balmy afternoon breeze was tinged with the distinct scent of orchids his mother loved, now carefully arranged in rows of driftwood that surrounded his parents' new home.

His mother, Mercy, was already standing on the porch with her arms outstretched to welcome him. She was a petite and elegant woman, with her gray hair cut short and neat. Age had made her lose none of the sharpness of her eyes; Lucas had believed since he was a child that he'd inherited his shooting proficiency from the sheer accuracy of his mother's gaze.

As soon as Lucas stepped onto the porch, she enveloped him in a tight embrace that seemed to defy her small frame. "I can't believe you're finally here!"

"Hello, Ma," he murmured into her hair, allowing himself to relish the familiarity of her presence.

"I've prepared the *tinola* you asked for," she said, patting him on the back. "And the village captain's wife sent some of her special pork *estopado*, too."

As they pulled apart, his father, Luis, came into view, stepping out into the waning afternoon light. A lanky, soft-spoken man with an artistic soul and a keen business mind, Luis had retired from his commercial ventures in the cities of Panay Island and now focused on assisting farmers in the province of Antique by investing in their cooperative efforts.

"Good to finally have you with us," Luis said warmly, clapping Lucas on the back as they exchanged smiles. "Hope you like the new place. We wanted something bigger for a possible cottage industry project with some local artisans. There's space here for that and more."

"Can't argue with that." From the wraparound porch, Lucas could see the stretch of farmland within his parent's property, bordered by a concrete-and-wire fence and rows of coconut trees. He gave a low whistle at the potential the space presented.

"Your father may have gotten the idea from the big coconut farm down the road," said his mother with a wry smile. "They've been making and exporting top-of-the-line food products for generations. Now he's thinking of expanding on that."

Luis nodded enthusiastically. "We're looking at coconut oil and soap, mats and ropes from fiber; and, of course, décor and accessories. People in this town already know how to make these products, so it's just a matter of harnessing those skills. That's what Galvez Farms did—and still does."

As he and his parents stepped into the spacious, airy bungalow, Lucas could practically hear the planning gears turning in his father's head as the older man spoke, but a familiar name quickly caught his attention. "Galvez?"

Mercy gestured for him to sit on the wooden dining table. An array of impressive-looking dishes were already laid out, among them a bowl of steaming chicken *tinola*, Lucas' favorite. "Yes, Galvez Farms is down the road from us, practically our next-door neighbor. You went to college with a Galvez who's now famous, didn't you? The singer?"

As hungry as he was from the long drive, the sumptuous appearance and smell of the soup barely registered. All he could feel was a tight sensation in his throat as he attempted a coherent response. "You mean Tara? Tara Galvez?"

There was a strange glint in his mother's eyes as she took the seat from across his. "Ah, yes, Tara. She's the one who looks like an angel, doesn't she, Luis, from her pictures on the Internet? The new owner of the farm?"

His father, seated at the head of the table, nodded thoughtfully. "Yes, Tara Galvez. She bought out the farm from her parents and brothers not too long ago. Seems like Miss Galvez is taking a break from the city life, too, just like you. Heard about it from their foreman during the last town cooperatives meeting. She's supposed to be here now, but no one has seen much of her. The people here are very protective of the Galvez family."

"With good reason, I suppose," chimed in Mercy. "Galvez Farms practically put this entire town on the map with their coconut juice and preserves."

"That's true," Luis confirmed. "As far as I know, Miss Galvez wants to keep the farm and the business running. She's even asked the foreman to hire more workers from the neighboring villages to help during harvest season. Got some fancy folks from Iloilo City taking care of the books and exports, too. The farm seems to have doubled production over the past two years."

"Talented and clever young lady," declared his mother, giving Lucas a long, unblinking look before she continued. "Shall we say grace?"

His mother led a short prayer before she encouraged them to get started while the food was still hot. Lucas had clearly heard everything his parents just said, but the new information that swirled in his head was overpowered by a flood of memories from more than a decade ago.

Tara.

He'd first seen her standing next to a tree, a vision with pale skin and long black hair fluttering in the breeze, during basketball practice. She'd been watching him play, and he'd been unable to look away for so many long moments.

As fate would have it, she'd had his sketchbook with her. Lucas could recall picking her up, rain drenched and shivering, from the puddle on the campus grounds after she'd slipped trying to follow him. Tara Galvez had the most beautifully expressive and intelligent eyes he'd ever seen. By the time they'd reached the classroom for shelter, he was a goner.

Later that evening, he'd walked her to the jeepney stop and given her his jacket to keep, but, in hindsight, he should have accompanied her home and never left her side.

He'd realized how special she really was when he read the poem she'd submitted, weeks later, to their college paper. As the illustrator for the publication, Lucas had felt a deep connection to her words, their meaning resonating as if she'd written the verses for him alone. Up until his final year at college, no matter how busy he was, he had never allowed anyone else to illustrate her poems.

Despite the undeniable pull he felt towards her, he never found the courage to talk to her again. He couldn't shake the fear that she would only see him as a shallow jock, incapable of appreciating the depth of her soul. By the time he finally mustered the resolve to approach her, it was too late—he was graduating and being drafted by a popular amateur basketball franchise, a mere step away from the country's premier league.

The idea of having Tara close by, *next door*…he could barely recall what he put into his mouth throughout dinner as his thoughts kept drifting, inexorably, back to her.

At the end of the meal, as they were tucking into small squares of *leche flan*, Lucas finally spoke. "I…I think I'd like to pay Miss Galvez—Tara—a visit. It's been so long, and I'd love to catch up."

"I think that's a wonderful idea," Mercy said warmly. "It would be nice to reconnect with someone from your college days while you're in town."

Lucas felt a flutter in his stomach as he replied. "Yeah, it would be great to see how she's doing. But I don't want to overwhelm her or anything. Maybe you've got some advice on the best time to visit her at Galvez Farms, Pa?"

Luis regarded him silently for a while before he answered. "Well, I know the foreman at the farm. He and his wife both work for Miss Galvez. They're all big fans of you and your team, too. He could give you some insight into when she might be available and what her schedule looks like."

"I'll prepare a basket of flowers and fruit for you to bring," Mercy added. "You know, just to make it a little more special."

After dinner, his mother led him down the hallways of the bungalow for a quick tour, the polished wooden floors creaking softly beneath their feet. The soft lights in his parents' new home fell on walls adorned with family photographs and mementos—from the younger years of Lucas and his brothers, to pictures of grandchildren captured in various milestones. Mercy finally paused before a wooden sliding door, pushing it to reveal a generous space decorated with light earth tones.

"Here you are, Lucas. I hope it's comfortable enough for you."

"It's perfect, Ma." The bedroom was beautifully done, but it seemed larger than necessary for just one person. "Everything in this new place has plenty of room, I'll give you that."

"It always helps to be ready for a few more family members, don't you think?" His mother's eyes twinkled as she spoke. "Especially little ones. They'll need plenty of space to run around in."

He grinned at his mother's not-so-subtle hint. Both his

older brother, who managed the family business of small supermarkets based in Iloilo City, and his younger brother, a surgeon who lived in Canada with his own family, had already fulfilled her dreams of a new generation of Delgados. Still, he sensed the underlying concern in her words.

"Slow down, Ma. You know I'm not even in a relationship right now. That might take a long while."

"It will take a long time, maybe never, if you keep hanging out with your showbiz lady friends." Mercy's teasing tone of voice was replaced by a more critical one. "Not such a good idea for a man your age."

He laughed it off, knowing that there was truth to her statement. "I know, Ma. Believe me, I can feel it in my bones. Literally."

His mother nodded seriously. She usually took his jokes in stride, but not this time. "You're not getting any younger, Lucas. It's time for you to find someone who truly understands you and your passions."

"With my kind of life, Ma, there are some things you have to put on pause."

"Well, then." Mercy squared her shoulders and made a move to exit the guestroom. "Whatever it is you decide, your father and I are already planning our Finals trip to Manila. A three-peat's not so far off, is it?"

Lucas smiled, grateful for her unspoken understanding of his situation and unwavering support for his chosen career. "Here's hoping. I'll tell Derek you said that, so he can work on his outside game during the training camp."

She nodded. "You do that. See you in the morning."

"Good night, Ma." He bent down to give her a hug and a quick peck on the cheek, before closing the door behind her.

Finally alone, he dropped his duffel bag onto the bed. He took a deep breath and allowed his posture to loosen, giving way to the tightness in his lower back that had bothered him since getting out of the car. His mother's words about his advancing age had hit him harder than he'd ever care to admit.

He knew it was only a matter of time before the secret was out, but that didn't mean he could still be as he was, if only for a little while longer. He could only hope to hold on long enough to finish the Philippine Cup Conference that year.

Lucas began to unpack the contents of his bag, his thoughts on Tara Galvez once more as he placed his clothes in the dresser. He had a collection of all her albums and singles, stashed away in his Manila apartment, hidden from the world on his bedside table.

As if on cue, his phone chimed with a notification, and he pulled it out to see that one of Tara's songs had been added to his Spotify playlist that had all her available music. He had watched her first live, sold-out performance online, all those years ago—a bootleg that he'd paid an exorbitant amount of money to acquire just so he could see her. Two years back, he had covertly attended one of her concerts, standing at the back of the crowd, too afraid to reveal himself but unable to stay away.

It was Tara who accompanied him during late-night drives after grueling practices or long games. The sound of her voice eased the burden of a career marked by losses and triumphs, trades and injuries. A life where much of reality was on pause, just as he'd said to his mother; a life where value and relevance depended on how much of a beating his body could take before it finally gave out.

OUR LOVE REPLAY

Lucas scrolled through his phone's playlist and selected the song he wanted, the familiar delicate strumming of Tara's guitar filling the room as he sat on the bed. He closed his eyes as she began to sing, imagining her standing before him.

Lulled by her voice, he allowed his aching body to settle onto the pillows and drift off into a dreamless sleep.

My heart remembers you
Even if everything else doesn't

My love endures for you
Even if all else is gone

~ Excerpt from 'Gone'
Lyrics and music by Tara Galvez
Fragments of Us, Esta Melodia Records

Chapter 3

THE SUNSET

Tara

She sat on the villa's front porch, strumming her guitar and scribbling down verses and notes as her mind raced to piece sound and feeling together. The weather was cooler today, Tara thought appreciatively, and lovelier to work outside in the fresh air for longer.

Just as she was about to start another verse, an unfamiliar voice cut through the stillness of the late afternoon.

"You stopped playing. I'm very sorry if I'm disturbing you." The voice was a deep baritone, male and seemingly sincere.

Her head snapped up, fingers stilling on the guitar strings. Her heartbeat quickened, and for a split second, she wondered if she was experiencing some sort of vision or ghostly encounter.

Was it not only yesterday that she'd deemed him a memory locked away in her heart? Now, he stood on the top step, silhouetted by the fiery colors of the waning sun, an apologetic smile on his face.

"Lucas?" The name escaped her lips before she could stop herself.

"Hey, Tara. It's been a while, huh?"

It was Lucas Delgado, standing at the edge of her porch—the very real Lucas, whom she hadn't seen in person for over a decade.

The charming, lanky boy she'd met in college had now transformed into a towering figure, his lean, athletic build filling out his polo shirt and jeans effortlessly. His wavy black hair, stylishly layered to frame his handsome features, was slightly tousled by the wind. Time and age had changed him, molding him into someone who exuded confidence.

"Yeah, it's been a while." Tara swallowed, taking that one precious second to regain her composure. Steeling her nerves, she turned to face him, placing her guitar into its case on the coffee table. "What are you doing—I mean, what brings you here?"

His eyes had not changed. They were as dark and deep-set as she remembered, their corners crinkling as a bigger smile formed on his face, the familiar dimple forming on his right cheek.

"We're neighbors," Lucas said. "At least, you're neighbors with my parents, Luis and Mercy Delgado—I'm just a visitor. They bought a small farm and built their retirement home just down the road. My father had always wanted to live here. He grew up in the next village."

"I've heard about them. They've been helping and investing in cooperatives for a while now. I didn't know they were your parents."

"They're kind of low-key. It was my father who arranged for me to come to the farm and pay my respects. My parents spoke very highly of you. When they said it was *the* Tara Galvez who owned the farm next door, I had to see you."

She stared at him for a few long moments, before she recalled this was her domain—and she wasn't acting like it. She got to her feet and extended a hand. "I'm sorry. I wasn't expecting anyone at all. Welcome to Galvez Farms."

He shook his head and took her proffered hand. His grip was firm and warm, as reassuring as she remembered. "No. I should be the one to apologize for barging in unannounced. My father actually arranged for your foreman to escort me and make the introduction, but I managed to convince Fred to let me come up here on my own when I told him we knew each other from college."

She would have given anything to see Fred's face when the foreman met Lucas. "I couldn't blame him, to be honest. Everyone around here roots for your team."

"I'd happily take all the blame for this intrusion. I have to admit I may have been a bit more pushy than usual. Please don't fire anyone. I'm a fan of yours, so it's on me."

The combined force of his touch and flattering words was enough to make the heat rush to her face. She let his hand go, trying to think of something weighty to say but finally settling on a simple truth. "It's okay. I trust the people here with my life."

He smiled, a mix of boyish sheepishness and gentle understanding. "So, does that mean I'm forgiven?"

"I'm not sure yet," came her measured response. "But it would be nice if you have a seat. Never let it be said I was rude to Lucas Delgado—or any of my neighbors, for that matter."

Lucas chuckled. "Fair enough. I brought you something from my mother's garden." He lifted a large basket off the top step and presented it to her with a small flourish. It was lined with red-and-blue checked cloth and filled with ripe yellow mangoes; a bouquet of white roses sat in the middle of the eye-catching arrangement. "She put this together for you. I hope you like it."

"It's very beautiful. Thank you." Tara accepted the offering, her fingers brushing against his. The contact sent an electric jolt up her arm, making her heart race. To disguise her flustered state, she glanced and gestured towards one of the rattan chairs. "Please make yourself comfortable."

She held the basket uncertainly, her hand still tingling from the brief contact with his. As Lucas settled into the chair, she added, "I have to admit, I didn't recognize you at first."

"Don't worry about it," he replied with a dismissive shake of his head and a reassuring smile. "It's been over a decade since we last saw each other, after all. I'm just glad you didn't mistake me for an intruder and bash me on the head with that beautiful guitar of yours. My face can't take any further damage."

She laughed at his self-deprecating humor, her anxiety at his unexpected appearance slowly fading. She decided to sit back down and was further relieved to see Marife, the head housekeeper of Galvez Farms, making her way to the porch.

"Good evening, Miss Tara," the older woman said, her eyes widening in surprise when she noticed Lucas. "Dinner will be ready soon."

"Fe, would you mind bringing some coconut juice for our guest?" Tara asked, grateful for the distraction. "Lucas, this is Marife. She looks after me here. You could say she runs the place. Fe, I'm sure you know Mr. Delgado."

She watched as Lucas stood up and introduced himself to the housekeeper, speaking to Marife with the same warmth and respect he had shown Tara moments ago.

No wonder Fred let him in unescorted, she mused, feeling a twinge of envy mixed with admiration.

As Marife bustled away to fetch the requested refreshment, Tara tried to focus on the present, resisting the urge to simply get lost in the moment without any word or explanation. She watched as the sunset made Lucas's bronzed skin glow, highlighting the thick waves of his hair.

"Thank you for the invitation to sit," he finally said, breaking the silence that had settled between them. "It's so peaceful here."

"It's a very special place," she agreed. "The only place I could ever call home, really. I spent almost all my summers here until I graduated."

"I never knew." Lucas gazed at her with a faraway look in his eyes. "I spent a lot of time in the next village when I was younger. One of my uncles still has a house there. I'm surprised we never ran into each other."

"Well, we're here now," she offered.

"Perfect timing, I guess."

Before she could respond, Marife returned with glasses of fresh coconut juice.

As he sipped his drink, Lucas continued talking as if they weren't nearly strangers to each other. "Your music is fantastic, you know. I've always known you'll be great at it, since you first told me about it in college."

"Thanks," she mumbled. "I'm surprised you're familiar with my work."

"You've got such a unique sound, Tara. And those lyrics? *Wow.* Sometimes, it feels like you're singing just for me. It's incredible."

She found herself unable to meet his gaze. Instead, she shifted the conversation to safer ground. "So, how have you been? Do you still draw? You're so good at it."

He let out a small sigh. "Not really, no. I train almost all the time now, and when I do get a break, I'm usually preparing mentally for the next tournament. There just hasn't been much room for anything else, especially in the past few years."

The twinge of sadness in his voice tugged at her heart. She wanted to reach out to him, but could only manage a nod. "You've done a pretty great job for your team. It's never easy when you've got a lot of people counting on you."

"I'm surprised you're familiar with basketball," he replied, a smile in his voice.

"Championship trophies on the news and fashion billboards on Manila highways aren't exactly hard to miss," she retorted.

He raised an eyebrow. "I'm just glad no one managed to convince me to pose for the underwear line. That would have been a sight."

She wrinkled her nose. "Ew."

They shared a laugh, the sound making her even more comfortable in his presence. As the sound faded, so did the last rays of sunlight and more so the years that had separated them.

"Will you be staying at the village for some time, then? My parents mentioned they've heard you're taking a break from city life, just like me."

She hesitated, before finally deciding to let him know. "I've been here for more than a month now, working on my music for my next album. It will be my tenth anniversary in the industry at the end of the year, and I wanted to do something special." She paused, looking away for a moment. "Not many people know where I am, and I'd like to keep it that way."

To her surprise, he grinned in response. "Your secret is safe with me. In fact, I'll be your personal bodyguard while I'm here—protecting you from prying eyes and paparazzi. Least I could do after disturbing you earlier. And free of charge, of course." He winked, and Tara felt her cheeks redden at his comically roguish expression.

"Free of charge, huh?" she countered playfully. "Well, I suppose I could make an exception for such a generous offer."

"Please think about it and let me know." Lucas stood up, preparing to take his leave. "Thank you for the juice, and for your time. I'm really glad you're here, too. As I said, the timing couldn't have been more perfect."

He extended both hands with a gentle smile. She wondered if it was a double kind of handshake he was offering, or an attempt to hug her goodbye. But it was his face that really caught her attention.

He looked happy, content, and open—emotions she found herself wishing she could hold onto just a bit longer. Maybe, just this once, she could indulge herself.

With sudden resolve, the words left her mouth before she could second-guess them. "Would you like to stay for dinner? I usually eat alone. It would be nice to have some company for a change."

Her heart skipped a beat as she watched his smile widen. "I'd love to."

Chapter 4

THE JOURNEY

Lucas

Nothing could have prepared him for the sheer sight of her.

It was all he could do not to lose his composure at the beauty of Tara Galvez. She had a striking, ethereal look on her album covers and press photographs, but seeing her in person again was something else entirely.

"Do you mind if we go inside before it gets too dark?" She gestured to the wide, intricately carved sliding doors that led into the roomy, old-world villa. Even a simple question from her sounded like a song.

He nodded and watched her lean forward to zip up her guitar case, unable to wipe the smile off his face as he did. She had a heart-shaped face, skin on the paler side, and expressive almond-shaped eyes framed by thick lashes. Her hair was a shimmering black, reaching down to the middle of her back.

As she made a move to lift the case, he extended a hand. "Let me get that for you."

Her gaze shifted to meet his, and he could feel his ribcage tighten at the effect of those eyes on him. He didn't need a whole team of overgrown Filipino-American players to stop him in his tracks; a look from Tara Galvez would be far more effective.

"Thanks," she said softly, turning on her heel. "Please, follow me."

"Lead the way." After picking up the guitar case, he reached for the basket of roses and mangoes with his other hand. As he straightened up, he tried to ignore the twinge of pain that shot up his lower back. Instead, he chose to focus on the woman before him.

When she walked, it looked like she was gliding on thin air. Combined with her stunning looks, the show business moniker for Tara, 'Asia's Acoustic Angel,' was more than fitting.

Upon entering the living room, Lucas noticed a framed, oddly familiar cut-out hanging on the wall. It took him a second or two to realize what it actually was.

It was Tara's first poem for their college paper, accompanied by his own illustration.

"Wow, I can't believe you still have this."

Standing next to him, she smiled softly. "Well, it was my grandmother who encouraged me to submit my poetry. She and my best friend, Jasmine, actually. They double-teamed me until I gave in."

"I'm glad they did," he replied, unable to help himself but smile at the basketball reference. He spied a yellowed photograph of an elegant couple a few frames to his left. Inching closer, he could see the gentleman's serious features, sleek dark hair, and sharp light-colored *barong*, the traditional Filipino men's shirt. Seated next to him, the lady had on a billowing dress, her hair piled high on her head. "Is that your grandmother?"

"Yes, with my grandfather." She moved to his opposite side, right in front of the portrait. "He used to be the singer of a four-piece *rondalla* back in the day. He gave me my first guitar. Since I was seven, we'd sing together during fiestas and special occasions."

"They look straight out of an old Sampaguita Pictures movie, don't they?"

"I used to think I'd never look as cool," Tara said fondly, her fingers caressing the edge of the frame. "I still do. I mean, c'mon. No one looks that good anymore."

"Well, it would be cool to recreate that photo like a lot of people do these days. I'd give anything to see you in that dress."

She raised an eyebrow at him. "Who'd be in that *barong*, then? You?"

"If it fits, who am I to say no to get a chance at looking like that? If you don't find me repulsive, of course."

She giggled, the sound reminding him of wind chimes. "You'll need kilos of pomade on your hair, for starters, but I think you'll make it work."

He could only stare, mesmerized at her laughter and her voice. He was willing to bet there was a matching grin on his face.

"Excuse me, Miss Tara? Dinner's ready."

His trance was broken by the soft, hesitant voice of Marife. He looked over his shoulder to see the older woman standing a few feet away.

"That's great," replied Tara. "Thanks, Fe."

As if on cue, a small parade of women flitted into the living room. With almost military-like precision, they switched on lights and insect repellent lamps, shut windows, and fastened screens against the encroaching night. It didn't escape him how many furtive glances they cast his way, punctuated by giggles and nudges. He responded politely, smiling and bidding each of the women a good evening. Two of them relieved him of the guitar case and the gift basket.

Marife ushered them through the living area and the wide archway that led to a vast dining room. The villa had smooth, shiny wooden floors and equally glistening pieces of carved mahogany furniture, each surface decorated with a basket or vase filled with white and yellow flowers. It was as if he had stepped into a different world, one of quiet intimacy, gentle beauty, and the calming yet beguiling presence of Tara Galvez.

"Please, sit down." Marife gestured to two set places of pearl-white china and polished silverware neatly arranged at one end of the long wooden table. Laid out before them was a lavish spread: the island's version of wonton soup called *pancit molo*, steamed duck with golden-brown sauce, grilled pork chops, and, of course, white rice. Further down, he could see a covered glass dish with familiar caramel-colored squares.

"Madam Mercy Delgado sent the *leche flan* for you, Miss

Tara," said Marife, as if reading his mind. "She hopes you'll like it."

"They're my favorite. Best ever." He pulled out Tara's chair at the head of the table.

She rewarded him with a smile before sitting down. "Please thank your mother for me, Lucas. With her gift basket and now the dessert, I feel very spoiled."

"I'll be sure to," he replied as he took his own place to Tara's right. "Knowing her, she's just getting started."

Tara laughed lightly. "Fe, can you please make sure we send across one of our premium baskets to Mrs. Delgado first thing tomorrow?"

"Of course, Miss Tara."

"And thank you for this wonderful meal. I really didn't need anything this grand."

"Of course you do, Miss Tara," Marife replied, her tone firm yet affectionate. "You deserve nothing less."

They watched as the other women trailed into the dining room bearing drinks. One placed a pitcher of ice-cold coconut juice before them, while another set down wineglasses and a bottle of red.

"From your grandfather's collection, Miss Tara. With Sir Lucas as our guest, I thought you would want to serve the *tempranillo*."

Lucas caught the eye of the women, winking playfully. "Thank you for taking such good care of Tara—and of me, of course. I hope this won't be the end of your generosity." They responded with titters and blushing nods before quietly dispersing under Marife's discreet prompting.

"Thank you, ladies," murmured Tara. "Good night."

Marife surveyed the table with a practiced eye. "Will you be needing anything else, Miss Tara?"

"I'm fine, thank you, Fe," she responded. "Lucas?"

He grinned at Marife. "I've got everything I need right here, Fe. Thanks."

They both bid the older woman good night and watched as she exited the room, finally leaving them alone. As the last remnants of daylight faded behind the curtains of the villa, he was glad to see Tara settle more comfortably around him, pouring wine and encouraging him to eat more of their delicious meal. He asked her questions about her music and concerts, watching as she spoke animatedly about her experiences on the road, performing in different cities and countries.

"Sometimes it's surreal, to think that my music has reached a lot of people and touched so many lives. It's both humbling and inspiring. Still can't believe it most of the time." Tara took a sip of her wine and tipped her glass in his direction. "And what about you? You're always on the move, too."

"I've found my own way, I suppose," he responded, shifting slightly in his seat to ease the discomfort in his right knee at being seated for a while. "Learned to adapt to being on the road most of the time. I was lucky to get traded to my team six years ago. They've become like family to me now."

Lucas watched as she listened intently as he spoke, longing to tell her it was her music that had been his constant companion, over and above the people around him. The hours passed effortlessly as they shared stories and laughter about their travels. The plates before them emptied and the night deepened, but he didn't care. Just as he'd said earlier, he had all he ever wanted with him, right there in that dining room.

It was a surprise when the clock struck midnight. Tara glanced at the antique carved grandfather in a corner of the dining room, the surprise flickering in her eyes mirroring his own. "I can't believe it's so late already."

"Happens when you're in good company," he replied honestly, unable to shake the feeling that their time together was too short. He knew he had to see her again.

"I should walk you to the door," she said as she got to her feet. "You drove here, didn't you?"

He nodded as he stood up. "My car's parked just outside the gates. Walked in with Fred, but then…you know."

He followed her as she made her way back to the living room, careful not to show any signs of his lower back protesting or his knee going partially numb after hours of being off his feet.

She looked over her shoulder with a smile. "I know. Guess it all turned out okay." Perhaps it was the effect of the smooth, decades-old *tempranillo*, but he could see a pinkish tint on her cheeks.

"It did." He paused just before they reached the front door, his heart pounding. He felt like a schoolboy again, mesmerized and dumbstruck at the mere sight of a beautiful girl.

"It was very nice of you to visit," she said, extending a hand. "This evening has been wonderful."

"Thank you for having me." He shook her hand and leaned down to press a quick peck on her cheek. "It's an honor to be with you, Tara."

The warmth of her skin beneath his lips was sweet and welcoming, carrying the scent and taste of vanilla and coconuts. Unable to help himself, he wrapped his arms around her.

She hugged him back, her arms going up and around his torso slowly. The embrace was awkward at first, but they soon relaxed into each other.

It was Tara who pulled away first. "Good night, Lucas," she said softly.

"Good night." He stepped through the threshold, allowing her to close the door between them. He turned to leave, but as he took his first step down the porch, a surge of hope welled up within him, and he couldn't resist turning back.

"Can I visit again tomorrow? I could keep you company, be your bodyguard while you work on your music."

Still standing on the doorway, she hesitated, her smile wavering for a moment before she finally nodded in agreement. "I'd like that."

A sudden rush of joy coursed through him, a giddy sensation of excitement at the prospect of spending more time with her. As he waved goodbye and walked off into the night, he found that, for the first time in a long while, the pain in his body no longer weighed so heavily.

What mattered now was the promise of tomorrow, as something akin to hope bloomed within his heart.

I was the one
Who looked at you
From across the room
The one who felt your pain
And never gave it back
I cared not
If you can't even see
Just in dreams
Be with me

I was the one
You looked right through
I was part of you
That shudder in the hall
That whisper at the moonless sky
That gaze on your back
That one
Loving you

~ Excerpt from 'That One'
Lyrics and music by Tara Galvez
Fragments of Us, Esta Melodia Records

Chapter 5

THE KISS

Tara

Being in the garden had always brought her a sense of tranquility, but today she couldn't shake the feeling that she was on the brink of something new and unknown.

Tara carefully plucked each golden blossom from its stem, her fingers brushing against the soft petals as she filled a basket woven from coconut leaves. With the white roses Lucas' mother had sent yesterday, she envisioned harmonious arrangements she could create throughout the house. It was a project that would hopefully distract her from thoughts of the very man himself.

Or from thoughts of his little kiss last night, and the way he'd put his arms around her for the first time.

Where is he?

She felt a slight shift in the breeze and looked up to see the foreman of Galvez Farms, Fred, approaching her with a hesitant smile, his hat clutched to his chest. Together with his wife, Marife, they had served the farm for more than three decades.

Ageless, sun-browned, and usually sprightly, he looked almost drawn as he stopped a few feet away, eyes downcast. "Good morning, Miss Tara."

She put her basket aside and got to her feet, dusting her hands and sliding off her gloves. "Good morning, Fred. Everything okay?"

He slowly raised his eyes to meet hers, shaking his head ruefully. "I shouldn't have let Mr. Delgado come to the villa alone yesterday. I mean, I know his parents…and he told me he knew you from college and he's your biggest fan. I don't know what came over me. I'm so sorry, Miss Tara."

At the back of her mind, a gentle reprimand would be suitable, but all she felt was a light-hearted sensation bubbling up from within her at the mention of Lucas' insistence.

"Don't worry about it," she replied with what she hoped was a reassuring smile. "I know you're a big fan of his, and so is everyone else in the village. It's not the first time someone's been star-struck."

"Still, I should have been more careful," Fred mumbled. "Your safety is very important."

"It's not a problem. Just be more careful next time, okay?" As the words left her mouth, she realized she hadn't felt intruded upon by Lucas' presence. In fact, it seemed as if he belonged right there, with her.

"Okay, Miss Tara." The foreman hesitated for a moment, before he continued, "Do you want me to put in extra hours? Or maybe you wanna cut my pay for the month?"

"What? No! Why would I do that?" She shook her head, amusement and exasperation warring within her. "Really, Fred. It's alright, I promise."

"If you say so."

"I say so. Now, please, don't worry about it."

Just as Fred was about to take his leave, the sound of approaching voices drew her attention to the garden path. Marife was walking towards them with none other than Lucas Delgado in tow. Even in the distance, his tall silhouette was unmistakable, making her heart beat a little faster at the memory of his lips, soft and damp, on her cheek.

"Good morning, Miss Tara." The housekeeper's round face was all aglow as she grinned up at the man next to her. "I met Sir Lucas at the gate on my way back from the market. He asked if I could let him in."

Lucas greeted Tara with a warm smile. "Good morning, Tara. Hope it's okay."

"Good morning," she managed to reply, trying to maintain her composure despite the heat that suffused her cheeks. "Of course it's okay."

"Hey, Fred," Lucas called over to the foreman, who remained rooted to the spot, still clearly star-struck. "I was thinking, maybe it's time for you to replace that old motorbike of yours. I spoke to someone from the village cooperative earlier today and they'll help coordinate the purchase for me. You know Dodie, don't you? Talk to him for me, okay?"

Fred and Marife stared at him, their eyes widening in shock. It was Marife who recovered first. With a squeal, she hugged Lucas tightly, jumping up and down like an overjoyed child. Her husband followed suit, more slowly but no less joyously.

Lucas patted them both on their backs, shrugging off their nearly incoherent words of gratitude with a smile. "It's the least I could do."

Tara found herself speechless as she watched the awkward, sweet exchange, deeply touched by Lucas' thoughtfulness and the ease with which he endeared himself to those around her.

"Anyway, I brought something for you." Once he was no longer in the group hug, Lucas turned his attention to her, holding up a brown bag. The freshly-baked aroma that wafted from the bag made her mouth water instantly. "It's *pan de sal*. I went to the next village first thing before they're all sold out. I hope I'm not intruding too early in your day."

"No, your timing is perfect," she said, mirroring his words from the night before, warmth spreading through her chest as she took in his easy smile.

Lucas' eyes twinkled, but before he could respond, Marife and Fred thanked him profusely once more, fussing over him one last time before they excused themselves, mumbling about their respective duties in the farm.

"Thank you." It was all she could say as soon as the couple was out of earshot. "That's very kind of you."

"My father called Fred yesterday morning, asking if he could arrange for me to visit the farm. He picked me up from my parents' house in his motorbike. While he was bringing me up here, we talked a bit about his family. I thought it would help a little if he had a new motorbike. I'm really grateful he made this happen…you know, getting me into the farm so I could see you."

Tara's heart pounded at his candid declaration, unable to understand why such a simple act could mean so much to him.

Lucas gave her a gentle smile as he continued. "You know, there was a time when I thought I'd give anything just to be with you up close. And now, here I am, standing in this beautiful place with you. Still feels like a dream."

It was her turn to get dumbstruck. Was this really happening, or have all the months in near isolation, with only her music for company, made her go crazy? Was this really Lucas Delgado, the very heart of every story told in her songs?

"Are you okay?" There he stood before her, concern etched on his face.

She nodded quickly, wanting to steer the conversation away from the intensity of the moment. "I don't usually have breakfast, but the bread you've brought smells incredible. I think I have the perfect coffee to go with it."

She was relieved to see his concerned expression get quickly replaced by a smile.

"That's great because this *pan de sal* is said to be the best in the entire province, maybe even the whole country." Lucas carefully took a piece of bread from the bag and, instead of handing it to her, brought it to her lips.

Tara felt lightheaded as she took a bite, savoring the flavor that seemed to be enhanced by his touch.

"Is it good?"

"Yes," she replied, knowing she was blushing, but unable to tear her gaze away from him. "It's wonderful."

"Another bite?" The teasing lilt in his voice made her blush deepen.

She nodded, her heart pounding so loudly she could barely hear anything else around them. "Please."

He brought the bread to her lips once more, and she eagerly took another bite. As he pulled the bread away, his thumb brushed against the corner of her mouth, flicking off a stray crumb. The slight contact made her shiver in the morning sun, his touch leaving her feeling both exposed and exhilarated.

"Oops, I missed another one." With a playful smile, he bent down and brought his lips to the corner of her mouth. His tongue teased the sensitive skin, causing her breath to catch in her throat.

She wasn't entirely sure if there was even a crumb there in the first place, but in that instant, she couldn't bring herself to care. All she knew was that her hands had somehow found their way to his shirt, gripping the fabric tightly, holding on as if she was about to get swept away. The bag of bread slipped from his grasp, forgotten as it tumbled to the ground and rolled into a patch of vibrant flowers.

His lips slid effortlessly to fully meet hers, moving lazily, as if exploring something delicate and precious. He paused for a moment, pulling back just enough to murmur, "Is this okay? Am I intruding?"

Without hesitation, she replied, "No, your timing is perfect." As if to further emphasize her point, she wound her arms around his neck and drew him closer. It struck her then just how tall he truly was, yet he seemed to have no trouble bending to meet her level.

As the kiss grew increasingly passionate, she became

dimly aware that he had lifted her off the ground, her back almost pressed against the rough bark of a nearby coconut tree, cushioned only by his hand. She wrapped her legs around his hips, the sensation of his arms around her body further fueling her desire.

His free hand roamed over her, fingers tracing the delicate lines of her collarbone and shoulders. She reveled in his touch, allowing a moan to escape her lips, as her own hands tangled in his thick hair, tugging as she ground herself against him.

"God, you're so beautiful," Lucas groaned into her ear, his breath hot and urgent. "So wonderful... Are you even real?"

His words, spoken with such awe and disbelief, sent a jolt through Tara, pulling her back from the edge of abandon.

"Wait," she breathed out, a wave of self-doubt taking over as she placed a hand on his chest, a plea for pause.

Instantly, he stilled, his broad shoulders heaving as he came up for air. Though the heat of passion still smoldered in his eyes, it was tempered by concern.

"Sorry," she whispered. "I just need to... I want to take my flowers inside before they dry out."

Without a word, he nodded as he carefully set her back down on the ground. He stepped back, giving her space, while absently helping her straighten her clothes.

Almost reluctantly, he separated himself from her. He looked away as he picked up the bag of bread and basket of flowers, extending both to her. "Do you want me to go?"

Instead of answering him directly, she asked, "Would you like to stay for breakfast? There's too much bread here for just me."

"I'd love to." He smiled tentatively and adjusted his grip, extending a free arm towards her. "Shall we?"

Tara nodded and hooked her arm through his. Together, they made their way back to the villa with unhurried steps. Nothing further was said between them, but the real, burning question lingered in her mind.

What did she really want?

Chapter 6

THE GARDEN

Lucas

He wondered what she was thinking, how she felt about their stolen moment in the garden, but he knew better than to ask.

Instead, Lucas chose to focus his attention on carrying the brown bag of *pan de sal* and her basket of golden flowers in one hand, while Tara held on to his other arm. At the corner of his eye, she looked seemingly lost in thought.

"This place is even more magical in the morning," he said as they reached the top of the porch steps. "It feels so serene, doesn't it?"

"Thanks," Tara replied softly, her voice barely audible as she let go of his arm upon reaching the threshold. "I've always loved it here in the mornings, when it's not yet too warm in the day."

She offered to make fresh coffee and led him to a large kitchen further inside the house. As soon as they entered the sunny room that seemed to occupy the entire back of the villa, she immediately busied herself, instructing him to put the bag and basket on the counter. As she worked, he stood near the windows, taking in the sprawling view of the coconut farm.

"Would you like to have breakfast outside?" Her eyes met his for the briefest of moments before darting away. She gestured to a small balcony built into the corner of the kitchen. "My grandparents used to eat there in the mornings."

"Sounds perfect."

"Please go ahead. I'll be with you in a minute."

He complied and took a seat on one of the wooden chairs. Before him, Galvez Farms extended as far as the eye could see, coconut trees waving gently in the breeze, while a smattering of birdsong provided a soothing, dreamy soundtrack. He could feel the tension and aches in his body slowly ebbing away at the peaceful scene.

She joined him minutes later, carrying a wooden tray with a pot of coffee and a plateful of bread. She seemed to relax as well, her shoulders softening as she took in the view.

As they drank and ate in silence, she would occasionally glance at the *pan de sal* in her hand, her cheeks flushing with color before she quickly turned away. He pretended not to notice, focusing a little too intently on his own drink and food.

"Your parents have been doing great work for the community," Tara said, after they had emptied the pot of coffee and almost finished all the bread.

Lucas nodded, grateful for the chance to steer their conversation towards a safe topic. "Yeah, they're really dedicated to helping out. My dad's always been passionate about giving back, especially to places like this. He taught me and my brothers how important it is to invest in local communities."

Tara's eyes lit up. "My grandparents started their export business years ago by partnering with locals to harvest coconuts and produce world-class juices and canned goods. They believed in supporting our people and our culture."

"My mother mentioned the other day it was Galvez Farms that put this town on the map. That's some legacy you got there."

"My family and I do our best," she replied with a smile. "Since I was a little girl, I've dreamt of having a place like this."

"And now you do."

She nodded, her gaze sweeping the scenery before them. "Still can't believe it sometimes, you know."

He took in the unguarded look of adoration on her face as she spoke, knowing he would give anything—do anything—for her to look at him the same way.

Silence came over them once more, but this time it didn't feel as charged or heavy.

"By the way, my mother has invited you for lunch at the house this Sunday after Mass. The service will be at the village chapel, so you won't have to worry about prying eyes. My father and some of the other men will be there to make sure everything is okay." He tried to sound casual, trying to ignore the cold sweat he felt popping up at the back of his neck.

"Really? That sounds lovely. I haven't been to the village in such a long time. I'd be honored to come."

"That's great." Relief coursed through him, paired with a sense of gratitude towards his parents. "She'll be thrilled."

"I need to come up with something for your mother to thank her for her gifts yesterday," she said, a thoughtful look on her face. "I think I ate four of those mangoes after you went home last night—and all the *leche flan*, too."

A chuckle escaped him at the thought of her hearty appetite. "That's won't be necessary. Just having you there would be gift enough for my parents. They're looking forward to meeting you after I confirmed you really were *the* Tara Galvez I knew from college."

That was the understatement of the year. Earlier that day, even before the sun had risen, his parents had grilled him about the previous night's events. From the look of joy on their faces, he knew they were already planning for future grandchildren. His mother was now probably mentally redecorating the guest room for a family, never mind the old bachelor who stayed in it.

Tara shook her head. "No, I insist. I'll make *biko* using my grandmother's recipe. I've got signed copies of my two albums, too."

"Alright, you win," he relented, secretly pleased at her insistence. "Go for it, then."

"Good. I'll be making the *biko* today, and you'll be helping me."

After they cleared away the dishes from the balcony, she led him to the living room. He hadn't noticed it earlier, but on top of the coffee table was a hamper overflowing with an assortment of drawing materials.

"These belonged to my grandmother," Tara explained in a soft, almost reverent voice. "She would use them to design dresses for me and the other village girls during the May *Santacruzan* parades. Go ahead, take a look."

Lucas gently sifted through the contents of the basket: well-loved colored pencils, delicate pastel chalks, and thick paper either loose or ring-bound into sketchbooks. He could barely remember where his own drawing materials were, if there were any left; years had passed since he'd last sketched anything.

"Thanks," he blurted out against the tightness forming in his throat. "You didn't have to…"

"I don't want you to be bored while you're here. I thought these might help keep you entertained. You said yesterday it's been a while since you drew something. Besides, the Wi-Fi in the farm is a little kooky and often unreliable."

He laughed. "You're right. This seems to be the perfect time to start drawing again, especially with you around. One piece of poetry from you and—boom!—I'll be drawing like a pro in no time."

"I guess you can look at some of my lyrics," she offered. "In strict confidence, of course."

He nodded, his eyes never leaving hers. "Everything seems to be perfectly timed for us, isn't it?"

She blushed and mumbled a response, her gaze flitting away. Sensing her discomfort, he decided not to push the matter further. Instead, he focused on her presence, following her around the house as she gathered together ingredients and utensils for the *biko*.

Just before lunchtime, she had him stirring the mixture of sticky rice, coconut milk, and brown sugar over the stove, supervising with a keen eye as she spoke of memories making the dish.

"Every time we made this, I remember my grandmother teaching me how to get the consistency just right. She'd say that the secret was in the wrist, but I think it was really in her heart."

Lucas smiled as he listened to her reminisce, marveling at how easily they fell into a familiar rhythm. Tara's approval of his cooking skills came soon after; she declared that the *biko* was perfect and only final touches were needed before she put it away to 'set.' She proceeded to drizzle calamansi juice and toasted coconut shavings on top of the rich brown rice cake before packing it up in a covered glass dish lined with banana leaves.

Lunch passed in a blur, with Marife and the other women beaming at him meaningfully before bustling away. When the afternoon arrived, Lucas found himself settling into a comfortable chair on the front porch, his inherited sketchpad in hand, while Tara strummed her guitar and hummed melodies to herself, pausing to jot down on her notebook.

Dinner came and went just as quickly, with a spread as equally generous as the previous evening's. This time, Tara didn't protest at the lavish selection of dishes set out before them.

As midnight approached, he reluctantly stood up from the table, knowing it was time to leave. "Thanks, Tara. It's been a wonderful day. Can't think of a better way to end it."

She smiled warmly at him as she got to her feet. "I agree. It's been perfect."

He followed her to the front door. Before he could step out into the night, he remembered the drawing he had completed that afternoon. He retrieved the loose piece of paper nestled within his sketchbook, which he'd carefully stashed away on a side table in the living room. "I wanted to show you this before I left."

The illustration was of Tara, in her light-colored shirt and jeans, black hair flowing in the breeze, standing amidst beds of white and gold flowers, surrounded by the cool shadows of coconut trees. He presented it to her, suddenly feeling shy.

Her wide eyes and soft gasp were affirmation enough. "Oh my god, this is…it's beautiful. You drew me exactly how I felt this morning—peaceful, alive, content."

"Thanks," he replied, his cheeks warming at her praise. "It had better be beautiful when I'm drawing such a beautiful sight."

Without another word, she stepped forward and wrapped her arms around him. He hugged her back gently, careful not to push her like he had during their kiss that morning.

"Good night, Lucas," she murmured into his shirt.

He pressed a kiss to the top of her head, inhaling the pure and sweet yet deliciously enchanting vanilla scent of her. "Can I see you again tomorrow? I hope I've been a good bodyguard today."

She giggled as she pulled back, reaching over to squeeze his hand. "Yes, you've been excellent. You make a great *biko*, too, so that counts. You're hired."

With one last look into her eyes, he turned and walked away. This time, she watched him go, calling out goodbye just before he lost sight of her and the villa.

Suddenly on his own without her, he was left with a feeling of emptiness and loss as he made his way through the night.

If only I could have a moment
I would stop time
To be with you
If only I could live in dreams
Then I would fly to you

All these could never be
Yet I won't stop loving you

~ Excerpt from 'Afar'
Lyrics and music by Tara Galvez
Fragments of Us, Esta Melodia Records

Chapter 7

THE MEMORY

Tara

THE EARLY AFTERNOON SUN WAS WARM ON HER FACE as Lucas drove from the village chapel to the Delgado house. On the front seat, Tara looked outside the window, focusing on the sights of vibrant greenery and distant mountains before her.

She tried not to think of her nerves at seeing his parents again after meeting them before Mass earlier that day. Mercy and Luis Delgado had been very charming, but the way they would look at her and then at Lucas in quick succession, then exchanged smiles, she expected them to eventually ask questions.

As they pulled up to a bungalow with a wraparound

veranda covered by a colorful assortment of orchids, she knew they had reached their destination. Seconds later, Mercy hurried out, a big smile on her face. Lucas gave her a sheepish smile before she stepped out of the vehicle to greet his mother.

"Welcome to our home, Tara. I told Lucas we simply must have you over." The older woman embraced her tightly as soon as she stepped onto the porch, and Tara hugged her right back.

Holding her at arm's length, Mercy continued, "Oh my goodness, you are even more beautiful in person. You really do look like an angel."

She blushed at the gushing compliment, lowering her head. "Uh, thanks, Mrs. Delgado."

"Mercy, please, dear."

"Ma, you're embarrassing her," Lucas said, grinning as he made his way around the SUV to join his father at the doorway.

"Let your mother be, Lucas," Luis admonished his son playfully. Turning to Tara, he added, "You should know by now that between Lucas and his brothers, a young lady like yourself is a very welcome addition to our family."

"Pa!" Lucas choked on nothing, his ears turning red as Tara suppressed a giggle, her own embarrassment momentarily forgotten. Mercy, however, was not as amused, and she swiftly elbowed her husband in the ribs, who tried to muffle a pained grunt.

"Sorry, dear," Luis muttered, rubbing his side. "I just meant to say that we are very happy to have you here, Tara."

"Thank you, Mr. Delgado…uh, Luis."

"That's better," said Mercy approvingly, taking her hand. "Come on, Tara. I'm sure you're hungry."

She nodded gratefully, allowing herself to be swept up in the gentle rhythm of the Delgado family's affection and care. The home of Lucas' parents was filled with natural light, its walls adorned with lovingly arranged photos and framed diplomas.

After taking her on a quick tour around the bungalow, Mercy led her to the cozy dining room. As she sat down to join them, she felt a sense of belonging, at being welcome without expectation or demand. She suddenly missed her own parents, who both still lived in her childhood home in Iloilo City, at the other end of the island.

After grace, Mercy served bowls of home-cooked native chicken *tinola*, saying it was Lucas' favorite, and generous slices of *lechon*, which, Luis said proudly, was cooked by the village men themselves.

"Best food in town, equaled only by the five-star dining experience at Galvez Farms," Lucas commented, giving an enthusiastic thumbs-up. Seated next to Tara, he obediently finished whatever his mother served to him. "Keep this up, Ma, and I might never want to leave."

"Here, have some more, Tara." Mercy reached over and slid a few more slices of crispy *lechon* skin onto Tara's plate. "Well, that's the plan, isn't it? What do you think, dear, is he worth keeping around?"

She swallowed before looking up from her food, only to feel herself redden as her eyes met Lucas'.

"He's a great bodyguard and very resourceful at getting nice food," she offered hesitantly. "He can also make *biko* from scratch. I guess he'll be quite useful to have around."

The expectant expressions of everyone around the table turned to mirth, Mercy's merry laugh joined by the deeper, almost harmonizing chuckles of her husband and son.

As the conversation rose and fell around her, Tara savored each mouthful of food, allowing the flavors to transport her back to those simpler summer days spent with her grandparents. When dessert was served—a rich, creamy-green *buko pandan*—her nostalgic bubble gave way to a burst of emotion as the familiar taste flooded her senses.

"Are you okay?" Lucas reached out and gave her hand a quick squeeze.

She nodded, a lump forming in her throat as she tried to give voice to her memories. "*Buko pandan* was my grandfather's favorite. He had it every Sunday, too."

Mercy smiled affectionately. "I made these with the ingredients from the basket you sent with Marife last week. I hope you like it."

Tara looked around the table with what she hoped was a reassuring smile. "I love it. It's really wonderful. It's..." To her horror, a lone tear slid out from the corner of her eye.

"Excuse me," she muttered, pushing back her chair.

She took a few unsteady steps away from the table, not daring to look at the faces of her hosts, before making her way to the living room. She settled on the sofa, taking deep, measured breaths as a few more tears rolled down her cheeks. She willed herself to get it together—breaking down like this was humiliating.

"Hey." Lucas crouched down before her, peering up at her face with concern in his eyes. She didn't realize he had followed her. "Are you alright?"

"Yeah," she mumbled. "I just needed a minute."

"My parents could come on a little too strong sometimes. Sorry about that."

She shook her head. "Your family has been nothing but kind to me."

He slowly stood up and seated himself next to her. She could have sworn she saw him grit his teeth, but the sight was gone just as quickly, replaced by his usual smile. "Have I done something wrong, then?"

She shook her head again, wiping at her eyes with the back of her hand.

"Shall I take you home? Or we can drive down into town if you'd like a change of scenery. I've got to be back at six, though. I'm playing in the fund-raising game between the junior and senior high school teams."

"No, no, it's fine. I'm fine, really."

He reached into his pocket and held out a maroon checked handkerchief, using his other hand to lift her chin. "Sure?"

"Really, Lucas—"

"Sure?" He goggled at her like a puppy dog, blinking furiously.

She giggled and sniffled as she swatted him on the upper arm. "Don't be silly."

He tickled her chin before letting go, eliciting a smile from her as she dabbed at her eyes with his handkerchief. "That's more like it."

A sigh escaped her as she felt her body relax; she found herself half-leaning against his body. His arm went around her shoulders as if it was the most natural thing in the world for him to do.

"It's the *buko pandan*," she confessed. "It tasted exactly

like the one in my memories—the one my grandmother used to make every Sunday. It tasted like…home."

She could feel tears once again welling up behind her eyes, but she blinked hard and chose instead to focus on the man holding her. Lucas smelled of the cologne that he endorsed; clean and sharp, with lemony notes.

"Home, huh?" he echoed, his voice pitched so low it was a rumble in his chest.

"Yeah…I'm sorry for being such a crybaby. I should apologize to your parents."

"No, you don't have to."

She shook her head and made a move to stand up, but he grabbed her hand to stop her.

"Tara, wait."

She hesitated before she slowly eased herself back onto the sofa. "What?"

He reached for her cheek this time, gently coaxing her to look in his direction. She obliged; when she looked into his eyes, she immediately knew what she saw in them would forever change her.

"Maybe you are home," he said quietly. "Maybe you are home with me."

Chapter 8

THE GAME

Lucas

H E KNEW ONCE HE UTTERED THE WORDS THERE WAS no turning back.
Home. That was the feeling.
He was simply adrift on a sea of existence when they were apart—and only ever alive when she was with him. The realization was both blinding in its simplicity and overwhelming in its magnitude.

Tara's eyes widened, her face coloring furiously. It was all he could do not to take her into his arms and kiss her breathless, never mind that his parents were in the next room.

"I…I don't understand," she breathed. "Lucas, I—"

"A-hah! There you two are!"

Before she could finish, Luis appeared at the doorway, straightening his glasses. If he had seen or heard anything, it didn't really show on the smile on his face. "We thought you wanted her all to yourself, Lucas, and spirited her away."

"I'm sorry for running out like that," said Tara. "I felt a little dizzy."

"Are you okay now, dear?" Mercy walked up to the doorway, too, and made her way into the living room. "Would you like to lie down for a bit?"

Tara shook her head as she gave his parents a reassuring smile, clearly a little awkward under their scrutiny. "Thank you. I'm fine now."

"We were just talking about tonight's game, Ma." Lucas smoothly took over the conversation as his parents settled into comfortable chairs next to them. "In fact, Pa, maybe you'd like to ask Tara what you mentioned to me the other day?"

"It's for a good cause, of course," said Luis. "The kids want to raise some money for their libraries and canteens. The high school really took a hit from the typhoon last November. We were thinking it might be nice if you'd perform a song during halftime, Tara."

"That's something that would inspire a lot of people," Mercy added gently.

"Really?" Tara looked taken aback by the suggestion. She turned to him, perhaps for support, but glanced away just as quickly. "I don't know, Luis…this is a surprise, for sure."

"Inspire is right, though," Lucas commented, clearly aware he was speaking from personal experience. "It would be the perfect morale booster for everyone here."

"We'll make sure no one announces your appearance

beforehand," his father assured her. "Lucas did mention how you wanted keep your privacy. We'll keep all the buzz to a minimum."

"I'll be there the whole time," Lucas added. "I'll still be on bodyguard duty, if you promise you'll watch me play." He finished with a wink at her, hoping the lighthearted gesture would put her at ease.

She only stared at him doubtfully. "It's been a while since I performed, Lucas…"

"Please?" he interjected. "As your biggest fan, I can say for certain you'll be fantastic."

"One song, dear." His mother reached over and patted Tara's hand. "Why don't you sing that truly heartbreaking ballad of yours, the one where there's a part that says 'be happy'? It's on the radio all the time. I believe the video has that really handsome actor, Paolo something? No, it's Pio-"

"'Never with You,'" said Tara quietly.

"Ah, yes, that's the one. Beautifully written, so haunting, don't you think so, Lucas?"

He nodded in agreement. "What do you say, Tara?"

"Alright," she agreed, her voice soft, almost drowned out by the excited reactions of his parents. "I'll do it."

"Fantastic!" Luis was already on his feet, reaching for his phone in his back pocket. "Everyone will be thrilled to hear your beautiful voice in person, Tara. I know we all are."

"You'll be so awesome," Lucas assured her. "We'll help you get ready, won't we, Pa?"

"Anything you need, anything at all. Just let us know." With the cool-headed control of a seasoned business leader, his father immediately went into planning mode with the game's organizers.

The rest of the afternoon passed by in a flurry of enthusiastic activity, the anticipation for Tara's performance palpable in the air. Marife was at the house by four o'clock with Tara's guitar. The Galvez housekeeper also brought a simple white dress and sandals, which Mercy happily received.

He and Tara crossed paths in the hallway, with her being led into the other guestroom by his mother to get ready, while he was on his way out of the house, his gear already in tow.

"I'm really excited to hear you sing tonight." He reached for her hand and gave it a tight, reassuring squeeze. "I know you'll be great."

"Thanks." To his surprise, she clung to his hand. At the corner of his eye, he could see his mother discreetly striding down the hallway to the guestroom, giving them privacy.

"You okay?"

"Yeah. Are you...I mean, will you be going with me to the game?"

"I'm actually going earlier with my father, to talk to the teams and warm up with them. The driver will take you and my mother to the high school gym just before six."

Her face fell. "Oh. I see."

"If you want, I can ask my father to go ahead without me."

Wide-eyed, she shook her head. "You've got to be there. Spend time with those kids. It's not every day they get to play with you on their team."

He grinned and raised her hand to his lips, pressing a light kiss to her knuckles. "I guess you're right. It's still an honor to be asked to play for a team, any team. Never outgrew that feeling."

She smiled, a little hesitantly. "I'll see you later, then. Good luck."

"See you later." As was their routine, he bent down to hug her goodbye. Instead of putting her arms around his torso like she usually did, she used the collar of his shirt to pull him down for a quick kiss on the lips.

The contact was over just as quickly, but he knew it happened—the hot brand of her lips on his, the lingering scent of her hair and skin. Most of all, his entire body jolted and stiffened, as if he'd been electrocuted.

If they were alone, things would turn out very differently.

Instead, he adjusted the strap of his sports bag higher on his shoulder and reluctantly let her go. With a final glance and quick wave over his shoulder at Tara, Lucas joined his father, who was waiting on the porch.

The violent, giddy pounding of his heart never stopped, not even when he drove off, not even when they reached the high school gymnasium and made preparations for the night's game.

Lucas knew, then, he had better do something about it.

I need to see you
One last time
I need to kiss you
One last goodbye

I need to tell you:
Be happy, baby
Be happy, always
Even if I'm never with you

~ Excerpt from 'Never with You'
Lyrics and music by Tara Galvez
Fragments of Us, Esta Melodia Records

Chapter 9

THE HEART

Tara

It was his smile that did it.

The last thing her emotional state needed was a public appearance, not to mention a live performance, but one smile from Lucas Delgado was all it took for her to say yes. As she sat with his mother at the passenger seat of the pickup truck, a mix of emotions swirled within her—lingering surprise, flattery, excitement, and, above it all, apprehension.

As the walls of the high school's covered court came into view, Mercy touched her shoulder, her voice and gaze displaying equal parts motherly pride and concern. "Just one song, Tara. You'll make everyone feel very special and loved."

She swallowed and nodded, knowing the older woman

was right. A song was nothing in the grand scheme of things, compared to the way the community had embraced and cherished her family for generations.

It was nearly sunset when they descended the truck and made their way into the gymnasium. Luis met them at the main entrance and relieved Tara of her guitar, guiding them through a sea of excited faces. The energy and noise was high, the sound system blaring with dance music; hundreds of students and adults were clustered on the concrete bleachers, talking excitedly.

The village's elected captain, David, a retired schoolteacher who had been friends with her grandfather, came up to them as she and Lucas' parents found their seats near the stage. Their reserved chairs, positioned in an enclosed area guarded by two burly young men, offered an unobstructed view of the basketball court.

"Thank you for agreeing to do this, Miss Tara," said David, shaking her hand enthusiastically, a proud smile on his face. "You have no idea how much this means to all of us."

"It's Mr. and Mrs. Delgado who convinced me," she replied, returning his enthusiasm with a smile of her own. "It's all them."

As they settled into their seats and watched the players take the court, Tara couldn't shake the edginess that settled in her chest, especially when Lucas jogged in their direction and gave them a jaunty thumbs-up before joining his teammates on the junior high bench.

Following a short welcome from the high school principal, the night's game was officially underway. When Lucas' name was announced, the crowd cheered wildly as he took his place against the center of the senior high school team for the jump ball.

Although she knew people in the gymnasium were merely expressing their adoration for Lucas, the noise only served to heighten her own anxiety. She fiddled with the soft material of her dress, trying to pace her breathing as she watched the players pass the ball around, ending with a boy from the junior high team making a flawless three-point shot.

As the final seconds of the first half ticked away, with Lucas' team in the lead, Tara took a deep breath, gathering her courage. As if sensing her apprehension, Mercy leaned over and put an arm around her shoulders.

"You'll be amazing, dear," she said reassuringly, giving her an affectionate squeeze. "I can't wait to hear you sing that beautiful song of yours."

As the final whistle for the game's first half sounded and the players moved to their benches, the packed building buzzed with conversation and curiosity as the event announcer made his way to the middle of the court.

"Ready, Tara?" Luis got to his feet, her guitar in one hand, while he held out his hand to help her up. The look on his face mirrored the pride she saw on Mercy's earlier. She knew she could never, ever let them down by chickening out.

She swallowed hard as she took the proffered hand and stood up. "I think so."

Mercy got to her feet, too, and gave her a quick hug. The wordless gesture was all the strength and reassurance Tara needed to get her feet to move and follow Luis up a few concrete steps to the wings of the stage.

"All the best, dear," he said, handing over her guitar. "Thank you again for doing this."

She nodded wordlessly before he left her on her own. She focused her attention on double-checking the tuning of her guitar, adjusting the tightness of the strings just so. A few feet before her, in the middle of the stage, a spotlight shone on a simple wooden stool set up behind two microphones.

The announcer cleared his throat before his energetic voice filled the court. "Our halftime show tonight is a very rare gift to us all. Our guest is a source of national pride, but she will always be a daughter of the province of Antique. Ladies and gentlemen, it is my honor to present the lady of Galvez Farms, the international music superstar, Miss Tara!"

Tara took a deep breath and stepped onto the stage, waving to the crowd as a deafening roar filled the gymnasium. She could barely see anything with the bright lights in her eyes, but she could make out that everyone was on their feet, clapping and cheering.

She arranged her face into a smile as she sat down on the stool, her fingers shaking slightly as she positioned them over the strings of her guitar. "Good evening. It's a pleasure to be here with you. Thanks to Sir David, Sir Luis, and all the school and village officials for inviting me."

As she strummed the first few notes of 'Never with You,' the crowd stirred. A hush fell upon them as they recognized the melody; then, as if an invisible conductor had given the signal, they erupted into deafening applause that drowned out her music.

"Tara! Tara, we love you!" a voice cried out, and soon the entire gym was swaying to the rhythm of her ballad, singing along with her.

The lights of the court went out, leaving only the stage illuminated. Cellphone torches and lighters came to life as people raised them high in the air, waving to the slow beat. As with every performance, she willed her mind to be still, giving in to the raw emotion that filled her heart every time she strummed a chord and sang a verse.

But, for the first time, this performance was different.

He was here, in the same building with her.

The only person whose smile and eyes had never really left her, even after so much time and distance between them. The very subject of her melodies, now living and breathing in her life, wrenched from what only used to be a dream.

As she sang, she thought of his determination on the court, his kindness off it, his artist's soul that resonated so deeply with her own. Could he see past the mask of her self-sufficient solitude, to the fragile heart that lay beneath?

A heart that had only ever been his, since she was eighteen years old.

As if by sheer magic, her gaze drifted to stage left and there he was.

Lucas stood in the wings, half in shadow. From what she could see, he was watching her intently, his dark eyes shining with unabashed admiration and something more.

Something that caused her breath to catch and her pulse to race.

Suddenly, he stepped onto the stage, moving toward her with purposeful strides. As he approached, he held out a bouquet of bright red roses, an equally bright and affectionate smile on his handsome face. Upon reaching her side, he dropped to one knee before her. The gesture was so unexpected, the look in his eyes so tender and genuine, that she felt a lump form in her throat, even as she kept singing.

"Kiss! Kiss! Kiss!" the crowd began to chant, their voices

rising in a fevered crescendo. The heat and urgency of their excitement mingled with the weight of her own feelings—overwhelming, undeniable, almost irresistible.

"Lucas," she whispered, her guitar slipping from her grasp as she stared down at him. "I…"

But before she could finish, the pressure became too much to bear. With a choked sob, she jumped to her feet and fled the spotlight, leaving her song and her heart behind.

Chapter 10

THE SONG

Lucas

THE BEAUTIFUL BOUQUET SLID FROM HIS HANDS. THE girls of the high school student council had giggled and worked so hard when they put it together earlier, knowing it was meant for a 'very special lady.' Now, their arrangement landed haphazardly on the stage, scattering petals and ribbons like a tragic foreshadowing.

Lucas knelt frozen, his heart pounding erratically as he watched Tara's back retreat into the shadows of the darkened gymnasium. As her silhouette vanished beyond the wings, he lurched to his feet, his body protesting with sharp jolts of pain through his abused knee and strained lower back.

Around him, the crowd that had been pulsating with

excitement now held its breath, their collective anticipation turning into a heavy curtain of unease. The raucous cheers for a kiss hushed into worried whispers.

He made his way down the steps and pushed through the mass of people that had gathered at the bottom of the stage, their faces blurred smudges on his periphery. His vision tunneled, fixated on the trail of Tara's hurried footsteps. He swallowed hard as he caught a glimpse of flowy white fabric disappearing into a side entrance.

God, she looked so beautiful in that dress.

"Lucas!" His mother's unmistakable voice cut through his fog of bewilderment, sharp and commanding.

The sight of his parents stood out from the chaos. Mercy was beside him in an instant, thrusting Tara's canvas bag into his outstretched hands. Luis followed suit, the familiar strap of Lucas' own sports bag wrapping around his fingers like a lifeline.

The words left his throat, hoarse and desperate. "I don't know what happened, Pa. She just ran…"

"She couldn't have gone far. Tara came in with your mother, so she'd be on foot." The quick, rational mind of his father was always a grounding force.

"Go after her." His mother's directive was laced with an intensity that brooked no argument, but her face began to crumble with worry and guilt. "She's fragile right now. I saw it, Luis. We could have prevented this…"

"Make sure she's okay, Lucas." Luis' voice was calm as he wrapped a consoling arm around Mercy's shoulders. His eyes behind the glasses spoke differently, prompting for urgency. "We'll take care of things here."

Lucas nodded wordlessly before he took off in Tara's

direction, slipping into the shadows and out through the side entrance. The night air was humid on his skin as he emerged into the inky, almost eerie, stillness that had settled outside the building.

"Sir Lucas!" Fred, followed closely by Marife, ran up to him, their faces bearing identical expressions of worry. "We tried to stop her, offered to take her home…"

"She told us to leave her alone," exclaimed Marife, tears welling up in her eyes. "I've never seen her so upset."

"Where did she go?" Lucas tried to keep his voice steady as his eyes swept the road, trying to orient himself in the sparse moonlight. North led to the farm, south down the mountain and into town.

"I think she's going back to the farm," Fred said quietly, gesturing to the northbound path. "Ever since she was a little girl, she always comes home to her family here…to us."

Marife's tears now flowed freely as she grabbed his hand almost painfully. "Miss Tara's got a heart made for the world to love but not to break. When her grandparents left us, she took it very hard. We thought she'd never smile again…until you came, Sir Lucas. Please bring her home."

"I…" His voice trailed off, his words quashed by the gravity of his own guilt. How badly he had put his own expectations on Tara. How stupidly he had thrown her to the public eye.

How desperately he'd wanted the world to see how much he loved her, in hopes she would see it, too.

"I'll make sure she gets home," Lucas finished lamely.

The foreman extended a small rectangular device to him. "This is for the farm gates. I'm not sure if Miss Tara brought hers. She never uses it."

"Thank you." He pocketed the remote and, with a nod to the couple, he turned and ran swiftly down the gravel lot to where the SUV was parked. His hands trembled as he rummaged through his sports bag for the keys, relief coursing through him as his fingers closed around the cold metal.

Lucas climbed onto the driver's seat, tossing his bag and Tara's to the space below the passenger dashboard. The vehicle roared to life beneath his hands, its headlights slicing through the darkness as he accelerated away.

"Come on, come on," he muttered as he drove, perspiration trickling down his temples, his heart pounding against his ribcage. His red and black jersey, a replica of his team uniform redone with logos of the local high school, was now drenched in cold sweat.

And then he saw her.

His heart leaped into his throat as he spotted Tara's white-clad silhouette several hundred meters from the gymnasium. She cut a desolate figure on the dark stretch of road, scurrying away like a wounded animal.

She flinched at the sudden intrusion of the car's harsh lights, her shadow splintering across the road like broken wings. His stomach lurched as she turned to him, eyes wide with the kind of surprise that edged on fear.

Lucas brought the car to a shuddering halt a dozen meters ahead, blocking the path. He was out in an instant, approaching her with measured steps.

"Hey, it's okay," he said, his voice a cautious whisper, holding out his hands. "It's just me."

She recoiled with the raw instinct of someone desperately cornered, wrapping her arms around herself, her slender body still racked with sobs. "Leave me alone."

"Please." The word hung heavy between them, suspended in the tension of the moment. "Let's get you home. You need to rest."

She stepped back, retreating further into the cover of night. The vulnerability and exhaustion in the delicate lines of her face broke his heart.

"I'm not going to hurt you, Tara. I'm just here to drive you home. Please, get in the car."

She trembled as she shook her head, midnight black hair cascading over white-clad shoulders. She'd never looked more like an angel.

"I can't..." Her voice was a murmur almost lost to the breeze. "I shouldn't have come tonight. I've let everyone down. I'm so sorry."

"Hey, hey, no." He found himself stepping forward, reaching out but not touching. One wrong move and their fragile exchange would be shattered. "You didn't let anyone down. This... this is on me. I wanted—no, I needed people to see what I feel for you."

He watched the soft moonbeams dance upon her tear-streaked cheeks as she stared at him in shock. He could see himself reflected in her own gaze—a mirror of unspoken pain, carefully guarded secrets, and a life wrapped in yearning.

"What you feel for me?" she echoed, the words fading into a look of disbelief on her face.

"What I feel doesn't matter if it's making you like this." He shook his head, overcome by an overwhelming tide of guilt as he tried to make sense of his own actions. "I'm so sorry. I should have given you space, not crossed your boundaries. This isn't a game, after all. It's you...and you mean more to me than any game—or anything, or anyone."

His own defenses, the barriers he'd erected to shield his career, his heart, his very soul from the inevitable injuries of life and love, crumbled beneath the weight of his own words.

"I wish I could be brave as you are." Her voice, usually so clear when wrapped around the notes of her songs, was now thin and shaky. "I'm afraid of the whole fucking world, do you know that? I'm afraid of opening up and being told I'm not enough, of being rejected and told my songs are no longer worth listening to."

"Don't say that—" he protested, but she wasn't listening.

Tara continued, her voice faraway as if she was trying to capture a poignant, distant memory. "I've traveled so far and wide, all over the world. I was fine always on my own for so many years. I don't need to open up, right? I have my music. It's everything to me, Lucas. It's all I have."

Her words stirred something within him, a protective instinct mingling with profound reverence for her honesty that allowed him a glimpse into her heart. This woman before him was not just an artist; she was every note of every song she'd ever written.

He closed the distance between them, his arms encircling her as gently as he could. He was ready for her to push him away, ready for her to put up yet another wall between them. Ready for her to reject everything he was willing to give.

Lucas Delgado had gone past caring whether or not he got hurt. This time, it would be worth it.

"No, you have people here who love you," he murmured into her hair. "You have the farm. And you've got me, too. You'll always have me."

He could feel the tension in her body, an instinctive

resistance heartbreakingly familiar to him. But slowly, she softened, her defenses faltering in his embrace.

She didn't say anything. Instead, she melted against him, burying her face in his shirt, her shoulders still heaving from residual sobs. He'd held her so many times before, but it was only tonight he realized just how small and fragile she really was.

"Let me get you home," he said softly. "Let me take care of you. Just for tonight."

She nodded, barely, but it was enough for him. He lifted her carefully and settled her onto the front seat. As he fastened the seatbelt around her, the soft click resonated like a lock falling into place around his own heart.

In that moment, the truth became undeniable.

He loved Tara Galvez. He always had.

His fingers lingered near her face, the urge to caress her skin almost overpowering, but he hesitated, respecting the trust she was tentatively offering him. Instead, he placed her canvas bag on her lap.

She glanced around uncertainly. "My guitar…"

"My parents will take care of it. I'll get it back for you in the morning. Don't worry, okay?"

She nodded, clutching her bag to her chest.

The road back to the farm stretched out before them, a still, empty path lined with gently swaying palm trees. In the moonlight, their shadows almost looked like the audience back at the gymnasium, moving as one to the beat of her music.

And he'd promptly ruined it.

Trying to ignore another wave of guilt that made his

chest constrict, he focused on using the loaned remote to open the heavy wooden gates of Galvez Farms.

"Is that Fred's?"

"Yeah. He wasn't sure if you had yours. My parents, Fred and Marife...they all told me to bring you home."

"They didn't have to worry," she commented quietly, her gaze trained on the darkness outside her window. "I'll always be safe in this village."

We thought she'd never smile again...until you came, Sir Lucas. Please bring her home.

Marife's words. A wealth of insight into the soul of the woman next to him, captured in such a short statement.

Home. It was a word that was slowly becoming synonymous with Tara's presence in his life.

"Doesn't stop us from caring," he replied gently, as he navigated the bends of the dirt road that snaked towards the main villa.

He parked as close to the house as possible. The engine's hum faded, leaving only the sound of their breathing to fill the quiet void between them.

"Do you know why I'm here, Lucas?" Her unexpected question cut through the silence like a knife.

He couldn't even think of a reply that didn't make him sound ignorant or insensitive. He chose an honest answer instead. "I don't know...Fred and Marife said you always came home."

"Did they? I suppose they're right, in their own way. This is my home...I chose it. When I'm home I'm not supposed to doubt myself. I shouldn't be afraid. But you know what? I'm scared as fuck."

"Tara, I—"

She cut him off—or she probably didn't even hear him speak. "I've been putting off my third album. I've been having nightmares that I don't have the material or talent anymore to keep going. I'm afraid that if and when I manage to get it done, I'll be heavily criticized. I came home to escape those doubts, Lucas, but I couldn't run from my own head. Tonight made that very clear."

He cast a sidelong glance at her; she was staring straight ahead, at a faint path of moonbeams past the windshield, her beautiful face drawn and almost deathly pale. The sight made his throat constrict painfully. What he thought would be a romantic gesture had caused a shitstorm he'd probably never be able to fix.

"When people's hearts are on you and your success, you can't afford to let them down. That's what's killing me. I can't even talk to my parents or Jasmine about it because I know they'll worry and most likely send me off for help. I don't want that—I just want to be with my music. But tonight, with all those people, with you in front of me…everything just fell apart." Tara sighed deeply, then cleared her throat. "Anyway, it's a miracle I'm back here in one piece. I've got you to thank for that."

He heard the finality in her tone, knew he couldn't push her any further. Instead, he nodded and undid his seatbelt to get out of the car. He was about to reach for the door handle when something stopped him—the need to know he was still allowed in her life.

"I didn't mean to put you through all this, Tara. I'm so sorry. I'll do anything to make it up to you."

She didn't respond at first. Instead, she undid her own seatbelt and slid forward on the front seat, her hands settling on the dashboard before she turned to look in his direction. In the faint moonlight, her eyes looked like deep pools of gold.

When she finally spoke, the words sounded muted. "Why did you do that at the game, Lucas? The flowers, the kneeling, the spotlight…If a showbiz performance was what you wanted, you should have told me from the get-go. I've been in the business for a long time."

He shook his head. "That wasn't a performance."

"Then what was it?" she pressed in a stronger voice, her brows furrowing. "Some kind of prank? I thought we were… friends. Why put up a show like that at my expense?"

"That wasn't a show," he countered, knowing at the back of his mind that whatever followed, he had better be prepared for the consequences. "I meant everything I did—and everything I said. From the day I first got to this place and saw you again, I knew I couldn't stay away. I wanted to be with you, Tara. I wanted to kiss you and hold you and protect you… and I needed you and the whole world to know."

He stopped, head spinning from adrenaline. Then he saw it: a flicker of something raw and unguarded in her eyes as she regarded him, stupefied.

To his utter surprise, her emotions broke free, stealing what little breath he had left away.

With a strangled cry, Tara threw herself at him fiercely, mounting him right there on the driver's seat. His hands instinctively rose to meet her as she kissed him—a kiss without any remaining facade of restraint.

He responded with equal fervor, the sweet taste of her lips igniting the fire of passion that had long since smoldered within him. The world outside the confines of the car ceased to exist; there was only her and her touch and her heady vanilla scent, the weight of her damp body on his lap a million times better than any fevered dream.

The kiss was hungry and desperate, quashing any hesitation he had left at his ragged, sweat-soaked state. Her fingers slipped beneath his jersey, tracing the contours of his abdomen. He responded enthusiastically by lifting the hem of her white dress, the fabric gliding against his hands as he cupped the softness of her skin protected only by the flimsy barrier of her underwear. Eager to taste her, he pushed his tongue into her mouth. She moaned in response, her hands tugging at his hair as she ground against him, a silent confession of her need.

He slid her upward, pressing his lips to the swell of her breasts through the thin fabric of her dress. His breath ghosted over the bare skin of her neckline, eliciting a shiver that he felt reverberate through his own body.

She writhed above him, her movements stirring his desire into an almost desperate hunger for more of her, all of her. Reaching around, his fingers found the heat of her, slick and welcoming. He stroked her then, fingers sliding in and out, watching her face contort with pleasure, listening to her moans fill the car—a melody sweeter than any song she had ever sung.

His breath caught when she reached down and tugged at his shorts. He lifted his hips and, together, they both managed to pull it down along with his briefs, releasing his throbbing arousal. He lost no time in pressing his maddening hardness against the dampness of her panties, his hands cupping the sides of her hips, asking for permission.

"Yes," she groaned, "always yes."

A muffled gasp escaped her lips when, in one determined movement, he pushed the tiny piece of fabric down, baring her just enough to join his body with hers.

"*Fuck,* Tara." The sensation of being inside her was so, so good. She was warm and wet and welcoming, everything he had imagined her to feel but amplified a thousandfold. "What are you doing to me?"

She didn't answer but clung to him tighter, their foreheads pressing together, remnants of her tears trickling onto his skin. She wound her arms around his neck as her hips began to move in slow circles. The friction caused jolts of electricity to course through his body, making him lose all sense except the feel of her in his arms.

"Lucas… Lucas…" she sang against his lips, fingers tracing patterns on the skin behind his ears, every motion of her lithe body a note that pushed him deeper and deeper into abandon.

He thrust back into her, his cock enveloped by the white-hot heat of her pussy, and he was lost in the sensation, drowning in the heady scent of her skin and their shared passion. He buried his face in her neck as they moved together in a pounding, increasingly wild rhythm that she controlled.

"God, you're perfect," he whispered into her ear, nipping at the soft skin now beaded with sweat. "Everything I've always wanted."

Tara responded by rotating her hips with increased urgency, throwing her head back uninhibitedly as her moans grew louder. His mouth found her nipples through the fabric of her dress, sucking each in turn to add to her pleasure, knowing she was close to the brink.

"Lucas," she gasped, and it was not just his name; it was

a plea, an affirmation, a surrender. Her body tensed in the most intimate of ways, and then her mouth opened in a silent, shuddering scream.

He felt the surge building within him as her body gyrated and shook in the throes of her release, the pressure and pleasure intermingling within him until he could no longer distinguish where one ended and the other began.

He followed her then, his own climax tearing through him, declared triumphantly to the quiet night by a hoarse shout he could no longer contain.

A simple truth he could no longer hide.

"I love you, Tara. I love you."

I feel my body steaming towards you
I burn in flames of passion
Until I am nothing more
Than trembling desire

I feel my soul steaming towards you
I surrender all of me
Until I am nothing more
Than your wasted possession

~ Excerpt from 'Nothing'
Lyrics and music by Tara Galvez
I Remember You, Esta Melodia Records

Chapter 11

THE SECRET

Tara

She was his now. It has always been so. She didn't know how long they clung to each other, still intimately entwined on the driver's seat as his confession hung in the air. His wavy hair was damp against her skin, tickling her cheeks as she breathed against him, momentarily spent. He smelled of sweat and citrus, his breath hot on her collarbone.

He was the first to move, slowly, almost reluctantly. He lifted his head, gaze meeting hers in the dim light as his hands caressed her hair, smoothing errant locks away from her face. "I've always loved you, you know."

Love.

One word, one thing she'd held on to, all these years. Her quiet sort of madness.

She had pined for this man half her life, watched and adored him from afar, robbed herself of the chance to experience something else with someone other than this tall, wavy-haired creature, whose piercing eyes had never stopped haunting her.

So much time, now wrapped up in this moment with him in her arms, Lucas saying the words she'd never expected to hear him utter outside of her dreams.

She didn't answer, allowing herself to go limp in his embrace as he carefully lifted her from his lap and settled her back onto the front seat. As they awkwardly fixed their clothes, the world around her came into soft focus, the windows and windshield of the car still fogged by their passion

He didn't demand an answer. Instead, Lucas caressed her cheek for a few precious, stolen seconds, before reaching for the door handle.

She caught his hand and brought it to her lips. His fingers still bore traces of her own scent as she kissed them tenderly.

"Will you stay?"

He smiled then, reminding her of the time she'd first invited him to dinner. "Of course. Let's get you inside."

With one last peck on her lips, he exited the car and opened the passenger door. He shouldered both his bag and hers, the sight making her giggle, and lifted her out of the vehicle. She pulled him close for a kiss before he set her back down. She led him by the hand, up the porch and into the house, locking the door behind them, sealing the world away.

With a deep breath, she silently made her way to a

staircase in a part of the villa he'd never seen before. He followed closely, at one point pausing midway through the flight of steps to wrap his arms around her and kiss the back of her neck.

"I love you," he said softly, again.

The words exhilarated and scared her.

For the first time in her life, she led a man to her sanctuary: a large, airy bedroom nestled in the far corner of the house.

"Is this…?" Lucas broke the silence as soon as she switched on the soft lights. His eyes took in the walls decorated with framed photographs of a younger Tara with her family and childhood friends, as well as more recent images of her portraits and album covers.

"Mine."

Tara took a deep breath and slowly shed her clothes, piece by piece, until she stood completely bare under his smoldering gaze. She felt exposed, but more than anything, she wanted him to see her. Wordlessly, she backed towards the bathroom, never breaking eye contact. As soon as she arrived, trembling and flushed, she turned on the shower and stepped under the warm cascade of water.

It barely took a minute before Lucas joined her under the spray. His lips met hers in a searing kiss, his naked body pressed tightly against hers.

Nothing had prepared her for the moment she could finally touch all of him. Her fingers traced wide shoulders and an equally broad chest, then slid down to explore a taut stomach and narrow hips. His legs were beautifully sinewy and strong and, between them, his arousal stood proud and unapologetic.

She heard him suck a breath in as her hands closed around the rock-hard length of him, tugging, caressing, claiming.

"Can I touch you, too?" he asked breathlessly between kisses. "All of you?"

"Yes," she murmured against his lips, her heart hammering in her chest at the idea of being so vulnerable.

He pushed her against the bathroom wall, his arms on either side of her, holding her up. He showered her with gentle kisses and caresses; on her lips, cheeks, nose, ears, neck, and collarbone, leaving a trail of heat with his mouth and fingers.

As he touched her bare breasts for the first time, her breath caught in her throat, thinking of the well-endowed actresses and models he was so often photographed with. To her surprise, he looked up with an adoring smile on his face, and his voice was filled with wonder when he said, "They're perfect—made to fit into my hand." She felt a sense of relief and happiness wash over her as he suckled her nipples like a starving man.

He kissed his way down to her stomach, spreading her legs as he did so. He knelt before her as if worshipping at an altar, the tenderness of his actions almost making her cry.

How she loved this man. But, even in the midst of their passion, she couldn't find the words to tell him.

And he was only getting started.

He positioned one of her legs over his shoulder, his hand stroking her pussy and the thin patch of hair surrounding it, his touch tickling her in the most intimate of ways.

"You're so beautiful," he said, his lips inches away from her heat. "So fucking beautiful."

She could only watch in awe as he proceeded to place

her other leg over his shoulder, supporting her against the wall with his own strength. Then his lips, tongue, and mouth dove into her, licking, circling, and sucking.

"Lucas," she gasped, grinding against his mouth, wave after wave of pleasure rippling through her.

He responded by using his tongue to trace the length of her slit, causing her to squirm and squeal, before he looked up into her eyes. "Let go, love. I've got you."

His mouth was back on her, bringing her to a slow, delicious, soul-rending climax that made her soar to a peak she'd never reached before. She didn't know how long she stayed there, eyes tightly shut, breathless and finally uncaring. She was only aware that his name lingered on her lips as aftershocks of her orgasm tore through her body.

When she finally opened her eyes, he was standing before her, supporting her limp form with a smile on his lips. Lucas looked tall and beautiful under the splashing water, his desire undeniable in his eyes and the rock-hard flesh between his muscled thighs.

"Kiss me," she commanded softly, putting her arms around his waist.

He obeyed without hesitation. As their lips met, she tasted herself on him, bringing forth a fresh wave of hunger. She knew she wanted to feel him inside her again.

"Let's finish what we started in the garden, Lucas."

This time, he paused, pulling back slightly to look into her eyes. "Are you sure? You just…you know."

"Yes. Always yes." Echoing what she'd said in the car earlier, she jumped into his arms, knowing he would catch her.

He eased her back against the cool tiles once more, her legs wrapped around his hips as he entered her for the second time that night. He suckled her breasts while he pumped into her, measured and deliberate at first, until his pace increased in urgency and passion. He growled against her skin, his teeth grazing and marking her flesh, until he shook and cursed as he climaxed.

Though dazed and trembling, Lucas didn't leave her wanting. He used one hand to reach between their bodies, using nimble fingers and his large, throbbing length to coax her body towards another shattering release.

Tara collapsed into his arms, unable to support her own weight from the sheer force of the pleasure he'd given her. To her surprise, he lowered her to her feet, one arm supporting her, his free hand lathering liquid soap all over her hair and heated flesh. He rinsed and kissed her in turn, then wrapped her in a towel and carried her to the bed.

"I'll be back, love." She heard the words in a dreamy haze, felt the softness of her own sheets against her skin. She reached out to stroke his damp hair, lovingly, trying to muster a reassuring smile for his benefit. She watched him turn off the lights in the bedroom and make his way back to the shower.

Kind, considerate, gentle, passionate Lucas.

A tear escaped her eye. If only she was brave enough to tell him he'd been the muse behind all her songs. If only she could admit that unspoken love had fueled her music for years. Instead, she let the steady sound of running water lull her to a peaceful slumber.

She didn't know how long she'd been asleep, but she slowly stirred to wakefulness with an overwhelming feeling of warmth enveloping her. At first, she thought it was merely her blankets, but as she shifted slightly, she became aware of the strong arm wrapped securely around her, holding her close against a bare chest.

The moonlight streaming through the curtains fell on Lucas' sleeping form, his features chiseled and unbearably beautiful in the thin, silvery light. Surely, this wasn't real. The sight of him lying beside her was, as always, just another fleeting dream.

With tentative fingers, she reached out and traced the curve of his cheek. As her touch grazed his skin, his eyes fluttered open in drowsy surprise. He murmured words of love, his voice thick with sleep, before closing his lids once more.

"Lucas," she whispered, feeling a surge of courage well up inside her as she leaned in and pressed her lips to his.

His arms tightened around her, his hands weaving through her hair and gliding over her back and buttocks. Even in his half-asleep state, he responded to her kiss with matching fervor.

She climbed atop him and deepened the kiss, rubbing her naked body against his, feeling him come to life underneath her. He eagerly explored her body with his hands, finding her breasts and then daring to reach between her thighs.

"Steady on, big boy." She playfully pushed his hands away. "Let me."

"Yes, ma'am." He chuckled and held himself still, allowing her to take control.

She slid down his body, leaving a trail of delicate kisses along his chest and abdomen. Her lips found his nipples, biting them gently before continuing their journey downward. As she reached Lucas's powerful thighs, her hands found the waistband of his boxers. With a determined tug, she pulled down the shorts, revealing his arousal standing at attention.

"Fuck, Tara." His voice was thick with desire as his hands slid into her hair, his fingers warm and possessive at the nape of her neck.

She closed her fingers around his cock, keeping her grip firm yet gentle as she began stroking him rhythmically. Her lips and tongue danced across his balls, raining kisses, licks, nips, and suckles that had his hips bucking. He groaned and cursed loudly, praises falling from his lips.

"Keep going, love," he urged her, in a voice strained with the effort of holding back.

She looked up, only to see his eyes melting into dark pools of passion. She finally took him into her mouth, knowing he was teetering on the brink.

She switched her focus, her hands now massaging his balls while her lips enveloped his cock. She tugged and sucked gently, increasing her pace every few seconds. His moans grew as he neared breaking point; his hands tightened in her hair, too, but she didn't stop.

Then he broke, hips shooting into the air as he climaxed, shouting with abandon, "Tara, Tara, fuck, I love you." His voice rang throughout the house as his release filled her mouth, and she swallowed it all.

She crawled up next to him and lay quietly as she waited for him to recover, his chest heaving as he struggled to catch his breath. She watched as his eyes slowly began to focus, finally settling on her face inches away.

With a tender smile, he opened his arms. "Love."

She hesitated for a brief moment, but she couldn't resist the longing in his gaze. She snuggled into his embrace, welcoming the warmth of his arms around her. He leaned down to kiss her hair and forehead as she listened to his heartbeat, marveling as its pace slowed down to sync with hers.

"Do you know why I'm here? In this village?"

The question, uttered in a rumbling whisper known only to lovers, came completely out of the blue, a twisted echo of her earlier confession.

"Lucas...I...I don't know. You said you wanted to take a break from the city, right?"

He must have sensed her growing unease, for he tightened his hold on her, his voice losing none of its soft timbre. "I came here to get away—away from Manila and my team, away from everyone's scrutiny. I figured this was the best place to clear my head and think things through."

She couldn't quite get the point he was trying to make, but she understood his meaning. She was here for the exact same reason. "Because...?"

"My career might be ending soon." The words escaped his lips in a rush. "Much sooner than most people believe it would."

Confusion coursed through her, followed closely by a sense of disbelief. He could be joking, but it was something so far out of character for a man like him.

"Why?" It was the only question, the only word that could help her make sense of this.

He sighed. "I've been injured. I've been hurt, a whole lot. Pulled back muscles that won't completely heal, broken kneecaps patched up, ribs that have taken so much damage they might snap. After our first Philippine Cup championship two years ago, the other teams made it their main goal to put me out of commission. They always assigned larger, rougher players against me just to cause more damage. It would be funny if it didn't hurt like fuck."

"But...you're still so strong," she fumbled, shaking her head. "Just as strong as when you first started playing in the league. Maybe even stronger."

"Maybe I'm good at putting up a show," he offered gently. "So good, no one could see I was falling apart right in front of them."

"No," she muttered against his chest, hearing echoes of her own secrets in his confessions. "No."

"I'm old, love," he continued wryly, "and broken. But you...you make me whole again. That's why I was so grateful when I saw you. Seeing you here made me feel alive and hopeful. Maybe I had another chance, you know? Maybe it wasn't the end for me."

Tara could feel her heart breaking as he spoke of the pain and vulnerability that had been hidden beneath his confident façade.

"Who else knows about this?" she asked tentatively. "Surely someone else does..."

"Yeah, my manager, coach, and trainer all know. They've done an excellent job at hiding it from the public and even my teammates, but it's only a matter of time before the signs become visible. Even the team owner is in on the secret. I wanted to drop my contract and suffer the penalties. He refused to let me go, though. These people still believe in me, for some reason."

"And your family?"

"I...They can't know, Tara. Especially my parents."

"I believe in you. I'll never stop believing in you." She pressed her lips against his cheek, nuzzling the thin stubble along his jawline. "Whatever you tell me will stay between us."

His admission struck so painfully close to her own fears. The crushing weight of expectations, the even heavier burden of keeping one's struggles hidden from those closest to them. She never realized two completely different lives on the surface could be so alike underneath, once the glitter of fame was stripped off.

Lucas turned his face to hers, capturing her lips in a kiss. "But you...I wanted to tell you the truth, from the very start. I don't want secrets between us."

She nodded in silent agreement and brought her arms up, encircling his neck, deepening the kiss.

He seemed to be done speaking, as he rolled her onto her back. He covered her body with his, his tongue making its sweet way into her mouth. His fingers traced a heated path along her collarbone, his touch making her squirm for more. Her breath hitched as he moved lower, caressing her breasts. His hand was replaced by his mouth, leaving a trail of kisses down her stomach.

He didn't have to ask; Tara opened her legs for him, just as she opened her heart to his love and trust that very moment.

Lucas gave a groan of approval, his hands warm on her thighs as his mouth found her core, lapping up her juices greedily with his tongue, his lips sucking her nub until her legs were in the air, until she was gasping his name in abandon.

It was her turn to hold her arms open for him. He went into her embrace, their lips meeting in a fierce kiss that tasted of her and him.

"Never let go, love," Lucas murmured into her ear, as he positioned himself between her legs.

"Never."

Then he was inside her, their bodies moving together in languid strokes. Her hips rose to meet his steady thrusts; as pleasure built within her, she brought her legs higher, wider, wanting him to take all of her.

"Yes, my love, yes," he encouraged, his voice thick and rough with passion.

She clung to him, her nails raking down his back as they kissed fervently, his strokes intensifying as her own pleasure built right along with his urgency. And then, just as she thought she couldn't bear it any longer, her climax crashed over her, an irresistible torrent of sensation and emotion.

"Lucas," she gasped into his neck as he pounded into her with a desire bordering on desperate.

She felt him tense up and fill her, heard him groan her name into the night, tasted his sweat on her lips as he kissed her once more before his head crashed onto her chest.

As she put her arms around him and stroked his hair, listening to him breathe against her own trembling body, she knew with all her heart that she now belonged to him in a way that could never be undone.

Chapter 12

THE DREAM

Lucas

HE AWOKE TO A WARM GLOW, BEFORE HIS EYES AND inside his heart.

Soft light filtered through the curtains of an unfamiliar room, the rays of sunshine almost golden. Lucas found himself holding Tara flush against his own body as she slept soundly, her chest rising and falling gently with each breath.

This was her bedroom.

He couldn't see a clock anywhere. He was certain his cellphone was buried somewhere in his bag, which he'd haphazardly dropped in a corner of the room the night before. As she stirred in his arms, he pulled her closer, feeling a wave of arousal wash over him when he realized they were both still naked.

He buried his face in the nape of her neck, inhaling the intoxicating scent of her hair. He felt her body shift against his, pressing her backside against his hips, causing his hardness to grow further. Unable to resist any longer, he began to pepper her neck, hair, and shoulders with tender kisses. "I love you so much, Tara."

"Lucas," she responded sleepily, snuggling deeper into his embrace. "You feel so good…so warm. Please don't stop."

"I won't," he promised, and began to kiss and nip at her upper back in earnest, rubbing his throbbing cock against her buttocks.

She moaned in response, reaching up to pull at his hair as she ground back against him. "I never knew it could feel like this."

"Neither did I, love. But we're together now…and this is only the beginning."

"Oh, yes," she sighed, as his tongue found the sensitive skin at the back of her neck. "Yes, we've only just begun, haven't we?"

He chuckled in satisfaction at the unspoken challenge in her words. He reached for her breasts, cupping and squeezing, fingers flicking over her nipples. He could wake up to this every day.

"Play a song for me?" he whispered into her ear as he reached for her hand and guided it between her legs. "Play this song only for me, love."

"Lucas, I…" She flushed, turning her face away.

"You're so ready," he encouraged, tracing the heat of her with a finger, eliciting a small yelp that made him laugh lightly. "So wet. I would eat you, but let's do it your way first." He nudged his cock against her back entrance, almost entering her. "Please?"

"Oh, Lucas…" She hesitated for a moment, but under the guidance of his hand, her fingers took a life of their own.

"Yes," he murmured in satisfaction, watching her hips begin to move under her own touch. He lifted himself up by the elbow to get a better view, entranced. "Keep going, love."

Bathed by sunlight trickling into her room, Tara's naked form was even more breathtaking than last night. Her black hair, spread on the pillow like wings, stood out in stark contrast to the creamy-white color of her skin. She had the most perfectly round and perky breasts, perched on a flawless torso that had a narrow waist and softly curved hips. Her face was angelic, but her body was irresistibly tempting—and, now, here she was before him, his name dripping from her lips while she rubbed herself.

Her moans reached a crescendo, her knees bending and spreading to give way to the pleasure she was trying to reach. He watched in wonder as her palm stroked in circles, fingers dipping in and out, hips bucking to the tune of a song only the two of them could hear.

"Fuck, love, you're so beautiful." Unable to resist, he bent down and captured her lips, tongue tangling with hers, groaning when he saw her other hand pinch her own nipples.

"I'm coming, Lucas," she gasped against his mouth, breasts bouncing against his chest, "I'm so close."

"I'm right here, right here." He was a team player, after all, so he joined in the last few beats of her performance. He reached for her wrists and gently positioned her palms over her breasts. "Go high, and I'll finish low."

He lowered his head between her legs, draping her knees over his shoulders, and dove right into the fray. He licked and suckled at the moist path left by her hand as she continued caressing her own nipples, writhing under their combined ministrations. Her juices spilled over his tongue and, in an explosive thrust of her hips and a scream of his name, she came on his lips.

He slid up to the pillows and took her in his arms, carrying on with his soft kisses to her hair, now damp and askew. She curled into his chest, mewling softly as her body shook from the echoes of her climax.

"I'm right here," he repeated, his lips brushing her temple, making their way down to the curve of her jawline. "I've got you."

"Lucas…Lucas…" she moaned into the crook of his neck as her arms went around him, her breasts melding perfectly to the skin of his torso as if they'd always belonged there.

The intimacy of the moment was not lost on him as he tightened his embrace, nuzzling her hair. But his body was a ravenous beast in her presence; just as she slid her leg to settle between his knees, his rock-hard cock reared its head in hunger.

"Is that…?" Her eyes fluttered open, thick lashes sweeping shadows around her face.

Fuck.

It was her gaze that undid him, as he felt his arousal respond by poking at her thigh.

"Yeah…he's a little excited. I'm sorry. It's just that you're so beautiful and he can't help himself."

A pure, tinkling laugh signaled her complete

understanding. Instead of saying something, Tara reached up to his hair and tugged his head down to hers. She kissed him full on the mouth, passionately and breathlessly, leaving no room for doubt.

Lucas eagerly accepted her unspoken consent, kissing her back as his hands slid down to cup her backside. He dipped a finger into her, circling his large palms over the soft cheeks of flesh. "Can he come in this way, love? I think he really wants to, if that's okay."

A blush crept up Tara's cheeks as she nodded, giggling. "Sure."

He got up and guided her into position, her body poised on all fours at the edge of the bed. He leaned in to plant a kiss at the back of her neck as he reached over to stroke her wetness, making sure she was ready.

And she was.

A surge of possessive need coursed through him as he straightened, already exhilarated at the sight of her buttocks on full display. With a deep breath, he found a firm grip on her hips and entered her from behind in one swift motion.

She gasped, her body stiffening. She felt hot and unbelievably tight.

"Are you okay?"

"Yes," she answered breathily. "You feel so good....oh..."

He began to move inside her, gradually gaining intensity until his moans were loud enough for the entire farm to hear. He used one hand to hold her steady while the other roamed her body, claiming every inch of her as his own.

"Do you like this version of our song?" His fingers reached between her legs, dancing over her clit in time with the rhythm of his thrusts.

"Keep playing," she moaned, and he obeyed, taking her higher and higher.

As his own peak neared, he increased the tempo of his thrusts and his fingers, until he had completely and clearly drawn the pleasure out of his body and hers.

As they collapsed onto the bed, he held her close, his lips seeking the damp strands that clung to her forehead. She reached up, too, threading her hands through his hair, eyes closed as she panted against him.

Slowly, he eased their bodies back up towards the pillows and pulled the blanket over her. "Are you okay?"

"Never better." She opened her eyes a touch, stirring in his arms to a more comfortable position on her side. "What time is it?"

"I don't know," he admitted. "But I don't care. I've got you with me and that's all I care about."

She sighed, smiling as she settled her head on his chest. "It makes perfect sense when you put it that way. I've only ever had you in my dreams before—*this* is way better."

He cupped her chin gently, turning her face back towards him. "I was in your dreams?"

"Lucas…" Her eyes darted away from his.

"You don't have to tell me anything right now," he said quickly, unwilling to put her on the spot. He let her chin go and embraced her. "I'm sorry."

"It's okay," she murmured. "I've never done this before."

"Sorry," he said again, stroking her back and hair.

Silence fell over them, and he found his eyelids growing heavy. He wanted to give in to sleep, but he also wanted to savor every waking second of having Tara in his arms, spent and flushed from his lovemaking.

"Lucas." Her voice was barely above a whisper, barely awake. "The first time you came here…what made you say that you felt as if I was singing only to you?"

"I don't know. There was just something in your voice that always made me feel like you were right there beside me whenever I listened to your music. It felt like the words you were singing were meant only for me to hear and understand. Crazy, huh?"

Tara exhaled slowly, her hands easing up to clutch at his shoulders. When she spoke, he could barely hear the words. "You're not wrong. My songs—all of them—have been meant for you."

She could have shouted them; the shock that went through his body was enough to stun him motionless.

She took a deep breath and continued, her voice trembling. "That song last night, 'Never with You,' it was for you. I wrote it when I first heard you got picked in the pro league draft."

He felt something warm and wet splash on his chest. She was crying.

She went on talking, in that haunting melodious voice of hers. "The reason it was so hard for me to sing last night was that I never imagined I would be doing it in front of you. And you were kneeling and all before me, with flowers…so I got out of there as fast as I could."

A disbelieving rush of joy shot through his body as he absorbed the weight of her words. "You were very fast, love. I thought I was fucked for sure."

She snorted through her tears, her light sobs giving way to giggles. "Well, you did get fucked, didn't you? Several times, I might add. Maybe a few more times if you behave yourself."

He joined her laughter and pecked her soundly on the lips, wiping her tears away with his thumbs. "I promise I'll behave if you kiss me."

Her lips found his in a breathless, passionate kiss. "I'm so glad I finally had the chance to tell you...I thought I'd get over it, but even after all those songs and so many years, things haven't changed."

He felt a smile break through his face, like dawn slipping through the darkest cracks of night. He felt it warm every fiber of what made him whole.

She did. Tara Galvez made him whole.

"You know why they haven't changed? Because, through all that time, I have never stopped loving you."

*It was as if
I danced with you
In the shadows
I danced with you
In the rain*

*I danced with you
To a beat
Only love remembers*

~ Excerpt from 'Rain'
Lyrics and music by Tara Galvez
Fragments of Us, Esta Melodia Records

Chapter 13

THE CONFESSION

Tara

Years. They measured time, but no one had ever told her they would also mean endless nights, hidden fears, and desolate walls.

The years had put her in a gilded cage of success and fame, where inside her heart had begun to wither. Sometimes she wondered why it was still beating.

Now, she knew the answer.

Her heart was still beating for him, *with his.*

And now, she needed more answers.

"You have…*loved* me for that long?" Tara still fumbled over the word. Writing about love was one thing; living it was something else entirely. "I thought you never even noticed me back then. I was a nobody back in college."

"Trust me, I noticed you." The gentle, reassuring smile on Lucas' face was the stuff of grand epic romances, of love lost and found. It was a smile that touched and overwhelmed her in equal measure. "You were never nobody to me. You were always the most beautiful girl I'd ever seen, and now… you're even more stunning as a woman."

He continued, his baritone like music to her ears, his tender caresses on her hair and cheek making her own heart sing. "Ever since the time you returned my sketchbook, I've wanted nothing more than to be with you. I've followed your career, bought all your CDs, and even attended your concert once, hiding at the last row like an idiot."

"I never knew…" Their years apart had made sure of that. "Why didn't you tell me sooner? Why didn't you send me a message or ask to see me after my show?"

Lucas moved to a seated position, easing her up along with him. The look in his eyes as he took in her bare breasts was enough to make her blush.

"How could I?" His voice was filled with awe as he reached out to run his fingers through her hair. "You are a star, Tara, and you shine like no one else does. Dumb jocks like me could only stand back and love you from a distance. But your music…it was my way of keeping you close. It's been the soundtrack of my life, ever since I heard your first song." His fingers made their slow journey downward, tracing her eyes, cheeks, and lips. "What was it? Ah, 'Rain.'"

She closed her eyes and let his words and touch wash over her. She grabbed his hand, keeping it on her cheek, loving its warmth on her skin.

"I've never had a meaningful relationship with anyone," he added wryly. "Didn't matter who or what they were…no one could compare to you. I just ended up listening to you sing, night after night."

With a soft cry, she threw herself into his arms. "You idiot, you should have said something. You should have *at least* asked for your damn jacket back."

"Now that I think about that jacket…have you still got it?"

She hugged him tighter. "It's in the closet, first door on the right."

Lucas laughed as he pressed his lips to her cheek. "It's not too late for us, is it? Tell me, is there someone who would want to put me six feet under for what we've been doing since last night?"

She playfully punched him on the chest, a smile breaking through her tears as she shook her head. "There's no one else."

"There's a chance for me, then, isn't there? Would you give me a chance?"

She didn't answer. She couldn't answer.

Instead, she slid out of his arms and got to her feet. Naked, she made a beeline for the closet and retrieved his old varsity jacket from its hiding place. She slid her arms through its voluminous sleeves as she made her way back to him.

He watched her every move, still as a statue from his perch on the bed. The desire in his eyes was unmistakable, burning brighter with each step she took closer.

"It still fits," she declared.

"It still fits," he echoed, biting his lip as he held out his arms to her. "Yeah."

"Sometimes, I still wear this," she said, crawling back

towards him. "You know, when it's cold…and when I dream of you."

She felt Lucas stiffen as she straddled him, her breasts promptly pushing up to his face as she put her hands on his shoulders.

"Dream of me, love?" He caught on quickly, his arms encircling her waist.

She smiled down at him. "Sometimes, I dream of what it feels like to be held by those arms, to be touched by those hands. The usual things a girl dreams about."

"Tell me more," he urged, his lips finding their way to a taut nipple.

"My favorite dream is this." She reached for his hardness, impressed at how quickly it responded, then guided it to her slick entrance. "Nothing beats this."

She sank onto him, sheathing him inside her. She gasped at the sensation of being completely filled, of being in control of something so raw.

"Let's see if we can beat your dream." He gave her a roguish smile full of promise.

They moved together, she clinging to him as he thrust up into her with determined strokes. The world around them faded away once more, leaving only the ebb and flow of their passion, the firm grip of his hands on her hips, and the sound of his moans echoing her own.

"This is fucking better than any dream," he said through gritted teeth. "Don't stop, love."

Encouraged by his words, she rotated her hips in a wider circle, pumping herself up and down, feeling an exquisite agony intensify with every motion. His hands on her tightened, seeking control of her movements, and she could feel him trembling beneath her.

"You're right," she gasped. "This is way better."

She leaned back, allowing her own pleasure to build unchecked. Her body was a symphony ready to be mastered, as she offered her breasts and clit for him to caress, desperate for his touch on the rest of her.

"Tara…Tara…." Lucas' words were urgent as his fingers began to work their magic. The pleasure built and built until it threatened to make her lose all control.

"Oh god, Lucas…" she cried out, teetering on the very edge, already lost in sensations far better than any wild dream could give.

Before she realized what was happening, Lucas had flipped her onto her back, her legs over his shoulders as he took over, pumping into her with a hunger she'd never experienced before. The sudden shift of position caught her off guard, and her climax caught her unawares, ripping through her without quarter, leaving her breathless and utterly consumed by a giant wave of pleasure, her arms flailing in the air for an anchor in the storm.

Lucas continued to pump into her, his body dripping with sweat. As his weight pressed down on her, she heard him pant in her ear, "Do you love me, too, Tara?"

She reached for him, one hand in his hair, the other around his neck, and met his thrusts with her own, lifting her hips as high as they would go, taking him deeper and deeper into her body until she heard him growl his release, a white-hot explosion that dripped down her thighs, a whisper in her ear saying this was better than any dream, better than anything.

And as they lay there, tangled together in the aftermath of their passion, she brought her mouth to his. As they kissed each other, Lucas' fingers fiddling with the fabric of his old jacket, Tara could still feel the lingering heat of him inside her, filling her with a strange sense of completeness.

"Everything about this... it's so much better than any dream, Lucas."

He reached up to trace her jawline, his eyes filled with such sincere tenderness that made her chest tighten. "Good. If you want the real me, I'm here for you. Always."

She wondered how long she could keep this up.

This artful, passionate deflection of hers.

She drew musical notes on his chest, taking her time to savor the texture of his skin. "Hmmm...maybe everyone is wondering what happened to us."

"Most likely they've already heard of the fireworks coming from your room." His teasing grin caused her cheeks to burn. She gave him an earnest shove, unable to suppress her giggles as he rolled away from her.

"Come on. We should go out before they call the police in from town to investigate." He reached down to help her up, and she let him pull her to her feet. They shared one more heated kiss before she moved to the closet while he retrieved his bag from the floor.

As they dressed, he glanced over at her. "I'm glad I brought clothes in. I hope it won't be the last time."

Only half-dressed, she crossed the room in a second and was back in his arms in a heartbeat. They fumbled with each other's clothing, lowering her panties and his pants and briefs just enough to allow their bodies to join together again.

She clung to him as they moved together on the bed

one more time. When they were finally spent, she reluctantly pulled away from him, knowing they had to face the world outside her bedroom door.

Before they stepped out, she turned to him, reaching for his face with a gentle hand. He paused mid-stride under her touch, turning his lips to kiss her fingertips.

"Lucas…I…I want to be with you…the real you. Always."

He answered with a smile and, for the moment, it was enough.

Chapter 14

THE PROMISE

Lucas

H E FELT LIKE A BOY AGAIN, FILLED WITH AN ODD kind of dread as he drove to his parents' house. Following Tara's abrupt exit from last night's game and his subsequent hurried departure to follow her, Lucas knew exactly what awaited him the moment he walked through those doors.

Questions.

But he was ready for anything, because he had her in his life now. He had this beautiful, passionate, maddeningly delicious woman in his arms, under his skin, in his very soul, just as she had him in hers.

This, too, made him feel like a love-struck teenaged boy.

Once he cut the engine, Lucas reached for his phone, buried deep within his sports bag on the passenger seat. It was the first time he had looked at it since yesterday afternoon, and it had been almost a full day since then. The screen lit up with a barrage of messages and a list of missed calls from Derek, his parents, and a number not on his contacts list. He sighed, locking the phone again before stepping out into the midday sun. He'd deal with it all later.

He'd barely taken a few steps towards the house before the phone vibrated. The screen showed Derek Torreblanca as the caller's name, which he quickly swiped to accept.

"Delgado, you're alive!" Derek's voice boomed through the phone. "How are you, man? I thought you were dead or something. I almost—almost—called Benny because you didn't take my calls yesterday."

Lucas chuckled at the mention of their team manager. "Well, I'm glad you didn't. The poor man would have overreacted and filed a Missing Persons report. I had a game with the village kids yesterday evening…and, then, spent the rest of it with a very special lady."

"What? Fuck me, you did?" The excitement in Derek's voice carried clearly through the line.

"You were right, you know. I found love here in the country, just like you said."

"Seriously? Who is she? Do I know her?" The questions came in rapid fire. "Do I get to be the best man?"

"Easy, easy." He tried to laugh it off, but the source of his hesitation was very clear: a shared vulnerability after a night of secrets and revelations. He didn't want to be presumptuous or betray Tara's trust by revealing too much too soon. "I don't want to jinx it, but I've met the girl of my dreams."

"Wow, that's amazing. And, yeah, you sound like someone in love."

Did he really? It felt like it, his body still humming with the desire to see Tara again—hold her, touch her, *be* with her.

"I don't know about that," he replied lightly.

"I can't wait to hear more when things work out, man," Derek said. "After all this time, you deserve to be happy. I'm glad you met your mystery lady."

"Thanks, Derek. You'll be the first to know."

"Great!" There was a hesitant pause, before his friend continued in a more serious tone. "We'll still see each other at the training camp in a few weeks, won't we? You're not just gonna ride off into the sunset, are you?"

"No, I won't leave you or the team in a lurch, I promise." Lucas spied a figure peering through the curtains of the bungalow. "Enjoy the rest of your vacation, Derek. Give my regards to your family."

"Will do. Take care, brother."

"Take care, man. See you in Manila."

As soon as the call disconnected, his mother appeared in the doorway, her eyes studying him intently, while his father followed behind her with a concerned expression.

"Lucas, is everything okay?" Mercy's voice was laced with worry. "How's Tara?"

"We've been trying to reach you since last night," Luis interjected. "Has Marife brought her guitar back?"

He took a deep breath and put on what he hoped was a reassuring smile. "Everything's fine, Ma. I found her last night on the road leading to the farm and took her back to the villa. I didn't leave until I was sure she was alright. She got the guitar this morning and was tuning it when I left."

His father shook his head, guilt evident on his face. "We shouldn't have asked her to perform. I feel responsible for what happened to that poor girl."

"Hey," Lucas said gently, placing a hand on his father's shoulder. "It wasn't anyone's fault but my own, Pa. I shouldn't have displayed my feelings like a lovesick teenager."

His mother moved closer to console him, wrapping him in a warm embrace. "Oh, Lucas, you can't blame yourself for wanting to show the world how you feel for Tara. I saw it on your face the moment I mentioned her name when you first got here. It was as clear as day."

"I'm glad you looked after her, as a real man should," said his father, gesturing for them to take seats in the living room. "How is she holding up?"

"She slept," he answered simply as he settled on the couch, the aches and pain of his body back in full force after the stress and emotional rollercoaster of the previous night. "She ate something this morning, too. The women at the farm will take good care of her."

"Maybe we should call her parents," Mercy suggested. "They live in Iloilo, don't they?"

Lucas shook his head. "No, Tara doesn't want her family to worry. She made me promise not to make a big deal of it. But I'll make sure she's okay, Ma. I'll keep checking on her."

"We'll make sure to look after Tara, too," added Luis. "If she still wants to see us."

"Of course she does, Pa. She felt guilty for walking out—she felt as if she let all of you down. She kept apologizing the whole time."

"It's all that fame…all that pressure on such a sensitive young woman," Mercy said, her voice cracking, tears brimming at the corners of her eyes. "Her being alone in that farm—it isn't natural. She should be out in the world enjoying her life. She should be with people who love her."

"You can start with me, Ma." Closing his eyes, Lucas leaned back and allowed himself to be vulnerable in front of his parents. "I've loved Tara for the longest time, ever since we first met in college. She's the reason I've never really had serious relationships...I helped her get home one time, during a storm. After that, I followed her around like a fool, but never talked to her again. Yeah, it's really stupid, but she's always had me."

A heavy silence settled over the room. He'd expected disbelief, perhaps uncertainty, maybe even mild judgment. When he opened his eyes, he saw only concern on the faces of his parents.

"Our hearts choose who to love without asking for permission," his mother finally said, reaching over to pat his hand. "Yours did, Lucas, and it chose very well."

"We're happy you found Tara again, after all these years," said his father, a small smile on his usually somber face. "Must be fate. It took some time, but you're with her now, aren't you?"

Lucas took a deep breath as he looked at both his parents in turn, not knowing how to react to such a sincere show of support. Perhaps they really did see the depth of his feelings, the road he'd taken just to reach this point in his life.

With a gentle smile, Mercy got to her feet. "Have you had lunch?

He shook his head. "I had some coffee and eggs at the farm earlier, but it's been a long night."

"Your mother has put aside some food for you," Luis

said, nodding towards the kitchen. "Maybe you can bring some for Tara, too, if you want to check on her later."

"Thank you, Pa." He stood up and excused himself quietly, retreating to the guestroom.

Once inside, Lucas sat down on the edge of the bed, his mind swirling with thoughts of Tara. His phone vibrated again, startling him out of his trance. It was that number—the one not listed in his contacts. Curiosity piqued, he picked up the call.

"Lucas Delgado."

"Hello, this is Jasmine Samontes," said the caller briskly. It was a woman's voice, crisp and no-nonsense. "I'm the manager of Tara Galvez."

Surprised, he stared at the screen for a few seconds before replying, wondering how in the world could Tara's manager have any business with him. "How can I help you?"

"Help me?" she scoffed. "You have some explaining to do, Delgado. How dare you pull a stunt like that with Tara!"

He bristled at her tone but forced himself to remain calm. "I'm not sure what you're talking about, Ms. Samontes."

"Last night's game?" Jasmine snapped. "My source told me all about it—how Tara ran off upset after you tried to pull some romantic publicity stunt. Are you in some kind of relationship with her? Have you been hiding it from the public? For how long?"

Taken aback by her questioning, Lucas hesitated before responding. "This is a private matter between Tara and me."

"Private?" Jasmine's voice rose in disbelief. "You made it my business when she ran off in the middle of a song she's performed a million times. You have no idea how sensitive

Tara is. You can't even begin to fathom what she's got at stake right now."

Lucas clenched his jaw, frustrated by her accusations but keenly aware of the truth in her words.

"I will never hurt her," he said firmly, clutching the phone so tightly in his hand he thought it might snap in half.

"Maybe you don't think you will, but if you keep putting her in situations that threaten her well-being, you'll have to answer to me. There's so much pressure on her for her tenth-anniversary album, Delgado. If you fuck things up for her, there will be hell to pay." He could hear her breathing down the line, clearly worked up and ready for battle.

Lucas took a deep breath. "I'll make sure she's not hurt or overwhelmed. I will protect her. I promise you that."

"Good," Jasmine retorted. "But just so we're clear, I don't know you. I trust you even less."

"Then know this, Ms. Samontes. I love Tara Galvez. I believe in her talent, and I believe in her."

Jasmine's silence hung heavy on the line for a moment before she spoke again. "You better not screw this up or I will destroy you, personally *and* professionally. She's my best friend, and if you really love her, make sure she doesn't spiral into self-doubt and never come back."

"Understood," Lucas replied curtly, feeling the leaden weight of his own promise.

"Goodbye, Delgado."

"Goodbye, Ms. Samontes."

As he ended the call, he stared out the window, heart pounding as the gravity of the situation began to sink in. He laid back on the pillows and closed his eyes, focusing on the image of Tara kissing him, telling him her songs had always been meant for him.

Lucas awoke with a start; the room was already filled with dusky shadows. Disoriented, he glanced at his phone next to him, noting the time—almost six in the evening. A message from his father informed him that both parents were away for their Monday night meeting with the town's cooperative heads. Hunger gnawed at him, and he realized he hadn't eaten all day.

Alone in the darkened house, his thoughts circled back to Tara, not realizing he was already dialing her number.

She picked up after three rings. "Hello, how was your day?"

"Truthfully?" A lump formed in his throat as he thought of her in the big villa on her own. His mother was right; this wonderful, beautiful woman deserved to be with people who loved her. "It hasn't been complete without you."

She laughed. "We only saw each other this morning."

"Well, I can't see you enough. Can I come over for dinner?"

"Yes," came her immediate response. "I'll see you soon."

After hanging up, he quickly took a shower and changed into fresh clothes. Soon, he was on the road to Galvez Farms. Once he reached the gates, he made use of Fred's remote control.

As he drove through the entrance, a night watchman greeted him with a respectful nod, showing no hint of surprise at his access privileges. "Good evening, Sir Lucas."

As he navigated the dirt road leading to the villa, he spotted Tara waiting for him on the front porch, silhouetted in the waning sunlight.

OUR LOVE REPLAY

He knew then he would never let her go or hurt her.

This was love. It didn't matter if it was old or new, fated or just coincidence. What mattered was the woman who stood at the end of the road.

As soon as the car rolled to a stop, he sprang out the door, bolting up the steps two at a time. As soon as he reached her side, she leaped into his arms, her laughter like the sweetest music.

He had that love now, and he was determined to keep it.

Believe me
When I say goodbye
In a halting whisper
Believe me
When I turn away
From the promise in your eyes

Believe me
That I'm never sorry
For loving you
Believe me
That I walk away
Before I no longer could

~ Excerpt from 'Believe Me'
Lyrics and music by Tara Galvez
I Remember You, Esta Melodia Records

Chapter 15

THE ETERNITY

Tara

It was nearly dinner time, reminiscent of their reunion earlier that month. She stood on the porch, her gaze fixed on the cloud of dust billowing behind the approaching car.

She began to wonder if this was nothing more than a beautiful dream, remnants of an old love only she could remember, a mirage born from the longing in her heart.

But no, it was all real.

The sound of Lucas' voice on the phone, asking if he could come over, was real. His touch from their night together, still lingering on her skin, was real. The taste and scent of him, all over her, musky and irresistible, was real.

And maybe, just maybe, he really did love her.

As the SUV came to a halt before the house, Tara's pulse quickened. She watched as he emerged from the vehicle, heartbreakingly handsome as always with a big grin on his face. A stream of giggles escaped her as she crossed the last few inches that separated them and sprang into his arms. He caught her effortlessly, kissing her as if they hadn't seen each other for an eternity.

Perhaps it felt that way. Perhaps love had a way of changing everything—the perception of time, memories, and the weight of waiting.

The world around them seemed to blur into nothingness as they stumbled through the threshold, still locked in their passionate embrace.

"Are we alone?" Lucas gasped as he came up for air. His eyes focused on her face before he breathed out, "And how is it that you get more and more beautiful every time I see you?"

"Y-yes," Tara stammered, her cheeks flushing. "I told the women I'd be fine for the evening."

He chuckled in satisfaction, his hands beginning to roam down her body as she turned to lock the door behind them. "I'm starving for dinner, but I'm even hungrier for you."

"Me, too," she said softly, leaning against the wood once the final bolt was in place.

"Good." He pressed his body to hers, hand reaching under the hem of her sundress. His fingers traveled slowly up her thigh, tracing the curve of her hip and waist, before finally settling on a lace-covered breast. "Let's take this slowly, love. Slower than last night."

"I'd like that," she whispered. "I'd like that very much."

So unlike last night's frenzied passion, they undressed

each other slowly. He lowered the straps of her dress first, kissing the bare skin underneath; her bra and panties followed, her most intimate places worshipped by his lips and tongue. She did the same, with his shirt, pants and underwear; her hands traced every inch of muscle and bronzed skin, their path followed by her mouth. There was no urgency; instead, there was an almost reverent sense of intimacy.

He guided her to the middle of the carpet and kissed her hand before he laid down on his back, wondrously naked, his cock jutting out proudly. He held out his arms to her, with the simplest yet most erotic command, "Ride me."

She straddled his lap and began to move her hips, grinding against him without penetration, arching her back as pleasure coursed through her veins. Lucas cupped her breasts, kneading the soft flesh, flicking the nipples with gentle fingers, creating a delicious friction that left her soaked and aching for more.

As if sensing her need, he positioned himself at her entrance, his hands firmly gripping her hips. Slowly, deliberately, he entered her, filling her completely, causing her breath to catch in her throat.

"I'm all yours, love. I've only ever been yours."

Something about the way he said the words—with such tender surrender—that made the dam of her feelings break.

Tara rode him, slowly at first, then faster and faster, her body creating a harmony of pleasure that soon reached fever pitch. Lucas followed her lead, pumping into her with a fervor that spoke of a love long denied, his hands gripping her hips like a lifeline.

And the tears came, streaming down her face as she called out his name. Love, ecstasy, pain…she wasn't sure anymore, trembling on the precipice of her most intense climax yet. She wasn't even sure who came first, only that it was a deep, grunting thrust from him that pushed her over the edge.

Heart racing, she collapsed on top of him, the scent of his sweat and the lingering musk of their lovemaking filling her nostrils. A few rogue tears slipped from her eyes, splashing onto his chest.

"Hey," he murmured, his fingers brushing the damp hair from her forehead. "It's okay. I love you." He guided her up to a seated position, cradling her in his arms as she pressed feather-light kisses to his heated skin.

"I missed you," she muttered into his bicep.

"God, I missed you too."

The sincerity of his tone made her chest ache, but she chose to focus on the ridiculous sweetness of their exchange. "We sound like lovesick teenagers."

"Maybe we still are, making up for lost time."

She buried her face in his shoulder, taking deep breaths against his skin, trying to stem the tide of emotions bubbling up within her.

"I don't want to lose any more time with you, Tara," Lucas went on. "I'll be here for as long as you want me, for as much as you need me. You set the pace—you command, and I'll follow."

His words almost triggered a fresh wave of tears, but she bit her lip to keep them at bay. "Why are you so wonderful?"

"Because I don't want to screw this up," he replied gently. "I don't want to lose you again."

Talking about her feelings had always been something she shied away from, but with him, she found the courage to slowly bare her heart. It was terrifying, but it was a start.

"We never really lost each other," she began. "Just like you, I haven't had what you could call a relationship. I've met men, sure, mostly while touring abroad. But… I'd pull away, knowing I couldn't offer them anything real."

"Tell me, love," he encouraged, stroking her bare back as he kissed the crown of her head.

"About six years ago, there was Andrew, hands down the most serious of them all. I met him in San Francisco during the kick-off concert of my North America tour. He followed me for three weeks, but I ended it in D.C., right before flying to Vancouver. It didn't feel right, stringing someone along, knowing I could never give them what they wanted."

"That's pretty fair," he murmured. "It sounds like the right thing to do."

She nodded and tilted her head up to meet his gaze. "Do you know what I did after breaking up with him?"

"What did you do?" His curiosity was tinged with warmth.

"I watched your game on my phone. You made two incredible three-pointers in the last few minutes, making your team back then win by a point. Until now, I believe that was the game that convinced your team now to take you in a trade." She smiled sadly at the memory; she'd regretted hurting Andrew more than she'd actually felt the loss of her short-term lover. Watching Lucas play had been the best thing to do to console herself.

"I'm glad you got traded. I never did like your old team. Their franchise player was—and still is—an ass. The refs should call him more often for travelling—he can't even dribble to save his life." She blushed, looking away when she saw his eyes widen at her comments. "I've hated men I didn't even know just because they fouled you or blocked your shot."

Laughter escaped her then, and she gave in to it with as much of her heart as she could.

Lucas joined in, his chuckle rich and infectious. "You've been stalking me, woman. That's very bad."

"Yeah. Not as bad as you, but equally guilty."

He brought his head down to kiss her lips, tightening his arms around her. She could still hear and feel the laughter rumbling in his chest. "Seems like we've always been connected, in one way or another, haven't we?"

She nodded. "I guess, but I still don't understand *this*… We'll never get the time that we lost back, Lucas."

He sighed. "It hurts like hell to think about it, but maybe that isn't how love is supposed to be."

"What do you mean?"

"I don't think we're meant to understand it, or question how it works," he said patiently. "We're supposed to live it, you know?"

She smiled, smoothing down thick locks of his wavy hair that stood up all over his head. "You should be the one writing love songs."

He grinned in response. "Well, I'm available for bookings, but for you I'm always free. Just say the word."

"Can you help me understand that kind of love, then? Teach me about the kind of love that we actually get to live?"

"I would do anything for you, Tara. Anything you want."

"Show me," she said, almost shyly. "Show me right here, now, on the floor."

He didn't need any further prompting; he guided her down onto the pile of their discarded clothes and made her lie down. His eyes darkened with desire as he explored her body with gentle touches. His palm and fingers worked expertly to make her wet, just as she saw that he was more than ready, too.

Lucas shifted to his knees, spreading her legs wide while he positioned himself between her thighs. Carefully, he lifted her hips and entered her. The sensation was overwhelming, filling her completely.

"Let me know how you want it." His pace was slow and steady, yet beautifully unyielding. His grip on her ankles was firm and controlling, yet somehow comforting in its dominance.

"Harder," she commanded, and he complied, driving into her with passionate vigor that made her moan in delight. "Faster," she urged, and he increased his pace, their bodies moving together rhythmically.

"Your hand," she gasped, and without hesitation, he placed one hand on her clit as he continued to slam into her.

Their crescendo built, her breasts bouncing and her arms reaching wildly in the air; she couldn't care less at her wanton state as she found herself on the brink of ecstasy. "Yes, Lucas, yes!"

She hit the peak with an explosion, her body trembling as she moaned his name again and again. The sound seemingly made his control slip away, and he was on top of her, fingers threaded through hers in an almost painful grip, pounding into her with such force that left her breathless and spinning towards a second orgasm.

Lucas came hard with her this time, his body stiffening, eyes closed as he shook uncontrollably and collapsed on top of her.

"You're a great teacher," Tara murmured, wrapping her arms around him.

He took her compliment with a gasping laugh and a groggy response. "Happy to teach you more, after dinner and all night long."

They took their time to get up from the floor and share the night's meal before retreating to her bedroom, where they made love again and again until dawn.

In the weeks that followed, they took their time to live in love.

The days were filled with simple pleasures: running around the farm and tending to her garden in the early morning, sharing breakfasts of *pan de sal* and fresh coffee, and sneaking into her room at midday to make slow, sensuous love.

Afternoons were spent with her music and his art, Tara sitting at the front porch strumming her guitar and singing as she weaved new melodies from their own unfolding love story; Lucas lounging from across her, always sketching with a smile on his face.

Evenings were for exploring the local villages in search of fresh fruits and street food, having dinner in the villa or in any of the tiny eateries they found along their drives, and making love in every corner of the house once they were alone.

It was everything she'd ever wanted—the only man she had ever truly loved, in the only place that had ever truly felt like home.

But no matter how hard she wished she could hold on to this time forever, she knew it wasn't possible.

The real world awaited them both.

Chapter 16

THE GOODBYE

Lucas

IT WAS HIS LAST DAY IN THE VILLAGE.
  Lucas tried not to think so much of the minutes ticking away as drove towards the main villa of Galvez Farms. The sunrise was beautiful, after all, and at the end of the road, he was going to see Tara again. He was determined to savor every precious moment he had left with her.

His heart fell when he saw the empty front porch. Over the past few weeks, she'd always been there waiting for him, a smile of her face.

As he pulled into his usual spot, Fred appeared with a wide grin. "Sir Lucas, thank you again for getting me the new motorbike. It's been really helpful in getting around the village more quickly. Not to mention Dodie picked a beauty."

Lucas had to smile at the foreman's enthusiasm. "It's very well deserved by you and your family, Fred. Least I could do for you and your wife looking out for Tara."

"Well, I just wanted to wish you good luck in the Philippine Cup. We're all rooting for a third championship. I may or may not have bet half a year's wages on you getting the Finals MVP, too."

Lucas chuckled at the statement. "In that case, I'll do my best not to let you down, or Marife will have my head."

"She'll hang me upside down on a tree covered by red ants, more like, but it's gonna be worth it." The older man rubbed the back of his neck before he continued. "By the way, Sir Lucas, do you need anything for Manila? Anything we can do for you before you go?"

Lucas shook his head. "I'm fine, but thanks for asking. I'll be driving back to the airport and return my car there."

"Miss Tara asked my wife to help prepare the *biko* for you to bring back to Manila. I told Fe she'd better make it extra special, you know, for good luck."

Emotion caught in Lucas' throat at the mention of Tara's thoughtfulness. Over these weeks, he'd grown to love her *biko*, which she'd prepared for him every Saturday. "Thank you. Please tell Marife I appreciate it."

Fred nodded. "Will do, Sir Lucas."

"Can you do me a favor, Fred, and keep an eye on Tara? If she needs anything…just let my parents know."

"There's no need to worry, Sir Lucas," the foreman said with a confident, reassuring smile. "Miss Tara is loved and protected in this village."

"That's very good to hear." Lucas extended a hand. "I'll see you all again soon."

"All the best, Sir Lucas." Fred shook his hand briskly. "Oh, if you're looking for Miss Tara, she's in her garden. She's been there for a while now."

"Thanks, Fred."

With a murmured farewell and a tip of his hat, the foreman was gone.

As Lucas made his way down the familiar path, the breeze made Tara's flowers dance gracefully in the sunlight. He could still remember her standing in their midst all those weeks ago, moments before their first kiss.

His beautiful, sensitive angel, welcomed by his parents into their lives with open arms. Every Sunday, they would attend Mass at the village chapel, followed by a generous lunch his mother had lovingly prepared. On their last Sunday together, Tara had sung for his parents, her delicate voice accompanied by the strumming of an old guitar that belonged to his father. In that moment, he'd realized just how perfectly Tara fit into his family—a gentle soul who thrived under the tender care and love that surrounded her.

Upon reaching the end of the path, Lucas stood at the edge of Tara's garden, watching her for a few moments as she moved among her white and gold flowers. She seemed to sense his presence, pausing for a moment before turning to smile at him over her shoulder. He approached her slowly and, as he reached her side, wrapped his arms around her from behind. He pressed gentle kisses to her cheeks and hair, breathing in her scent.

"Hi." Tara turned in his embrace and angled her face up to his, eyes fluttering close.

He brought his lips down to hers, in a kiss that felt like a wondrous eternity wrapped in a few fleeting breaths.

Everything he had ever wanted, now in his arms. The constant aches he felt from his injuries were nothing—nothing—compared to the searing emptiness brought about by their impending separation.

"Uh, I've got the bread," he mumbled, clinging to the reality of their breakfast routine in hopes of not losing himself to the pain. "Left it in the car. I got worried when you weren't on the porch."

She gave him an apologetic smile as she shook her head. "It's okay. Sorry, I lost track of time. I wanted to get some flowers for you."

"Why?"

"Because I felt like it." With a heavy sigh, she stepped out of his arms, her gaze drifting to an overflowing basket of blossoms on the ground.

"Something wrong?" He reached her hand before she could move further away. "Are you okay?"

"Of course not. How could I be, when you're leaving tomorrow? No more Saturday *biko*, Lucas, no more Sundays…" Her voice caught as she averted her eyes, her shoulders shaking.

In a desperate, helpless bid to comfort her, he fumbled for words. "I'll come back—weekends, whenever I can. We can see each other in Manila, right? I'll get you flights and courtside tickets to all my games… You could even stay with me in my apartment if you like, or I could stay with you, or I could book you into a hotel…"

"Sounds like you've got it all figured out," she said quietly, slipping out of his grasp.

"What do you want me to say, Tara?" He could only stare at her back uncertainly, heart pounding. He wanted nothing more than to grab her and ride off into the sunset, never to be seen again, just like Derek had said.

He watched as she deftly plucked a white chrysanthemum from its stem, weighing it in her hand.

"I don't know," she finally said, her voice barely audible above the gentle rustle of leaves. "Just tell me, Lucas, what do you really want?"

He blinked at the question, taken aback by its simplicity. It sounded so obvious, but as he searched for an answer, he realized just how little he understood what it truly meant.

"I don't understand, love," he admitted.

She walked up to him, her eyes glistening with unshed tears as she put the white flower in his shirt pocket. Her hand lingered over his heart, then reached up to caress his cheek.

"What do you really want?" she repeated, her voice stronger this time.

"I want you," he replied, choosing the clearest, truest answer he had. "I've always wanted you. I want a life with you in it."

Her gaze held his. "I've always wanted you, too. A life with you in it. But I don't know what kind of life that would be. I still don't."

He felt a strange sense of relief wash over him. "Neither do I, but maybe we can find out together."

"Together..." she echoed, the word almost disappearing into the wind. "You make it sound so easy."

With that, she let go of him, moving out of his reach and into the middle of her garden, ensconced in the safety of her flowering plants. Between them stood pots upon pots of roses. It looked like Tara was protecting herself with their thorns.

"I don't know what else to say, Tara."

She sighed as she delicately ran her hands over clusters of white blooms. "Do you remember what I told you the night of the game?"

"Tara, I—"

"I've been running from my own head. I've been hiding out here, hoping I don't fall apart long enough to make music that still means something. To make sure I still mean something. You made me believe I meant something, and I'll never forget that."

"But you know what I really want?" she sobbed, wiping at her eyes almost angrily. "I want a life where you're happy and healthy and loved. I want a life where I can give you all of myself without getting scared."

"Scared of what?" His throat tightened, feeling the pain of the vulnerability she had somehow trusted him to know.

"Of everything, Lucas. Of falling apart again and again, thinking I'll never be good enough. Of you getting hurt again and again, right in front of me. I'm in fucking pieces, and I'm scared you're going to get torn apart any day, too. We found each other after all these years, and for what?"

"For *us*," he answered hoarsely. "For us to be together. For you to be loved by me."

"What about you—your heart, your art, your body? Don't you care about what happens to you? Because…I do. I care."

In that moment, realization struck him like lightning—she loved him. She had never said it, but he knew it as surely as he knew his own name. He closed the distance between them and reached for her hand, pulling her gently out of the cluster of plants.

"I love you, Tara. Please, tell me you love me too."

"Will you stay with me if I do?" she countered softly.

"I'm far from perfect, but I'll take good care of you."

He smiled at her, as bravely as he could. "You've always been perfect to me. Always. But staying here…it's not that simple."

"I never thought it was," she murmured, smiling back with sad eyes. "I thought I'd try anyway. Someone taught me to take chances even when we're scared shitless. He taught me about real love that way."

He understood the weight of their choices—the life they could have together, and the life that pulled him away. Not knowing what else to do, he embraced her. "Sounds like a very wise man."

She didn't resist, hugging him right back. "Yeah. I'm going to miss him when he's not around here anymore."

He kissed the top of her head. "He's going to miss you, too."

Tara laid her head against his chest, ear to his heart, not saying anything for a while. After some time, she pulled away just enough to look up at him. "Will you stay the day?"

He nodded, not trusting himself to speak with the growing lump in his throat. He stepped around her to retrieve her basket from the ground and held it out her. The exchange reminded him of the first time he'd visited her in the garden. The first time they kissed.

"Shall I get started on the coffee?" Tara took the basket and tilted her head in the direction of the villa.

"Please. I'll get the bread."

After retrieving their *pan de sal* from the car, he went into the kitchen to see her preparing their breakfast as she did every morning these past weeks. Standing on the balcony, he watched her move gracefully about, her hair swinging like a silk waterfall as she worked, her hands performing each task with her customary elegance.

This could be the last time they shared their quiet, unhurried rituals, so he tried to memorize every detail of her: the way her shirt clung to her slender frame, the gentle curve of her wrists as she poured water, the delicate sweep of her eyelashes as she blinked.

When she finally set down their tray of coffee and bread before him, he reached across the table and took her hand.

"I love you," he said simply.

She smiled in response. "Eat up. Good thing the *pan de sal* hasn't gone cold yet."

He didn't let her hand go, even as she tried to wriggle it out of his grip. "Tara, will you…would you like to join my family for dinner this evening? My mother's cooking my *despedida* meal, and my uncle and his wife are joining us, too."

She lowered her head, gaze fixated on the wooden surface between them. "I d-don't think it's a very good idea. For me to come over a-and all, especially tonight."

The stammer and sadness in her voice were enough to break his heart. "Why?"

"You know why." She managed to pull her hand out of his, using it to rub at the corner of her eye. She was crying quietly.

"Tara, please…"

She averted her eyes towards the field of coconut trees. "This isn't easy, Lucas. I don't want your parents to worry about me. You know how they are. I don't want to ruin your last day with them."

"I'm sure you won't," he insisted, pleadingly, almost desperately.

"Won't cause a scene like the first time I was there?"

"It's not your fault."

"Of course it's my fault." She shook her head vehemently, tears sliding down her cheeks. She shakily tried to wipe them away, but not too successfully. "The game, too, that was my fault. I care too much and I end up losing too much. I know that very well and I know exactly what's gonna happen."

He could only stare at her, at a loss for words. She was everything he had ever wanted. Now, he was the source of her pain.

"Please don't make this any harder than it already is," she sobbed. "Please, Lucas. Just do me this favor."

He stood up, made his way to her side, and knelt next to her so they were eye to eye. "Kiss me, then. Let's forget everything. Let's forget that it hurts. Just for now."

Eyes wide, she hesitated for only a second before she threw herself into his arms.

Their lips met hungrily, breakfast and the world around them forgotten.

He carried her up to her bedroom, where they undressed each other. He reveled in the feeling of her soft skin beneath his fingertips, etching every curve and contour into his mind. He tasted every inch of her body, lapping up the sheer sweetness of her like a dying man.

He took her on the middle of the floor, pumping into her as she cried his name out and gasped for more, rubbing her clit and her nipples in turn until they were pebble-hard from the pleasure of his touch. She straddled him on her bed, riding him slowly, drawing out every sensation as he thrust upward to meet her; soon urgency took over, and they both gave in to moans that shook the villa. He took her from behind as she leaned over her windowsill, bare breasts bobbing wantonly in the air, the gauzy white curtains wrapped around their heated bodies.

As they showered together before lunch, it was her turn to kneel before him in the bathroom, on the tiles that had witnessed so many passionate encounters. She gave his cock all the attention he so craved, rolling it between her breasts before putting the length of him into her mouth; as she massaged and tugged at his balls, his release exploded in her lips, punctuated by his own strangled shouts.

After lunch, she packed up the special *biko* for his trip, in a beautiful box woven from palm leaves, decorating the packaging with flowers from her own garden. His heart twisted painfully as she gave him tips on how to keep the rice cake fresh the moment he reached his Manila apartment.

That afternoon, they didn't bother to retreat to the porch. Instead, she led him back up to her room, where they made love again and again, clinging to each other as their borrowed time came to a hazy, heady standstill, measured only in caresses, kisses, embraces, and promises of a love that would endure.

It was nearly sunset when they collapsed on the middle of the bed, arms and legs entwined, shaky and sweaty and breathless, but never quite sated. Eventually, as the shadows grew longer and the minutes shorter, they rose to dress, languidly, prolonging the inevitable farewell with stolen kisses. Half-dressed, he took her one last time against the walls of her bedroom, her legs wrapped around him. When they reached the peak together, night was upon them.

They finished dressing, then made their way down to the living room, where the box of *biko* awaited on the coffee table, sealed and ready for the journey ahead. Tara picked it up with a smile and carefully placed the parcel in his hands.

"It will last you a while…I made it extra special, too, with lots of coconut flakes and calamansi syrup."

"Thank you." It was all he could utter, after all was said and done in their love story.

Tara linked her arm through his as they made their way out to the porch and down the steps. "Don't ask me again, Lucas."

"I won't."

She nodded, seemingly appeased, as she watched him put the box onto the passenger seat of the SUV. When he closed the door, the sound rang out with poignant finality.

He took a deep breath as he turned to face her. "I guess that's it."

It was goodbye.

"Yes, I guess." She smiled as she reached out to caress his cheek. "Knock 'em dead, Number One, okay?"

He returned her smile, nodding at her request. "Do you think…it would be okay if I saw you tomorrow morning before I go? So you can kiss me good luck?"

She laughed, the sound mournful and broken, and shook her head. "Oh, Lucas."

"No?"

She held out her arms and he went into them. Without another word, their lips met, tenderly, each tracing the other. He pressed his mouth and nose to her forehead, closing his eyes as he took in her scent. He could drown in it and die happy.

"No," she whispered into his neck. "I want to remember us as we are now. So, good luck, Lucas."

"I love you," he replied, the words catching on the night breeze. "I'll call you…every time I can. I promise. Will you let me know once you're back in Manila, too?"

She looked up at him and nodded. With one last look into her eyes, he, finally, painfully, reluctantly, let her go.

Without another word, Lucas climbed into the car, knowing that he was leaving behind a part of himself. He drove away; before making the turn towards the farm gates, he stopped the vehicle and stepped out, unable to resist looking at her one last time before the sight of her was swallowed by the fading light.

Tara stood at her usual spot on the front porch, waving him off. She blew him a kiss, and he caught it, holding it close to his heart, even as the winding road took him farther and farther away from the woman he loved.

I still look at the screen
Hoping it would be your message
Hoping somehow you found me

I still look at the screen
Hoping your picture would be there
Happy, smiling, truly alive

With tears in my eyes
In the quiet hours of dawn
Though I know
You will never be there

I still look at the screen

~ Excerpt from 'Screen'
Lyrics and music by Tara Galvez
I Remember You, Esta Melodia Records

Chapter 17

THE DIAMOND

Tara

THE NOTES FROM HER GUITAR HUNG IN THE WARM air as she strummed and hummed, piecing together fragments of a new song.

Tara sat on the front porch of the villa, savoring the gentler touch of the late afternoon sun. Gone were the days of soft breezes; the encroaching heat of the summer months reminded her of how quickly time had changed everything.

Glancing at her phone on the porch table, silent and unmoving, she felt a familiar wave of guilt. Lucas had tried calling her often, but she had refused to take his calls. He'd sent messages too: telling her he'd made it back to Manila, thanking her for the *biko*, updating her about their training camp and the start of the Philippine Cup Conference. But eventually, his messages dwindled to short weekly texts and then nothing at all.

A small part of her was relieved that he had decided not to keep messaging her. It was an odd emptiness akin to what she'd felt before he came into her life, and in some ways, it was a comfort. No melody or words could fill the void, no adoration from fans could replace it. Since then, she'd stopped going out of the farm, immersing herself in her music instead.

Despite occasional invitations from Mercy Delgado, who sent formal messages through well-meaning villagers bearing notes to her at the farm gates, she remained secluded. Mercy had asked how she was and if she'd want to visit their home, anytime Tara was free.

Tara had once penned a response back, delivered by Marife and Fred along with a crate of Galvez Farms' new line of flavored *nata de coco*. She had thanked Lucas' mother for her kindness, but Tara's songs had a deadline. It had hurt to push away the family who had shown her nothing but love.

Love.

It was the strangest emotion, imbued with as much power to destroy as to shape the world around her. Love had made her music come to life; it had also shattered her heart into a million pieces. At the end of it all, she was still alone.

"Excuse me, Miss Tara?" a gentle voice called out.

She looked up to see Marife ascending the porch steps with another woman in tow—Lucas' mother. A strange sense of *déjà vu* washed over Tara as she recalled the first time she saw Lucas that year, standing on these very steps. Her heart clenched at the memory.

Quickly setting her guitar aside, Tara stood up, feeling a

pang of guilt at the concern etched on Mercy's face. Instead of the anger or frustration she had expected, she was met with only a mother's worry. As Marife murmured an apology for disturbing her, she could only nod in response, unable to find her voice.

"Would you like something to drink, Mrs. Delgado?" the housekeeper asked politely.

"Thank you, but I'm fine," Mercy replied. "Good afternoon, Tara."

"Good afternoon, Mrs. Delgado." The formal address left her before she could stop herself. "Would you like to sit down?"

With a quiet nod, Marife retreated, leaving the two women alone on the porch.

Mercy nodded her thanks and took a seat on one of the rattan sofas. Her tone was gentle yet probing when she spoke. "Tell me, Tara, how are you? We've all been so worried about you, especially Lucas."

At the mention of his name, tears welled up in her eyes. On her own, she could pretend—but with the very reality of Lucas' mother sitting in front of her, the pain of loss hit her almost like a physical blow.

"I'm so sorry, Mercy." She sank into a chair, her voice cracking as she tried to hold back her emotions. "I'm so sorry for not accepting your invitations."

The older woman shook her head, her eyes searching Tara's face. "It's entirely your choice whether or not you want to visit us, dear, but you shouldn't let it bother you. Luis and I are more concerned on how you're holding up…being here on your own, running the business, making your music. It's a lot to take on."

Unable to bear the concerned scrutiny from Lucas' mother, Tara closed her eyes, feeling hot tears brimming over once more. "These past few months have been so hard, trying to convince myself that I don't need anyone. I thought I could just carry on with the life that I've been used to for so many years. But the truth is, nothing's been the same."

"Since Lucas left?" Mercy asked gently.

Tara took a deep breath, allowing tears to escape to relieve the pressure inside. "I miss him. I miss being part of your family. I just couldn't be part of a life where he keeps getting hurt and broken...I wanted to take care of him, to make sure he is happy and healthy, but now he's so far away..." Her voice trailed off as she realized that even Lucas' parents didn't know the full picture of his health.

Mercy took a seat beside her, putting a comforting hand on her shoulder. "Is that why you've pushed us away? You're afraid of what being part of his life—of loving him—might cost you?"

Tara nodded, her chest heaving with sobs.

"He's been fighting through all that damage to his knee and his back like a true warrior," Mercy said, sighing softly. "It's hard seeing Lucas put on that brave face all the time, of course. It never gets easier, even after a few years."

Tara stared at her. "How did you know?"

"Lucas is my son, Tara. I know when he's hurting, when he's sad, when he's happy. I started seeing the signs a while back, whenever we visited him in Manila or when he'd visit us at our house in the city."

Mercy paused, her gaze steady. "I never asked him about his injuries, allowing him space to admit the truth when he was ready. Lucas is a smart man, Tara. He knows exactly what he's doing, and when he's ready, he will tell us the truth."

She reached out and took Tara's hand, giving it a comforting squeeze. "I'm glad Lucas has told you about his injuries, but I am even happier that he found you. He really does love you, Tara. I've never seen him so happy, so fulfilled, when you were together."

Tara could only shake her head in disbelief. "I'm sorry."

"For what?" Mercy tilted her head, studying Tara's face. "Sorry that you loved my son too? Sorry that you came into our lives and made us feel what it's like to have another daughter, one as talented and beautiful as you?"

"I just…I couldn't be someone who could keep loving Lucas even if I see him slowly being broken on the court. I feel so helpless about that. I just wanted to be there for him, but not in the way he wants…"

"Lucas loves you for being yourself, Tara," Mercy told her patiently. "He loved you even when you were just a face on a music video and a voice in a song. He has done nothing but adore you all these years; I've seen his collection of your records in his apartment, heard him play your songs on his phone when he thought no one could hear."

"Mercy, I love him, too…loved him since I was a girl. He's only ever been the one for me."

The older woman nodded, her eyes and smile filled with understanding. "You have no idea how much and how deeply Lucas loves you. Maybe you should give him a chance to love you as best as he could. It might surprise you."

Through her tears, Tara felt a small smile tug at the corner of her own lips as a memory surfaced. "Lucas told me the night of the basketball game that he felt whole again when he was with me."

"Yes, he does feel like that," Mercy confirmed, her own smile getting bigger. "It was written all over his face, the first time I told him you were at the village."

Tara breathed out slowly and squeezed Mercy's hand. "I just want you and Luis to know…I had the best time of my life with your family. I've never felt so welcomed and loved. I'll always be grateful. And I hope…you're not disappointed in me."

"No, never." Mercy reached out and smoothed her hair. "We're very proud of you, Tara. Whatever happens, you'll always be welcome in our lives."

"I appreciate that." Wiping away at the remnants of her tears with the back of her hand, Tara gave the older woman a grateful smile. "I'll be leaving the village soon, maybe in a few weeks, so I'm glad I got to see you. I was just putting the finishing touches on the last song for my third album."

"Ah, I see. And where will you be going, back to Manila?"

Tara nodded. "I'll need to arrange the songs with producers and then hit the studio. After that, I might take a page out of Lucas' book and stay with my parents in Iloilo. Once the album is out, I'll be busy for a few months with promotions…and then, that's it for me, I guess."

"Will you be coming back here or…?" Mercy's voice trailed off as she regarded Tara curiously.

"I don't know yet. My recording contract will be over by then, so it would be nice to have some real time to myself for a while. Perhaps we'll see each other when you pass by Iloilo."

Mercy nodded and leaned in to kiss Tara on the cheeks and forehead, before giving her a big hug. "Perhaps we can spend a Sunday together. Luis and I would love to hear you sing for us again. We missed you."

Tara returned the embrace tightly. "I missed you both, too."

As she pulled away, the older woman reached into her bag on the coffee table and produced a colorful envelope that appeared to be meticulously hand-painted. Upon closer inspection, it was made of dried coconut skin, with a discreet logo on the corner bearing the name 'Delgado Homemade Products.'

"Lucas was going to give this to you," said Mercy as she got to her feet, carefully placing the envelope on the table. "He'd hoped you would join us for his *despedida* the night before he left."

"He did ask me, but I didn't think it was a good idea at the time." Tara felt a lump in her throat as she recalled how many times she'd refused him. "I suppose it's too late for regrets now."

Mercy picked up her bag and made her way to the steps. Before descending, she turned to Tara and gave her hand a squeeze. "It's never too late."

She shook her head. "I'm just glad he and his team are doing so well at the tournament. That's enough for me."

Mercy gave her a long look before she spoke. "Someday soon, we'll all break and get hurt, and we'll be able to piece ourselves back together when there's someone holding us up, someone holding us together. That's love, Tara. Don't deny yourself of that love."

"Maybe someday," she replied simply, giving the older woman a reassuring smile.

After they exchanged goodbyes, Tara watched Mercy

walk down the steps, heading in the direction of the farm gates. As the distance between them grew, she once more felt a sense of desolation that had become all too familiar to her in recent months.

She turned her attention to the envelope Lucas' mother had given her. She carefully opened it and pulled out a folded piece of paper. Her breath hitched as something small and shiny rolled gracefully out, landing on the wood with a soft clink.

A ring.

It was a golden ring adorned with a delicate diamond, the gem shaped like a basketball.

Surprised, Tara unfolded the paper to reveal a familiar scene in pencil and pastel: herself standing amidst a garden of white and golden flowers, bathed in the soft glow of morning sunlight. But this time, Lucas was there too, drawn kneeling before her just as he had done at the basketball court. The difference was that in this picture, he held out the very same ring that now lay before her. At the bottom right corner, the drawing was signed and dated—the last day they had spent together.

Tears welled up in her eyes as the realization hit her like a tidal wave. Lucas had wanted her to join him and his family for dinner that same night. He'd asked repeatedly, insisted and pleaded upon it.

He had intended to propose.

And, yet, she had never given him the chance—never gave herself a chance to make her songs, her dreams, finally a reality.

She remembered her own words to him, said in the very

same garden. Real love was about taking chances even in the face of fear.

Love, she thought dazedly.

One word, an emotion; it had haunted and taunted her for years. She'd desperately tried to capture it in her lyrics, through her stories told in song. It had never been enough, because she'd never lived it.

Now, she finally had it. All she had to do was be brave enough to walk into its unknown embrace.

"Lucas," she whispered, the name disappearing into the wind, melting in the heat of a summer she'd thought would only be filled with memories and lonely nights.

She fell to her knees on the porch, her heart threatening to burst from her chest. Through the torrent of tears blurring her vision, Tara Galvez finally saw the truth—a love for Lucas Delgado that could not be denied any longer.

Chapter 18

THE GIFT

Lucas

THROUGH THE FLOOR-TO-CEILING WINDOWS OF HIS high-rise apartment, he stood and watched the city below come to life as night approached. Lucas knew he should have been exhausted after a long day of practice and strategizing with his team, but instead, he was wide awake, consumed by a gnawing emptiness.

Stand and watch. That was what he did.

Two days ago, he stood and watched as his shots met only the board and then nothing, the ball bouncing to the hardwood floor in defeat as he missed two free throws in the final minute of Game Six. He stood and watched as the opposing team won the game by one point, forcing the

Philippine Cup Finals series into a sudden-death Game Seven.

It was *déjà vu*, too. They were playing against the same team they faced in last year's Finals, where the double-overtime seventh game had been nothing short of brutal, leaving physical and emotional scars.

"Fuck this," Lucas muttered under his breath, rubbing at his sore ribs. One well-placed elbow and he was done for.

The silence of the apartment was broken only by the rhythmic ticking of the wall clock. Sighing, he glanced over to check the time, taking in the carefully curated display of team photos and framed victory jerseys on his living room walls. Each and every one of them spoke of his success as an athlete.

He had paid enough for it—with time, discipline, pain, loneliness, and pretension. He had played the game in and out of the court, now here he stood, watching the world go by, wanting—needing—only one thing.

Her presence in his life.

All he could do was remember what he had lost, what he now desperately missed.

The warmth of her mouth on his, their kisses shared during meals and drives. Their lovemaking, passionate and tender, in the hidden corners of her villa, her skin flushed and glowing under the moonlight. Her sweet vanilla smell seem to have followed him, too, wrapping him in a gentle embrace he longed for. The way she would say his name became the melody that haunted his dreams.

Lucas closed his eyes and let himself be carried away by the vision of her stirring *biko*, focused and content; he could see her snipping at the flowers in her garden, sunlight filtering through her long dark hair, turning it into a halo of soft light.

His hands itched to draw her again, to bring her back to life on paper, but he knew that he couldn't. Not after leaving the last drawing—the one meant to accompany his proposal—along with the ring at his parents' house. It was a cowardly act, but he was better off without those reminders of what could have been.

As he watched the sunset cover the city in orange hues and dark shadows, memory of that day more than three months ago came flooding back. The day he'd returned to his apartment and unpacked the box of *biko* Tara had sent with him. He recalled the large plastic container nestled in a woven basket, adorned with flowers from her garden.

But there was another gift hidden among the petals—a silver compact disc with only his name written on it in black marker.

He'd eaten his way through the *biko*, all on his own, in three days' time. He never had the heart or the courage, however, to listen to the CD. He'd stashed it away instead, in a final act of self-preservation.

He hesitated for a moment before making his way into the bedroom. He located the CD inside the top drawer of his night table, now part of his collection of Tara's albums. His heart pounded as he inserted the disc into the home theatre system, unsure of what was in it but knowing that hearing her voice, beautifully immortal in recording, would be the only way to keep her close.

There was a soft whirring sound for the first thirty seconds, then her voice came through, tentative and sweet.

"*Hi, Lucas.*" There was a pause as he heard her take a deep breath. "I don't really know what to say. That's pretty strange, isn't it? After all, I rely on my talent to mince words and stuff like that."

There was another pause. Tara laughed softly. "What am I doing, anyway?"

A short silence followed, then guitar chords began to fill the air.

"I call this song 'Untold.' I started writing it a couple of nights ago, when I couldn't stop thinking about you and…you know, being with you. I had the best time ever these past weeks, Lucas. I'll never forget how kind you've been to me. Thanks for everything."

She breathed deeply once more. "Well, here goes nothing. Hope you like it."

Tara began to sing.

You said that you were sorry
That you don't need me no more
You said that you were leaving
And walked right out the door

Baby, how many times have you hurt me?
I truly have stopped counting
How many times have you left me?
Standing alone while it was raining

You said that all was wrong
That nothing works when we're together
You said we would only be lying
If we keep talking of forever

OUR LOVE REPLAY

So go on, tell me
Whatever you want to say
Go on, be true
There seems to be no other way

Tell me I'm not the ideal
I know all your reasons why
Tell me I'll never be strong
That I'm always lacking in your eyes

Tell me everything that hurts
This forever hopeful heart of mine
Tell me how to make you stay
But, baby, just don't tell me goodbye

Her voice broke at the end of the song. The closing chords melded to the subdued whirring of the CD, then there was nothing.

Nothing, except for a lone tear escaping his eye, burning its way down his cheek.

Nothing, except for his emotions that he hadn't allowed to surface in far too long, and his love, now gone unanswered by a phone number that would not pick up, a message recipient that would never respond.

He sat on the floor in front of the speakers, unaware of how much time had passed since the CD stopped playing. He stared at the city lights reflected on his walls, lost in the regret of not staying when she'd asked him to.

I'm far from perfect, but I'll take good care of you. It had been her greatest declaration of love. Now he was left with nothing.

Suddenly, the doorbell rang, breaking through the stillness of his darkened apartment. Startled, he realized he rarely had visitors, especially at this hour. He considered the possibilities as he rose to his feet and fumbled for a lamp switch nearby; perhaps it was the team trainer or even their manager checking up on him. But when he opened the door, his heart skipped a beat when he saw neither of them.

Instead, he saw Tara.

He blinked hard, trying to determine if he was dreaming or hallucinating from the pain in his body—or perhaps even his heart.

But she spoke, her voice unmistakable, "Hi, Lucas. I'm sorry for bothering you. I know it's late—"

She couldn't finish her sentence before he wrapped his arms around her, as if holding her tightly enough would ensure she wouldn't vanish into thin air. To his relief, she didn't disappear; she was solid and real in his embrace.

"Lucas," Tara whispered, her breath warm against his chest, "I missed you. I really missed you. I'm sorry if I hurt you."

He couldn't find the words to respond, still in shock at her sudden appearance. Instead, he buried his nose in her hair, inhaling her familiar vanilla scent, reveling in the warmth and feel of her body pressed against his.

Without another word, he guided her into the apartment, locking the door behind them. In a heartbeat, their lips met in a passionate reunion, her hands tangling in his hair. As they kissed, he heard something fall to the floor with a dull thud but paid no attention to it, utterly consumed by her touch.

"Love," he finally managed to say between kisses, "I

missed you, too." He then proceeded to shower her cheeks, nose, and chin with tender pecks, eliciting giggles and strangled sobs.

Tara clung to him, her slender arms wrapped securely around his neck. He welcomed her weight, but reality loomed over him like a dark cloud.

Hesitantly, he released her, steadying her on her feet. "Are you real?"

She nodded, smiling slightly. "Look, Lucas, I'm so sorry for this...I just wanted to—"

"Stop apologizing, love, please." Taking her hand, he led her to the couch and motioned for her to sit down. "Would you like something to drink?"

"Water, please," she said, wiping her cheeks with the back of her hand.

He hesitated for a second, reluctant to let go of her even for a moment. But he hurried to the fridge to retrieve a bottle of water, returning as quickly as possible to sit beside her.

"So...how are you?" As he handed over the water, he spied her backpack that had fallen on the carpet earlier. He'd been too preoccupied to pay attention to anything but her presence in his apartment.

"I've been traveling since early morning. I left the farm after midnight." She took a long sip of the water before continuing. "I came straight here to see you."

"Why?" His one question was a mixture of shock, happiness, and disbelief. "Why didn't you call me at least? I could have picked you up from the airport or asked someone to drive you over."

Tara offered him a sad smile as she look him straight in the eye. "I wasn't even sure if you wanted to see me or talk to me after everything that happened. But I know how it feels when everything's hanging in the balance, when your next move could either make you win or lose it all—everything you've worked hard and sacrificed for."

Just like in her recording, she took a deep breath and went on, the emotion in her voice going straight to his heart. "I came to tell you that whatever it is you feel now, and whatever happens tomorrow, you won't be in it alone."

He inched closer and took her hand, relieved when she didn't pull it away. "How did you find me?"

He wasn't sure if she giggled or snorted—perhaps both. "Jasmine knew where you lived. She knew about what happened between us at the farm. She made me promise I'd let her know whether or not this would work out, that is, my 'crazy romance heroine stunt.'" She made quote marks with her fingers as she mentioned the phrase.

"This is a stunt?"

"I told her I wanted to see you after the game two days ago," Tara explained. "She tried to talk me out of it. We ended up with a compromise. If you break my heart, I would let her 'destroy him professionally and personally.'" She rolled her eyes as she said the last few words.

Lucas chuckled. "Not the first time I heard those. She warned back then there would be hell to pay if I hurt you."

"Yeah, she told me she called you the day after we… um…" She blushed and looked away. "Anyway, she knew what was going on the whole time."

He nodded solemnly. "Very scary lady."

They smiled at each other, before he decided to take her in his arms again. She went into them with a contented sigh.

"Lucas…I'm not sure if your mother told you…" As she

spoke, her fingers danced over his heart just as she rested her body trustingly against his.

"Told me about what, love?"

"About my decision to...slow down."

He smiled down at her. "She did mention a few weeks ago you told her you've decided not to renew your recording contract."

Tara nodded, explaining that she'd finished writing her songs. Lucas listened as she went on about the work needed for her album and what would follow its release—media appearances, press conferences, promotional shows. She had turned down the offer of a grand concert tour throughout the country and worldwide.

"I'll still be writing music once this is over," she declared, a note of excitement in her voice. "But on my own terms, maybe as an indie."

"Won't there be at least one concert for your tenth anniversary?" he teased. "One I could see from the front row?"

"For three nights, around this time next year. We've decided to name it after my third album, *Our Love Replay*."

"Our love," he echoed. "Replay."

She pulled away to look up at him. "Lucas—"

"I love it," he murmured.

She smiled at the compliment. "I knew you would."

Nothing more was said as he leaned in to capture her mouth. They kissed deeply, hungrily, until the room was covered in the sultry embrace of night. As they broke away for air, he carefully guided her down onto the carpet, his hands deftly unbuttoning her blouse and jeans before helping her out of her panties. He quickly undressed, his desire almost at breaking point at the sight of her beautiful and vulnerable beneath him.

He lowered his lips to hers, exploring the curves of her body he so desperately missed. His mouth found her nipples, teasing them until she let out breathy gasps of pleasure. Moving lower, he trailed kisses along her stomach, his tongue dipping into her navel before continuing its journey downward. Spreading her legs, he licked and nipped at the delicate flesh between her thighs, until she was writhing with the need for release. With his lips, tongue, and fingers, he brought her to the peak.

"Lucas," Tara gasped, her body trembling with the force of her climax, "I love you."

Still reeling from the force her confession, he covered her body with his and entered her in one powerful thrust.

"Did you just…?" When she nodded, whispering those three precious words once more, he lost himself in her completely.

"Say it again," he urged as he moved within her, thrusting faster and deeper as his hands cupped her breasts. "Tell me again."

"I love you," she cried out as she clung to him, meeting his hips with hers. "I have always loved you."

As Tara's moans grew louder, reaching a crescendo that echoed throughout the building, he joined her in a release that left them both breathless and shaking.

The night was a symphony of love, their bodies intertwining on his bed again and again, in the middle of which they shared a late dinner of *siopao* and vegetable *chop suey* on his dining table, the end of their meal marked with her riding him on the wooden surface, taking him to new heights.

As morning light filtered through the curtains, he stirred, his arms still wrapped around her. He took in the sight of her peaceful face, her lashes resting gently on her cheeks, her breath a soft whisper against his chest.

She was real—and she loved him.

In that moment, he felt invincible.

Slowly, carefully, he eased her from his embrace, tucking the blankets around her. He longed to wake her, to share his own decision with her—the one that would shape both of their futures, regardless of the outcome of tonight's game.

Instead, Lucas sent a message to his team manager, informing him that he was on his way to their meeting and asking for one last favor. He wasn't sure whether or not Tara would like to be at the game, but the choice was ultimately hers to make—just as she'd chosen to love him.

He scribbled a note and left it with his extra key next to her phone on the bedside table. With one last lingering look at her, he kissed her on the forehead. "See you after the game. I love you."

As he locked the door behind him and stepped out into the world, he knew he was finally ready to take one last shot.

I want to go home
To the days of years past
When the breeze was soft
Laughter was easy
Love was a possibility

I want to go home
To the days that never were
When I saw you
Found you
Loved you

I want to go home
To the days when you were there
When I had your voice
Your light
Your heartbeat

I want to go home

~ Excerpt from 'Home'
Lyrics and music by Tara Galvez
I Remember You, Esta Melodia Records

Chapter 19

THE VICTORY

Tara

Her heart raced as the black Volvo came to a stop outside the sports arena. The noise of the crowd inside was already reverberating through the air around them.

Tara glanced at Simon, the assistant manager of Lucas' team who had accompanied her on the trip. The car itself had been sent by the team's owner, for her exclusive use before and after the game.

"Here we are, Miss Galvez." Simon opened the car door and stepped out into the crisp air, holding out a hand to assist her. He had a quiet, confident demeanor that calmed her.

As she took his hand and stepped out, she noticed that it

wasn't the main entrance she'd seen countless times on television. This entryway was more discreet, shrouded in shadows.

"VIP access only," Simon explained, catching her curious gaze. "Reserved for league and team officials, and the occasional high-profile personality." He smiled at her knowingly. "Of course, you're a VIP too, Miss Galvez. Everybody knows you. My wife loves your songs."

"Thank you," she murmured. It felt strange to be considered important when all she wanted to do was to support the man she loved.

Following Simon down a dimly-lit corridor, Tara felt the air grow heavy with tension. She slowed her steps as they approached a small door, which seemed to be positioned directly under the bleachers.

"Straight to courtside," Simon declared, almost proudly.

"Could you give me a minute?" She gripped his arm just as he reached for the knob. She needed a moment to collect herself before facing the public eye once more.

"Of course," he replied, stepping forward to peek through the tiny door left ajar. "The teams are already on the floor warming up."

The thought of seeing Lucas play up close was enough to propel her forward. Determinedly, she took Simon's arm and walked out with him.

Stepping into the dazzling lights of the arena, Tara was momentarily blinded by their intensity. The noise from the warmup and enthusiastic crowd washed over her. The audience waved red and white balloons, streamers, and flags, creating a sea of vibrant colors. Among the banners, she spotted many with Lucas' face on them.

"Right this way, Miss Galvez," Simon said, patiently

guiding her to her seat. As she glanced around, searching for any glimpse of Lucas among the players on the court, a familiar warmth enveloped her.

"My dear, surprise!" Mercy Delgado pulled her into quick hug.

"It's so nice to see you here, Tara," said Luis as he appeared at his wife's shoulder and embraced her, before gesturing to three adjacent seats meters away from the bench of Lucas' team.

"Thank you, Simon," Tara said, her earlier anxiety ebbing away at the presence of Lucas' parents.

"Anytime, Miss Galvez," Simon replied with a smile, before joining the bench of his team.

Mercy took Tara's hand and gestured for her to sit down. "How have you been, dear?"

Tara smiled. "I'm fine, thank you. I came to Manila to support Lucas." Her heart swelled with pride as she admitted this truth aloud.

"Ah, we are so proud of you and happy with your decision," Mercy beamed, her eyes shining with approval.

Her gaze wandered back to the court, trying to catch a glimpse of Lucas in action. Just then, a sudden hush fell over the arena, followed by an excited chatter that spread like wildfire. A courtside reporter had spotted Tara and called out her name, sending ripples of excitement through the audience. "Tara Galvez is here!"

"Look, dear." Mercy gave her a gentle nudge and pointed to the giant screens hanging above the court. Tara's face appeared on them, causing people to cheer and whoop with delight. Heat rose to her cheeks, but at the encouragement of Lucas' parents, she mustered the courage to stand up and wave, acknowledging the crowd.

As she did so, her eyes finally found Lucas standing at the free throw line, his attention drawn by the noise. Their gazes met across the distance, and she felt her heart skip a beat when he gave her a smile and a wink. He dribbled the ball towards the baseline close to where she stood, and mouthed, *"For you,"* before turning and making a flawless three-point jump shot, making the crowd roar in approval. She applauded along with the rest of the arena before resuming her seat.

The noise in the building grew thunderous as the game commenced. Her eyes remained fixed on Lucas, watching as he expertly maneuvered through the sea of opposing players, his every move an intricate dance of agility and skill. As she watched him glide across the court, just as she had all those years ago from under the acacia tree, she felt the weight of her past doubts lifting, replaced by a newfound sense of freedom.

It wasn't lost on her how the opposing team used ruthless tactics to stop Lucas—double and even triple teams, deliberate fouls from players off the bench, and an in-your-face defense from his shooting guard counterpart. Midway through the game, there was a charging foul that could have very well broken Lucas' ribs. By the time the last two minutes rolled about, Tara's breath had nearly left her body, more so when the scores tied.

"Come on, Lucas!" she cheered, her voice joining the chorus of thousands.

Lucas' team had possession of the ball thirty seconds before the final buzzer. A teammate tossed him the ball from the inbound line. The seconds ticked by as the shot clock started running down. Twelve to shoot. Eight. Someone stepped in front of him; he evaded easily. Six. Two players tried to block his way. Four seconds.

She watched with bated breath as Lucas lined up for a pivotal three-pointer. His hands came up, lightning-quick. The ball soared through the air, arcing gracefully before hitting the board, then spun around the hoop. Pandemonium erupted when the ball swished through the net.

"*Delgado. Three points!*"

As Lucas raced past her, his eyes met hers for a brief moment, and he blew her a kiss. The crowd's attention shifted momentarily to Tara, their eyes wide and curious, before snapping back to the action unfolding on the court.

The other team had six seconds to shoot. The ball moved quickly, almost desperately, towards the outside line, for an attempt to tie the score. It never had a chance, with Lucas in its way. The guard made the shot, clean and well-aimed, but Lucas leaped into the air and blocked the ball, sending it out of bounds.

The buzzer rang out like a triumphant anthem, signaling the end of the game and the three-peat of Lucas' team as the Philippine Cup champions. Red and white confetti and balloons cascaded down like a euphoric rainfall as the arena filled with the raucous sounds of victory.

She jumped to her feet with the rest of the crowd, clapping and cheering at the top of her lungs. Lucas' teammates hoisted him onto their shoulders, and their coach joined him in a jubilant ride around the court. Next to her, she watched Lucas' parents embrace each other tightly, tears streaming down his mother's face.

As the celebration continued on the court, league

officials presented trophies to both teams, with short speeches honoring their efforts throughout the season. And then came the moment: Lucas was awarded the Philippine Cup Finals Most Valuable Player for the third year in a row.

The Commissioner of the league held up a hand for silence, a diplomatic smile on his wizened face. "Our three-time Philippine Cup Finals MVP, Lucas Delgado, will be making a statement. To our ladies and gentlemen of the press, we would be happy to answer all your questions at our postgame press conference later tonight."

Still cradling his MVP trophy in one arm, Lucas shook the Commissioner's hand and took the microphone the other man held out, ready to address the crowd.

"Thank you, everyone!" Lucas began, with his familiar infectious grin. "I am truly humbled by your support and love throughout this incredible journey. First of all, I must thank my incredible teammates, our owner, and coaching staff for their tireless effort and dedication in leading us to our third conference championship in a row."

"I want to congratulate you for giving us a fantastic Philippine Cup Finals series," he added with a smile, bowing his head respectfully towards the opposing team's player and coach. "You guys pushed us to be better, and for that, we are grateful."

Lucas paused for a few seconds, his gaze taking in the sea of faces before him. "I'm sure everyone has heard one or two rumors about how I would end the Philippine Cup, aside from partying with my team." The statement was met with appreciative laughter and whistles from all over the arena.

"Ladies and gentlemen, please allow me to put these rumors to rest. I will not be joining the Arabian Falcons in Abu

Dhabi as their coach, or in any other capacity. I had a generous offer from Sheikh Khalfan, which I had to regretfully turn down. My heart is in the Philippines and in this league."

Tara could hear excited murmurs rising from the crowd.

"There is no trade in my future, not in the next tournament or the following season. I won't be a free agent, either, and I won't be coaching in any league or college in the foreseeable future. My contract is with my team, and that is where it will end."

A hush of disbelief descended on the crowd, followed by a roar of questions that people were asking each other. The media and sportscasters surrounding Lucas kicked up into a frenzy, pressing around him on the court.

He took the reaction in stride, gracefully acknowledging them with a patient smile. "I am ending the Philippine Cup with my retirement from basketball. Tonight was my last game. Being a part of this championship legacy has been the greatest honor of my career. I would like to thank the millions of fans all over the world, especially the ones present in this arena tonight. None of this would have been possible without you."

Lucas looked up to the bleachers; on the giant screens, Tara could see the sincere gratitude in his eyes. "I will still be the league's biggest fan, but I would no longer be playing or working in it. It's time for me to become a spectator and cheer on my teammates, especially the tireless Derek Torreblanca, from the sidelines." He grinned as fans whistled at the mention of his teammate's name.

"But rest assured, I will always love the game that gave a young boy from Iloilo more than he ever dared to dream."

He held up his MVP trophy in the air. "Once again, thank you very much, from the bottom of my heart."

The arena exploded with sound again as more balloons and confetti rained down, accompanied by the unfurling of a giant banner bearing Lucas' jersey number one. The court announcer's voice boomed through the speakers, declaring that the team was retiring his number in honor of all that he had achieved. "Please join us in giving a farewell ovation to our three-time Philippine Cup Finals MVP, Lucas Delgado!"

Tara rose to her feet, clapping and cheering until her hands stung and her voice grew hoarse, as the true meaning of Lucas' decision settled on the fringes of her overwhelmed mind. It was a slow, dawning realization that warmed her heart.

He had made his choice.

Through the throng of photographers and reports rushing to surround Lucas, his eyes searched the crowd and met hers.

"*I love you,*" he mouthed.

For the first time in her life, Tara felt truly unafraid, truly free, as she gave him her answer.

"*I love you, too.*"

Chapter 20

THE BEGINNING

Lucas

The dashboard clock read 1:58 AM as Derek's car rolled to a stop outside his apartment building. From the passenger seat, Lucas gave his friend a tired, contented grin.

"I thought that press conference would never end," he said, shaking his head. "I almost fell asleep in my bird's nest soup."

"Yeah," Derek concurred. "They should have served the meal before the questions."

"I second that." Lucas reached for his bag in the backseat and gave his friend a grateful clap on the shoulder. "Thanks for the ride, man. Officially my last one as your teammate."

"Anytime, although not the last as my friend," Derek replied, grinning. "You bastard, I can't believe you finally did it, though. And without telling me."

He swallowed hard against the knot in his throat, unable to suppress his guilt for keeping such a secret. "My body's just… it's not holding up anymore. Tried to keep moving through it for a while, but in the end, I had to make a decision."

Derek's smile faded as he took in Lucas' somber expression. "That bad, huh? I mean, I've seen the wraps they made you wear sometimes, but, damn. Never thought it was that serious."

"Kneecaps and ribs are shot," Lucas admitted quietly. "My back muscles feel like they're barely stitched together. The double and triple teams this conference didn't help, either."

"Jesus, Lucas…" Derek sighed, his eyes reflecting a depth of understanding only a teammate could possess. "Must have been hell keeping that from us."

He nodded. "It was, but thanks for getting it, Derek. Best to quit while I'm ahead, right? Before time really catches up with me."

"Can't argue with that. We're not exactly spring chickens anymore." Derek grimaced as he ran a hand over his right knee. "This screams with every rebound, too. After I jump and then my feet hit the ground…fuck."

"Tell me about it," Lucas chuckled. "You should get that properly seen to one of these days, maybe rest it for a while before the next conference. When I spent that time at my parents' house, I barely played—just ran every day to keep the tank in shape."

Curiosity flickered across Derek's face. "So, that mystery woman you mentioned before…it was Tara Galvez, wasn't it? She had quite the effect on the crowd tonight…I knew she was gorgeous, but *man*, in person? No wonder you couldn't stay away."

"Yeah, it was her," Lucas confirmed, feeling a smile tug at his lips at the admiration in Derek's voice.

"Good for you, man," Derek said, giving him a hearty slap on the back. "No more staring at your Spotify playlist like a lovesick puppy, then?"

"Guess not." Lucas picked up his sports bag and pushed the passenger door open. "See you in a few days at the party, yeah?"

"Wouldn't miss it." Derek gave him a parting wave and thumbs-up. "Talk to you soon. Good night."

"Good night. Thanks again." Lucas shut the door and watched Derek drive off into the night. He lingered on the pavement until the red tail lights blurred into the distance.

His last ride as Torreblanca's teammate was right. They still had a team victory party next weekend, not to mention a basketball camp for kids over the summer, but tonight really did mark the end of one chapter and the beginning of another.

The phone in his pocket felt like a tiny anchor, grounding him in this moment of transition. Pulling it out, he quickly scrolled through a few new messages. One was from his older brother in Iloilo, who had to stay home with his heavily pregnant wife, their second child due any minute. His younger brother had already called earlier from Toronto, amidst cheers and shouts of congratulations from an entire community center filled with supporters. An earlier message from his father confirmed that both his parents were back at their hotel and enjoying room service.

And there it was, punctuated by an emoji with a heart on its lips, Tara's brief yet affectionate text from a few hours ago: *'home, luv u'*

Lucas ambled towards the entrance of his building, nodding to the night security guard stationed at the lobby, who promptly beamed and called out merrily, "Congratulations, Sir Lucas!"

After thanking the guard and wishing him a good morning ahead, he took the elevator to the top floor and quickly made his way to his apartment. He fumbled for his keys at the entrance, but before he could find the right one, the door swung open.

Tara stood at the threshold, wearing his bathrobe. She was a vision of casual intimacy, her unbound hair contrasting sharply with the white terrycloth.

"Congratulations, Number One," she breathed, stepping into his space, her arms winding around him.

"Thanks," he managed, voice rough with surprise at seeing her awake and awaiting his arrival. He pulled her closer and crushed his mouth to hers, for a taste of his real victory. She moaned in satisfaction, reaching up to wrap her arms around his neck as she deepened the kiss, using her tongue to trace the inside of his mouth.

Breathless, he broke away only long enough to secure their privacy. His bag dropped forgotten to the floor as he drew her back into his arms, but something glinted sharply on the coffee table, demanding his attention.

Her diamond.

"What...how did you get this?" Lucas crossed the living room for a closer look, heart thundering in his ears.

It took only a few strides and one trembling touch to confirm it was the very same ring. He quickly lifted his fingers away from the coldness of the gold band, sinking onto the couch as apprehension washed over him.

Tara's touch was cool on his burning cheek as she took a seat beside him. "Your mother brought it to me, along with your drawing."

He shook his head, surprise, disbelief, and nerves churning in his stomach. "I didn't want to be presumptuous, or to pressure you..."

"You were very persistent in getting me to that *despedida*, to be fair," she commented gently, leaning her head against his shoulder. "But I suppose I had more stubborn in me that day compared to you. The heart tends to have the instinct for protecting itself when badly hurt."

"Was it because I didn't stay when you asked me to?" He lifted her chin to look into those heart-stopping eyes. One look all those years ago was all it took—and he'd been hers ever since.

She nodded, blinking hard and fast as her gaze reluctantly met his.

He leaned in and pressed his lips to hers before saying, "I'm so sorry.

She cupped his face in her hands. "I forgive you, but that doesn't mean you're not a big, bumbling idiot, because you still are."

"I hope that's not because I decided to retire without telling you. I wanted to tell you last night, and this morning, but...everything just happened so quickly." The words spilled out, honest and vulnerable. "Since I left the village all those months ago, I couldn't stop thinking about what kind of life I really wanted to have. Basketball has given me so much, but not without a price…was I willing to keep paying it, with every single fucking bone in my body?"

"Oh, Lucas." She reached up to tenderly cup his cheek. "It's your life, your choice. I'm here to love you right through it. Even if you decided not to retire, I'll be right here, too."

"No," he countered fiercely, "it's not just my life anymore. It's ours, together. I want a life with you in it. A life where I don't keep hurting you or myself all the damn time."

Hope painted her features with a luminous glow. "It sounds like a great life, Lucas."

"More than you know, love. I've invested in my parents' businesses as an equal partner and even now we're looking to expand, to grow with the community, especially in cottage industries. I've put capital into Antique's local cooperatives, too, to help the people who had looked after your family and mine."

She nodded, her eyes lighting up. "Yes, that would make a lot of people very happy."

"I'm glad you agree." He nuzzled her nose with his. "I love you."

"Love you too."

He reached for the ring and looked closely at her face, trying to gauge her reaction. "Tell me, love, would you like to have this?"

Tara looked thoughtful for a moment before responding, "I don't know, was this meant for me? Because the man on the drawing clearly knew what he was doing. I'm not getting the same vibe right now."

Lucas lowered himself to the floor on one knee, not bothering to disguise his wince as he felt something crack in protest. Heart pounding, he held the ring out to her. "Is this better?"

Tara stood up before him, a playful grin spreading across her face as she took the diamond and held it up to the light. "Well, to be honest, I want you. But if it's part of the deal, why not? If I get to have you stay with me forever."

He wasted no time in pulling her into his arms, joy quickly replacing his earlier doubts as they collapsed onto the couch. "Is that a yes?"

She nodded. "Always yes, remember? Since our first night together, I have always said yes."

"God, yes, you did." He pulled away to gently take the ring from her grip and slide it onto her waiting finger. Overwhelmed, he kissed her passionately, lingeringly. "I love you."

"Alright," she said, in a soft yet businesslike voice. "I accept. Let's seal the deal, love."

Before he could fully comprehend her words, she climbed onto his lap with a graceful fluidity that took him back to their first time together in the SUV outside her villa. Her hands deftly unbuttoned his shirt while he fumbled with the belt of her robe, revealing her naked body underneath as he pushed the soft terrycloth off her shoulders.

"Always prepared for you," she murmured, as she offered up her breasts to his hungry gaze.

His hands hovered above her, itching to touch, but before his fingers could reach her flushed skin, she had already slid down to her knees on the floor. She skillfully removed his shoes, pants, and briefs, and managed to tug off his polo shirt with his assistance. She parted his legs and took him into her hands, not needing much effort to bring him to full arousal.

"God, Tara," he groaned as her hands wrapped around him, stroking the length, kneading the balls. She traced the contours of his thighs and pelvis with the tip of her tongue, every flick sending his hips bucking off the couch.

"More, love… please," Lucas gasped, the plea torn from the very edges of his reason, as she sucked and pumped him into her mouth.

And she gave—more pace, more pressure, more depth. She didn't just seal a deal—she claimed her rightful possession of him and his heart.

"Ah, fuck…" Lucas cried out as his climax shattered through him with a force that shook the entire building. He didn't care if his voice carried beyond the walls of the apartment; let the world know he belonged to Tara Galvez now.

When he came back down, spiraling from the heights of ecstasy, he found her gazing up at him, her chest adorned with the evidence of his release.

"Looks like I'm yours now," she declared, her voice a velvety, teasing caress. "Completely."

"Fuck, Tara, what are you doing to me?" With a growl, he reached for her, guiding her onto her back upon the coffee table.

He knelt between her legs and brought her ring finger to his lips, sucking and tasting the salt of her skin mingled with the metallic tang of the gold band—it was an odd yet intoxicating cocktail. His other hand reached for her pussy; he groaned as he watched her hips arch hungrily towards his touch. He drew steady circles with his palm, drawing slick, sweet wetness.

Using both hands to spread her legs wider, his mouth descended on her heat, his tongue tracing the lines of desire that his touch had just charted. His tongue lapped up the taste of her, making her writhe above him, his name on her lips.

Knowing she was close, he paused to move her to the floor next to him. Slowly, he lifted her legs and entered her, filling her in a languid, unhurried rhythm. His hands cupped her breasts, his touch gliding over the sticky sheen of his own cum.

"Lucas….Lucas…" she sang, her hands clutching at the carpet as she met his hips with hers, breasts bouncing to the beat of his thrusts. "You feel so good…"

"Look at me, Tara." He put his arms around her torso, bringing her up against his own body without missing a beat. "I want your eyes on mine."

Obediently, her lashes lifted, her arms encircling his neck as their eyes locked. The world fell away, leaving only their bodies joined in passion.

"Sing for me, love," he whispered as he thrust up into her, increasing his urgency as he crushed his mouth against hers.

"Always," she murmured against his lips, matching his rhythm stroke for stroke.

As he buried himself deep one final time, he declared, for all the world to hear, "I love you."

"I love you too," she gasped, her body shaking in the throes of passion, and then their voices rose together in ecstasy, in the sweetest symphony of their love story yet.

Epilogue

THE STORY

Lucas

THE STAGE LIGHTS WERE DIMMED TO NEAR DARKNESS but the studio audience was charged with an energy bordering on frenetic. The setting took him right back to the first time he'd watched Tara's concert live all those years ago, from a similar discreet seat in the back row.

Lucas watched as the crew of the noontime TV show quickly moved equipment and props around the stage during the commercial break, speaking in hushed, urgent tones. People around him whispered amongst themselves, their voices melding into a low hum of excitement.

"Oh my gosh, I can't breathe," dramatically declared a young woman a few rows in front of him. "I haven't seen Tara in forever. I'm literally dying to hear her new songs. D'you think they'll be even better than the ones from her second album?"

"You bet," a female voice answered. "I heard they're already making videos of a few singles. I can't believe she won't be touring, though. I saw her in concert last time; she was *sooooo* great. We were all crying by the time she finished singing 'Home!"

"Did you see her at the Philippine Cup Finals last summer?" another voice chimed in. "She was cheering on Lucas Delgado. Something's definitely going on between them."

Giggles erupted from the surrounding seats, followed by murmurs of agreement. "They'd make a gorgeous couple! They should have accounts all over social media. People would follow them like crazy—I would!"

"Lucas is hot," someone else commented, this time a male voice. "It's a pity he retired too soon. Sure, Derek is cute, but he doesn't have Lucas' hair and abs. He just isn't the Daddy Lucas is."

"Wouldn't surprise me if Lucas and Tara are together," said the first girl, her voice laced with the authority of an avid fan. "He announced his retirement at the end of the conference, right? And then, a few weeks later, Tara makes this press statement that she and Esta Melodia are parting ways. What does that tell you?"

As the speculation swirled around him, Lucas smiled in the safety of the studio's shadows. They were right, after all, but it felt a little odd hearing strangers exchange theories about his new life with Tara.

"Three, two, one… And we're back!"

As the floor director's countdown ended, a spotlight illuminated stage left, where one of show's regular hosts, a statuesque actress and model, stood beaming at the camera.

"Ladies and gentlemen, I have been a fan of our next very special guest since day one. This singer-songwriter, Asia's Acoustic Angel, has been my musical idol for a decade! And now, for the very first time on Philippine TV, to perform the carrier single of her latest album, *Our Love Replay*, please welcome Tara Galvez with '*Untold!*'"

The studio erupted into thunderous applause, and Lucas could feel his own anticipation mirrored by the entire audience. As the lights and cameras shifted, he saw Tara sitting serenely on a wooden stool at center stage, cradling her guitar. The live-feed screens all over the studio focused on her ethereal features; her long black hair framed her face in soft waves as her eyes regarded the audience, a gentle smile on her lips.

Tara began to strum her guitar, the poignant chords resonating throughout the studio as everyone and everything else fell silent under her thrall. Each chord weaved a story of passion and longing; each lyric told a tale filled with bittersweet moments and heartfelt confessions. As the song reached its crescendo, it seemed as though the entire audience held their breath, completely entranced at Tara's performance and collectively experiencing the raw emotions that poured from her music.

The last note of her song hung in the air like a heartbroken farewell, and for a moment, time seemed to stand still. Then, as if released from an invisible grip, the world around him came alive in a rousing standing ovation.

"Wow, Tara, that was absolutely breathtaking!" the host gushed, dabbing at her eyes. "Your voice is truly one-of-a-kind, and your poetic soul shines through in every note and word you sing. I wish I had even a fraction of your talent."

"Thank you so much," Tara replied, her cheeks flushed.

"More, more! We want more!" chanted the crowd, their voices merging into a single plea for an encore.

Lucas watched the flurry among the crew—urgent whispers into headsets, the stage manager conferring with the director and producer, and the host tapping her earpiece as she awaited instructions. It was a unique kind of chaos only Tara's performance could inspire.

As he absorbed the scene before him, an image began to form in his mind—Tara, sitting onstage, bathed in light, calmly accepting the admiration and adoration that surrounded her. Lucas had started drawing again, every day, and he never ran out of subjects. Some of his drawings had even made it to the labels of Galvez Farms and Delgado Homemade Products.

Grinning widely, the host raised her hand to silence the boisterous crowd. "Alright, alright! It seems we have a unanimous decision for an encore." She turned back to Tara, eyes dancing with excitement. "It seems they simply can't get enough of you, Tara. What do you say? Do you have another love song in store for us today?"

Tara smiled, her eyes twinkling. "I think I might just have the perfect song. It's a little something I wrote many years back when I first fell in love. That feeling has always stayed with me, so I tried to capture it in each and every song I wrote."

"A feeling?" echoed the host, leaning in with unabashed curiosity. "Do tell."

"Love and longing have always been universal emotions. They're what connect us all—our shared experiences of pain and joy, of loss and discovery." Tara's voice was soft and wistful, her gaze drifting towards the studio audience.

"Isn't there always that one person, for each of us? The one whose presence transcends all songs, all stories, and all memories? No matter how much we try to capture them into words or even pictures, it's never enough."

"Wow," interjected the host, a hand over her heart, "that's so profound, so romantic. Some of us could only wish to find that kind of love." A nostalgic sigh swept through the audience, as if each person were recalling their own versions of the elusive someone Tara spoke of.

In that moment, the host's gaze fell on the ring on Tara's hand. "OMG! Tara, are you engaged? Because I'm absolutely certain that is a beautiful diamond right there."

Tara's cheeks blushed a gentle pink, but she met the host's probing stare with a coy smile and a playful wink.

"Maybe," she responded, sending a ripple of excited murmurs through the crowd.

"Alright then," the host conceded, her smile never faltering. "Let's talk about your encore song. What have you chosen to perform for us today?"

Tara's smile widened, her eyes scanning the audience until they locked onto Lucas', even through the glaring stage lights and shadowy corners where he sat. He wondered if she could really see him, but it didn't matter—he knew that her heart could now see clearly into his own.

"Today, I'll be singing the first platinum single from my debut album, *Fragments of Us*," she began, her voice tender and dreamy. "It's called 'Never with You,' and I'm dedicating it to someone very special in the audience today."

She paused, her eyes fluttering down to her guitar as she positioned her fingers on the strings. "I wrote this song for him a long time ago. Now, he's here to listen to me sing it."

As the opening chords of 'Never with You' filled the air, Lucas felt his heart swell with awe, love, and pride for the woman who had captured him so completely. How far they had come—together and apart—and how beautiful the promise of their tomorrows they now had the freedom to create.

Tara's gaze lifted once more, her smile dazzling the entire studio as she began to share their story with the world.

"This is for my fiancé, Lucas."

About the Author

Shirley Siaton writes edgy and evocative stories and poems. Her worlds are in a deliciously dark cross-section of the romance, neo-noir, action, fantasy, new adult, and contemporary genres.

She has several books of fiction and poetry released since February 2023. Her first book is the free verse collection *Black Cat and other poems*. She also pens juvenile literature as Shirley Parabia.

She is an award-winning writer, poet and journalist in English, Filipino and Hiligaynon, lauded by the Stevan Javellana Foundation, Philippine Information Agency, and West Visayas State University. Her essays, short stories, and poems have been published internationally in print and digital media. Her multi-lingual plays have been staged in the Philippines.

Shirley is a black belt in Shotokan Karate and an international certified fitness coach. Originally from Iloilo City, she is based in the Middle East with her husband and two daughters.

On the Web

Shirley's official website:
shirleysiaton.com

Complete reading guide:
shirley.pub

Subscribe to Shirley's VIP list for free exclusive updates:
newsletter.shirleysiaton.com

www.ingramcontent.com/pod-product-compliance
Lightning Source LLC
LaVergne TN
LVHW040034080526
838202LV00045B/3335